VIRTUTIS

VOLUME 1

THEO BENNETT

"Ai morti, agli esclusi e a coloro che non mi perdoneranno mai"

VIRTUTIS: VOLUME 1

Paper Back ISBN: 979-8-9869097-2-1

E-Book ISBN: 979-8-9869097-1-4

Concept Art by Matheus 'The Gillotine' Seban

"E così... la domanda più grande per un guerriero. Che ne è dell'amore?"

"L'amore è il valore più alto. Ma non può esistere da solo. Deve essere legato alle virtù. Deve essere leggero e delicato da muovere, ma pesante nelle fondamenta del cuore di un guerriero. Scorre tra le virtù di un uomo come se tenesse un uomo vero."

CHAPTER 1

113 BCE

Virtutis gripped his Spartan dagger, set on revenge. Blood streaked down his face and chest, dripping into the midnight soil. Shadowed barbarian corpses hung from the trees, the slow creaking from rotating dead weight merging with the sounds of his short, unsteady breaths. Veins protruded to the surface of his robust warrior body; he adjusted his toes in leather sandals to steady his stance.

Standing at his full height, he lowered the dagger and dipped his chin, hoping the ruse would make him appear vulnerable. His muscles twitched in anticipation, a call for his enemies to attack.

Frustration pumped through his body like static traveling through his blood. His eyes scanned the darkness for his wife's abductors. Breath held, he strained to hear her pleas. Any cries that may make it past the groans of the twisting rope-bound bodies or the thudding of his racing heart.

Fog closed in, impeding his vision. He stepped forward, feet sinking into the damp clay. Heavy, tired legs weighed down his footsteps, making them slow, less reactive, and amplifying his already irritated state.

I must find her.

A breeze blew against his back, swaying and rotating the hanging dead surrounding him.

Ropes creaked louder, and white noise wailed, sweeping away the trail of her existence. He wanted to scream her name, but it would only widen the growing chasm separating them. Instead, his mind wrapped around the word he wanted to call, a vice clinging to hope.

With only the moonlight to assist, he scanned the horizon; a black shape darted toward him, then disappeared into the hazy fog.

He whipped toward the sound of rapidly approaching, pounding footsteps. Before he could lift his blade, a massive weight slammed into his chest, knocking him backward.

His back hit the dirt with a grunt; the impact dislodged the dagger from his grasp. A Black Wolf with its ivory fangs and stale breath pinned his chest—pressuring, suffocating, snapping its jaws inches from his face. His forearm pressed against its fur throat, muscles straining against the beast.

With its prey dominated, the wolf paused. Its hazel eyes—almost human—peered into Virtutis's, boring deep into the crevices of his being. Drool dripped from its snarling jaw into Virtutis's mouth, sliding down the back of his throat, permeating his Spartan soul.

The Black Wolf lifted its head. With jaws open wide, it howled a chilling sound, ominous yet beautiful. It closed its eyes, savoring the moment. Instincts took over; Virtutis seized the opportunity. With the last of his fleeting strength, he twisted his body and simultaneously swept his arms, forcing the wolf's paws from his chest.

Desperate, he rolled out from under the wolf. His back to the beast, he was exposed, weak—a necessary risk and his only chance for escape. A futile attempt. The Black Wolf crushed a heavy paw between his shoulder blades, shocking Virtutis and forcing his face into the dirt. A cold, wet nose sniffed behind Virtutis's ear, sending a shiver like life departing a dead man's body down his spine.

Blinded by dirt, he flung an outstretched hand that fumbled in desperation for the dagger. Finally, he wrapped his fingers around the cool metal of the hilt. Hope surged.

Sharp teeth buried into his shoulder, hot knives ripping through tender flesh. Virtutis gasped a voiceless scream.

The Black Wolf shook him with violent disregard, an attempt to stun its capture for an easy kill. Under death's grasp, Virtutis let the wolf whip his body from side to side.

The jaws released to grip again. Virtutis turned, launching into an upward attack, burying his shoulder into the neck of the beast. He wrestled the Black Wolf, sweeping its legs with his foot, slamming them to the ground.

Virtutis scrambled on top of the wolf, poised to deliver the final strike.

Eye to eye, he jammed the blade against the Black Wolf's neck, increasing the pressure.

"Father! Father!" a familiar voice echoed from behind. "Wake up!"

Virtutis jolted awake. His vision cleared.

What have I done?

Reality surfaced. He had straddled his son with a dagger pressed upon his innocent throat. His son's eyes widened in fear, then narrowed, confused.

Virtutis felt tiny arms wrapping around his neck as icy fear crawled through his body.

"Father, stop. Please. It was another dream."

His soul sank into a sadness that buried all faith—in his future, in his sanity, in himself. He'd almost slaughtered his fourteen-year-old son, Stoa, while Augustus, the youngest by eight years, held witness over his shoulder.

Virtutis threw the dagger across the room of his loving home, attempting to distance himself from the nightmare—a nightmare that could have resulted in his son's death.

It spun away without mercy, etching its way into his memory forever.

Bewildered, Virtutis slumped in shame, falling back on his haunches.

He had brought the very threat of death into their home, a threat he had sworn to defend them from now lay sprawled upon the stone floor in the shape of a dagger.

"Stoa, my son." He opened his arms toward Stoa, but he scampered away in fear.

Augustus released his hands from his father's neck, then stepped away. A weary expression twisted his features.

"I am sorry. I didn't mean to hurt you."

They darted looks between them. He searched for forgiveness. "Son?"

Stoa backed away farther still, holding his shoulder, rubbing the back of his head, then finally, his throat. He brought his hands in front of his face and turned them; there was no blood.

Virtutis's head sank, his eyes filled with tears. "Stoa?" Standing, he offered a gentle hand.

Stoa took another step back, then turned and ran out the door in a panic.

Virtutis's heart crashed; his actions haunted him, leaving his stomach hollow.

Gripping Virtutis's arm, Augustus pleaded, "Father, leave him. He only tried to wake you. You were tossing and turning and wouldn't open your eyes. You were screaming. We shook you, and you attacked him."

Virtutis's body felt heavy. His mind searched for reasoning.

Fighting depression and confusion, he stared, fixated on the doorway, hoping Stoa would soon return, so he could make amends and stop the tide of hurt pouring over his drowning heart.

"Augustus. I am sorry." Virtutis shuddered, then added, "You know I would never hurt either of you."

Augustus embraced him.

Virtutis closed his eyes, grateful for the endearing gesture. He checked, then rechecked the doorway. Stretching Augustus out to arm's length, letting him read his face. Eye to eye, Virtutis forced logic to return.

"Back to bed, son." Tender and careful, trying not to show his grief, he scooped his young son into his cot. "Please, sleep. I will look for Stoa." He waited, placing a gentle hand on Augustus's chest, then tucked him in.

"Yes, Papa." Augustus's sincere, innocent eyes turned toward the doorway.

Stoa reappeared, standing in the dim sliver of moonlight as a shadow, casting guilt over Virtutis's soul.

Stoa's lean frame crossed the dimly lit room. His arm extended, showing he had retrieved his father's dagger. It caught the light, showing its often-deadly blade.

Virtutis's chest expanded, broadening his posture, hands open at his sides, ready.

Stoa entered the house, his presence making the one-room house seem smaller.

"Father, you taught us to protect our family. But what do I do? Tell me. What do I do when I need to protect us from our own flesh and blood? From our own father?"

Stoa edged closer.

Virtutis cracked his neck to the side, battle-ready, then relaxed his palms outward to calm himself, breathing out deeply.

"You are right. I could have killed you," Virtutis replied, his voice calm but focused. He glanced over his shoulder at the cot in admittance of shame. "Or Augustus."

Fighting the sadness of a potentially violent confrontation, he stepped away from the cot, putting his back against the wall, taking the fight away from the innocent. Augustus was subjected to more than his fair share of trauma for the night.

Stoa rotated the dagger between his fingers with deadly precision. Skills passed down from father to son.

Virtutis raised a heel, poised—actions that made his gut tighten.

The shadows blackened Stoa's eyes, making it hard to read his intention.

He then reversed the handle toward Virtutis's heart, offering a choice of responsibility—holding his father accountable.

Virtutis studied the handle of the dagger, unsure if he dared to reclaim it, unsure if he could trust himself. But he could not falter more in front of his sons.

He reached for the dagger.

Stoa held it firmly by the blade, not letting go.

"I know who you are, Father. This is not you. You haven't been the same since Mother was killed. You're distant. It's been years now—years." Stoa's face leaned toward the light, pent-up tears of anguish glistening down his cheeks.

"The Black Wolf, he haunts you. But now, through you, he haunts all of us."

Stoa let the razor-sharp blade go.

Virtutis was left gripping the instrument of death. Its weight felt heavier than a stone, knowing it could have been dripping with Stoa's blood.

Stoa's words repeated in his head, slicing his soul. Not able to look Stoa in the eye, he stood and silently sheathed the dagger.

He tried to talk, but there were no words; he couldn't shift the distaste from his mouth. Ashamed of how he could no longer articulate who he had become, he walked through the moonlit doorway, detached from the present. Numb.

CHAPTER 2

Virtutis sat by the riverbank where his wife's body rested beneath the hard clay and rock. He longed for her connection more than ever. The more he tried, the more his longing washed away downstream.

"Forgive me, my love."

Eyes closed, he remembered their first embrace by the rushing water and their passionate love that had grown their family. He searched for peace but found none.

The hair on his arms stood on alert.

The power of the Black Wolf's jaws lurked freshly in his mind—how its teeth pinched through flesh and the vice-like grip that had ensnared him.

He shook his head, shaking away the threat, trying to regain a firm presence, searching for a better solution.

Virtutis hoped she wouldn't judge him for his actions; the thought of letting her down sank his head forward. The boys were her pride, her joy.

Not wanting to disrespect her memory, he fought a battle within himself all night until dawn, trying to honor her, but the last images of her life were too vivid to erase.

Each time he re-witnessed her death, her face tormented in pain, it provided a passage for the Black Wolf to slip back into his mind—thoughts he needed to suppress for his sons' sake.

Exhausted and distraught by the look on Stoa's face when he had his blade pushed against his throat, Virtutis made his way home in the dead of night.

He sat on his blanketed bed, and it sank beneath his weight.

The same bed where he had made love to his wife and where she had given birth to his sons. In its comfort, and on many occasions, she had used her gentle hand to repair his body.

Now it served as the place where he mourned alone, where he had lain for months—a warrior escaping death's door, trying to heal the open gashes from tempting the Black Wolf's deadly jaws.

Shadows from the corner fire shifted over the interior of the humble, clean house.

The fire sparked with a crack, alerting his senses further. Virtutis snapped his head around, reaching for his dagger, ready to defend. A familiar shadow shifted. His muscles relaxed at the unthreatening figure of his trusted friend, he sat.

"Odigos, I didn't see you enter," Virtutis said.

He removed his hand from the blade.

"After twenty years, have I become that unnoticeable?" Odigos smiled. "I saw you arrive a while ago," he replied, stoking the fire further, then adding wood to a low burn.

Virtutis rubbed his thirty-year-old hands with a twist of his palms. He saw her image dancing gracefully in the flickering flames. A constant omnipresent haunting, he wished he could step into the fire and join her.

He halted his breath, checking that Stoa and Augustus still slept in their beds along the far wall. Beneath them, a hatch door served as a reminder of their narrow escape two summers before. A summer that had burned its way into every cell in his body. A summer that ended in murder.

"You are lost in your own head again." Odigos stood, observing the accumulating fire. "Are you still having nightmares?" He looked over his shoulder, lifting an eyebrow, sincere in his care.

Virtutis, suspicious, bit the inside of his lip and passed his fingers over the scar on his face, a scar from the night it all went terribly wrong.

"Did the boys talk with you? What did they say?"

Odigos pursed his lips and nodded once. "Stoa came into the barn after what happened."

Virtutis's shoulders slumped forward. With a weighted tone, he forced himself to talk. "The dreams are more intense these days, more regular, and more concerning."

Stoa shifted under the blanket.

Virtutis scoffed and shook his head in regret.

"He will come full circle," Odigos assured. "He's old enough to understand things are difficult. He knows you could never hurt him, but you also taught him to defend his family."

"Sometimes, I wonder." Virtutis's right knee jittered to conceal his worry. He used his hand to secure his nerves; it stopped. "I am restless. Before she died, I could fight and return home to her and the boys; I knew who I was. But now, the way she died... I'm tense, and the boys feel it. Stoa is right. I am not the father I was. I am not the father that I should be."

"Yes. At times, you look numb. I see Hades in you. Something small will set you off; you become—" Odigos paused, choosing his words carefully. "But these reactions are normal considering the circumstance."

"Circumstance? Circumstance is a place where cowards lay blame."

Virtutis gazed at his crooked fingers. "I blame myself, not circumstance. I threatened my son; she died because of me. These are mine to own."

"Few would have survived this long. But all the same, blame is pointless. So is shame. Shame is a cloak cowards use to hide from the wolf pack."

"You are correct. A warrior must act. He must find resolve. Sometimes, I am myself; then, it's like a dam of flames bursting under my skin. I can't be here. I am lost in my own mind. With the nightmares and how unpredictable I am, I know I need to go. The boys are safer with you. I could have killed him. I am as far from a warrior as I can be."

Odigos sat at his side, wiping his hands with a cloth; he was missing two fingers on his left hand—severed by barbarians.

"What do you think will bring resolve?" he asked. "What is it you need to do?"

Virtutis glared at his spear and shield hanging on the far wall.

"I have tried solitude; it buried me further into my head. I even thought of suicide; it calls my name with such sweetness, but I can't. It disgusts me. The confusion of all this angers me; it haunts me."

"You are Spartan. You cannot change that anger strikes. This is who you are," Odigos defended.

"Yes, but I must see past being Spartan. Today's world is different. The ashes of Sparta have shown us this. Who knows how many of us are left? As boys, we were all scattered to the wind. I could barely carry my father's spear but dragged it halfway across those mountains," he answered, nodding to the left.

"I remember." Odigos's chin tilted in agreement. His hand combed over his long hair before scratching the back of his head. "You are rabidus from your mourning, and your calling is that of a warrior. You must do what you must do."

Virtutis rotated his wrist. It crunched multiple times—overused from refining the effectiveness of his spear. "There are no tribal wars." With a sudden flick of his head, he cracked his neck. "I have decided," he stated airily. "I have chosen my fate."

The firelight danced intrigue through the house, adding a warm glow to each surface.

"I will fight for the Romans." Virtutis tried to disguise how labored he felt.

"The Romans?" Odigos turned his head. Virtutis knew the decision would catch him off guard.

Virtutis contemplated his decision, staring into the fire, refusing to face his friend.

"The Romans will always have someone to fight, and I do not lack willingness."

"As you must," Odigos replied, staring at the flames. "I will do what is required. I am at your service. As always, I will care for your sons."

"Thank you, old friend. There is no greater service than that to family. And you are family." A shared moment of gratitude and respect passed between the two. Odigos was indebted to Virtutis for saving his life, and Virtutis to Odigos for many years of loyalty.

"At least we will have more money for the farm. A mercenary's wage is more than modest," Odigos said.

Virtutis sighed. "I wish it were that easy. But to depend on a wage that may never arrive, and from wars I may not survive, I am afraid, will only lead to disappointment. Besides, I have never fought for money, only virtue."

Virtutis rubbed his beard's stubble, changing the subject. "Promise me you will keep teaching them from the scrolls? Land, money, and people will come and go, but the depths of a virtuous man will guide their way forever."

"Of course." Odigos dipped his head in agreement. Their gazes landed on the chest tucked in the room's corner.

Virtutis sensed his friend was holding something back. "What is it?"

Odigos, always composed, said, "Virtutis, as descendants of Sparta, we are ridiculed rather than regarded. The Romans will not hesitate to use you or put you to the sword. You know this."

"Yes, I know, but things are different now. They even protect our lands. We are part of Rome, whether we like it or not," Virtutis replied.

"That is true." Odigos exhaled long and deep. "I will teach and train the boys. You know I will do everything in my power to protect and educate them. You have my word."

Virtutis studied Odigos's back while he stoked the fire. He finished by playing with a stick in the embers.

Odigos continued, "I remember when we were young. I fished and farmed, but you trained as a warrior. You would run, roll, move, spin, and throw that spear all day. I was in awe of the mastery you acquired in such a short time, and no man in the village could match your skill. Many tried, but few could test your ability. Even as a young man, no one here wanted to suffer such a foolish wage."

"Yes, I think you were the wiser of us." Virtutis found a little of his humor. "At least frolicking fish serve our bellies. Fat barbarians just leave a smell, even after you drag them into bloody ditches and bury them."

Odigos stood, chuckling. "There is the Virtutis we know." He placed his three-fingered hand on Virtutis's shoulder.

"We can leave a small predicament, only to find a greater predicament in life. Who knows what is worse? Our own, or someone else's?"

"I am not sure of the Romans. No one can be. They are thirsty for war and quenched in conquest." Virtutis leaned back on his bed with a sigh, stretching his spine, before becoming hypnotized by the fire again. Odigos was correct; his young life had revolved around training to be a battle-hardened warrior; now, life was much more complex.

He didn't notice Odigos leave.

Another crackle of fire jarred him from his thoughts.

Quiet and gentle, he tucked in Augustus, ensuring he was safe. He pressed his lips to his forehead, a kiss from both him and his boy's mother. He looked up, hoping she could see the Virtutis she had known—the caring and protective husband and father.

12

He studied Stoa, not wanting to disturb him, then placed his dagger on the faraway table.

The bed provided enough comfort to sleep. Exhausted, he closed his eyes.

The following morning, he woke to the sounds of the boys playing in the nearby fields. He sat up. The morning sun broke through the door opening; its radiant energy told him he had fallen into a short, deep sleep. A sleep for which he was grateful, despite the heaviness in his limbs.

The scent of last night's lamb and fresh bread flooded his senses. He lifted his face to the ceiling in gratitude for what he had, then shook his head in disgrace at who he had become. His unpredictability created a stain on his skin.

Firming his finger-grip on his knees, he demanded the best of himself in what could be his last moments with his sons.

Deep in his soul, he knew his pathway was set, and theirs would be their own. His stomach twisted. There was no unwinding his torment.

He retrieved his dagger, placing it in its sheath. "Grant me courage. Let me show the way."

Calamity and energy called from outside.

"Papaaaa! Raaaaaa!" Augustus roared, running through the doorway, his untamed hair making him appear more savage-like. His wiry body, covered in fresh dirt, carried the hardness of playing warrior on the verge of reality. But his youngest son, behaving normally, not afraid, relaxed his tense muscles.

Virtutis's heart pounded.

Outstretching his arms, he gathered Augustus in a bear hug. He spun him around, inhaling the last joy of his child's purity, happiness from an innocent soul.

Stoa stood cautiously at the door, watching over them, establishing it was safe.

Almost at his father's height, he had the chiseled features of a soon-to-be-man. His arms and shoulders were well-formed, legs solid and powerful from hard labor and learning the ways of a Spartan's oldest son. His knuckles had also hardened from handling the technical teachings of the spear from his father. Having shown him the dark arts, Virtutis was wary. He knew another episode like the previous night would lead to a confrontation with Stoa.

Virtutis's stomach sank after seeing the distance between them was more than physical. Trust had drifted away like a relentless tide in an ocean of uncertainty.

Virtutis brushed his hand over the dagger, making sure his tunic covered it. Last night's trauma wouldn't be relived.

He lowered Augustus with one arm in a squat while focusing on Stoa. Augustus continued to fight and squirm but settled, sensing the mood change. He blew his hair from his eyes, then bit his bottom lip.

"Stoa, son." He kissed Augustus on the top of the head. "I am sorry I hurt you." His voice was soft, apologetic, and genuine.

He sat back on the bed and gazed back and forth into their innocent eyes, his breath thick with regret.

Augustus's bottom lip quivered.

His eldest son remained distant and stoic.

"Boys, I am leaving. I have chosen to offer my services to the emperor and to fight for the Romans. Like before, you will remain with Odigos. He will care for you; he is someone we all trust."

Augustus shuffled backward, looking to Stoa for comfort as he often did.

Not finding any, he turned back to his father.

Stoa's narrowed eyes didn't break from Virtutis's gaze.

"Are you leaving because of me?" Stoa asked, taking a step forward as though he were demanding the truth.

"No, son. I am not." Virtutis searched their faces for forgiveness. Forgiveness for abandoning them. "There are things within myself that I must resolve. You know this."

He put his hand on Augustus's shoulder. "Stoa, come here. Stand with us."

Stoa walked forward, his posture closed and eyes still unsure.

Controlling his disappointment in himself for Stoa's tentativeness, keeping the walls of regret from falling into the pit of his stomach, he remembered how each night he installed the best of what he understood about life in his young sons.

"What must a warrior do?" Virtutis tested, hoping to regain their core family virtues.

Stoa fronted bluntly, "To protect his family. To pursue a virtuous life."

Virtutis's eyebrow lifted. The confident Stoa was back, determined and focused.

"Yes. Good. There are things I must do to regain my own way, as a man and as a warrior." He lightly squeezed Augustus's shoulder. "This is something I must do for all of us."

Risking rejection, he placed his hand on Stoa's shoulder. This was for them both in equal measures.

Stoa tensed under his touch but didn't move away. The father and son bond that had been so important over the years was healing itself.

"There is no good time for a father to leave his family, definitely not his sons. But you are sons of Virtutis, with the blood of Sparta running through your veins. Stoa, I have taught you the ways of war, how to protect those close to you—to protect your family. I want you to do the same for Augustus and pass on my teachings."

The boys stood slightly taller, their father's words elevating their confidence.

"For now, I need you both to work the farm, feed the animals, and cook and clean." He looked at Augustus. "Even you, little man."

He puffed his chest out. "Yes, Father, I will."

"You will both help Odigos, and you will also learn from him. He's a loyal man. A man of virtue."

Virtutis looked up through the overlapping clay tiles, imagining the heavens above. "And your mother will always be here guiding you."

Stoa inhaled, lifting his eyes to the ceiling, then narrowing them, steel-like.

Virtutis added a caring but firm shake upon their shoulders. "You know how to fight, how to stay alive. Your short swords are sharpened and ready if you need them. Use them if you are forced to."

His words regained ground, filling the room with a presence he'd once commanded as a father. "Always use your wits. Be attentive." He rolled his shoulders back and cracked his neck. "What is the family creed?"

The boys looked at each other, then back at their father. "Courage grows at a wound. From a wound grows strength," they recited confidently. Virtutis smiled proudly, with a bittersweet pang in his chest.

"And what does that mean?" He tested their ability to remember a father's stories.

Stoa stood firm. His young shoulders became broad, forearms firm and veiny like those of his patriarch. He held his father's gaze, focused and serious. "It means no matter the wound, flesh, bone, or to our hearts—we will heal. The process of mending creates formidable strength."

"Yes, Stoa. Very good." Virtutis grinned.

"Father?"

"Yes, Augustus." He scanned his younger mirror image with pride.

"If you die there—in the war—will you heal?"

Virtutis shuffled with interest. It was a good question. "I may die, son. After all, it is war, right?" They nodded in agreement. "As for

16

healing after I die, I believe we do not. When we die, there is no coming back."

Augustus's face frowned with questions. "But you said Mother is here? Did she come back?"

"How intelligent you are, son. No, she will not come back. She lives within you, her lessons and impression of who she was ingrained into your very core. Listen to yourself; aim to be a good boy, and she will console you like she helped shape me into a better man."

Augustus narrowed his eyes, thinking.

Virtutis continued, "As for a man's journey, we must live each day with virtue. We want to look down from the heavens, knowing we did our absolute best on every occasion. Knowing we were real men— the best men we could have been. Correct?

"A true man resolves his affairs with the living before he dies because the dead... are dead." He winked. "A good man acts with rectitude. He keeps his promises. He loves with a full heart. He is honest. He takes responsibility." Virtutis reflected on his own search.

"And he must find ways to forgive and heal himself." He looked at Stoa. "For his family."

Stoa placed his hand over Virtutis's forearm with a gentle embrace. "I forgive you, Father. I don't fear you. I am not afraid of anything, not even the Black Wolf." Stoa widened his eyes.

Tears welled over Virtutis's own. Stoa remained stern, matter of fact.

Augustus searched Virtutis's face. "Father... the Black Wolf?"

"Yes, son?"

"Tell us a story." Augustus became energized.

The hairs on Virtutis's arms rose, and a chill covered the back of his neck. The mythical stories were passed down, proving to be true.

"The Black Wolf." His hand unconsciously rubbed the back of his neck in an attempt to control his emotions. "He will meet us all on our passage toward death. Young, old, rich, poor, just or unjust—he has no favorites. He will arrive when least expected."

Images of his nightmares flashed through his mind. He shook his head to rid himself of them.

"The Black Wolf will be waiting at the end. I am not sure if he has no intention of making your life a living Hades. How we approach living our life creates our hell or our heaven. Who knows what awaits us on the other side of death? Most men's problems are created when they try to run from the Black Wolf. But you must understand, we can't simply run from death.

"Death will take us all; we must face it eye to eye. We must confront it. We must make the right decisions and live our truth. The Black Wolf is playing its role. A role that involves us all at some point. Many fear it, so they cower away." He tapped his finger on Augustus's temple.

"They run away in their minds first because they are afraid, and soon after, their actions follow. It is not the wolf that creates torment." Virtutis straightened. "It is our thoughts and actions as men that create it. If you die in fear, the old ways say we could also be that way in the afterlife, forever. So, we must be fearless when we face the Black Wolf. The Black Wolf is not death, simply the passage to death's white wall. That's why we must train the mind and live with virtue."

Virtutis stared long and hard into Stoa's eyes, testing him. "What are our virtues?"

The boy puffed out his chest and replied, "Courage to face ourselves. Righteousness, doing the right thing, no matter the consequence."

"Compassion for everyone, even our enemies," added Augustus.

Pride filled the cavern in his chest that had been carved out by the thought of leaving them. He'd witnessed them recite the virtues almost daily since they could talk, but today it was different. They continued, determined.

"Consideration for everything around us. Sincerity in our actions and words. Empathy," stated Stoa.

"Forgiveness," finished Augustus with a nod. "And most of all, gratitude."

18

"Well done, my sons." Virtutis narrowed his eyes. "And so... the greatest question to a warrior. What of love?"

Stoa lifted his head assertively but waited for Augustus, giving his younger brother a chance to answer. A manner of teaching his brother and how his father had taught him—a method that worked.

Augustus started. "Father. Love is the highest value. But it cannot exist by itself. It must be attached to virtues. It must be light and gentle to move but heavy in the foundation of a warrior's core. It flows between the virtues of a man as if holding a man true."

"Very good, Augustus. Take your time; your memory is good," Virtutis encouraged.

"A man must show the power of his love through his words, actions, and decisions."

Virtutis looked Augustus up and down with pride. "Yes, son. Who do you love?"

"I love you and my brother. I love my mother."

"Yes, and one day, you will love a woman who is not family. Then you will know the meaning of the words you speak because they will be tested as you make her your family. Loving outside your family is another world to discover within yourself."

Augustus fidgeted, the confidence sliding from his face.

"You are not wrong. There is simply much more to come. Don't worry, my son, you will experience this love soon enough."

"Yes, Father. Always more to come."

Augustus shrugged and sighed with the weight of never knowing enough. Stoa put a comforting arm around his brother's shoulders and gave him a compassionate smile.

"Father, you are a warrior, and a warrior must fight. If you fall, may it be to a lofty mountain. If that lofty mountain is a man, we will avenge you. You have my word."

Virtutis pulled his head back in awe. Stoa's response was untamed, almost unsettling, but honest.

"I have raised two warriors, haven't I?"

"We are warriors." Stoa tipped his head with confidence.

Virtutis sat, stunned, proud.

"I am blessed to be your father. Just do not forget about the harvest."

Stoa looked down at his feet. "Yes, Father."

"You can't fight if you are weak. You must eat. To eat, you must farm. Agreed?"

"Yes, Father." The boys shifted their stances.

"Farming will teach you much about yourself." Virtutis asserted his opinion harder. "You will not only be tested by the obstacles in life but also by how you look at the obstacles.

"Here on the farm, you will encounter them within yourselves, and the warrior skills I have taught you will come to serve you sooner or later. I hope in due time, the virtues I have taught you will reflect in your life."

Virtutis stood, his presence towering above them.

"One day, my sons, you will make a great impression in the world. Your lives will shift from the shadows of your father and become your way. You must not look to me; instead, you must set your own expectations, for they will not be the same as mine. Choose your own paths. Times, people, and situations change, some for better, some for worse. You must treat each day with a degree of wonder and fascination. Take nothing for granted, and do not be overwhelmed by the unexpected."

Virtutis searched their faces. "What did you hear from my words?"

Stoa looked up with sureness. "We will not only be tested by the obstacle but also how we look at the obstacle and how we overcome it."

"Yes!" Virtutis embraced them like the father he once was. The father he should be. In the corner of the room, a shadow shifted, sending shivers down his spine. He held his sons close, not breaking his gaze, his breath frozen still and followed by more emptiness.

He pushed the boys back, focusing deep into their eyes.

"Tell Odigos to fetch Urion."

He scanned the shadows again while footsteps scampered out the door.

He stood, collecting his shield, spear, and shoulder bag, preparing himself for his journey.

Not feeling his feet, he walked across the cabin floor, his face meeting the sun's warmth at the doorway. The events of his life were now leading toward faraway wars, not his own, determined to wage a battle against himself if he must.

Holding his spear on his shield, he clunked them together; the sound filled him with courage.

Outside in the morning sun, Stoa and Augustus stood by his large, black warhorse, Urion.

Odigos had tied Virtutis's saddlebag. It was time; he was ready.

Virtutis patted the hindquarter of his trusted companion.

"Odigos, if I send someone for the boys and they mention their mother's name, it is me who is sending for them. If they cannot mention her name, kill them without hesitation and leave immediately. This is imperative. Do you understand?"

"Sir." Odigos nodded.

The black warhorse's eagerness energized the yard. Bobbing his head, keen to leave on an adventure, the warhorse snorted his readiness. "Yes, Urion, we ride toward battle. But there is no battle today. Easy."

Virtutis rose into his saddle and looked down at his sons. Odigos stood behind them as promised.

With a heavy heart, Virtutis pushed through to his goodbye.

"Sons, you know enough to live a good life. What you do not know, you will learn. You are forever in my heart. Look to the stars. Under them, we will always be connected."

Augustus sobbed at the finality of the moment, and Stoa placed a reassuring hand on his younger brother's shoulder. "Goodbye, Father."

Stoa straightened, lifted his chin, and widened his eyes to show his father the look of Sparta. "Fight well, Father."

Urion snorted and bowed his head. Virtutis let his body flow with the underlying current of tension. His gaze remained fixed with Stoa's.

"Father, wait!" Augustus sniffed, wiping tears from his eyes. "After you fight for the Romans, will you become a gladiator?"

Virtutis's head tilted in surprise.

He inhaled with a wide-eyed fury.

"Gladiator!" he boomed in a battle tone rarely heard at home.

Urion scuffed his hooves into the dirt.

Virtutis lowered his voice to a growl. "I am Spartan." He whipped the reins, spinning his warhorse under tension like before battle.

He steadied the horse and faced his sons. "Spartans live and die as free men. A gladiator is a slave." He jolted Urion's reins, making sure he had the boy's attention. He lowered his voice and growled, "I will never be a slave!"

Any other children would have looked away, but Augustus and Stoa lifted their chins in awe at their warrior father. Virtutis looked down with the sternness of the dying Sparta breed. A defiance cultivated in his bloodline, one that had evolved and survived the challenging test of time.

Again, he rotated his warhorse full circle, displaying its true magnificence.

With a final stare and holding back a river of emotion, he tapped his heels into Urion's side. The great warhorse nodded his head. With a final look at his sons, man and beast turned and galloped towards war.

Late in the afternoon, like a dampening fire—beyond his outburst in defense of his Spartan honor—Virtutis's heart sank. The realization of his departure settled in, and the fire in his chest extinguished into smoldering ashes of loneliness.

With each step farther from home, the cracks of regret widened.

He had no choice but to trust he had prepared them for the things they had not seen, and they would have the intelligence to figure them out.

The wind gusted, stirring dust into his already glistening eyes.

He rode on with sorrow, fighting the urge to turn back the whole day while riding into the unknown in search of a renewed warrior code to hold him steadfast. The quest for battle would soon block out the pain of the old and the pain of the new.

The coolness of the night enveloped them. He pulled back Urion's reigns, commanding him to stop. After building a small fire, he pulled up the hood of his cloak and laid down, staring, hypnotized by the flames. Before sleep could take him, a shadowed shape of a wolf appeared in the flickering orange and yellow glow.

He rubbed his eyes, reassuring himself it was his imagination.

"I will have your head, you little black pup," he called to the blaze.

The journey continued. Over the next few days, his mind became stronger and more present; his body became one with the steady flow of the saddle's movement. He accepted leaving behind his sons.

Through the distant horizons, he continued to fight the battles of his mind, confirming his quest, wanting to be whole. Together, they rode.

CHAPTER 3

The stale odor of latrines and smoldering fires wafted across the plain. Virtutis took refuge in the tree line, surveilling the Roman camp. The enormity was enough to intimidate any man or beast.

Urion weaved his head anxiously. Virtutis let him express himself, then, with calloused hands, gently controlled the reins. He leaned forward with a calm pat on Urion's neck.

"Easy boy," he said. "You can stay here for now."

Spear in hand and shield latched over his back, he left Urion hitched to a tree with a long lead to let him graze in a small patch of grass.

He walked through the perfectly organized tents extending as far as the eye could see. Roman equipment was neatly assembled—battle-ready. The proximity to the great Roman war machine stimulated the warrior within.

Ahead, a long line formed comprising men waiting to join the auxiliary. He recognized some tribesmen from the surrounding regions. Others he did not recognize were very strange-looking, but he paid no particular attention to them, hoping they would not pay any back.

He joined the line; it edged forward under the beaming sun, gradually working its way toward no return.

He caught the looming approach of a large figure from the corner of his eye.

Virtutis focused ahead while an enormous man pushed in front of him. Extra-long leather belt straps for carrying knives and small axes crossed his shoulders.

The gargantuan blocked some of the sun, casting a shadow over Virtutis's feet.

Virtutis held back the willingness to surgically dissect his back with his dagger for such disrespect—he bided his time. There was no need to draw any unwanted attention.

He looked at the blue sky, narrating the quest to himself, holding his resolve.

After what felt like hours of baking in the afternoon sun, the man's odor became unbearable. He couldn't control himself any longer and had no regard for the attention he'd receive.

"Like a wet boar on a hot day," Virtutis muttered.

The man-mountain turned, and Virtutis looked up under a putrid, unforgiving breath.

"What did you say, little man?"

Virtutis glanced over his left then right shoulder before focusing on the man-mountain. "Me?" Virtutis replied with a disingenuous smile.

With blood rising, he furtively slipped a hand under his tunic, placing his palm over the dagger's hilt.

"It's a good day," Virtutis added.

The big man grunted a huff and turned back in line, frustrated. "Let's get this done! There are more mosquitos than men out here!" he boasted to the men up front, wanting to be the joker and the bully. "I have come to pluck barbarian virgins, fight, and get paid!"

The silent line shuffled sideways, agitated.

Virtutis cracked his neck to the side and rolled his tongue between his teeth, wanting to spit in distaste. Barbarian women or not, he would cut down any man before he'd let a woman be taken in such a way. He would dismantle any man from such heathenism, regardless of size.

The beast let loose his intentions down the line. "After twenty-five years fighting for the Roman Empire, who knows? Maybe there will be a bath in Rome big enough for me and my cobra when I am done! When we finish with the local ladies, we will be ready for the nobles' wives!"

Chuckles echoed down the snaking queue of men while Virtutis swallowed spit, using discretion over dissection.

The line filed closer. He finally reached a skinny rat-like clerk taking names and issuing orders.

Virtutis gripped his spear before stepping up to the table. "I am here to join the auxiliary."

Without looking up, the clerk asked, "What is your specialty?" His squeaky voice suited his stature and features.

"Spear and shield. Horseman, with my own warhorse, sir."

Virtutis inhaled deeply, requesting the clerk to acknowledge his presence.

"What is your tribe?"

"I have no tribe."

The clerk's gaze slid from Virtutis's head to toes with sly interest. "Are you sure it is not Maniots? With a spear like that, you look like a Peregrinus Spartan."

"No, sir." The disrespectful prejudice surged fire through his veins. "I am Virtutis. From Peloponnese."

"Oh, another farmer who thinks he can fight? A waste of the empire's money. Wait here." The clerk slid back his stool and stood. "I need to piss."

The clerk disappeared around the side of the tent, and Virtutis relaxed the grip on his spear.

Not being able to help himself, Virtutis looked down at the unattended desk. The list of names was divided into groups he couldn't make sense of.

"Spartan!" the clerk snapped.

Calm under unsaid insinuation, he lifted his eyes to the clerk who fumbled his robe with arrogant hands and then patted himself dry. "Eyes to yourself, Spartan. We have more than enough horsemen. You can sell your plow horse and report to the light infantry who are leaving tomorrow for reinforcement."

Virtutis adjusted his stance and felt his veins pulse in his neck. "Sir, my warhorse and I are trained for war. We cannot be separated; we are one."

"You fight where you are told, and as I have already explained, we have enough horsemen," the clerk replied forcefully calm, his rat-like eyes flicking down, then up. "Or you go back to the farm—Spartan."

There was no compromise. Without signing his name to the auxiliary, his quest would be over before it began, but he could not betray Urion.

Virtutis smoothed his features.

"If I can arrange my horse, I will return tomorrow with my decision."

He turned and walked from the tent.

"You have until morning. Maybe you should stay in Peloponnese. Do not waste my time again," the clerk called to his back. He heard the clerk rustle papers. "Spartans have always been and will always be untamable. Next!"

Virtutis paused in the tent doorway and fought the urge to turn back and stab the clerk through his beady eye. He shook his head, then walked into the sunlight, letting his veins settle into a cooler pulse.

Virtutis found Urion, who had unleashed himself and was grazing in a meadow behind the tents.

He waited and watched, contemplating his actions, unsure of what to do with such a loyal creature.

There will be a way, he reassured himself. There has to be.

Urion's big tongue curled grass inward, followed by teeth chomping, his long face lax in delight. Bees and butterflies flapped their wings, escaping for their lives only to be blown off course from snorts of ecstasy in his chopping joy.

He was almost goofy—ready for the next mouthful.

Virtutis laughed under his breath, pitying the occasional bee that could have been digested, sounding a titt, titt with his tongue.

The feasting warhorse lifted his head, dropped his weight forward, then kicked his back legs in a small buck, galloping over. Strong and proud, Urion tossed his happy head while letting out a short, excited neigh. Powered by his bulky legs and chest, he came directly to Virtutis, slowing and lowering his head in a gentle reunion.

Virtutis placed a hand on Urion's neck and stroked his loyal companion.

"How are you, brother? Giving those bees a run for their honey?"

Urion, almost human-like, twisted his head, slightly confused about where the punchline had fallen. Virtutis laughed and patted his side with a firm, open hand.

"Come on. Let's find somewhere to sleep."

Without holding the powerful warhorse's reins, they walked side by side through the camp. Virtutis noticed the attention of Roman soldiers pulling toward them. "Seems like we are the center of attention, brother."

Without looking around, they focused ahead and made their way to the far side of the camp where the ragged-looking auxiliary were building their camp.

Virtutis observed a fortified structure to the side and took a second glance.

It was a prison—different from the other discoveries of the day. Virtutis and Urion stiffened at the imposing sight.

A large wooden fence stood twice as high as an average man. Inside, small wooden cages held captives of all shapes, sizes, and ages.

Urion snorted.

"They are most likely deserters. Criminals. Some slaves, or perhaps unlikeable characters of innocent differences."

Through the fence in the corner, a large wooden cross had been erected where the prosecuted would be sentenced to lashes or, for the more heinous crimes, death.

No doubt a Roman statement allocating a prison next to the auxiliary—a constant reminder that this was where deceit led if you dared to defy the Roman rule.

The idea of having all freedom revoked in such a manner made his palms slick. Urion's unease grew, shaking his neck and whipping his tail.

"We'll be fine. Prison is not for us, brother. Just do the right thing, and we have nothing to worry about." Virtutis clicked his tongue in reassurance, walking them onward. "That fate for us is impossible." Virtutis's stomach turned.

In truth, he was afraid of captivity, but not at all of death.

They found a calm spot away from the main encampment.

"Is this us?" Virtutis asked, forcing a wry grin.

Away from the calamity of too many people, the warhorse shook his head in confirmation.

Virtutis dug his spear into the ground and gently looped Urion's reins over it. Sprawled on his back in the grass with his hands behind his head, he watched the clouds form shapes in the blue sky. Occasionally, one would pass in front of the sun and provide a much-welcomed break from the afternoon heat.

Urion pushed his nose into Virtutis's side.

"What? Something to say?" Virtutis acted annoyed, then smiled. "Do you remember when I found you? I was only fifteen."

Urion's head nodded as though he understood.

"You were just a small, black foal. A flash flood in the mountain rivers had swept you away, almost drowning you." He grinned with a scoff. "Saving you almost cost us our lives, you know? Sometimes, I question my actions, but it was worth it, don't you think?"

29

Again, Urion nodded.

"I named you Urion. He who is sent from heaven. Although you landed in a puddled predicament."

Virtutis couldn't help but feel the weight of having to find a solution to getting Urion home safe. Selling him was not an option.

He sat up cross-legged as if switching positions would help him think.

"Virts!" A familiar voice interrupted his thoughts. Virtutis sat up taller and craned his neck. A small figure bounced sideways around the low, nearby tents.

Virtutis's eyes lit up, cheeks softened, a posture reserved for those close to his heart.

He spun himself around to stand.

"Arquitos," he said in a low tone. "You little rabbit of a man. When did you arrive?"

Arquitos bounded towards him with his boyish features, accepting the compliment with enthusiasm.

He bucked his teeth to the front of his mouth like a rabbit to heighten the humor.

"Yeth-terday!" Arquitos replied.

Virtutis chuckled at the much-needed humor, easing into their typical exchanges formed from a boyhood friendship. "I am going to be running for the Romans!" Arquitos stated proudly. "I heard about a huge warhorse walking with a Spartan." He made a large mountain motion with his arms, finishing with an entertainer's sideways wink of the eye. "I figured it was you!" He cackled.

Virtutis calmed the situation with a short silence. "I am happy for you, brother. If anyone can run a message to the ends of the world, it would be you."

Virtutis beamed with genuine pride at the lean man's accomplishment.

"Arquitos, you deserve it," he continued. "You made it happen like you always said you would. I am sure your infectious attitude and determination will also prevent you from becoming rabbit stew."

"If I'm the rabbit in the stew, then you must be meat stewed with beans with a hot airy joke like that!"

"Ha! Nonetheless, brother, your father would be proud." They grew quiet, reflecting on their old lives. "How is he?" Virtutis inquired.

"Good. He's good. Father is getting fatter by the day," he joked. "And the plantation is almost built."

"That is good to hear. Arcos has a way with business and politics." Virtutis noticed Arquitos looking at Urion, who was seemingly listening to their conversation.

"Did you sign with the horsemen?" Arquitos asked.

"No. I am to sign as reinforcement to the infantry. We leave tomorrow."

"Infantry? Why would they turn away Urion?"

"I don't know," Virtutis replied, his mood souring. "Brother, I need help. I am looking for a rider. Someone who can deliver Urion back to the farm. Someone reliable and capable."

Arquitos scratched his head. "I will find someone. Leave it to me! And about the infantry, I will find out what I can tonight and report back to you by morning." Arquitos looked up at the late afternoon sun. "I have to meet the captain soon for my first message dispatch."

He lowered his tone and puffed his chest, displaying macho pride.

"Well, we best not keep the fastest rabbit on earth from his job," Virtutis replied.

"No, sir! I will find you when I am done. However, you will never see me coming!"

Virtutis laughed again under his breath. "Like you will never see my spear, little rabbit-top."

"Oh, Virtutis, I am just your humble runner. There's no need to be so Spar-tos."

31

They eyed each other up in defiant jest.

Arquitos bowed, then ran between the tents like a hare, intentionally getting in people's way to show off his skills and practice his dodging.

Virtutis exhaled. The youthful excitement brought him a much-needed perspective on one of life's simple joys—belonging.

As he sat back down, Urion immediately double-dipped his head alongside Virtutis's shoulder. The Spartan placed his arm over the stallion's large muscular neck for a reassuring pat and brushed his long mane, stopping it from getting up his nose. "If only you were as fast as that rabbit-boy, huh? My fat-bellied, black bolt of lightning."

Again, the warhorse's neck twisted around, one eye figuring out the meaning behind the words. He nodded and let out a snort of air as if he understood.

Night fell over the camp, and fires lit up in the distance. Virtutis reached into his shoulder bag for a wheat biscuit to weather his hunger, sharing a little to be crunched without mercy.

Curiosity stirred Virtutis to stand. A curiosity greater than the long day of excitement.

Urion turned his ears forward; his muscles twitched in alarm.

"Rest here for a while. I'll be back soon. No unhooking from my spear, huh?"

He checked his dagger, leaving behind his spear and shield, not wanting to stand out amongst new friends.

CHAPTER 4

Naturally suspicious and inquisitive, Virtutis placed his cloak over his head and ventured into the camp's various areas, using the shadows for added cover.

Colorful languages floated across the smoky darkness with their sing-song variances.

The aromatic cooking of various cultures mixed with scents from the smoldering embers dripping meat made him realize how hungry he was. His growling belly yearned for more than a wheat biscuit.

Attentively, he studied the many cultures of people gathered—he was amongst a land of warriors. He was far from home, and this was the opportunity he hoped it would be. A world where he could unleash his anger and hide his aching heart behind it. A world where he would confront the Black Wolf and end the torment.

His mind and body tired. He rounded a large tent of military authority and headed toward his campsite.

Two large guards stood staunch with their hands braced on their swords.

All at once, the hairs on the back of his neck stood on end, and a chill crept over his arms. The wind carried the familiar sound of anguish. Unable to see, he lifted his head higher to listen. A commotion of voices made it impossible to discern what was being said. But then, above the ruckus, a man screamed in desperation.

"Hel—"

"Help. Aghh. Let me—"

He shifted in the shadows, inching closer.

The familiar tone sent a shiver down his spine. Again, it cut through the air, adding to his agitation.

"No…" he whispered to himself.

It became muffled, disappearing beneath the chatter of men around the campfires. Men appeared to ignore the sound like it was common practice, but it only confirmed something very wrong.

With one foot in the light, almost risking his cover, he backed into the shadows.

A man in a robe dragged a limp body from the tent, dumping it on the ground in front of his guards. "Take this spy away. I'm done with my interrogation. Lock him up. No one disobeys our empire. He will be executed tomorrow; do what you may."

Virtutis focused on the body. It can't be. Arquitos's body was being dragged toward the prison pen.

His fists clenched until his knuckles turned white. He is no spy.

Virtutis's veins swelled with adrenaline. His mind raced between reaction and reason.

Wait. This is not the time.

He tracked the guards from afar. When they moved, he followed, maintaining a safe but striking distance.

The guards dragged Arquitos a few steps, then stopped to beat him.

Arquitos groaned, rolling helplessly on the ground, unable to defend himself. There was little he could do apart from accept his beating.

The willingness to react fired within Virtutis's legs, urging him to stop the barrage, but he could do nothing to help. Yet.

Looking down at the unlit ground, he turned from the scene, composing himself.

Arquitos, stay alive. If I act now, we are both dead. Hang on for your life.

Arquitos fell limp, his clothes ripped and offset, his fun-loving energy leaked from him with his blood.

Virtutis's heart dropped further when he noticed blood dripping down his legs. The boy-like, lean runner, a gentle soul with dreams of being in the Roman army, had been stripped of his decency.

Now, he would be executed for resisting—for fighting for his innocence.

Virtutis's frown deepened, his gut twisted in disgust—Arquitos had been raped, and tomorrow, they would put him to death.

Without time to debate, Virtutis cut across the camp, running past the back of Roman legion's tents, an area that was off-limits. His feet light and perfectly poised in a silent sprint, he used the shadows well and did not stop to ask permission. There was an occasional shout to stop, but he was too fast to be recognized, and commotions fell under the intensity of his mission.

Running through the darkness without hesitation, he knew what had to be done.

He owed no one his loyalty outside his own conscience.

The day had not yet closed its cycle, and he was already tempting his fate against the greatest army in the world. His body flew into action, knowing he could be torn apart by the empire's merciless talons.

They would shred him limb from limb for what he was about to do—if they caught him.

The gods had placed events in front of him. There was no time for doubt.

One thing he could not stomach was betrayal. Betraying an intended oath to an empire or betraying his friend.

He huffed as only a Spartan could.

I am sure the empire has been betrayed by greater men.

Virtutis stood hidden by the prison. The guards arrived at the large gate and paused to talk to the night guard, laughing while dragging Arquitos. They dumped him on his stomach in the back of the yard and opened a small wooden cage.

Standing back, one of the guards placed his hand on his chin, pretending he was in deep consideration. "Hey! I have an idea! Grab his arm and a leg."

They picked up the tiny limp body and started swinging him back and forth with sickening snickers of joy. "On three, let's fly the little rabbit!"

They swung him back. They swung him forward.

"One!"

They swung him back.

"Higher!"

They swung him forward, getting more excited.

"Two!"

"Higher! Higher!" Their sick excitement raising their voices. Arquitos's body swung back almost above their shoulders.

"Three!"

Their hands opened wide as though they had finished a great show, letting Arquitos fly through the air. He landed headfirst with a thud.

His shoulders folded, batted against the back of the cage. He grunted in the dirt, where he remained unmoving.

From the shadows, Virtutis's veins flamed in raging heat.

He clenched his jaw in frustration.

One day, I will string you up to bleed like the little Roman pigs you are. I will cut your throats myself. Every one of you.

The Romans stood looking at Arquitos, dusting off their hands as if they were ending a great day's work.

"Look at that, straight to sleep. How anyone can have a good night's sleep before they are about to be executed? I have no idea!" They laughed and tied the door off in a lazy manner. Arms swinging with glee, they chuckled their way back to their posts.

Virtutis put aside the desire for quick revenge. He needed to remove himself from the situation and think.

Instead, he made his way back to the camp where the fire had damped itself down.

Already sensing the tension, his warhorse had unhitched itself from Virtutis's spear and stood ready.

Virtutis gathered a rope from his equipment bag and tied a loop at the end.

Checking the knife at his waist, he then ran low and fast back to the prison pen, stealthing through the darkness behind him.

"Thitt-thhitt," he hissed at Urion.

Urion walked silently to his hand.

Virtutis positioned him by the fence, attached the rope to the top of the saddle, climbed up, then scrambled over the fence.

Dropping to a crouch, he left the rope hanging to the ground and settled still, waiting, watching.

Torchlight cast its way across the prison, causing the human eye difficulty distinguishing between the wind's shadows and real movement. The night remained devoid of sound, and Virtutis moved to the cage where Arquitos lay unconscious. "Brother." He looked around to see if there was a patrol and whispered with more intent, "Arquitos! Arquitos! It's me, Virtutis."

There was still no movement.

Virtutis crawled to the front of the cage, sliced open the rope-tied door and pulled it back. He quickly checked Arquitos's health and shook him gently with no response.

"Arquitos! Arquitos!"

Again, nothing.

Knowing time was running out, he dragged Arquitos out of the cage.

Although quiet and controlled, their movement did not go unnoticed by other prisoners.

Virtutis held his hand out, signaling he knew they were watching, but he urged them to remain silent.

Knowing he was at the mercy of desperate men, he crawled over, cut through the ropes holding the wooden doors on three of the closest cages, and gave each group a whispered instruction. "Wait for the signal. I will tell you when to go. You do not move before I give the order, understand?"

Gaunt faces, awash with disbelief, nodded in reply.

Virtutis returned to Arquitos's limp and lifeless body.

He rolled him to his back and, with a quick movement, gently lifted Arquitos's leg. Positioning his shoulder on his stomach, though keeping a leg hooked, he pivoted to his other elbow, being sure not to crush Arquitos's head. He then hoisted him over his shoulders and stood from a lunge—a practice they used to carry deer back after hunts.

Shuffling Arquitos with a jolt, Virtutis ran to the base of the fence and placed his foot in the rope loop. He held on with one hand, the other still securing Arquitos's elbow and leg together like a staple to avoid losing balance.

"Thhiistt!" he whistled.

The rope tightened, and Urion walked away, creating a steady pull.

They rose to the top of the wall in a smooth, controlled movement.

Virtutis quickly placed his rope hand on the top of the fence and stepped up in an awkward low lunge, balancing with little room for error. "Thit, thit." Urion slowly stepped backward.

Sweat poured from Virtutis's brow. His palm and fingers gripped with all their might to maintain balance on top of the fence; Virtutis knew they had to move.

No doubt, the alarm would soon be raised, and the camp would swarm with guards searching for the escapees.

The rope loosened, and Urion returned underneath them. Virtutis timed his jump the best he could, trying to step down to the saddle, but it was still farther than his reach.

Without an alternative, he leaped in faith.

He slipped, falling back against the fence and crushing Arquitos in the process. It was by far a lesser consequence than death.

"Sorry, old friend," he said in a hushed voice. He shifted his stance, adjusting Arquitos's body, guiding his weight sideways onto the groove of the saddle.

With a whistle, he signaled to the prisoners to attempt their escape.

He hooked the rope to the bottom of the fence and threw it back over to aid them—a reward for their silence. It was in their hands now.

Arquitos lay belly down across the saddle, silent, still unmoving. Virtutis guided Urion by foot into a nearby pasture to examine the unconscious Arquitos.

Hearing hurried footsteps approaching, he crouched, drawing his knife. He adjusted his eyes, one of the prisoners was running toward them. The man held the rope, perfectly wound and tied off.

He held the rope out to Virtutis in two hands with a bowed head of gratitude. "It is better to return a man's rope while you can. Tomorrow's rope could have well been the one that snapped my neck."

He turned, not waiting for a reply, and disappeared into the night.

Arquitos rustled and moaned, finally waking.

Virtutis had no choice. Daylight was upon them. They had to leave.

"Come on. Up you get."

He secured Arquitos to the saddle using the returned rope, attaching it to his wrist with a knot.

"Virtutis," Arquitos said drowsily.

Yells came from the prison.

Torches flared and flamed in the distance.

"Arquitos, return to the farm. Odigos will get you to the sea, then return home. Tell him my wife sent you." Virtutis took Arquitos's hand, shaking it. "My wife sent you. Do you understand?"

"Yes. Yes, I understand," Arquitos replied, bewildered. "But Virtutis, I need to tell you about the infantry. You must come with us."

Shouts grew louder. Men running close by startled Urion, making him twitch.

"Arquitos, the Romans will burn us alive; they know who I am and where I am from. If I leave now, they will hunt us down. Then we are all dead men. Even the boys."

The shouting continued. The searching Romans were getting closer.

Virtutis hushed any further comments. "You have to go."

He moved to the front of Urion, patting his muscular neck.

"Take Arquitos home. We will see each other again one day, I promise." Urion let out a snort, unsettled. Virtutis scanned the area.

We're out of time.

A scream pierced through the night. The type of scream from a man who realizes he is about to be slaughtered.

The Roman guards had captured their first victim.

With an uncharacteristic action, Virtutis rounded on Urion, slapping him on his hindquarter, startling him into a trot toward the trees.

Dagger drawn, Virtutis darted into thicker cover, staying between Urion and the Romans.

The great warhorse stopped ahead in the moonlight, turning his body halfway, so Virtutis could see him. Urion dipped his head hesitantly.

Arquitos struggled at first but forced him to ride on into the darkness.

Shortly after, the increasing distance absorbed their image.

Virtutis turned toward the camp, dodging hunting Romans. Finally, he made it back to his ember-less fire.

His spear stood waiting, dug deep into hollow ground.

Alone under the stars, his heart slowed, and his ears recovered from searching for threats.

Loneliness settled into his heart. He drew a breath of uncertainty, hoping the events were fated by a larger destiny.

A cover of darkness settled over him. Wolves chattered in the forest.

Out of protection for himself and his sons, his mind turned his heart black. A thicker skin of distrust grew over his face.

Now on the hollowed Roman ground, reality had bared the truth—nothing would ever be as it seemed. His admiration for the empire drained into an unforgiving feeling of emptiness.

He swore never to be a victim of such betrayal.

Virtutis lay exposed to a new world, imagining Arquitos and Urion with his body and mind aching.

He threw his blanket over his chest, searching the stars, not worried for his own life.

Sleep conquered his weary eyes just before sunrise.

An unquenchable thirst grasped his throat.

He gagged and scrambled to a deep well, pulling a slippery chain, the weight heavy, draining all his strength. Exhausted, he finally grasped the bucket, lifting it in haste to soothe his pain, but the bottom of the bucket dropped out. Water splashed over his feet and seeped into the desert sand.

He snapped awake. Parched. Dry. Confused.

The rest of the early morning held torment.

The sun rose, bringing even more uncertainty.

He stood, not knowing if his allegiance to service would protect him or if the light of day would bare the truth of last night's events. His Spartan spear clasped firmly in his hand, he stood with a purpose—a stature willing to own new consequences. With an appetite for destruction, he prepared himself for the war ahead, under no illusion there would be no mercy.

CHAPTER 5

Virtutis packed what campsite belongings he could carry into his shoulder bag. Then, with each firm-fisted shove, he pushed the uncertainty to the pit of his stomach.

He walked toward the auxiliary infantry. His bag weighed heavy, like his mind.

Peering between the gaps in the prison fence, six Roman guards hung from crosses, wrists bound in leather straps. Heads hanging low. Dead.

Perhaps some were innocent? Either way, they got what they deserved.

Then he realized he was no better and only a stone's throw away from the same fate, if not worse.

Each step made him further question his part in the Roman army. The idea of his family being hunted and slaughtered and him being left forever haunted by the Black Wolf outweighed the fear of his corpse on a cross.

What is done is done. He had to save Arquitos. It was a matter of honor, a matter of friendship, and one of loyalty. For his conscience's sake, it was worth it.

The mental pressure made the line for the auxiliary move faster.

It was time.

Virtutis refocused his thoughts while he stepped up to the tent.

"Spartan! I did not think I would see you again." Stale wine tainted the clerk's breath.

Virtutis stood tall, the skin on his face thick without expression, his heart black without emotion.

If he were to die here, he would make sure to kill the clerk first. A blade through his beady eye would do.

Under his cloak, Virtutis caressed his dagger with a dark, endearing touch. "I am ready to sign up. No horse. Someone stole him last night."

The clerk fidgeted on his stool, uptight. "Yes. Last night some prisoners escaped, but we will find them. If your great plow-horse is to be found, it is likely with them, no? He will be taken into Roman care and given to someone who can control him. So do not worry. We will soon make a real warhorse out of him. Or..." He eye-balled Virtutis, squinting in delight, wetting his lips, taunting. His breath smelled of ale-filled arrogance, considering himself untouchable. "Or, he will wind up on my dinner plate." He bared his rotting bottom teeth with a cynical smile. The clerk searched Virtutis's face, no doubt liking the thought of providing any discomfort against the Spartan descendant.

Virtutis kept his face impassive. "Thank you, sir. I am sure you will enjoy yourself either way," he said, disarming the verbal attack.

The clerk snickered. "Sign here... Our mighty Peregrinuss-Spartan turned mercenary."

Saliva swirled inside Virtutis's mouth. He pushed it around his gums and between battered teeth. It tasted like blood. Wanting to spit it out, he paused, thinking of his boys.

He signed his name. By the time the ink was absorbed into the papyrus, paranoia had bombarded his brain.

Maintaining physical composure, he scanned everything in the tent, searching for signs of a setup.

He drew a breath.

Movement slowed around him while his mind raced faster than frenzied wolves chasing a wounded rabbit.

A guard adjusted his shield and shuffled his feet, his face grimaced with the obligation of his duty.

The clerk looked on offended. "Next!" He shouted.

Things seemed normal.

There was no sign of threat, but he kept his guard high.

His eyes narrowed, turning toward the sunlit exit, an exit that would normally shed relief but now held a tightness in his stomach. The dryness in his throat forced an involuntary cough, reminding him of the sand from his desert dream.

He left the tent, passing his hand over the stubble of his shaved head. He trusted no one. From this day forward, he would have to be careful of every word he spoke and every man he met.

By noon, he found his unit. Men shuffled around, changing their attire.

Pulling on a tunic, chest armor, and a red Roman cloak, he shed his old clothes and life with them. A snake slithering out of its skin.

"Shield and spear are to be traded," the armory clerk said.

Virtutis said nothing, laying down his shield and spear, collecting a short sword, larger shield, and Roman spear. With a sleight of hand, when nobody was watching, he swapped the spear out for his father's weapon of choice, taking back his ancestry. He would not be without his body and soul's extension.

Falling into formation under a crimson banner, he became just another soldier—a chameleon with an unquenchable thirst, hoping to camouflage himself in red blood.

But it did not move so fast.

Slow days of marching rolled into weeks.

Going through the motions, he walked stony roads, grassy meadows, and mountain forests. All the while, an emptiness in his soul came and went. Summer rains fell, and the hot nights brought mosquitos, adding a fight against the small, relentless enemy.

He rarely talked to anyone, and rarely did anyone talk to him. Where he could, he found solitude away from the camp. His sleep was broken with the Black Wolf clawing at the trap door beneath his sons' cots.

The hot midday sun held no shelter. Virtutis sat alone, sharpening his spear. Testing the blade's razor edge with his finger, he lifted his head, checking the other members of his unit taking shade. Some sat with tunics over their heads. Others lay on their backs, resting. He continued to grind and, with each passing of the sharpening stone, began to accept the hollowness of the Roman ideal, determined not to let it influence who he was destined to be. On the other side of virtue were the inflictions of the iniquitous. Virtutis wondered where the scales of his journey would tip him next and, ultimately, who would be the judge.

A thick-set figure walked through the groups of men. He approached direct, intentionally crossing pathways.

The thick man's shaved head made his face seem rounder than most.

"May I join you?" His accent was too foreign to know where he came from, his tone foretelling he wanted a detailed conversation, a conversation Virtutis had little interest in.

Refusing to look up, Virtutis opened his hand, irritated by the forced invitation.

The man released a sound of relief. "My name is Fatu Khan."

He continued refining the blade. "Virtutis," he replied, focusing on his weapon.

The two men sat without talking, sweating in the smelting sun.

Uneasy, keeping Khan in his peripheral, Virtutis studied Rome's newest mercenaries. Listening to their words and behaviors created differences, separating them from one another. Then, when the eagle looked away, they fought for authority within the ranks. Pressured men divided, with selfish egos on one side and selfless patriots on the other. In the middle, the uncertain were unknowingly viced in a merciless beak that would eventually be pecked apart.

Virtutis eased pressure over the sharpening stone to a gentle caress, refining the razored edge of the spear. He paused accepting the situation and prepared for what he must, but one thing he knew, he would not be trapped in the middle.

A change in the distant trees caught Virtutis's attention. Birds flurried away, fleeing from an unseen predator.

Virtutis checked on Khan, unsure about his motives.

With one hand holding the shaft of the spear, he pulled a cloak from his bag with his free hand to clean the tip of his spear.

He felt Khan's eyes watching, but still, he did not entertain any dialogue.

Movement started within the scattered groups.

Their commander strutted through the men. Ridden with sweat dripping from his brow, he secured one hand from the top of his excessive chest armor while the other hand rested on his sword. He stopped and straightened. "Get up; let's move! We have barbarians to war with!" he yelled with deep-toned belittlement, like trying to motivate children. His intention to motivate felt as delusional as his choice of words.

The men slowly made their way to their feet, uninspired.

Khan grunted as he stood, letting out a sigh. "Let's see how long he stays alive for?"

Virtutis did not bait at the comment, although he agreed.

They made their way into loose formation and marched into the unknown.

The night slowly pulled her veil over blue-red skies as the high-horsed commander led them into harsh hinterlands by the full moon's light.

Footsteps and lungs of unaccustomed men searching for air over unstable, steep trails filled the trees with murmurs of complaint. At times, the terrain forced them into a single file as the commander ordered the flag bearer in front like he was a warning for any potential threat against the great empire. Virtutis did not like the vulnerability of their thin and exposed position. He checked his dagger and repositioned his spear to mid-shaft, letting men walk past, intentionally falling behind the main group.

Khan followed suit, maintaining distance, Virtutis knowing he was watching his every move. Khan's breathing was heavy. It blocked Virtus's hearing—a sense he often relied on—frustrating him to no end.

Virtutis dropped his head, listening through Khan's noise deep into the night.

"Stop," he whispered, placing the back of his hand on Khan's chest, halting them both, also holding up the men behind them.

Virtutis crouched on instinct; Khan and the men followed his lead.

He drew a long breath through his nose, smelling the air. He held it while glaring into the shadows, justifying his instinct.

The faint smell of fire, a stench he knew too well.

Ash war paint. War paint from the tribal customs of barbarian fires.

Images of his dead wife came flooding back, making his stomach churn.

The night birds had stopped their song, and the crickets fell silent. Clouds covered the moon on and off, plummeting the tiring Roman Auxiliary reinforcements into frequent complete darkness as they walked deeper into unknown danger.

Above, clouds cleared, and Virtutis noticed a small break in the moonlit tree line.

"Down here." He descended to a narrow trail. The rocky slope, layered with shingles, was hard to navigate with limited vision. Virtutis used tree branches and a bare hand on the rocks to subdue the noise while holding his spear ready. The sound of Khan and the men followed suit.

Virtutis stopped to regroup. He searched their hardened faces. Eight. Making him nine.

"We go back to where we came from but stay below the trail," he said, urgent but blunt. "Be quiet and watch your feet." He squared up to Khan with a cynical grin. "Or you might step on a barbarian. When the time is right, follow my lead. We do not know what we will find. There will be no time for plans."

Together they scrambled through the trees and over rocks, backtracking until Virtutis halted downwind.

"Up here." He pointed his spear to a slight incline that led above the trial. He listened hard, but still, there was an alarming silence. "Quickly, we don't have much time. We have to catch up to our men before it is too late."

Latching his spear over his back, Virtutis climbed, grabbing tree branches and stumps for support. His sandals occasionally slipped under pressure to gain high ground. But his anger toward the barbarians far outweighed any obstacle.

Conquering the steep incline left the men panting, trying to keep up the pace.

"Wait," Virtutis ordered. "Gather your breath." Once recovered, Virtutis added, "Good. Control your breathing from here. Stay high and don't go down any farther. Be steady. And no mistakes."

Under the forest canopy's cover, over moonlight-speckled terrain, they pushed forward, gaining on their allies being led to their death without notion.

Their stealthy movements were soon covered by the auxiliary. A random cough, an occasional clunk of metal, and whispered chatter drifted up from below. They had reached the larger group.

Virtutis slowed his steps with caution.

Clouds drifted in again, blacking out the moon.

A bird sounded its call. A song Virtutis recognized from many years ago.

He crouched, letting out an uncontrollable deep groan. Wolf-like.

They were here, hidden. Some kind of barbarian force was poised for an attack.

Reaching down, he scrapped his hand around, finding a rock.

His men gathered behind him.

The night became pitch black.

In one fluid motion, he launched the rock on top of the barbarians, hoping it would sound a warning. Hoping it would buy the commander enough time to react.

The slap of the rock hitting leaves and branches and ending in a thud on a tree trunk abruptly ended the signal. Shields clunked, ready to defend. Then a sudden silence held the forest hostage. Not a breath was heard.

"Attack!" a lone voice screamed.

Unable to see into the darkness below, Virtutis cracked his neck. Listening, waiting to make his move.

The forest came alive with barbarian war cries like Hades had broken the peaceful gates of Earth, set on ravaging the soul of men.

Clashes of metal on metal and men fighting for their lives echoed through the forest.

Patient, Virtutis waited.

The initial screams and commotion changed to the reality of war. Men shoving and pushing, the battering of axes on Roman auxiliary shields, and the wailing of barbarians being stabbed. A song of life and death that Virtutis knew too well, providing a compass for a stealth attack.

"It cannot be that easy," Virtutis said under his breath. He looked back at Khan. "The barbarians were smart enough to wait this long. They must be more prepared." He unlatched his spear. "With me, stay close."

Fast and low, Virtutis led the men closer to the battle.

His grip on his spear was loose, but he was ready to react. The clouds lifted, opening moonlight that shone on an untamed battle.

He let out a quiet huff. Between his elevated position and his men trapped on the trail, barbarians were lined up undercover for a full downhill assault.

He stopped on a large rock above the rear of the war-hungry barbarians.

49

A spark followed by a small fire exploded into life.

The barbarians had set a fire trap. Five men surrounded the blaze, dipping their arrows into the flames. The tips started to shine their lethal light through the darkness. Darkness, severed by the light of death's messengers.

If the fire landed on the trail, it would mean panic, and panic meant death.

Virtutis had to act now.

He spun the clumsy Roman shield from his back, bracing it over his forearm.

Into the dark, directly over the fire, he leaped.

Not knowing how the landing would go, he exhaled, relaxing his body. He prepared for the worst, bending slightly at the knees, ready for impact.

Crack!

His feet slammed into the flames, snapping wood and spitting embers in all directions, his Spartan eyes gleaming from the depths of Hades itself.

The archers stepped back, frightened, surprised.

Virtutis took advantage of their hesitation. He extended his spear, sweeping it in a cutting motion, its razor-sharp edge severing all flesh in its way.

Three barbarians fell, squirming in agony.

Fire snapped at Virtutis's legs, forcing his exit from the fire. He pulled his spear back, stabbing the closest throat.

Fumbling, the last remaining archer turned to nock his arrow, but Virtutis was too quick, thrusting his spear straight through an unprotected spine. The barbarian collapsed. The flaming arrow buried its head into the earth and was swiftly swallowed by a river of red.

"Behind us!" a barbarian yelled. A roar that woke the earth.

A horde of broad, camouflaged barbarians rose from their ditches. Half of them turned toward the fire. Virtutis glanced over his shoulder.

The fire flickered on a smooth towering wall of limestone, a crag of no retreat.

Isolated, with too many figures to count, Virtutis spun his spear. He thought of his sons and the Black Wolf clawing at their door.

With his shield lifted, he peered over its protection from the onslaught of ominous silhouettes.

He cracked his neck, releasing all tension, then lowered his stance.

A howl echoed through the forest.

He scoffed out his nose from the back of his throat.

Finally, his quest to be reborn in the face of death had begun.

He studied the approaching barbarians for weaknesses. He had to attack the flank. To stay center would mean a quick death.

He stepped to the left, backing himself in front of a broken boulder, limiting the degree of attack.

"Ahhhhh!" roared a familiar voice.

Khan came barreling from his right, bracing his shield in front, barging the barbarians.

More shouts came when the rest of his men started to engage to his far right. Khan was soon caught in hard contact and had no choice but to use his sword and shield in a more conventional manner. The attacks encroached on him from the front and sides, forcing him backward.

Virtutis stepped forward. He had to control the left flank, or Khan would be engulfed by an unconquerable swarm.

Using the full length of his spear, Virtutis stabbed at the head of the nearest barbarian, forcing him to raise his shield. He swiped the tip low at bare ankles. The barbarian fell to his knees, providing a launching pad for Virtutis's foot. He exploded forward, springing off, getting high above the attack. He darted his spear at any exposed head. Landing, he swept low with the spear's shaft, causing more to fall or stumble. Lifting his stance, he threw the spear into the chest of an off-balanced victim. Drawing his short sword, he barged and sliced his way without staying still, probing and stabbing at anything that moved. His pace was faster than a man could think, his strikes precise, without doubt.

Bodies littered his wake. He moved to support Khan's side but did not stop. Barbarians dropped like a fistful of rocks scattered into a bloody stream.

Khan screamed a war cry Virtutis could not understand, the sound imposing an intimidation that unleashed fierce energy over their enemies. They fought side by side. His men soon found formation. Together they pushed the barbarians back down the hill, corralling their foe into a position of no escape.

It became a slaughter.

The road to Rome running red without mercy.

The Roman auxiliary reinforcements yelled in triumph, surviving the deadly ambush. But it was not without casualties. Many men lay dead or wounded on the trail.

Virtutis signaled to Khan. "Attend to those who we can save. The rest—give them the option of a quick death; either way, they will be dead before dawn."

The moans of dying men filled the forest.

Virtutis stepped over the corpses, offering respect and assistance where he could.

An anguished hand reached out to him from a nearby ditch. He kneeled, looking into the shadows. A young barbarian boy, arm outstretched, pleaded for mercy with his eyes. The hairs on Virtutis's arms stood on end. It could have been Stoa. The boy groaned, gasping for breath. He collapsed, limp and dead.

Through the night air, the Black Wolf howled, waiting to feast on the souls of dying men. This boy would be one.

A horse neighed ahead on the trail. Through the darkness, the commander sat tall, armor intact, sword drawn and unused. Virtutis stared at him through the mist of warm blood rising.

"Maybe he fell asleep on his horse and rode away from the fight?" Khan said.

Virtutis walked through the ditch up toward the rock without responding.

"Where are you going?" Khan asked.

"To get my spear," Virtutis replied.

"Fall in!" the commander shouted.

Virtutis did not look back. He continued up the hill and pulled his spear from the chest of a dead barbarian, his face black with ash, eyes still open, and the look of surprise still fresh.

"The Black Wolf had no time with you, did he, brother? May you find your peace in the afterlife."

"Fall in!" The commander's frustration grew. Virtutis squeezed his spear, looking back down to the trail. He could sever the commander's throat from here. It being so dark, he would never see it coming. Virtutis scoffed and returned down the hill, stepping over the dead boy in the ditch.

The auxiliary line started to amble along. Even with a slow pace, a young infantryman limped, struggling to keep up. Unannounced, Virtutis came up beside him, scooping his arm around the man's waist from in front of his arm, lifting the body weight from under his armpit, relieving pressure from his wounded leg.

"Walk," Virtutis said. "Walk, or you will be left to die."

Near dawn, ragged, beaten, and hungry, they made camp by a stream.

Khan had sparked up a fire away from the men. Virtutis helped the injured man to the main camp and returned to sit with Khan without a word.

Khan broke the silence. "More than half of us are dead, and more than half here are injured." He shook his head. "There is uncertainty and doubt. The men fear they will never reach our post before being slaughtered. We must do something."

Keeping his silence, Virtutis stood and left to find solitude. The image of the dying boy in the ditch triggered a wave of regret that he had from leaving his sons, making the nights hard to face. He chose to stalk the shadows and venture into the depths of the forest, seeking solace in the silence.

The next months were filled with close victories and scattered defeats. Many of the injured died. But with each battle, Virtutis's killer instinct grew, almost elegant. However, he was riddled with discontent with the commander's tactical decisions on terrains he knew nothing about.

Virtutis's actions and experience gave him a reputable influence that waged an internal war over battlefield leadership. Regardless of battle plans or orders, men would find Virtutis and follow his lead. In the mayhem of fighting for survival, he dolled out blunt orders, saving lives and tipping the blade of war when defeat was breathing down their dirt-ridden necks. And while the nights calmed the sunlit battlefields, the true fight in Virtutis's mind had only just begun. The Black Wolf's fanged smile shuddered him awake from his dreams' shadows while razored claws tore at his soul.

With little conversation, Virtutis often retired to solitude, cleaning his spear and short sword.

Khan sat nearby with a few men, watching as if protecting an asset—their only hope of survival.

Virtutis saw many meetings in the middle of the night. Meetings where men fought for security and control of their density while withstanding the limitless Roman thirst for conquest and power. Leaving behind them dust that settled over streams of drying blood, soaking the earth that leaked from unknown fallen men. Rivers ran red with the blood of fallen men's open veins.

In the heat of summer, the commander left cold impressions wherever he walked, causing respect to fall away like dying leaves from inadequate decisions. Decisions that killed many good men. Unnecessarily slain before their time.

After a close victory tallied by many casualties, Virtutis limped back to his camp. Before cleaning his spear, he watered a rag to wash his bloody face. He sat over a sharpening stone with his spear. His back-and-forth grind was accompanied by a low, deep groan. The mantra of a man possessed.

Khan soon interrupted his hypnotic state. He sat closer than normal, for the first time, intruding.

"What do you want?" Virtutis asked, short and gruff.

He tilted his head sideways, listening before releasing words into the cool breeze.

"The commander is dead," Khan said. "And the senior officers have also been killed." Khan's words seemed to hang in the air between treason and coincidence.

Virtutis said nothing, rotating his spear to sharpen the other side.

Khan sighed. "The men have been unhappy for some time. There was nothing we could do to stop them." He scratched his head. "It has left us a long way from support. We have no leadership, and we are without guidance. As a force, we are depleted and vulnerable."

Virtutis picked up his blood-soaked rag, wiped away shards from the spear tip, and then tested it with his finger. "And what has this to do with me? The men have done what the Romans did to us. Neither you nor they can be trusted. The only true thing is the reality of the blade. It is either dull or sharp. Does it maim or kill?"

Khan jostled his posture. "Virtutis, the men—they trust you. They will follow you."

Virtutis placed his spear down gently, reaching for his shield. "The choice is not theirs to make. I am no leader. I am a warrior, a soldier under the command of Rome." Virtutis fired his eyes at Khan for the first time, holding the gaze until Khan looked away, conceding the unsaid truth of mutiny.

Virtutis wiped his beaten shield, then folded up the rag before packing it away. "I will not involve myself in such conspiracies." The thought alone shot warnings through his bones.

Khan followed with a desperate tone. "Without leadership, we will perish. If we fall apart now, we will all die. The barbarians will pick us apart." Khan's tone rose, putting his case forward without begging. "We want to live. If we waited any longer to take action, the commander would have killed us anyway. You know that to be the truth. If you need me to attest to any treason, I will confess. You have my word. We cannot get any weaker. We will all die."

"Khan. I will die facing my fate in battle, not in treason. I have seen the truth of these men. Sooner or later, someone will spear me in the back." Virtutis felt Khan's frustration, his attempts to add to his disappointment.

"My oath is yours. I will protect your back, and so will the men. They too will swear their oaths to you."

"I understand the situation, Khan, but this is not for me. If I assume any type of leadership, I'm a dead man." He thought of his sons but did not give away such information. "If these men do not murder me, I will be hung by the Romans for conspiracy."

"I don't think so, Virtutis. The men respect you. They will follow you. They will show loyalty." Virtutis sensed Khan's pressure to resolve. "To be prosecuted by the Romans, we would have to survive this first."

Conflicted, Virtutis could understand why Khan played his treason card but again said nothing.

Khan stood. "There is not much time," he added before excusing himself. Virtutis studied his back while he returned to men gathering around a campfire.

Soldiers rallied to talk long into the night. Khan looked agitated and used fierce body language, slamming his chest and shaking his head.

Virtutis kept his distance, having no desire to hear anything they were saying.

He dearly wanted his mission to remain the same—he just wanted to fight. But, without a leader, there would be no more fighting, only a massacre. Either way, all of them would likely be hunted and killed for treason.

The truth was clear. The future unforeseeable.

He threw his cloak over his shoulders and gathered his spear and shield. Then, without notice, he walked into the forest, leaving the safety of his fire.

In a small clearing, where the stars shined through the treetops, he sat and curled under his cloak to keep warm. He watched the stars blink, hoping they would soften his thoughts. They did not. Resting back, he gave in to the stress and chaos of war's unpredictability. The tiredness of the day's battle began to surface like deep fatigue. Knowing he shouldn't, he turned sideways and placed his head on his arm.

He closed his eyes.

Leaving him vulnerable to man and beast deep in enemy territory.

CHAPTER 6

A bellow-like growl agitated Virtutis's sleep, a tone so deep it vibrated his internal organs.Instinct told him not to move.

A firm nudge hit his back. Followed by the backs of his legs. The front of his neck. His feet, his groin, and his abdomen were all being sniffed and nudged.

He focused, trying not to react. He pulled a little breath through his nose, slow, cautious. Staying controlled, keeping his heart rate steady. Commanding his veins not to pulse with a Spartan response.

A large sniff at his ear caused a deafening sound in his eardrum. He wanted to react, but he maintained his composure.

Something tugged at his sandal. He let his leg get pulled straight and tossed from side to side. Eventually, the sandal came loose, followed by the ferocious growling of competition and the chopping of jaws.

His heart pounded hard and fast with the realization, causing intensifying chaos in trying to control his body's reaction.

Wolves. Maybe a pack.

He dared not move. Not yet.

The stench of wet fur and dripping saliva crept up his nostrils.

His spear and shield were an arm's length away. Any sudden movement could result in him being ripped apart. Then they would attack and render him helpless.

He allowed the wolves to probe more, sensing their size. They pushed him around the dirt with their foreheads, playing out their investigation. They used their paws to scratch and dig around Virtutis's limbs, looking for any reaction.

Soon they would snap. Soon they would bite.

He rolled with the movements, just enough to keep them unaware that beneath their play, he was calculating his escape.

Another deep growl came from further away, making his liver shiver.

Now half on his side, belly down, Virtutis opened the eye closest to the ground. He blinked away dirt, trying to focus, but grit fell back in, cutting at his eyeball and causing him to blink more. A wolf pack surrounded him.

Cold blood surged inside of him, numbing his legs. Tears from his bottom eye finally washed away the debris.

Little by little, inch by inch, the wolves stepped back, watching their plaything, fixing their hazel eyes for any movement.

A chorus of sounds erupted from the pack.

Some whimpered and whined with disappointment, wanting to continue playing and eventually attack. Others growled, keeping any chance of retaliation under submission.

The temperature plummeted.

He opened both eyes.

Growling and snapping of jaws came from all around. The fierce owners of the night, offended by him, played coy.

He fired into action, leaping for the protection of his shield and spear, gathering them with a roll.

Taking a battle stance, firming his fighting posture, he rotated with one bare foot, grinding a base in the dirt. Turning steady with his spear low and long, his shield covering half his body, he measured the distance, judging possible attacks while setting a parameter.

The wolves howled louder.

Virtutis regripped his spear.

Their attack could come at any time. But they held their distance. Why?

Through the darkness appeared more and more eyes.

The pack was larger than Virtutis could have ever imagined. He swiveled around, trying to find an exit—a simple escape did not exist.

This would cost him his own flesh and blood.

He prepared himself to fight, forever if need be.

He lowered further into his stance, grinding the side of his bare foot deeper into the earth, lifting his back heel just a little. He narrowed his eyes with an unyielding focus.

A silent submission came across the pack. Something imperious was coming.

A pair of eyes appeared from the darkness. They grew larger until the shape of a black wolf's head came forth. Its forehead and jaws became dwarfed by a bigger-shouldered frame with powerful legs.

Its teeth longer than a man's dagger.

Virtutis steadied, his veins bulged, ready.

The wolf pack retreated, opening a gap wide enough for the Black Wolf not to cause any reason for their death.

The giant wolf looked down, holding no regard for Virtutis's crouched readiness to fight.

The wolf's breath like vapor leaked outward from the corners of his mouth. His jaws opened like a large cave waiting to collapse without mercy. He licked the side of his lips with a huge tongue.

Virtutis's head tilted slightly.

Knowing there was no escape, Virtutis showed an intentional sign of disregard, rejecting eye contact with the alpha. Instead, he stared around, provoking the wolf pack with a Spartan snarl, testing their obedience, causing chaos amongst them.

They snapped their jaws and clawed at the dirt, wanting to rip his flesh apart.

He stood upright and lowered his shield. Then cracked his neck, attempting to display calmness, sending a message that the pack was in no way his equal.

Lifting the shaft of his spear high with a spin and an accurate slip of wood over familiar skin, he stabbed it deep into the ground.

Spartan-hearted, he stepped forward, directly under the mouth of the wolf.

He opened his arms wide. "If you want to take me, I am ready. I have no fear."

The Black Wolf bared his teeth, ground his bottom jaw by pulling it back, and finished the motion with almost puckered lips of pleasure.

Virtutis, with a defiant nod, lifted his posture higher toward the large hazel eyes of death's passage. "There is no right or wrong time to die." He rolled back his shoulders, extending his chest forward. With a jolt, he extended his arms. "I am ready." Virtutis lifted his chin more. Exposing his neck. "Take me now!"

The Black Wolf's eyes focused on the veins in Virtutis's neck. He jerked his head away—away from temptation.

The giant teeth snapped from a powerful jaw.

Virtutis did not flinch. "My father told me tales of the Black Wolf and how he hunted Spartan warriors with fear in their blood. But you never got my father's, and you will never get mine."

Virtutis smiled, knowing he had won an advantage.

The wolf tried to regain his intimidation. Rounding on his tasty Spartan prey, he crossed his front legs over each other and wound his body around behind Virtutis. His fur was coarse, harsh against human skin.

Virtutis shifted his body, facing the wolf straight on. He lowered his chin, leveling his head.

"Well, if you do not want to kill me now, what is there left to do?" Turning away from the confrontation, Virtutis pulled his spear from the blood-hungry earth. He twirled it with ease and pivoted his bare foot to face the wolf's massive body again. "Are we done?"

The Black Wolf's energy shifted to frustration and anger.

Virtutis scoffed, gripping his spear just in case of attack.

Infuriated, the Black Wolf pounded his paws back and forth, thudding the ground beneath them. The closest wolves scattered from his reach, whimpering away in fear of consequences meant for Virtutis that could result in their death.

Virtutis backed away, then turned, leaving his back to the wolf.

The wolf attacked, pounding his head into Virtutis's exposed spine. He tried to roll in defense, but the wolf's teeth pierced his shoulder blade.

He arched in pain. Frantic, trying to crawl with his arms and legs, he remained pinned.

Virtutis woke bewildered, face buried in the dirt. Rising to his knees, he found his feet.

His heart pounded while he stood alone in the forest.

From above the trees, the moon lit the way back to camp. The earth under one exposed foot gave comfort. Where is my sandal?

Breaking from the trees, the coldness of the Black Wolf's presence removed itself from Virtutis's veins, and a little warmth returned.

Fires lit the encampment in defense.

Virtutis caught the attention of the few soldiers who stood on guard. They sounded the alert before they recognized Virtutis's figure. Their tired, pale faces remained pinched, perhaps spooked by the distant howling.

"Lower your weapons," Virtutis reassured. Their faces echoed relief.

Virtutis walked straight to Khan, nose to nose. "Tell the men to be ready at dawn. Anyone not willing to give their oath can leave. Anyone not following our code after they swear their oath will feel my spear through their heart. Any dishonesty or lack of loyalty will mean certain death. Understood?"

Khan nodded. "Sir."

Virtutis had accepted. For now, he was a commander.

"Sir?" Khan's voice broke into pieces as though hesitant to speak. "Your sandal? Where is your other sandal?"

Virtutis walked on, replying, "Waiting for me in the belly of the afterlife."

He found space away from the men, looking to the shadows beyond the trees. Lifting his eyebrows, he bit his lower lip, then released it slowly. Had he really just escaped death? The encounter with the Black Wolf left him rattled.

Regardless of what he did or did not experience, he had assumed command.

He would take the fight to the barbarians and the Black Wolf.

There was movement in the shadows. A cold presence cast itself over the camp. He shivered, pulling up the hood from his cloak.

"If you want a duel of death, my little black pup, I will show you the way."

He drew his sharpening stone, preparing to finish his ritual, looking sideways. Khan issued the new orders.

A small group of men gathered their belongings, huddled together briefly, then ran into the shadows, unwilling to follow the new command.

There were howls and barks in the distance, followed by brief screams from men being torn apart. Eventually, the night drowned the cries of the dying men.

A different silence fell upon the forest, its intimidation serving a new purpose that would force his men to cling to his leadership and his cause.

CHAPTER 7

Virtutis overlooked the camp with withdrawn, sleepless eyes. He rotated his shoulder, sore from jabbing his spear, tender from his nightmare. He scanned the forest out of habit while he hatched plans with men he had no closeness with. The coldness of reality filled his mind; leadership was a curse to a warrior. He could not defeat the enemy of his predecessor, nor could he send a message down the Black Wolf's spine by himself. But one thing was for sure: His mind needed to be clear—he would not fall victim to those he led by living in an illusion of war and the games it played in the minds of unprepared men.

His calloused hand spun the spear shaft, mimicking the spinning of his mind and the crucial first decisions of command. So many realities spun and twisted doubt in the events around him that he could not control.

No decision is as deadly as the wrong decision.

He huffed.

Enough.

Khan approached somewhat cautiously, carrying a new pair of sandals and a shoulder bag.

Virtutis outstretched his hand, receiving the offer.

Khan nodded, pleased as if he'd brushed off a little of his tension.

"What's in the bag?" he asked.

"Maps and papers. The last of the commander's documents," Khan replied.

Virtutis felt a wall of protection build over himself. Protection of what he did not yet know about military command, putting the shoulder bag down until he was alone.

"Are we organized?" Virtutis tied his sandals, not looking up.

"Yes. The wounded are taken care of. We have sent those closest to death back into the woods. They will be guarded by the least wounded. They will await further instructions. The rest of the men are in good condition and ready for orders."

"Good. Do we have information about the barbarians?" Virtutis cocked his head to the side, cracking his neck and looking past Khan to the camp. Surveying. Listening.

"The runners saw them in the upper cliffs yesterday. It looked as if they had regathered, maybe preparing for an assault? Most likely, they will come to finish us off once they are prepared."

"How many?" Virtutis looked directly into Khan's eyes, forcing the shorter man to inhale through his nostrils before responding.

"One hundred, maybe one hundred and fifty? Our numbers have dwindled. We merely have seventy now, and taking away the injured, we're left with... thirty-five."

Virtutis shook off the outnumbered difference. He thought deeper, tilting his head, maintaining his eye lock.

Spartans never considered the odds. He planned to kill them all— and he would ensure they found a fiery hell.

"How far up the hill? In the tree line or further up in the rocks?"

"They are up in the rocks," Khan replied. "It is impossible to attack them. They would cut us down. It is too steep, and the rocks are loose. There are side tracks up, but they would make it a narrow attack."

"Agreed. But they expect us to run. We do not know this place like they do. We must go for the throat, or we die."

Khan let out a deep murmur. "Ahem."

"Send ten bowmen and three runners out again to confirm. Be sure that one runner comes back with the confirmation. The other two can wait and watch, but they must move together. If there are any barbarian movements, a runner comes back to inform us, but one must always follow while leaving a trail. Whoever comes back to report returns immediately to rejoin and reinforce the who is waiting, and so on."

Virtutis spun his spear. "It's imperative we know every move they make. If the barbarians try to descend, tell the bowmen to cut them down and push them back from the tree line, if possible, or at least slow them down. After you issue those orders, send ten men to gather as much dry brush as they can, bail it only on one end. Each of our men must carry four bails and their weapons. Tie them to their backs, if you must."

"Sir?"

Virtutis looked at the clouds moving quickly across the skyline without looking down at Khan. "Do as I say. Do it quickly. Our time is running out."

"Sir." Khan snapped his head as he turned, gliding down the hill with a purposeful stride that carried energy to complete his orders.

Virtutis focused on his men dispersing into action. Taking flint rocks from his bag, he struck them together with a spark, testing their ignition. Click. Click-click. Satisfied, he stood, preparing his spear and shield, then wiggling his toes in his new sandals.

Taking one final look, he snapped his neck to the side, ready for a destiny he had never contemplated.

The energy amongst the men was different now.

Virtutis scanned their faces. Their eyes lifted without question, adjusting postures to a new purpose.

"So, it seems our destinies are intertwined." Virtutis tilted his head, gripping his spear. "May the gods give you the strength to stay the course."

Virtutis walked beside smoldering fires to the far edge of the camp. He waited. Men attached to bales of brush—almost ready.

66

Virtutis readjusted the grip on his shield and spear, then broke into a jog, striding down the sloping valley, pushing every man's urgency to play catch-up, intensifying the already tense change of pace.

From the plains of hard clay and occasional shrub, Virtutis led them into the mountain cliffs' lower tree line. His heart rate accelerated from the anticipation of his first action as commander.

He circled the trees for cover without slowing, holding a fast pace. Unforgiving.

After several minutes, he paused in a small clearing. He inhaled long through his nose, clearing his mind.

His heart rate dropped, but it maintained a forceful pump, expanding his veins. Veins that flowed like rivers over his feet and up his lower legs—full, primed in readiness. The reality of the speed he felt was far from his nightmares' torment.

Khan came dodging around crouching men covered in bundles, doing his best to catch up. He seemed alert and ready to follow instructions. But still lacked air in his lungs.

Virtutis shook his head. "Out of breath again, Khan? If you are winded so easily, how can any man trust you?"

"My axe is not fueled by air. It is fueled with the spirit of taking as many with me as I can," Khan said. "So far, no one's been left alive to complain about my breathing."

Virtutis contained his grin.

"Align the men with bundles below the tree line, so they are ready. Space out evenly but leave a gap there"—Virtutis pointed—"on the right side that leads around to the trees. When they stack the bundles, make sure they stack more toward the top and lighter toward the bottom, like a triangle. Send the bowmen to the opposite lateral position on those upper rocks." He pointed his spear at closed rock formations. "There on the left, as the flames move upward with the wind, the bowmen must follow behind and let loose on instinct. Tell them no barbarian gets through the flame wall. Light the bundles when I give the command. They cannot escape this way. Understand?"

"Understood." Khan stayed low, ordering quiet commands.

Virtutis spun his spear, then held it firm, hoping the plan would hold as well. He turned his head, checking their positions. Confirming the preparation, he rose from the cover of the trees and walked into the open to secure a better look. Loose rock shingles crackled under his feet. He glanced upward at the crest of the flat ledge where the barbarians had supposedly fortified themselves.

Whispering to the wind, he sent his declaration of intention: "While you are not easy to get to, you have no escape."

Virtutis looked back toward Khan, still hidden from view, and slowly swept his spear low, signaling to begin.

Men crawled out of the trees with their bundles of brush, placing them up the rocky terrain in two wide triangle formations, leaving a narrow space on the right-hand side.

Virtutis watched small weeds move in the breeze, assessing the wind. He nodded back to Khan, then took cover back in the trees.

Men scrambled back after laying the brush.

Virtutis made his way toward the right flank, hitting the butt of his spear on the backs of men crouching in turn. "Come, come—you stay here—come," he repeated down the line until he was jogging with fifteen men behind him. Cutting, climbing high up into the tree line without pause, they poured over rocks and fallen trees.

Virtutis stopped. He pointed with his spear. "There, there, there— and there. Hide well. Make no sound. Attack only from behind or the side. Not from the front." Inspecting his men, he noted a tall, lean warrior.

"You, Skinny. Take these flint rocks, return to the bottom, and light the fires so the flames feed upward. When you are done, come back here with the runners. Tell the bowmen to let loose as soon as the barbarians stir but to pace their arrows well."

The skinny soldier looked down at the stones.

Virtutis spat out a harsh whisper, "Now!"

The runner turned with haste, disappearing down the pathway.

"The rest of you position yourselves—go!" he said with a grumbled tone.

His men dissolved into the trees without a sound. The skinny runner had disappeared.

Virtutis studied the trees and high rock-faced cliffs and scaled a plain. His nostrils flared. It did not take long for the smell of smoke to drift through the air. By the time he had concluded the next part of their attack, Skinny returned with the runners.

"Skinny, you and the runners gather rocks. Once you have filled your shoulder bags, climb over the path up there on that ledge; stay hidden. When I give the command, attack their backs."

Skinny was the first to move.

They immediately began searching for rocks.

He lowered his head, listening.

Shouts from above echoed down, with the odd arrow hitting rock from a steady barrage of attacks. Smoke came thicker in waves, testing his vision under the involuntary act of eyes welling up. Virtutis felt the energy of the once-cool forest change to a hot desert day. Veins on his forearms bulged in readiness with the grip on his shield. He shot his spear out long, sliding it through his grip and back again—testing his battle-ready control.

Gripping the shield tighter, he flexed his wrist. Smoke wafted thicker over the trail's exit from the mouth of the plateau above. If it were thick here, it would be intolerable further up. Virtutis stood at the opening of the narrow pathway, forcing anyone coming down to narrow their attack, an attack that would meet his readied spear.

Rocks scraped loose under reckless feet, perking up his ears.

Screams echoed through the valley from high above. Tumbling rock meant one thing—the barbarians had started their escape.

"Hold your position." He crouched, looking over his shoulder briefly, speaking just loud enough for his men to hear. "When it is time, attack at will."

He lifted his head above his shield so the runners perched on the upper rock wall could hear. His voice came cruel and deep from the back of his throat: "Skinny... rain rock and hollow their heads."

A large figure materialized from the haze with sounds of huffing and puffing and thudding footsteps landing carelessly under a weight almost breaking rock.

Virtutis sized up the barbarian coming down with an almighty force. Virtutis's eyes widened, heart pumping full.

"Romannnnn!" the barbarian screamed, eyes streaming from the smoke. He lifted a monstrous axe high above his head, and using the steep slope and his body weight to advantage, he launched an attack over Virtutis's head, striking his shield.

The loud clunk of steel ended in a chink as the axe's blade chipped and ricocheted to the side. Absorbing the brunt of the force, Virtutis twisted his wrist to offset the impact. The weight of the axe head pulled its master further forward, exposing the tender undercarriage of flesh that Virtutis attacked.

In one smooth motion, he rounded his shield and slid his spear effortlessly into the underbelly of the massive man. Feeling the spear could push farther and pass through his enemy's body, Virtutis resisted. Oncoming masses of barbarians stole his attention.

Retracting the entire shaft with a practiced motion, he let the barbarian fall to the ground dead. Then, squaring up to the narrow trail, Virtutis stepped back, using the corpse for his back foot so that he stood level. "Lucky for me, you are a man-mountain, brother."

Virtutis twisted his foot, digging in his heel and forcing a gurgle of blood through the man's paling lips. Liking the sound, he dropped his weight harder into a crouch.

Lifting the shield high, he could still see the flurry of animal-skinned warriors coming to meet their death.

Enemy attacks burst from the smoke, two abreast, the line behind them deep and long so as not to fall off the side of the mountain.

Virtutis opened his shield, extending the spear and stabbing the first attacker on the closest side, retracting and impaling the next with a shorter stab. The two fell even. By the time they hit the rock, face down, the next attacks were shuddering down on Virtutis, thudding against his shield. Holding his strained stance, their weight shoved him back, forcing his back-foot-prop corpse to succumb to the pressure. It rolled away, dislodging his back heel to slide off unbalanced.

Virtutis tripped, falling backward, rolling over his head but regained his feet, attacking forward instantly.

He stabbed, probing all living flesh and dodging assaults of axes and swords, yet he continued to face upward.

Bodies fell, and Virtutis moved with dance-like timing. Fast and furious, he weaved, slipping and sliding his way over the rock, dead bodies piling up in front of him. With his eyes focused, Virtutis evened his breathing while his spear continued to act as an extension of his body, always searching for the next victim. The warm blood of his enemies dripped down the cliff walls. Together their daggered dance edged Virtutis back little by little, giving away ground, yet he never exposed his spine, not after it had been exposed to the Black Wolf.

Virtutis moved in death's waltz, acting so close to life's fleeting movements, escaping blades that cut through the air with often-chinking steel on steel. A symphony only he could conduct. A ballet that only he could perform. The solo Spartan echoed his message down the valley, and in return came the long, deep, guttural howl of the Black Wolf.

"Haaaawwwwoooooo!"

Virtutis lifted his chin and pulled back from his stabbing strikes, forcing all to pause.

"Ah, my little black pup." He snickered harshly under his breath. "How are we playing a song of death today?" He spun his spear, spraying unrecognizable blood that held no favor, lowered his stance, and launched a more intense attack—his warrior skill rising to a challenge that only he knew the wager. His feet continued to move in death's dance, one they'd memorized long ago.

The rhythm of the attackers grew; the battleground widened. Focused, he pulled back farther.

Rocks started hitting flesh and bone.

From his peripheral vision, men came rushing from the trees below. They stabbed, weaved, and pivoted. The pace of the battle swayed; attackers dwindled in numbers.

A bigger picture returned to Virtutis's vision as his men ran blades through the barbarians, leaving them heaped in anguished groans.

Sensing no new threats, Virtutis stood and wiped his forearm across his face, relieving his skin of blood and sweat. He licked his lips, tasting the salty tang of blood that was not his own. Swishing it about, he spat out the conquest.

Above, Skinny and the runners looked down from their vantage point, stunned.

"What are you waiting for? We are not done yet."

At pace, he dodged littered bodies running up the trail, leaving the battle behind, dead bodies dissipating like the thinning smoke.

Not breaking speed, Virtutis's eyes stalked around for possible threats. Shield and spear ready for anything, he regulated his breathing so his ears could pierce through the sounds of the wind and dying men for any enemy attack, hunting like the wolf himself.

A woman screamed.

He slowed his arrival onto a large open space.

Barbarian fires, lean-tos, and supplies lay scattered, along with fallen arrows that were not impaled in a dead or squirming body.

In a far corner under a rockface, a scuffling, screaming woman fought one of his bowmen. He left his post and broken rank early, pinning her down, attempting rape.

Taut chills ran through Virtutis's stomach. His feet slowed to a fast, furious walk.

The woman cried as the bowman's body buried into her, hands tearing at her clothes while mauling her neck with his mouth.

Virtutis's feet did not touch the ground. His wife flashed before his eyes—her honor, her gentleness, her virtue.

His spear's tip caught the man's shoulder.

"Bowman," Virtutis whispered in a grated tone from the distaste coating his throat. His blood rose hotter than hell.

The rapist lifted his head, surprised, panting from his assault.

Virtutis used his shield like a battering ram, striking him clean away. Clank!

The impact freed the woman. She scampered backward against the rock wall, gathering her clothes to cover herself, afraid, frantic.

Her eyes gleamed up at Virtutis in fear he knew all too well—fear of torture, rape, and slavery.

Virtutis retreated, giving her space, but did not drop neither spear nor shield. "We do not harm women or children. I will not harm you. Neither will my men." He spoke the words slowly while the warm blood of her clan still dripped from his spear.

Turning to the still-stunned bowman, Virtutis kicked him away, pushing with the edge of his shield, shoving him in shame.

"She was trying to escape!" The accused scampered back. "I was going to kill her. I was."

"This is not who we are." Virtutis hovered over him. "This is not what we do!"

Throwing his shield to the side, Virtutis reached down and pulled him up by the tunic, his dangling, scrabbling feet hitting Virtutis's shins while his fisted grip at the man's throat made direct eye contact inevitable—escape impossible.

Virtutis sniffed. "You smell like a dog. You think like a dog—and you will be fed to the dogs. Better yet, what about a wolf? How would you like that?"

"No, no! It was my right!" The man squirmed, his attempt pathetic as he begged for justice. "Kill or capture—she is mine. I want... I want justice!" He squirmed more, twisting and turning, his fingers clawing at Virtutis's tightening grip. He shrieked, terrified; his pupils shrunk to pinpoints.

Virtutis did not blink, his bloodied face already wearing the mask of death.

"Justice? You will learn very well of justice." He lowered the rapist. "You want to stand for justice? You may stand—it is your right."

Purposefully, Virtutis let the condemned drop toward his feet. The man gasped for air. Inch by inch, he lowered the man, pressing upon the tip of Virtutis's spear until it slit the skin and entered under the man's sternum.

He cried out then shuddered, gasping in silence. Blood ran a rivulet from the corner of his mouth.

The pain on his face jerked, smoothed, then twitched. Finally, he fell away, his legs giving up the fight. The weight impaled the man's punctured lungs, killing him—and any intention of jaded justice.

With a push and twist, Virtutis yanked his spear free and let the bowman fall to the ground.

A scurry of footsteps stopped. He dipped his head over his shoulder. His execution had been witnessed by most of his men, including Khan.

Their energy swelled.

Turning his back on the woman, he faced his men, lifting his head in a subtle tilt of challenge. Knowing he had to make his stand, he confronted anyone willing. "No children or women are to be harmed." Authority rasped in his booming voice, filling the stoned space. "Any man who violates this will be executed. This is not what we do. This is not who we are. Any man wishing to have his say, speak now."

Silence spoke. Stillness confirmed.

"A warrior only skilled in killing is a mere savage. If a warrior cannot determine the difference between man, woman, or child because of the rage in his blood, he is a savage. I am no savage."

Still, no warrior moved.

Virtutis knew well the intimidation he carried.

Khan stepped forward, turning toward the gathered men.

"Anyone who does not agree can also find clarity in my axe!"

Virtutis kept his stance and spear suspicious, ready for further statement. He scanned his men. "Very well. Search the camp," he ordered. "Skinny—send the runners to scour the smaller trails and report any loose ends. Mark the trails as you go. Send out five bowmen and five swordsmen to follow the markings shortly after. Any barbarian who escaped and is on the run will hide, then move. We have a better chance to finish or capture them if we flush the trails first."

"Sir!" Skinny turned, selecting his men.

Khan stood, waiting for orders.

"Khan, tend to this woman. The rest of the men can search the camp." He motioned to the woman in distress. "Take her, care for her, and give her what she needs. She may stay, or she may go."

Khan nodded once and approached the woman with his hands open in calm negotiation.

She spat and swore.

Virtutis collected his shield from the ground and latched it over his back.

He sighted a steep ridge that looked unworthy of escape; its narrow ledges and harsh, vertical cliff told sign of no entry—so he thought he must.

CHAPTER 8

I nstinctive and alert, Virtutis climbed smoothly with a steady one-handed grip—his spear ready in the other. He paced himself, his legs heavy from hours of that deadly dance. He pushed only controllable limits, so he would have sufficient energy to kill if there were confrontations. He often stopped to listen, his movements a fluid momentum over steep cliffs that threatened deadly falls. His breathing eased.

Thwack!

A large rock bounced off his shield just below his shoulders. Any higher, and he would have been a dead man. Scampering, he slid closer into the rock face for protection. Ears alert, he held his breath. He waited.

Nothing.

He listened longer.

Nothing.

Unhitching his shield, he placed it over his head. Then, risking steps over the narrow passage, he proceeded with caution.

Bam!

Another hit reverberated through the shield.

"Ahh—enough!" Lowering his shield, he exploded.

In quick stride, fearlessly, he ran to the edge of the cliff face.

Falling rocks clipped his shoulders. One nipped an ear. Another thudded against his thigh. Scaling higher, neither looking up nor down, he focused on the next movement, finding hidden cracks to place his hands and feet and propel him upward. He tempted the gods themselves.

Thwack!

A rock shocked pain through Virtutis's shoulder, stinging up to his neck and down his arm. Taking necessary cover under a ledge, he watched the boy scurry up and away.

"Barbarian bastards!" Virtutis gathered the pain under control. Rounding the last slope of flat rock, he slowed with caution.

A boy armed with a rock and a large man with his sword drawn stood at the plateau's edge.

There was no escape.

Virtutis looked at the boy, imagining his sons, how they too would fight without fear in this situation, and how he would want them to live on. The clouds parted, and the sun shone through, illuminating the mountain scape like a sign. For some reason, he felt he owed a debt to the gods for all the lives he had taken.

Virtutis bent, placing his shield and spear on the rock and holding his hands in full view. "No more killing needs to be done. The battle is over."

The large man swung his sword in figure eight. "I am King Waldhar! I am Alemanni! I will die fighting! Fight me!"

"I decline the challenge. What is done is done. You and the boy may go free. You may choose death another way."

"We are Alemanni! Pick up your spear! Fight me, Roman scum!"

Virtutis stepped back to the end of his spear. His hands were still free, non-threatening.

Waldhar lunged forward.

Virtutis held his nerve without flinching, steadfast.

"Fight me, you coward!" Waldhar picked up a rock, throwing it at Virtutis.

The missile whistled past, missing by a hair. Waldhar had lost his mind.

"Have it your way, Roman. I will kill you where you stand!"

Virtutis watched Waldhar's footsteps. He approached like a demon.

Slowly, patiently, Virtutis stood his ground.

Picking up his spear crossed his mind, but the way the spear lay captured his warrior curiosity.

His attacker slowed.

Virtutis tilted his head.

Why would a king foolishly die? What would that teach his son?

The king's footsteps came closer. Rocks shook, stones dislodged. Sunlight flickered off his sword's blade.

Judging the king's distance, timing the threat, Virtutis stomped on the butt of his spear, lifting the spearhead. Waldhar aggressively used his own momentum to drive himself to death.

The head of the spear sliced through his belly and out his back in one slick motion. He staggered, spear at midweight, balancing in flesh and bone.

At the last second, Virtutis stepped sideways, escaping the massive impact of the sword that pounded into rock, misguided and misjudged.

Evading the entire attack, Virtutis locked onto the shocked boy.

Virtutis paused.

The whistle of the mountain breeze broke the silence. They stood above the world, the valley below reflecting the beauty of life. A beauty that begged the persuasion of Virtutis's mercy. The boy was the same age as Stoa, perhaps older.

"There is no need for this to go further," Virtutis said, unarmed. "There is no honor in killing a defenseless man, is there?"

The skinny boy threw the rock.

Virtutis's instincts awakened, primed for a child's game, and he dodged forward, grasping the boy's outstretched arm. Pivoting him off balance, he threw him flat on his back and followed with a knee to the boy's chest.

He struck the boy's skull with his fist in one swift movement. The boy's eyes rolled back into his head, rendering him temporarily unconscious.

Virtutis left him subdued, turning to retrieve his spear.

Still alive, the barbarian king coughed blood while pivoting backward on his knees, held up by the spear.

Virtutis rounded to in a final face-off. Their eyes connected in the way warriors did in the last rites.

Waldhar coughed. "My son. He must live. Take my sword, my… my ring." Dark blood flowed from his mouth.

Virtutis studied the king's face, contemplating. Maybe the gods had placed this as a chance to rectify or show gratitude, thus improving the odds of his sons living a full life?

"You have my word. Your son will live." Virtutis placed his hand on the spear shaft. Ready to end it. Ready to send the king on his passage.

With his last breath, the king demanded, "Do it, Roman."

Life enveloped between them like an exchange of grace, of soulful purpose—the purpose of warriors.

"If it is any comfort. I am no Roman. I am Virtutis—Spartan. We will dine in the afterlife one day, King Waldhar, if the gods will it to be so. May your journey be swift."

Gripping the shaft, Virtutis pulled, retracting the spear in one motion.

Gasping for air, the king smiled, his body weight propelling him forward.

Virtutis stepped forward, bracing Waldhar's dying body against his leg, preserving his dignity, preventing the fall from grace. Then, with a soft grasp on his shoulder, Virtutis turned the king gently onto his back so he might witness the clear blue sky in his final seconds. As should be the death of a king.

Virtutis gave the final touches of death's passage by closing Waldhar's open eyelids with his palm and crossing his arms over his chest. Paying respect.

The boy stood witness to the last seconds of his father's death.

A howl from the Black Wolf echoed from the valley below.

Virtutis looked at the king's expressionless face. "You will not be a wolf's dinner tonight, Barbarian King." Virtutis knew he had a responsibility. "Boy," he said firmly. "Help me bury your father. No harm will come to you."

The boy did not move.

Virtutis gathered rocks, placing larger ones around the body first. All the while, Virtutis kept a stern watch over the boy. Who knew what he could do when emotion was so high?

Eventually, the skinny lad started to help.

Together, friend or foe, they buried the king high toward the heavens.

"That is enough. You have little time. Use it wisely," Virtutis said.

Virtutis collected his shield, clamping it over his back, then gathered his spear.

His leg began to stiffen from the rock that had hit his thigh, but he refused to show any weakness.

Sensing the boy's calmness, Virtutis twirled his spear for a different grip. He placed the tip of it under the king's sword, flipped its weight into the air, and caught it by the handle. Then he slid the weapon into his belt.

"We must leave," Virtutis said sincerely. "Down here." He pointed the way with his spear.

Together, they slowly made their way back down the steep rock. Virtutis, impressed by the boy's ability to hold his resolve after losing his father, let him take ownership of his descent.

Before dark, they slid down the last steep rock face onto the plateau, where men searched the area for barbarian loot.

In the corner, captured women and children huddled together.

Turning the boy to face him, Virtutis removed his father's sword from his belt but kept his ring in his pocket.

"Your father's dying wish as a warrior was that you live. This is now your sword. I am honoring his death with my word."

"He was already dead. The Romans poisoned him," the boy said. "So, your conquest of my father the king was not as it seems."

Virtutis searched his face.

"If he was already dead, why were you escaping?"

"We were not escaping. He wanted to die close to the gods. If he did not die today, then tonight I was to end his pain, sacrificing him for our kingdom under the full moon. But then you arrived, and fate played its part. No one is above the fate of the gods."

"He used my word to keep you alive?"

"Our king was an intelligent man. That's why the Romans poisoned his wine. It took them twenty years to get close enough. And even in the face of death, he thought of the future."

Virtutis looked beyond the boy into the trees and up to the sky, his mind catching up to the events of the day.

"Who would have thought barbarians were so smart?"

"Not all Alemannis are barbarians. Before the Romans came, we thrived in these lands, but the wars forced us into the mountains to be hunted. They have destroyed our homelands and divided our tribal agreements by bribing the weak and taking their sons. Those who are left are now mixed—the poor, the weak, and the fatherless. My family had the remaining hope for any type of retribution. Now, I am the last."

Virtutis stared hard at his face. "You are a smart boy."

"I am my father's son. He shaped me for this day." The boy looked at the blade. "He said intelligence is only as good as the eyes that see more than one reality and that we must possess a mind that is patient enough to seek the truth."

Virtutis looked on in silence.

Had the death of his wife blinded the truth with aggression? And did he, in fact, wage war against people who played no part in her death? Was there more than one truth?

Virtutis looked at the women and children gathered in the rocky corner. Was fighting for the Romans wrong?

"You may stay with us tonight," Virtutis said. "No one will harm you. You will be fed and cared for. If you choose to leave, you may. But take the east mountain trail. All the other directions are filled with legions, and you will be slaughtered. The choice is yours."

Looking down at his father's sword, feeling the weight of it, the boy lifted his chin.

No hint of trepidation or timidity of responsibility marked his features. "I am Benductos of Alemanni."

The boy, Benductos, held Virtutis's interest, almost to the point of awe.

"We will cross paths again, Spartan, and this sword will either be of service, or it will sever your head from your neck." Benductos inspected the sword's handle, reading its markings. Finally, he interrupted his thoughts with a decision. "We will leave at first light. You have my word we will not cause any trouble." Virtutis watched him join his people, giving them what comfort he could.

Virtutis motioned to Khan, who was keeping a watchful eye.

Khan came to him, his face curious.

"Give them what they need," Virtutis ordered. "Food, water, blankets. When they leave in the morning, you may give them their weapons back."

Khan looked puzzled. "Sir?"

"We have no war with them. They will not return. Benductos gave me his word as king."

"King? That boy? There is no kingdom left to govern."

"It is not a kingdom that makes a king, nor how many people he rules. It is how he serves his people." Annoyed, almost boiling, Virtutis searched Khan's face. His stomach churned with doubt in Khan's words. "Do as I ask." Virtutis unlatched his spear, calming himself. "What of the surviving barbarian warriors?"

"We have separated them. They are down in the gully, tied and gagged."

Snapping his neck to the side, he rotated his stinging shoulder. "Good. I shall attend to them myself. Guard the boy—with your life, if you must."

"Yes. But we have secured the area. Only our men remain."

"That is what I mean," Virtutis replied. "Post guards and rotate them often through the night, so all men can rest. If we are to get out of these lands alive, we will need all the energy we can gain."

The adrenaline of war wore off and pain radiated from Virtutis's leg. He limped down the narrow trail to the gully. His thigh tightened; ignoring it, he straightened himself up.

Benductos's conversation repeated itself in his head, challenging his narrative of who he was fighting. Maybe the only difference of who he was today was where his lands fell on a Roman map?

Caught between thoughts of treason and duty, he hoped the night would bring him resolve.

He placed his palm over his dagger; he remembered it spinning on his stone-cold floor, knowing how capable he was of undeniable treason toward his sons. What else was he capable of?

Trying to find something to calm his mind, he searched the skies. Stars blinked in the changing night sky. Animals called out, displaced from the fire that stirred nature's desperation.

A black bird, perhaps a crow, swooped prey from the brush in front of him, adding a screeching to the already unsettled night.

Something did not sit right—this was no barbarian force waging war on Rome. Women and children in the camp seemed more like an imposed genocide.

As a foot soldier, he made no moral decisions. He fought who he was told to fight. But now, the pressure of understanding and his position posed new problems—that of consciousness, that of virtue.

Coldness filled the forest valley below.

Guards stood over the captured souls waiting for their fate. "Leave us. Climb to the camp and take your rest. You will have no part in this."

Virtutis waited until his men were far up the trail when yaps and yelps sounded from the battlefield. Wolves closed in on the dead as he closed in on the bound and gagged with his dagger.

Smoke still wafted through the valley as Virtutis arched his back, relieving tension between his shoulder blades while looking up the mountain. A sudden break in the smokey air opened to the full blue sky. Virtutis took it as a sign to move through the betrayal he felt from his daggered duty of bound men. He hoped no one had witnessed his treason.

In the foreground, Benductos began to lead the remainder of his father's kingdom down the trail. The boy stopped and looked back. Benductos nodded in acknowledgement before he turned and slowly descended into a new destiny of his own.

Virtutis addressed his warriors with Khan standing beside him.

"We must move lightly. Take only your shoulder bags and your weapons." Virtutis threw his Roman shield, which spun with a clunk into the bushes below the ledge of the rock-scaped camp.

"There will be little time to stop, and rest will be limited, and we will have use of the upper mountain passes to get to the outpost."

Khan shifted his stance, uneasy. "We are going up there?"

"There is little choice. Down here, we don't know what we would encounter. Even the Romans will be suspicious. The best way is to get to the camp and report for duty before we are under any suspicion by either side. At least we will be able to defend ourselves."

Some of the men shuffled their feet and nervously glanced at each other.

"If you have done something wrong and cannot hold your resolve, go. If you are innocent, we leave immediately. There will be no more discussions."

"I am ready," Khan said. "Prepare to leave!"

Men hustled to the ready, knowing they stood little chance by themselves.

Virtutis looked to the sky, sucking in a long breath through his nose. "Wait." He stopped Khan before he left to harass the men.

"Send a runner back to the wounded. Tell them they are on their own. They must find their way back to the camp. They will not be able to make this journey injured."

"Do you know your way through the passes?" Khan asked.

For the first time, Virtutis was not resistant to the questioning of his command. He found Khan's inquiry to be authentic. "I have the map, but there are no pathways drawn. We will have to find our way."

Khan motioned to two redheaded men talking closely together. "Those two skinny boys."

"Who are they?" Virtutis asked.

"Hunters. They are twins. They can track anything, and they can climb. I've seen them track goats and come back with a gutted and skinned carcass more than once. If anyone can lead us through the passes, it would be them," Khan replied.

Virtutis watched them carefully before accepting. "Call them over."

Khan grunted to get their attention. "Aye… You two. Over here."

They approached apprehensively but still had big smiles as they joined the private meeting.

Virtutis scratched his head. They seemed more like jesters than warriors. "What are your names?"

"Remus," one said, grinning. His messy, almost-dreadlocked red hair covered his forehead, and a long tail from the back of his head landed on his shoulder.

"Rufus," the other answered, also with a smile from ear to ear. His hair was short apart from a thin platted tail down his back.

"Why are you two so happy?" Virtutis asked. He looked them over, noticing they both had the same woven leather band on their wrists.

"We are alive, aren't we?" Rufus said with a shrug.

"And we are together. That's all we need..." Remus added.

"Family," Rufus finished his brother's sentence.

Virtutis looked at Khan, suspicious of their mental state. "Can you lead us over the mountain? There are no maps. We must cross soon enough to miss the snow."

"The mountain pass?" Remus asked.

Rufus nodded. "We could."

"It's a steep climb. We'd have to tie off at some parts," Remus said. The twins were quick to talk between themselves, not engaging with Virtutis or Khan while they made their decision. They fired details back and forth so fast that not even Virtutis could intervene or understand.

"Yes. We can do it," Remus said.

"But we need to leave soon," Rufus added.

"Now," Remus asserted.

"Yes, now. It's not safe to wait," Rufus finished. "The snow."

"The ice," Remus added.

"Enough." Virtutis held a hand up. "You will both take point."

"Now?" Remus asked.

Virtutis stared down at the happy duo sternly without blinking.

"Now," Rufus answered, shoving Remus to get ready. "Let's not keep the commander waiting."

"Easy. We leave as soon as you are both ready. Our lives are in your hands." Virtutis said, setting them straight in their responsibility. "Khan and I will follow your lead."

The twins smiled, then chuckled with excitement, less nervous now.

"Great. Let's go." Rufus smiled.

"Rope. We need extra rope," Remus said as they walked away.

The two scavenged the camp for what they could find, allocating ropes to the men. It did not take long for them to signal they were ready.

CHAPTER 9

The first day was steep but easy climbing. The tiered group of warriors scrambled their way, zig-zagging up above the tree line and into the occasional cloud. They maintained a slow but grueling and steady pace. The night fell with starlit beauty, the full moon illuminating their way. Khan was correct in his recommendation; the twins could not only climb, but they selected routes that all the men could navigate. One would take the lead while the other would explore ahead and return with the best trail upward, alleviating the need for stops. Their trust in each other also gained the trust of Virtutis.

More concerned with his men's fatigue than the dangers they faced climbing under a cloudless night, Virtutis called out, not knowing who was closest. "Rufus, Remus. We rest at the next plateau."

"Yes, sir," they called back in unison.

Virtutis shook his head.

The flat ledge they took refuge on offered some shelter from the wind.

"Khan. Drop back down the trail. Take three men and rotate the guard in case there is anyone else using the pass. Spread out when you sleep so that you are not bunched and no fires."

"Sir," said Khan.

Still confused who was who, Virtutis called a name. "Remus. Come here."

Remus bounded over with his untearable smile, eagerly twisting the tail of hair with his fingers.

Virtutis, for the first time, returned a small smile, liking their genuine character and not really knowing what he was looking at. "You have both done well today. Rest well. Tomorrow will be harder to navigate."

"Yes, it is steeper. We may have to climb around the cliffs to get to the next pass. In the morning, we will look—or we could go tonight. There is enough light with the full moon," Remus suggested.

"We will see in the morning. I will come with you. Meet me here before dawn. Go and rest."

"Yes, yes," Remus replied as if his brother was answering with him.

Virtutis walked farther up the trail alone, wanting his solitude and needing to rub his swollen leg without any of his men seeing he was injured.

After some time repairing his body, he pulled up his cloak, placing the hood over his head and resting back against a rock bed to close his eyes. Sleep took him fast and deep.

The trap door under Stoa's bed was torn open, his bed thrown over, and the table tipped against the fire, threatening to ignite. Smoke filled the house, flames burst into life, and Stoa stood in the foreground with his sword in hand while Augustus placed his back against the corner of the wall. A growling and snorting reverberated through the house. Stoa launched forward to the attack. A black shape swamped him whole, leaving Augustus alone, petrified. Cornered, fear turned to action, and he screamed as he lifted his sword high to strike.

Virtutis sat up gasping. He grabbed his spear, sprawling backward and stabbing it into thin air. Its point was referencing the shining northern star, Polaris. Many would consider it a beautiful night, but now it was riveted with anxiety and worry.

Unsettled, Virtutis sat awake, watching over his men.

Another sleepless night.

His thoughts started to race with his sons and the decision to leave them. He needed to move to occupy his mind. He crept down and shook Rufus, who innocently woke from a pleasant dream, opening his eyes without a worry in the world. Remus chuckled in his sleep, something about bread, then the stirring of his brother woke him.

"Let's go," Virtutis whispered. "We have to make good progress today. Get ready. I will be back soon."

Virtutis walked through the camp unnoticed. He descended the trail and found Khan awake, sitting and staring at the stars.

"I was worried I'd have to wake you," Virtutis said, spooking Khan. He stood, grabbing his axe.

"Again?" he said, huffing. "When will I learn?"

Virtutis now considered spooking Khan as more of a game rather than an inconvenience.

"Change your post with one of the men. We have some trails to look at."

"Moonlit goat trails without breakfast. How romantic," Khan muttered.

Virtutis and Khan arrived at the campsite where Rufus and Remus stood ready. Together they made good time up the even slopes until the trail plummeted beyond the light of the moon.

The twins stopped looking down. Rufus picked up a stone and threw it in, listening for the bottom. It did not come.

"What do you think, Rufus?" asked Remus.

"We can do it. We just need to tie on."

Remus turned to Virtutis with a smile. "Over that side is where we would start our descent tomorrow." He pointed to the far side of the cliff. "But first, we have to go up and over. There are many ways that have dead ends." He scratched his head, then pulled his hair tail with a twist for assurance. "So, if we climb around the cliff, it's faster to backtrack. It will save us a day or more in trying to guess where to go."

Virtutis looked over the edge. "It's a long way down."

Remus laughed. "It's also a long way up!"

"Half-empty down." Rufus giggled.

"Half-full up," Remus finished. "We can do it. It's a little cold, but it looks like there's no ice. There is enough moonlight."

"We will have to tie off," Rufus said, "just in case we have to leap a little."

"Swing, anybody?" Remus asked, smiling.

"Oh, yes. Thank you for the offer, kind sir." Rufus laughed, bowing his head.

"Are you certain you can make it?" Virtutis asked, concerned about their sanity.

"We swore our oath of service, our family to yours. If we get it done fast, we are less likely to have to eat one another if the mountain freezes over. It's no fun eating family." Remus laughed, dropping away to the straight face of reality.

"Very well." Virtutis nodded. "With the help of the gods, you will succeed."

"Yes! We are close enough to them. Maybe they will give us a hand," Remus chuckled. "Or fart in our faces."

"Ha! At least it would warm the rock!" Rufus continued. "Commander, would you please tie off the rope?"

"We will let you know when to release it," Remus said.

Virtutis took the rope and tied it securely to a nearby rock.

Remus and Rufus continued with their banter, not bothering to check if the rope was secure.

"I dreamed of Mama's bread last night. With goat stew," Remus said while they started their climb around the rock face, their words obviously calming each other.

Below, the drop seemed to grow darker than before. Virtutis stared hard into the pit, letting his vision adjust, but still, he could not see the bottom. He listened while they talked away their nervousness with simple joys and humor.

Khan came closer to see the action. "These two give a whole new meaning to the word crazy."

Virtutis did not respond while he tested the rope for security.

Rufus led, inching his way forward, hugging the cliff wall. Remus followed, giving space and following the pattern of hand and foot placement his brother left behind.

Rufus disappeared around the corner while Remus paused before moving his lead hand. "Untie the rope," he said. "I will connect it here."

Virtutis removed the rope from the rock, and with a gentle touch, he threw it over to Remus.

He caught it one-handed and began adjusting it to loop a new structure.

There was a scuffle.

"Ice!" yelled Rufus.

A scurry of rock, followed by a snapping of tightening rope.

Remus only just braced himself with one hand before the tension hit his waist, the force and motion sweeping his feet from support and almost pulling him off the wall. In the chaos, he let the rope slip from his grasp, recovered his grip for a second on loose rock, then it slipped off, adding more pressure to his single-handed grip.

Rufus swung below uncontrollably, twisting and turning.

The swing spun him awkwardly, and Virtutis heard a thud as he slammed into the rock face with a snapping sound and then a cry of pain. "Aghh!" He swung back into the moonlight like dead weight.

Remus tried to pendulum him back using the rope below his waist for momentum while still holding on for dear life with one hand.

Virtutis dove into his belly to help with an outstretched hand, but Rufus was just out of reach.

Rufus swung back into the darkness, out of sight.

The weight and angle of his return came fast, catching the side of an oddly shaped rock that hooked the rope just beyond Virtutis's assistance. Rufus screamed again. The rope had trapped his wrist

91

against the rock. It snapped backwards, broken, leaving him unable to pull himself up with the angle and crushing tension.

Rufus's position, while stable, continued to add weight to Remus's failing grip.

Remus, too far away for Virtutis to help-tried again and again to retain a two-handed hold, but his grip kept slipping.

The dangling Rufus became heavier by the second.

His eyes, wide with fear, met Virtutis's as he hung over as far as he could while Khan braced his feet.

Rufus's face dropped into a sincereness Virtutis had never seen in a man before—that of sacrifice.

Rufus swayed with his entire hand jammed, the other arm seemingly broken from slamming into the wall.

Virtutis felt time slow down.

"Cut it," Rufus said calmly. "My arms, I can't move. I am done."

"No!" Remus shouted. He screamed in pain from holding the pressure, from the thought of losing his brother.

Virtutis reached his arm behind to Khan. "Axe!"

The silence of hesitation fired a warning within Virtutis; he laid with his back to a man who had conspired and killed his commander. Now, as he lay with his hand outstretched behind him, the back of his skull exposed, fate had already positioned three dammed men.

The axe came handle first in a precise grip and with it a sigh of relief.

Virtutis looked for the best place to cut the rope, but there was none due to the lay of the rock. The only rope he could cut clean sat directly under Rufus's wrist.

Remus could only hold the weight for so long.

Virtutis searched once more, but there was no slack to hitch and pull-no vantage to stop the inevitable.

He had to act.

Rufus's eyes swelled with tears as he nodded to Virtutis. "Cut it."

Only Virtutis knew what had to be done to set him free.

Virtutis thought of telling Remus to cut it himself with his own knife. But it would be better to have the guilt of death over his own head than Remus carrying the torment until the end of his days.

The hand and the rope had to be cut, together.

"No, no, no…!" Remus screamed, trying to regrip his free hand to no avail.

Time had run out.

Virtutis took action.

He swung the axe hard and on point, cutting through Rufus's wrist, splitting flesh and rope, and sending him floating out of sight.

The sound of chipped rock fell away into the depths.

Rufus did not scream or yell, leaving the mountain wind to whistle its tune of death forever in their minds.

Rufus's severed hand held for a second. First, his family wristband fell away, then the rest of the hand dropped, chasing a belonging that it would never obtain again.

Virtutis sunk his head over the side of the cliff. He lifted his eyes to see Remus regaining his feet, then a fresh handhold that pulled him to safety.

"Remus, come back." Virtutis opened his hand to help his return.

They exchanged a brief look, but instead of returning, Remus continued to scale around the corner, disappearing into the night, leaving no trace of his or his brother's existence, as though what had just happened was a figment of Virtutis's imagination.

Virtutis pushed himself from the edge and sat up. He looked at the blade of Khan's axe, not knowing if he should wipe away Rufus's blood or not.

He looked back at the cliff hoping Remus would return, but in reply, a cold wind blew across his face.

Remus, without a rope, without support, without half his soul, would no doubt be joining his brother down in the depths of death.

With the icy cliff, there was no way for either Virtutis or Khan to follow; they walked back to the main camp, stunned, silent.

The sun started to peek its eye over the far-off lands of Germania.

Virtutis looked into the sun, not making eye contact with Khan. "We need to move. Who knows how long it will take to get through the pass without the twins. If he is alive, I am not sure Remus will return." Virtutis looked at Khan's axe. "And I don't blame him."

"You did the right thing. I would tell you if you didn't. I will alert the men it's time to move."

"I thought of making Remus cut the rope, you know?" Virtutis looked back into the sun without blinking. "It was better to be my decision. I wish that pain upon no man. Together they were one; now, one is merely half." Virtutis thought of his wife, adding to his already guilt-ridden emptiness.

Khan said nothing. Then barked orders for them to assemble. Within minutes, they continued their trek up into the narrower trails that provided the challenge to follow with fewer markings.

Leading his men upwards, navigating on instinct, Virtutis replayed the last moments of Rufus's life, regretting his decision to wake them up due to his lack of ability to live with himself. Once again, the Black Wolf had indirectly claimed a life by haunting his dreams. A haunting Virtutis feared had only just begun building its momentum.

At a junction, three passages taunted Virtutis. Unsure of where to go next, he let the men rest and eat.

"Where to now?" he asked Khan.

"Your guess is as good as mine." Khan shrugged. "The twins were correct. Working backwards was the right way."

Up ahead, Virtutis studied the pathways. "We will need to send runners up each way. When they return, we will decide which is the right choice."

"Agreed, there is no use sending the men back and forth," Khan replied. "They are already fatigued. If forced to fight, we would be at a greater disadvantage."

"Tell them to rest. I want to see up ahead first."

Frustrated, Virtutis climbed hard and fast to the top of the middle trail, not only searching for the passage through but finding space to release his scorched mind, which burned with the responsibility of Rufus's death. Legs on fire, heart pounding, he wanted to lash out. He yearned to fight, to kill. Anything to release the fury he felt for himself. All the while, he knew it was not right to feel that way, but an animal instinct overrode all logic.

Out of oxygen, gasping for air, he wildly searched for a release. He picked up a large boulder with all his strength, juggled it to gain control with a grunt, and threw it over the closet cliff with all his anguish. "Aghhhhh!" he yelled, his pain echoing back at him repeatedly.

The rock bounced and split in two. As Virtutis watched it explode, beyond the debris, he saw the trail that would lead them to the other side of the mountain. His gaze followed it back to where his men were camped, waiting like ants.

Below them sat the cliff where he'd last seen Rufus alive and where Remus disappeared; the sight plummeted him into a deep sadness. A sadness no one would ever see.

Heavy under the strain of guilt for pressuring others to explore just to escape his inner torment, he rock-hopped back to the camp.

Khan sat resting his feet on his arrival.

Virtutis did not stop. "This way. We move now."

The men instantly reacted, scampering to collect their limited belongings before falling in. Khan soon made up ground, arriving puffing at Virtutis's back.

Scaling up, rounding the first counseled bend on all fours, Virtutis came face to face with a ghost as he stood.

"Remus. You are alive." Virtutis adjusted his feet for balance.

The men's halted climbs and murmurs confirmed Remus was not a spirit.

A pale broken boy stood before him. His familiar smile and lightheartedness had been ripped from his soul. "The trail is this way." Remus's voice was coarse and raw. His face without emotion, without life. His eyes bloodshot, lost.

He turned, showing Virtutis his back before he could say anything. Quiet and shocked, Virtutis and his men followed Remus up through narrow, perilous trails.

Remus did not stop through the night; he climbed on and on.

The next morning the sun was a welcome relief to straining eyes. But there was still no relief from Remus's steady pace.

On a flat trail, Khan brushed close to Virtutis's shoulder. "We must stop soon. The men are wary, and we all need to rest. They need food and water."

Virtutis did not take his eyes off Remus walking ahead. "Rufus died upholding his oath, not just to me but to all of us." He cracked his neck from the tension of his own mourning. "Remus finished the mission, then regardless of his loss, he came back for us." Virtutis rubbed his hand over his head. "Remus holds true his oath. So we will hold space for him. However, he needs to mourn; we will let it run its course." Virtutis stopped in his tracks, eyes locking on Khan. "If he chooses to walk into the fires of Hades, we would walk with him."

Without waiting for an answer, Virtutis continued to follow Remus.

By the third day, Remus swayed, stumbled, and fell, exhausted. Virtutis rushed to his aid, rolling him over. Remus's face was withdrawn, lips blistered and dry, near death.

Virtutis pulled out his waterskin and dripped a gentle stream into Remus's mouth. "Is he dead?" Khan asked, his eyebrows knitted together. Remus looked up at Khan before closing his eyes.

"No, but he is in between this world and the afterlife. His soul is tormented by the desire to be with his brother. Perhaps he will return," Virtutis answered, hoping that even though a part of Remus was dead, he would not die. "We will camp here. But we leave again at first light," he ordered. "Bring me two spears, a blanket, and a rope."

"Sir," Khan replied. He ordered the men to camp farther down the trail, leaving Virtutis with his space so he did not have to take it.

Throughout the night, the runners came to attend to Remus, bringing water with herbs to help his fight for survival. Each time Virtutis heard them approach, he left them without conversation to take refuge alone until they had finished.

At first light, Virtutis held the front of the stretcher with Khan behind. Together they led the men into the valley below, cutting over between passes without being detected by Roman soldiers.

For seven days, they carried Remus, giving him a chance of survival like he and his brother had given them. Virtutis rarely made eye contact with anyone other than Khan. It was not driven by more than regret or responsibility for cutting away Rufus. Moreover, it was the reality of the Roman inquiry for the killing of their commander and avoiding closeness to people he may be leading to slaughter.

Like a distant mirage, the Roman outpost appeared, and it was time to declare what had happened to the highest authority, General Lucio.

CHAPTER 10

Virtutis stood in General Lucio's tent without armor and only his hidden dagger. There was a table between them with a low lantern displaying a map of the Germanian Hinterlands. Layered curtains cast shadows over the general's face, making his intentions harder to read.

"Virtutis. We did not expect any of you to return alive from the Hinterlands." General Lucio's voice came slow with a hint of stress from obsessive screaming.

"We have been fortunate," Virtutis replied. "We had to find our way back over the mountain passes and were lucky the barbarians are unorganized, or we would have been slaughtered." Virtutis fixed his eyes, scrunching his toes in his well-worn sandals. He knew very well that nothing could prepare him for a Roman interrogation of recent events.

"Fortunate indeed," the general replied, filling his cup with wine before taking a sip.

Virtutis waited in the long, drawn-out silence. No doubt, the atmosphere was intentional.

He wanted to scratch his overgrown beard that held the remanence of dried enemy blood, but he resisted. With a subtle glance, he looked down and over his shoulder to guards standing like statues at the inner entrance, barely moving, making little sound. Their swords gripped, ready to execute.

He relaxed his hands at his side, concealing any discomfort about being in the beak of the eagle. Under the cover of composure, potentially false accusations tightened his stomach.

A movement drew attention to behind the general—someone lingered behind a curtain.

"For someone not trained in military leadership, you seem to be resourceful," the general probed.

Taking his time to respond, Virtutis relaxed his stomach so as not to create an involuntary tone of guilt. "It is true. I know little about military leadership. Only tribal infighting." Virtutis's fingertips, eager to fidget, twitched. Once. Slowly, he furled and unfurled his hand, moving past the tension.

The general took another drawn-out sip that sounded like a long swirl before swallowing. "When a situation arises such as this and men appoint their own commander, it is normally a consequence of treason. It is very coincidental that the commander and his men were all killed in the same battle, don't you think?"

"Yes. I caught one of the traitors. I executed him with my spear," Virtutis replied, using the rapist he impaled as a martyr. "I believe it sent a clear enough message for now." Virtutis maintained his calm; though he did not enjoy twisting the truth, a rational defense was needed. Taking a risk, he continued, "General, I am as concerned for my life as any other. No doubt, in time, there will be more to deal with. For now, things seem to be in order."

The general gripped his armrest with a sideways glance. "Are you admitting that men under your order killed the commander?

"At the time, they were not my men. I was a foot soldier like everyone else. We were defeated by the barbarians, left for dead with less than a quarter of us alive, and outnumbered four to one. We had to fight or die. So, I led. If I were involved with such a conspiracy, why would I be here? I have nothing to hide. I believe the men who committed this act fled after the battle."

"You assuming leadership is enough of a confession in being involved in a conspiracy."

"Like I said, if so, I would not be here. A guilty man would not dare take any type of responsibility. I would like to think I am honest enough. I did not conspire. Being appointed as temporary leader was not for my own benefit other than to stay alive, nor was it to benefit anyone else I know. The empire is not something to play games with; she will tear you apart."

"Yes, she will. Not before she destroys a man's soul for betraying her." The general drew his hands together, elbows poised on the arms of the chair, fingers steepled over his rotund belly. "You seem an intelligent man, Virtutis. Very aware. I am astounded you knew nothing of such a plan."

"I knew nothing of the plan. But there was tension enough to provide the environment. We are part of the auxiliary; we are simply the hired help and easily discarded. These men are from all different tribes, and I am discovering they are also very different in their opinion."

"This execution of the traitor—you took upon yourself to deliver justice?"

"Yes, I did. We were at war from within our own ranks. Justice had to be swift."

"I see. You are very well versed in debate."

"I have two boys and had a loving wife. If I can raise Spartan boys and negotiate with their mother, I should be well versed in debate."

For the first time, the general shifted in his seat, showing he was paying more attention.

Virtutis's gut tensed again at the man's growing comfort.

"No truer words have been spoken. However, if Spartan life were something to aspire to, they would still exist, don't you think? As for taming the will of a child and the heart of a woman, those are two accomplishments I have yet to achieve. However, in either case, I take what I want."

Virtutis imagined the smirk from the shadow, disliking the comment.

"You hold yourself with a degree of wisdom when you speak," Lucio continued.

"I am not wise, sir. I simply try to not have any division or delusion between my words and reality."

"Do you think the Roman commander who died in battle was delusional?"

"I think he was a poor leader. Delusional in some ways, yes. Either side would have killed him eventually."

"Are you saying Roman commanders are delusional? And he was killed because of perceived delusion?"

Virtutis held his breath. But not in search of words. He searched for confirmation from the deeper darkness, trying to identify a rustle— a shift in the background behind the curtain.

"Men are men. Roman or not. Delusion does not favor a robe, nor does it favor its choice of death. The commander was delusional, but I do not know enough Romans to say that they are that way inclined."

"You are surprisingly sharp, Virtutis. And you killed the so-called King Waldhar?"

"At first, I thought he would have been better kept alive for interrogation, but he did not want to be taken alive. He would not surrender."

"So, you killed a king. I wonder could you kill a...?" General Lucio muttered something under his breath.

"Sir?"

"Nothing, just commenting on your ability to eliminate those who oppose Rome's purpose. Your spear is very handy. And the king's son? You set him free?"

"Yes, he is a boy. There were no people left for him to lead. I showed him mercy."

"Mercy is for the weak." The general's words held a knife's edge.

"There is no weakness in showing mercy in this case. The boy was not a criminal. His father was at war with Rome. He did not choose to be the king's son. Being guilty by association is like killing a man for loving Hera more than Zeus."

Aggression deepened the general's voice. "You should have executed him. We are at war. He is an enemy of Rome, and nothing other than the success of the empire should be considered. He is a criminal."

"Understood. But not all enemies are criminals. I have met some honorable enemies in tribal wars. However, I am a warrior and was new to a command—and I know little of the Roman way. As for the king, he was beaten in fair combat. I was not prepared to slay the child, for he was unarmed and not threatening. I was unaware I would be under any type of implications of such matters."

"Wise choice of words. Using your lack of experience to save a barbarian savage."

Virtutis did not engage further in the matter. Rather, he stood waiting for the topic to change.

The general poured more wine and straightened in the chair as though he was forcing an uneasy decision or waiting for a cue. "Spartan, you may keep your role within the auxiliary, for now. But you will be issued a new commander in the coming weeks."

"Sir, if I may?" Virtutis interrupted.

"What?"

Virtutis searched the shadows behind the general. Knowing that letting a Roman commander regain control meant he and his men would be an unwanted commodity; even more so, he would be in less control over his destiny if this was the case. "Sir, a Roman commander cannot lead these men. Like I said, things are tense; these men could sway in any direction. They need more than fear of prosecution and Roman discipline. It will only end in mutiny."

The general twitched, straightening further in his chair as if to stand.

Virtutis had moved from the beak of the eagle to between its razor-sharp talons.

The general leaned into the light instead, causing his night guards' attention to shift. "Speak up then, Spartan. But choose your words carefully. After such a rise to authority, this could be taken as a threat."

Virtutis held his resolve, feigning no intimidation.

Pulling what could be his last breath into his lungs, he controlled his delivery: "The barbarians are always shifting their forces; they are dominant in the hinterlands. So, Rome sends more troops to outnumber the threat, but more numbers in these mountains will only create poorer execution by unprepared commanders. No doubt they will suffer the same fate. By the time they learn how to navigate these terrains, they are already under the blade, and so are most of their men." Virtutis motioned at the map on the table. "May I?"

"Be my guest." The general swept out a hand in magnanimous detain.

"It is better to have a mobile force here in the mountains." Virtutis pointed to the area on the map he had just escaped. "Traditional legion fighting will only give the enemy more opportunities to prepare, so it is best to use tactics they do not expect. Traditional tactics should be saved for the legions in areas where they are stronger. Let us flush the barbarians out and bring them to you here"—he pointed and swept his finger across the parchment—"and we can finish them off here."

"And you can provide that?"

"Sir, I can. All I request is time to train these men and your word that as long as we win, I remain in command. My word to you is if I fail, I will be dead anyway. I will bring the barbarians to their knees—or die."

General Lucio came forward into the light. His head was bald down the middle, making his chiseled face and withered skin carve a permanent frown, forcing roads of wrinkles around his eyes. Roads paved with blood in the name of Rome.

"I have heard many stories about Spartans." His words hung between them, his head pushed forward as if reading a threat, should Virtutis be plotting a rebellion. "I thought they had long but perished."

103

"I have no concern with what has been, nor what will come. My only concern is to serve and fight. I am a man of the world. Sparta has been perished for decades. I do not hold on to anything that does not serve me."

"Yes, I am surprised you are still alive with the reputation and disdain the world feels for your kind."

"I have no expectation to live long, and death is something I do not fear. I do not entertain what others may think of me." Under threat, Virtutis's mind became sharper, reminding him of the warrior he was. "Those who judge me must pass the tip of my spear before they get close enough to influence my mind."

The general took a long pause like he was waiting for a sign, tapping his knee with his fingertips.

"Well, Virtutis, the Spartan." He shifted in his chair. "If you were not interested in leading before, I am intrigued to know why you are now. However, you may have your request. You have one month to train your men, and we will give you one hundred reinforcements."

Virtutis bit the inside of his lip so his satisfaction would not be noticed. "Sir," he affirmed his orders.

The general stood, trying to intimidate, using the step to seem taller. "If traitors remain in your ranks, I want their heads—see that it is done." He gulped more wine as though he was unhappy with the agreement. "I accept your offer. Success—or your life trying." The general sat back into the shadows again. "You may leave."

Virtutis turned toward the opening of the tent, glancing up at the guards in full armor. His heart pounded with adrenaline; a cold wind crawled over his skin, making hairs stand up on end with realization.

He recognized the guards. The vermin who imprisoned Arquitos.

Which meant the general was Arquitos's rapist. The man who issued his death sentence.

Virtutis shuddered a vengeful breath. He wanted to turn and stab him in the neck. Darkness gripped his heart, the skin on his face tightening, hard and thick with truths only he would know. Not only was genocide being conducted against the mountain tribes, but the orders came from a man with such a despicable absence of human dignity.

Not feeling his feet touch the ground, Virtutis trudged back to his camp, his mind flustered in thought. Collecting his shield, spear, and blanket, he walked deep into the woods.

Finding an open space through the thick forest below the full moon, he drew his spear. He stabbed, slashed, and spun, growling a vengeful moan while he practiced a dance of death. The general's voice cutting away at his mind, he let his movements flow for hours until he calmed.

Composed. For now, there was nothing he could do but plan.

CHAPTER 11

Standing in the night shadows, Virtutis knew he needed allies. Men he could trust who were not under the influence of Rome. However, he questioned the overall loyalty of everyone under his command. Were they loyal or desperate to survive? With each complication of past events relived, so returned his guard.

In complete darkness, Virtutis watched from outside the parameter of Khan's campfire. Five men huddled close to the flames. They spoke in low tones, so their words could not be heard—tones that rung the possibility of distrust, possibly treason.

Virtutis approached undetected.

"Have the new supplies and reinforcements arrived?" he asked. Khan jumped to his feet, spilling stew down his front.

Virtutis scanned his face for guilt, ignoring others, knowing the look of deceit is best cut from the eye of the whisperer. He waited. Removing Khan now, on suspicion, would only be more detrimental to his new leadership.

Not breaking eye contact, Khan replied, "Sir, we have not seen you in days." He wiped his hand slowly down the front of his tunic, embarrassed. "Yes, the swords, shields, and spears have arrived. And twenty new men."

Twenty? The general had already broken his word.

"Also," Khan added, "Remus has disappeared. We can't find him."

Virtutis thought of Rufus falling away without a sound. Trying to break his feeling of responsibility and guilt, he focused on the fire's embers; it flashed a memory of home. He hoped he would see his sons again. His face remained cold as he forced himself back to the plan.

"If he is caught by the Romans, he will be killed for desertion," said Virtutis.

"We looked everywhere," Khan said, reiterating Virtutis's concern. "He's a hunter; he knows how to disappear. But there is talk of a hole in the woods, where they drop deserters. Death is the last thing anyone would be worried about."

More guilt passed over Virtutis like a cold chill. He looked up at the night sky, wondering when he would pay the price for his deeds, as a crackle sparked from the fire.

"I pray to the gods he is safe. See that all men are ready for training tomorrow morning at sunrise. Each man is to remove the spearhead from their spear so that only the staff remains. No food, only water."

"Sir, it is late. There is no way to get organized by morning. The men are still recovering and are most likely drunk."

"Find a way. There are five of you here. Make a decision on how to do it. I will see you in the morning."

Virtutis pulled his cloak around his neck and walked into the bustling camp in search of a particular man, suited perhaps, for a very specific mission.

Tucked away in a corner of the camp, a small group of runners gathered for their meal. Virtutis halted in the shadows, interested in their mannerisms.

Skinny, from the battle with the barbarians, sat silently. It was rare that a warrior would seek such company.

Virtutis listened to their story of throwing stones to help destroy the barbarians. Occasional laughter would break out, poking fun at each other. The conversation turned more serious with the discussion over the execution of the bowman. All the while, Virtutis listened to every detail. It was a small group, but a group nonetheless. They seemed loyal to each other.

Breaking from his night camouflage, Virtutis approached. "Evening, brothers."

They startled, heads snapping, posturing—surprised.

"May I sit with you for a while?" Unlike Khan's group, his unannounced entrance was received openly and more relaxed.

They opened their circle in invitation, shuffling their seating.

"Sir, would you like some stew?" an older runner offered. His head was bald, his legs powerful and flexed without intention, and his upper body lean.

Once seated in a squat, the man began ladling steaming stew into a bowl. Joking to himself, Virtutis wondered if the stew maker was perhaps a minotaur.

"Yes, stew would be good." Virtutis smiled. "I am grateful for your hospitality."

"Commander, it is our honor." He looked around the faces of his companions, no doubt unsure of the reason for his arrival.

The bowl smelled of herbs and broth. A comfort entered Virtutis's nostrils, bringing on a suppressed hunger.

"Call me Virtutis. There is no rank amongst such honest stew."

The men laughed, their tone the same as when Virtutis was in the shadows, confirming it to be authentic. The tension in their bodies relaxed slightly.

Virtutis pulled his cloak over his head—not to shelter from the cold but to sit and participate as a common soldier. He sipped, chewed, and listened.

They talked of their homelands, wives, and their aspirations after the war. The conversation forced him to think about the innocence of Augustus, then he was quickly riddled with shame about his last confrontation with Stoa. He looked over at the men circled around the campfire and hoped that somehow if he maintained the respect of the common man, the gods would influence the image of their father finally able to live a life of virtue and substance as a warrior, rather than a jittered man in a lonely bed.

Skinny sat still, quiet.

Virtutis directed an intentional change of topic. "Skinny, what is your name?"

"Mercalis, sir." His soft voice held no sense of shyness nor lack of confidence. His chiseled face was almost hidden by scraggly hair, and his lean frame gave him the edge of physical fitness over many larger warriors.

"You are from?" Virtutis asked.

"Attica."

Virtutis lifted an eyebrow. "That explains your running ease. Not just a warrior."

Mercalis chuckled. "That is a statement I have not heard, sir. Most people consider a warrior more valuable than a runner."

"Our runners will be the most valuable resource we have in the auxiliary. Warriors are bred to fight, runners to inform. If warriors do not know where and how to fight, they quickly perish. Thus"—he looked over the men gathered—"part of the reason I am here."

His comments left a silence. He sipped his stew. "How much information and how many messages did our dead Roman commander ignore?"

"Is that a question, sir?" the older half runner, half minotaur, asked.

Virtutis turned his head, so he could find the stew master's brown eyes. "What is your name?"

"Stoades, sir." He nodded, pleased with the personal acknowledgment.

"Yes, Stoades. It is a question."

"We did not relay much information, nor did we send many messages. The only thing keeping us fitter and not fatter was the amount of running away from the enemy we did."

The men snickered, murmuring in agreement.

His comment almost caused Virtutis to join the laughter, but he chose to keep listening. He sat, grateful for the openness and hospitality. With his eyes remaining shaded, he gazed past the group to what looked like less comfortable fires.

Agitated energy and footsteps approached through the camp. A scraggly warrior arrived out of breath with orders.

An all-too-common lack of fitness for Virtutis's liking.

Orders huffed from the winded soul. "Attention. Tomorrow at dawn, we are to meet at the northern end of the camp." He pulled in more air, gasping to regain his breath. "Bring your spear and water."

Baiting, Virtutis could not help himself. "A spear? Or only the shaft?"

"The shaft! That is what I said, didn't I?"

Irritated, the warrior searched the circle closer. "Who said that? Khan will have your head!"

"Khan will have my head?" Virtutis pulled back the hook gently.

"Yes. And I am happy to cut it off and take it to him." The man's hand clenched the hilt of his sword.

The warrior glared in Virtutis's direction before he spat on the ground and ran to the next fire.

Virtutis scoffed through his nose, a measure of how much the warrior's threats deserved his attention.

The men sat finishing their stew, occasionally chewing the tender meat that floated in the savory liquid.

Virtutis stared at the flames, again thinking of his boys. He knew he had to leave the comfort of the runners before his mind became too idle.

"Thank you for your stew and conversation. Stoades, meet me at dawn. I have a mission for you."

Stoades nodded enthusiastically. Virtutis turned to the silent Mercalis. "Skinny, would you join me for a private conversation?"

"Sir, of course," Mercalis answered.

Hood remaining over Virtutis's head, they walked through the entire camp unnoticed.

"Have you family back home?" Virtutis asked.

"Just my brother and sister are alive now."

"Why did you sign up for the auxiliary?"

"The Romans were only getting stronger. Our village was destroyed, and we lost all we had. I knew I had to survive amongst them. After my service, I will be a free man."

"Is there any such thing as freedom?"

"Moments, maybe. Amongst family, amongst friends."

Virtutis liked the genuine and authentic conversation, so he risked honesty. "I agree. There is freedom in belonging. My wife, she gave me that freedom, but I never knew it until she was gone."

"She is dead?"

"Yes. I hope she is waiting for me in the afterlife. However, I will only know when I am there."

Uncomfortable with divulging too much of his personal life, Virtutis curved the conversation into more simplistic topics as they walked.

After almost completing a full circle, Virtutis slowed. He needed more than an ally. He needed eyes where he could not see and ears where he could not hear.

"We will talk before dawn at my camp, before Stoades arrives. You are not to be seen with me again."

"Sir?"

"There are many roles in service. I have one that requires risk but also gives a man great power without association or retribution if he plays his part well."

"Sir. I am at your service. I will do what is required."

"Good. Tomorrow night we are to begin training in the dark arts."

"Dark arts?"

"You will see in time."

Voices lifted in conflict in the distance from the runners' fire.

Mercalis reached for his dagger.

Virtutis caught him, putting a hand on his arm to stop any rash movements. "Back, with me. I want to see."

They retreated into the shadows, making their way closer to the other side, while the commotion grew.

The out-of-breath warrior had returned with fire in his eyes—drunk.

Dust stirred. Feet scrapped for balance. He pushed and shoved, asking questions. He drew a dagger, pointing, threatening.

"Where is the runner? What is his name?" He grabbed Stoades. "His name!"

Receiving no answer, he pushed Stoades to the ground, holding a knife to his throat. "Tell me!"

Virtutis knew this beast; it had a sickened mind, like the one within himself that once straddled his son. He closed the space from behind, Mercalis creeping alongside.

The other runners stood their ground. Not flinching, calm. They armed themselves behind the warrior's back, picking up knives, a short sword, and even firewood.

Virtutis held back his discomfort. "Mercalis," he whispered, "they will not move until they are sure he will not kill Stoades."

Stoades gulped, speaking through the pressure from the dagger now dangerously close to his jugular. "We do not know his name, nor where he is from. He ate with us, then left. He came with the reinforcements."

Virtutis whispered to Mercalis without taking his eyes from the fray, "If he kills Stoades, spare him no pain. If he releases him, I will deal with him in the days to come. Understand?"

"Understood."

Virtutis knew very well the drunk warrior was not going to kill anyone, for if he was going to, he would have begun killing from the start.

Mercalis carefully walked back into the group, drawing his dagger to the side, concealed. With a quiet brushing of the runners with his arm, he moved close enough to maim or kill.

By fate, the warrior released his grip on Stoades's throat. Standing, he turned directly into Mercalis.

For a mere second, they faced off.

Virtutis could see Mercalis's face contemplating action, but he backed down, bowing his head, keeping the dagger hidden.

Virtutis smiled from the shadows, turning his back on the scene.

He picked goat's meat from his teeth with his finger while he walked.

He could trust Mercalis. And from what he saw from the runners, they too held a loyal resolve. When threatened with their life, they could have easily betrayed him, but they held their tongues well. Well enough for Virtutis to consider them for his plans.

Virtutis sat by his campfire, considering his troops' training plan. It would be harsh. Harsh like the sun threatening to tear her hot impression into their new reality. Despite having no experience in troop development or Roman strategy, he had no doubt where he needed to start.

Early, as requested, Mercalis arrived at the edge of the darkness.

Virtutis, liking his caution, stood and walked to the cover. "Did you sleep well, Mercalis?"

"No, sir. It took a while for the situation to resolve itself last night. But we managed."

Virtutis tilted his chin. "Is it resolved?"

"Yes. We left him alive as you ordered."

"Good." Virtutis let out a breath through his nose. "Do you know many men here?"

"Not many now. Most of the men I knew were killed when the barbarians first attacked. And over the mountain passes, I kept to myself."

"Why?" Virtutis asked.

"Who knows who is who? Or what they have done?" Mercalis replied.

Virtutis admired his honesty, an honesty that only confirmed his instincts about the stability of his leadership.

"True statement. I am glad you survived. The gods only give those who live opportunities. Those who are dead are dead."

"Yes. I agree."

"We do not have much time. It is important the men now see you only as a runner. Your warrior skills will keep you alive better than the other runners. You are valuable, even if you are skinny." Virtutis caught himself joking, comfortable, which made him feel awkward.

"Sir?" Mercalis asked.

"If you are a runner, people will talk freely around you; you are no threat. But if a situation is threatening, you can take care of it." Virtutis looked Mercalis straight in the eye. "I have three requests of you. First is to be known as a runner. The second is to train the other runners in secret. Teach them to attack and defend themselves better. They must stay alive. If they die, so does our information, and if our information dies, so does our ability to see beyond the battles. Third, you are to be my shadow without me knowing it, and you will be my eyes and ears where I am not."

"I am going to be your spy?"

Virtutis checked his dagger at his side. "Yes."

A gust of wind blew through the camp, making the fire crackle and spark.

Mercalis stared hard into the campfire, then nodded. "Very well. I accept your request."

"Good," Virtutis said. "It's important people do not see us together often. They are not to know the depths in which we speak or your role in my command. You must always protect yourself and say as little as possible about the matters of war and your personal life. Especially with the runners you are training. They must trust you but never really know anything of you."

"Why not trust them?"

"Runners and messengers are not warriors. I have not known one who has not turned when I have caught them. That's why you must train them in private. They must become warrior runners."

"Understood." Mercalis changed posture, placing his elbows on his knees.

Virtutis relaxed, content, more comfortable he'd made the right decision with his selection. "Mercalis. If words do not escape your mouth, you will never be condemned for the decisions of command— that lies with me."

Mercalis shifted, uneasy. "With the wrong information or decision, I could kill you at any turn. That is giving away more trust than any man I know."

Virtutis lowered his chin. "Yes, but at least I know where it has come from. It is either you or me, correct?"

"Yes."

A sincere gaze cut through the night between them.

"I cannot do this alone." Virtutis scanned the darkness. He pulled up his hood.

"I understand," Mercalis said. "I am with you. I am at your service. Thank you for the confidence, commander."

"Call me Virtutis. We are brothers, and our lives are now intertwined. There is no rank in brotherhood, just survival." Virtutis offered his hand.

Mercalis drew breath into his chest and reciprocated. Perhaps overwhelmed.

They secured their brotherhood with a strong forearm grip, purpose and trust gleaming between them.

"This is our bond. From here, we are bound in life and death," Virtutis said.

"This is our bond, life and death," Mercalis affirmed.

Virtutis had to risk his position for the sake of his sons. After their bond, there was no reason to distrust Mercalis. He squeezed his forearm with solitude.

"If anything is to happen to me, return to my farm. My sons are there and my trusted friend Odigos. Tell them I sent you. They will ask for my wife's name. Her name was Cynisca."

"Cynisca. Yes, brother. I will not fail you."

"Good. Now disappear. There are eyes a plenty." Virtutis released his grip, eyeing suspiciously beyond the fire.

Mercalis left before their conversation could be discovered. The darkness absorbed his figure.

Virtutis returned to his seat, warming his body by the flames, waiting for dawn to break. A dawn that held a future he could not yet see. He only hoped it would lead him to his ultimate destiny—that of resolve.

After a sleepless night, Virtutis walked away from his fire. His eyes watered, looking into the blinking eye of the sunlight as it broke over the mountain. He pulled crisp morning air through his nostrils, fueling his lungs, and cracked his neck to the side, remembering the feeling of the sun's warmth on his neck. He imagined Rufus lying somewhere, deep down, never to be reclaimed.

Footsteps crunched over morning frost. Virtutis took a chance to seem self-assured. "Stoades," he said. "Please, warm yourself by the fire."

"Sir, thank you," Stoades replied.

"You held your tongue well last night. Although, it was nearly cut out." Virtutis turned and sat across the fire. "I trusted you initially, but the composure you showed was admirable."

"I was not that composed. Just too shocked to talk," Stoades said, unashamed.

"Either way, you protected me and my identity. I am grateful."

116

"Sir," replied Stoades, nodding his head.

With little time to spare, Virtutis had to include Stoades into his plan.

"Stoades, I am a warrior. I took risks to keep us alive. Now I am to command these men. But there is still much division and distrust."

"Agreed. Even though we made it here, doubt and deceit flow freely."

"That's where I need you. You are a runner. But you must learn how to think like a commander. If we are to continue to survive, I need someone I can trust to help navigate my command. The men will only trust success. Any hint of hesitation, and we are all dead men, again."

"How so?"

"In battle, you are to adapt messages if needed. I cannot control the changing enemy strikes that occur in battle from a single vantage point. The Barbarians shift and move their point of attack. In the blood bath of battle, by the time I receive information, the vantages would have already changed. And most important is the intention of decisions if I am not capable of doing so. I am a warrior. I get lost in battle while a commander often navigates tactics."

"I understand. But I am not sure I am able to do so." Stoades said.

"You are able," Virtutis affirmed. Standing to collect his spear, he checked the trees for anyone watching them. "If our men are to fight as good as three men, you must think as good as three. A messenger, a warrior, and a commander."

"I understand, sir. I will try. But still, I am not sure I am the best choice for this responsibility."

"You will learn. We must learn together." Virtutis held a steady stare on his new protégé. "Stoades, I trust you. That is all we need at this time. If you are willing, then the rest will come."

"I understand." Stoades's face looked shocked at the context of the responsibility.

"Do not worry about what you do not know and what you cannot control. Let destiny take its shape."

"Yes, sir."

Virtutis leaned in closer to the fire to expose more of his vision. Stoades reflected his caution, also leaning in.

"Our success will largely depend on the auxiliary's ability to be mobile and adaptable, both in warfare and within from Roman mind games," Virtutis explained. "This will take specific training, and we have little time. We need to know our skills and temperament. These first days we must create conflict that quickly shows us who our men are under pressure. No warrior can be judged by what he says he can do. He might be good in training, but only his ability in a life-or-death moment will demonstrate what he is made of. The true test is in the heat of battle, don't you think? We have to make things as close to this as possible."

"Yes, truth."

"So, let us try our best to create the tension needed in order to see our men clearly. You are my eyes and ears; you must see and hear everything I cannot observe. If we are to survive, we must know these men."

"How do we do that?" Stoades asked with wide eyes.

"We run them; then we make them fight. We take away who they think they are, so we can see who they really are."

CHAPTER 12

Standing just outside the camp, Virtutis analyzed the early stirring of haphazard warriors arriving in dribs and drabs, some still waking up, others having been up for some time. As a whole, they were unprepared, disconnected, and lazy.

Khan appeared from the back of the group, wiping sleep from his eyes.

The runners grouped to the side, attentive.

Virtutis snapped his head, wanting to crack his already cracked neck, unimpressed.

"Follow me." Initiating an easy running pace pressured his men to follow suit, ready or not.

It was not long before Khan started sucking a full barrel of air behind him. Virtutis shook his head, picking up the speed, wanting to leave him far behind.

Keeping his hand in a light grip, perfectly balancing his spear, Virtutis ran freely.

In between inhalations and exhalations, Virtutis's ears searched for breathing patterns of those behind, searching for oxygen limits before they themselves encountered them.

Wrestling as a young man, had taught him much about the oxygen capacity of his opponents. Oxygen fueled the head; without it, thinking became limited, making any man or beast vulnerable.

The sun moved through its summer spectacle, breaking into a full declaration, providing harsh light for the eyes, and adding heat that parched the sturdiest throats. At the base of small hills leading to high mountain trails, anticipating the environmental change, Virtutis increased the speed even more, pumping his legs, attacking the upward slopes.

He grinned. We all think we have great problems until we can't breathe.

He rounded a bend, looking back down. His tactic worked, separating the men into fragmented groups littering the path up the mountain.

The runners were the only group able to keep pace with him. They opened the distance between them until the rest of the men became tiny ants spread out as far as the eye could see.

After a steep incline, the trail split in two. He stopped, gathering the runners cantering down from behind. Straight to command, Virtutis put the plan into action.

"Stoades, stay just in sight of the closet group and lead them to the right. I will give them orders from there. Mercalis, you are with me. The rest of you double back down the rocks unseen. I want to know where the clusters have stopped, how many in each group, and if they are out of water and exhausted. Relay information. You will need to loop back and forth with updates. Understood?"

Stoades smiled. "Yes, sir."

Virtutis laughed under his breath, having his fun. "It is time the snake bit off its own tail for breakfast."

Taking the right fork, Virtutis and Mercalis hid above the trail, waiting. Soon enough, Stoades came pacing through, disappearing far enough to bait the warriors in pursuit.

From above, Virtutis gathered small stones while Mercalis watched, remaining hidden.

Virtutis hammered the trail with stones, making the group scatter to protect themselves.

"You are all dead!" Virtutis called. He continued to throw stones at their feet. "So, I guess your afterlives are with me."

Jumping down off the high rock, scattering the warriors with his descent, he waved them closer. Mercalis remained hidden, listening.

There was huffing and puffing around the corner, surprising even Virtutis.

Someone was coming louder than an ox pulling a cart through deep mud.

Almost laughing, Virtutis saw the commotion first. "Khan... you ox."

"Ahhufff, ahhhuff." Khan had burst around the bend like he was dying. Seeing the group, he stopped with his mouth wide open.

Virtutis was half humored and half concerned.

"Are you alive?"

Out of breath, Khan pulled air and dodged his eyes around the faces, trying to read the situation.

"Sir. Yes, sir, I am good." He put his hands on his knees. "What did I miss?"

"Nothing," Virtutis said with a raised eyebrow before addressing the group. "There is a cluster of men approaching from behind you. They will be led up the left fork on the steep pathway. When they are almost at the top and exhausted, overpower them and take their water and weapons. You can cut over to the track up there." He motioned toward a narrow goat trail easily missed.

"After you have the water, come back here, and you will receive your next orders. And don't go too fast; it might kill Khan. Go on; be prepared."

Khan let out a smile for the first time, which Virtutis pretended not to notice, looking over the ox's shoulder in dismissal.

The warriors did not waste time getting ready for their ambush, finding short sticks to accompany their spear shafts.

They cut up the track out of sight.

Virtutis motioned to Mercalis to break cover. He dropped down, ready.

"Head down, meet the next cluster. Tell them to hide until I arrive. Cut over the rock faces so you are not seen. Then head down to the last cluster and prepare them for a battle. Tell them to slow down. They must protect their reserves, stay together, and use their brute strength."

"Sir?"

"The slower group will be the heavier, more powerful group. Give them the advantage of information."

"Yes."

Sure-footed, he scampered over the rock space.

Virtutis's sandals, now well worn, eased while running ridges and secured his steps as he scaled steep pathways.

He caught glimpses of his analytical childhood war games, watching his men pitted against each other over the mountain terrain. Using the runners to give information and direction, he caused confrontation, testing their abilities under stress and confusion.

The day progressed with many small fights, leaving bodies battered and broken.

Above the chaos, fearing his men would turn savage and seeing a black blanket of a moonless night starting to form, he called the runners to return to his lookout command. Satisfied with the runners' effort and control, he had seen enough to start training. Out of respect for their effort, he let them rest. "Drink, gather your breath. There will be only a few final orders for the day."

Holding back his own conclusions, he posed to his runners. "What did you find about the men and their responses to today?"

Stoades gulped down a mouth full of water, spilling from the corner of his mouth in surprise at being asked.

Virtutis waited, interested now even more.

"The leaner men ran the hills using stealth and surprise. The larger men stuck together," Stoades said, wiping his mouth.

One of the younger runners in his teens, eager to join the discussion, moved forward, perking Virtutis's ears.

"Warriors who knew each other found ways to regroup and stay together, backtracking and not following orders."

"Interesting. You saw all of that?"

"Yes, they have always broken rank." Stoades sipped more water, almost suspiciously.

Virtutis glanced at Mercalis, who remained silent, not causing any attention. So far, he was right about his gut choice about the warrior runner.

"Stoades, call a truce. They can return to the camp and rest. Tomorrow, we start at dawn. Please do it quickly. If we leave them too long, revenge and savagery is all that will be left. I can feel it festering."

The runners evaporated into the coming night.

With low visibility, Virtutis climbed a little higher, searching for space to gain perspective on the day.

He reflected on what he saw. Seated high on a rock overlooking the hinterlands, he closed his eyes, gathering his thoughts before he started his downward run back to camp.

Calm chatter from exhausted men, who rested after being pushed to their limits, made the camp quieter than previous evenings.

Virtutis rounded through the shadows. Khan sat alone with his feet elevated, sipping on broth.

Knowing his target was self-occupied, he lurked from behind, using the darkness to his advantage.

Khan hummed a low tune, grumbling something over and over again from the deepest parts of his throat.

Virtutis waited a little longer to listen to the strange gargling sound.

"Lovely bedtime song, old ox."

Khan jolted his feet from the stool, spilling his broth once again.

"Sir!" Looking down at his tunic, he scrunched up his face. "Every time, I swear you frighten the life out of me."

Virtutis broke from the darkness into the firelight.

"You're alone? Where are your men?"

"They are not my men," Khan replied, adamant in defense. "As for friends, I would rather my own company than the consistent speculation of a destiny we cannot escape. Doubt is deadly."

"Speculation?"

"They have had four commanders before you, and none of them survived. Confidence in leadership, regardless of our survival, is still not an easy accomplishment."

"Why are you here, alone?"

"If I die, I would rather do it in a fight that people would remember, not stabbing someone in the back and pretending it didn't happen." Khan moved over by the fire, collecting an extra bowl from his bag. "Our battles have been exciting. I like it. Broth?"

An uneasy twist held Virtutis's stomach; endless deceit felt rampant.

Could these men be planning to assassinate him like they had his predecessor?

"Yes, thank you."

"Sit, please." Khan offered one of the short-cut logs as a seat.

Virtutis sat open to hear more if it was offered. Khan hugged the bowl, wiping it with his almost-clean tunic, filled it, and handed over the steaming dish.

Virtutis opened with an easy subject to see if Khan would speak freely, not forcing talk of treason. "How are your feet? Will you be ready for tomorrow?" he asked, tasting the broth. Though heavy with meat, it tasted strange.

"Yes. I think so. I am not sure about that run, though. Some of us are not Greek goats, you know?"

"Yes. But you did well. Even if the enemy heard you puffing all the way from Rome."

"Ha! It's my nose. It's broken. I can't breathe or smell anymore. Running is difficult. I am not tired; I just can't breathe!" Khan threw his hands up as if he was a lost cause. Then, remembering he had spilled broth, looked down to wipe his tunic again.

Virtutis took advantage of the lack of attention, emptying the stew beside him. Khan looked up, not noticing, catching a new thought with a smile. "My wife loves my broken nose, you know? Says she can bathe once a fortnight now. Which is funny because that's what I thought she did before I broke my nose." He chuckled. "Oh well, I am grateful for my broken nose when I am home, at least. Ha! The puffing only lasts for a minute or so."

Virtutis cracked a smile at the genuine openness of Khan's humor at himself.

"You are an interesting man, Khan. It is good that you think lightly of yourself." Virtutis stood with the empty bowl in his hand, choosing not to push the topic of mutiny yet.

"I only wish I was that interesting. If I can stay alive for another year or so, who knows, right?" Khan added.

"Yes. Who knows?" Virtutis looked around. "Can I use some water to wash the bowl? I have no water with me."

"No, you are my guest. I will wash it with mine. My wife taught me how to wash bowls well."

"Thank you, Khan. I am grateful for the meal."

Khan shifted his head to the side, squinting his eyes as if confused.

"I am grateful for your company. It's almost as if you like me."

"We will see." Virtutis adjusted his shoulders, checking the darkness for movement, deciding to risk a third ally with any great details.

"Meet me before dawn at my camp. I have a job for you."

Khan postured up, then scratched his head. "As long as it is not running to the top of that mountain again, I will be of my best service."

"How about just a good chance to fight?"

"Well then! Count me in! Like an ox!"

Virtutis stood, handing Khan his bowl. "Yes, Khan. Like an ox."

From the light of the fire, Virtutis embraced the least prestigious path, finding comfort in the dark outskirts of the camp.

Khan's deep gargling song started again, fading away with Virtutis's every step.

Throughout the night, Virtutis crept through the darkness with his hood up, listening. Watching. Thinking.

While his new position served a purpose, it was also a distraction from the sadness that would come and go. Loneliness entered the spaces between his quest, the responsibilities of a commander, and the preoccupation of being poisoned or executed at the hands of lesser men rather than dying in battle on scrapping the edges of death's greatest lessons. If he was to continue as commander, he would need to gain the confidence of his men and promote the members of his leadership through equally shared experiences.

Uneasy, and even though his camp was set up and the fire was burning, he felt more comfort taking his cloak and blanket into the night away from the security of his troops.

He sat in the forest, looking at the stars and thinking of his sons, wife, Urion, and the burning injustice Arquitos had faced that stripped him of his decency.

Restless while the moon quartered her beauty, he took his small sharpening stone and ground his dagger. Swaying, he found a rhythm. There was a howling in the distance while he meditated. A meditation set on murder.

A situation of revenge needing attending to.

126

CHAPTER 13

Virtutis's face and arms were covered with damp ash to hide the reflection of any light that may give him away. He walked in the shadows behind the last row of perfectly aligned tents in the legion's encampment.

Under the cover of darkness, the movement and footsteps of others were louder.

His ears caught a warning—a wild dog growled, but it crept away unseen, daring not to approach. Occasionally, soldiers shared stories and laughed, and a few groups sat cluttered around the campfires.

Virtutis inhaled through his nose twice, fueling his cold, calculating mind armed with a sharp, vengeful dagger.

While he could not get to the general, an assassination so close would unnerve his untouchable attitude.

Intimidation held the empire's enemies at arm's length—but not tonight. Not for Virtutis with double-edged revenge on his mind. He took advantage of the relaxed and recovering camp far from the front lines of battle, giving him access to the general's area. Open. Exposed.

Hidden, he studied two guards standing at attention under the light of tall lamp flames outside the general's quarters.

He moved on—they were not the mark for his dagger of death.

Tucked behind the general's tent stood four legion's tents, used by his personal guard.

Virtutis sat down on his heels, watching. Waiting.

Tent flaps wavered in the night. One of the guards who'd beaten Arquitos flicked open the canvas door. He proceeded to the darker shadows and let out a groan as he relieved himself with his right hand.

Virtutis closed the gap from the deep dark.

Drawing his dagger, he came from the right side.

With the guard's right hand still guiding mid-stream, he was unable to oppose Virtutis's dagger. Exploding upward, the tip entered under his chin, rendering the man's throat to nothing but a gargled surprise.

Virtutis made sure he stayed out of range of the continued urination, and he watched the last seconds of death while he twisted his dagger with pleasure.

The whites of the guard's eyes flashed in a painful surprise, a dead man standing, unable to retaliate.

Virtutis allowed the limp body to fall to his knees, twisting him at the shoulder and guiding him to his back before removing the blade. He checked the surroundings for unwanted attention, then placing his hands under the guard's shoulders, he dragged him further into the cover of darkness.

Maintaining a low crouch, he listened and searched for any stir of activity.

Nothing.

He walked over the daggered deceased to his next target farther in the shadows. One of the three remaining tents held his last prized revenge.

He waited. The chattering of wild dogs gave way to the sound of teeth tearing warm flesh not far behind the bushes. The wild dogs had sniffed out fresh blood, and they fought and feasted, drawing attention.

The guards at the general's entrance turned but held their post. A tent flap whipped open, giving way to the second target.

Virtutis sniffed the air—the scent of a dead man.

A large guard, bare-chested and brave, shook his head in anger. "Filthy mutts!" He swiped a nearby lamp, drawing his sword from inside the tent. "Can't a man get some sleep without you scavenging mongrels fighting over scraps?"

Virtutis followed him, letting him walk his last steps into the darkness, away from witnesses, and into death's dagger.

Lamplight inched its way toward the frenzy of feeding dogs at the man's approach. "Yah!"

Dogs scattered in all directions, unveiling his dead, mauled comrade.

"What the hell!"

"Unpleasant, isn't it?" Virtutis whispered, entering his dagger deep under the man's ribs, right by the spine, finishing with a familiar twist.

Virtutis's opposite hand wrapped around the guard's jaw and mouth, quietening any response. He rotated the neck, forcing the body to follow momentum to the ground like a bull turned by his horns.

Keeping his hand over the guard's mouth, Virtutis drew the dagger before the man knocked on death's door.

Virtutis sprawled over him sideways, locking eye to eye while he angled the dagger high, gutting the pig from navel to diaphragm.

The guard gasped, pulling air through his nose, choking blood back against his throat.

Virtutis sliced him quick, making sure the guard was still alive, making sure he felt every pain of his death.

The guard weakened, shivering with cold, almost falling beyond agony.

Virtutis removed his hand and allowed the man a last breath.

Blood spurted from his mouth. "You … S-spartan…"

Eye to eye, Virtutis watched him bleed out, closing the conversation with a final word.

"Arquitos."

CHAPTER 14

Dawn broke over the second day of auxiliary training. Warriors stirred, scurrying to be ready for anything. Virtutis's skin goose-bumped all over from the midnight swim where he'd washed off blood and charcoal.

He briefed Khan and Stoades on the day's plans, including the importance of running information and adapting orders.

Sensing commotion coming through the middle of his men, Virtutis dipped his head to listen, then looked over Khan's shoulder.

A Roman messenger darted his way into their group. "Virtutis? Who is Commander Virtutis?"

"I am."

"General Lucio has requested the attendance of all commanders at his council. Immediately." The messenger's hands shook, his feet shuffled and his beady eyes, too small for his head, darted back and forth uncomfortably.

"I'll be on my way shortly."

The messenger rubbed his neck. "Sir, the request is immediate, or… or he will have our heads."

"Understood. You may return. I am on my way."

Fear eased in the messenger's eyes. "Sir, thank you."

The message laced a layer of Virtutis's own conundrum of guilt but not of remorse. Being summoned would either be the end of his revenge or the beginning. He was certain no one had witnessed him last night, but certainty in the darkness of vengeance is like the certainty of a Roman's word.

"Khan, you know what to do with the men. If I am not back by sundown, I am dead, and you should find your way back to your wife without delay."

Khan's eyes searched for clarity, his brow flickering, a frown and eventual acceptance. "Sir, I have everything under control. Watch out for Glycon."

"Glycon?"

"The snake. The one who climbs the empire's standard to try to sit with the eagle; it influences his mind. If it is not the ambition of the eagle who tears you apart, the snake will poison your flesh, and his words will trick your logic."

Virtutis searched Khan's face. "You believe in mystic?"

Khan snickered a laugh, then dropped into a more serious gesture. "I believe others do. Real snakes and eagles are one thing; the power of deceit and betrayal imposing upon a man's mind is another."

Virtutis nodded. "Truth. See to it that the men are well tested today. I will return as soon as I can."

He turned to Stoades. "If I am not back in time, and you get to tactical training, report all messages to Khan. He is in command now."

"Yes, sir." Stoades looked bothered.

"What is it?"

"Last night, there were murders, so be aware. And well…" Stoades paused in thought.

"Carry on. Speak your mind."

"If the Romans take the command from you, we are as good as dead." Stoades revealed desperation on his face, desperation that Virtutis did not consider before now, that of more responsibility.

"It will be what it will be, Stoades. We do not control certain decisions. Die now, or die later—only the gods know our fate."

Virtutis noticed Khan looking agitated. "One thing at a time, Khan. You are the ox. Focus on the training today, nothing more."

Virtutis dipped his head to something else that unsettled him. "Skinny?"

Mercalis rustled his sack over his shoulder. "Sir?"

"Mind your own business and make sure you are eating more food," Virtutis warned. "This conversation is for leadership, not the ears of runners."

"Sir, yes, sir."

Virtutis hoped he covered his tracks with caution—Mercalis had knowledge no other man knew. Knowledge that unlocked advantages over himself, knowledge that put the lives of his sons at risk.

By the time Virtutis was on his way, the general's runner had already disappeared. The walk was long, owning a hundred possibilities that led Virtutis to formulate a simple response—the assassinations were unfortunate events, and whoever the culprit was deserved maximum punishment.

Nearly a legion of men stood at attention along the main entrance to the general's quarters. Tensions hummed, creating energy that forced each man to look straight ahead. From afar, a man might perceive discipline or duty, but fear held each soldier's attention with a gulp in their throats.

The general had been threatened.

Now retaliation would be very, very real.

The general's guards had been replaced by four praetorians standing at attention around the perimeter of the tent with hands on their swords—their armor intimidating, helmets shadowing their eyes.

The ground was covered in fresh blood, no doubt what remained of the personal guards.

Virtutis's feet warmed from his sandals deepening into the moist, red mud. The scent of death rose as steam became captured by the morning sun. For Virtutis, a familiar smell.

The smell of slaughter.

"Halt!" the praetorian guarding the tent entrance ordered. "Roman Commanders only. Auxiliary are to remain here until summoned."

Virtutis put his fingers to use by adjusting his belt. He stood, feet slightly apart, looking directly into the eyelet shadows of the merciless helmet. "Is here satisfactory, centurion?" he asked, knowing the insult of a lesser rank would boil blood.

Virtutis brushed his tunic to the side, removing an obstruction, and brushed his dagger with his palm.

There was no break in their silent standoff.

From the general's tent, voices fired back and forth in fierce discussion—overridden by screaming authority. The talk was further silenced by a clash of metal on what could have been a table.

Turning his body, Virtutis pretended to look at the outskirts of the camp. Leaning into his left ear, he stretched the limits of his hearing, attempting clarity.

It was in vain.

He balanced the inner tension, heightened by the unknown depth of the Roman snake pit.

But why were Virtutis's men not assembled? Maybe they were considered incapable of such a crime?

The tent entrance erupted with the exiting of six Roman commanders.

Stepping back, Virtutis let their abrupt energy pass. He locked eyes with the last commander and received a glare that could kill. A glare that spewed offence at the mere fact of Virtutis's birth—and an attitude that cut a man down for speaking out of turn.

A praetorian opened the tent door for the general—a general red in the face, aggressive. Murderous.

"Spartan! With me. Now."

Virtutis followed close behind the Roman leader, who shoved his way past a praetorian and on toward the edge of the murdered guards' tents.

"The thing is, Virtutis." He slurred insults. "Anyone who finds themselves in a position of power or authority can quickly adopt complacency."

The general stopped abruptly, pulling away his white robe and moving to urinate.

"One of my guards was pissing. Pissing!" He laughed, making Virtutis very aware of how insane the man was when agitated. He continued to relieve himself.

"The man stood at the back of his tent, and someone assassinated him while he held his snake in his hand." His words held more humor.

Virtutis watched the back of the general's neck. Just above his robe stood a vein. One prick, and it would be over. If he used his dagger now, it would be done.

The general looked down at his business, then sideways, catching Virtutis's attention.

"The walls should have been up. Guards should have been in place. But they were all complacent. And it almost cost me my life. Whoever I have crossed did not hesitate, did they?"

The general looked down and continued to watch his streamed display. Virtutis looked at the ground; the general was pooling a urine insult over his guards' drying blood.

Virtutis shifted. Uneasy. Not looking down at the general's business. "How do you feel pissing away the blood of a man who swore a duty to protect your life?"

The general snickered, finishing. "There is little willingness in such duty, Spartan. Not all men are seeking the great ideal of service to provide them with purpose. This is war; the willing are as rare, if not as dead, as Sparta." Ice ran through Virtutis's veins at the man who pissed so proudly on another man's life. The general was a man who truly believed he could rape men, women, and children at will, and now indirectly insulted his ancestry. "You see, Virtutis, the only thing that will keep men in long service is fear of never reaching retirement. Every now and then, we must use a situation to send a clear message of who is the authority. Don't you think?"

Virtutis remained silent. Staring at the general's vein on his neck as he continued his verbal assault.

"This was not a random assassination," the general said. "Those two guards have often carried out sentences from my orders. It would most likely have been someone from within our own ranks. Perhaps we are not that different, you and I, in taking control of what we feel is rightfully ours?"

"Some things are beyond all control. Even if they seem controlled or ordered, human nature is as predictable as a donkey, even if you think you know its temperament," Virtutis replied.

Realizing he had urinated on himself, the general started to shake his hand in the air, finishing by running the back of it on his tunic. Unimpressed with himself, he spat where a dead man's last breath took place, adding insult.

Virtutis ran a roughened fingertip over his dagger.

The general laughed. "And here I am. With a Spartan Prefectus, whose company I prefer over my own lazy, failing Roman guards."

The comment caught Virtutis by surprise. Before he could manage a response, the general slapped Virtutis on the shoulder.

"Come, let us walk. We have something to talk about. I have a special assignment for you in the coming days. You will accompany a precious delivery from Germania to the sea. You will escort a person as fast as you can. It should take ten days to get there and back if you travel light."

Virtutis rebutted the offer. "Sir, I have little time to prepare my troops. I am not sure they will be ready if I am not here. I am no messenger or delivery boy."

The general spun, looking up over his nose and curling his lip. "This is not an assignment of choice, Spartan."

The two stood, assessing one another.

Virtutis resisted the urge to reach for his dagger, breathing deep and slow.

He swallowed the taste of revenge—rather to regurgitate it elsewhere when the time was right.

"Sir… as you request." He gave a slow, reluctant nod.

"Good. I knew you would accept." The general flicked the back of his hand as if to shoo a fly. "I will send for you. You may go."

Virtutis caught himself, gulping vengeance at the gesture, choosing instead to turn and begin his walk away.

"Outstanding," the general spoke as if to himself—though loud enough to be heard. "Whoever said you cannot tame a Spartan?"

The words filled Virtutis's empty stomach with a fiery appetite.

For blood.

He returned to the auxiliary, cracking the knuckles in both hands, attempting to edge out the tension, crunching the urge to kill.

He tried to focus on something else.

The legion's campsite had begun to shape itself into a reflection of war from the inside out.

Axes rang out, hammers hit, and commanders cursed their cohorts into the machine Rome was famous for.

An ox pulled a cart across his path, loaded with corpses—the general's failed guards.

Virtutis searched for more calm.

And vowed to follow his quest as a warrior and a prefectus. He would not submit to revenge any time soon.

Virtutis pulled the dagger from its sheath. Holding it gently, he studied the engraved ivory handle and razor-sharp edge—and waited until the hot lava that ran through veins from his heels to his temples cooled down.

He looked back to the wagon pulling away.

A single hand bounced free, dangling in gesture. An ultimate service to the empire.

A hand that could well have been his own.

Sheathing his dagger and organizing his belt, he followed the blood-dripped path back to his men.

If he could not kill the general now, he would secure himself until a safe opportunity revealed itself.

CHAPTER 15

At the empty campsite, Virtutis's men had already left for training in the mountains. He gathered his spear and took a swig of water, gulping back more than half, spitting out the rest in an attempt to wash away the disdain for the general.

It failed.

He tucked a small leather pouch into his belt and broke into a stride, leading him over the flats and up the mountain trail.

His mind grew busy with hatred, burning hot. Searing like the blacksmith's forge.

Sheathing his dagger was an easy action—sheathing the mockery from the general was not.

He tried everything to shake the fixation. The only thing that would save him from further festering was the next task. He had to distract himself.

He lifted his heels and sped up his pace, a pace that forced his mind to focus and his heels to barely touch the ground. The air through his lungs refreshed his brain, the pain building in his legs lending short-term relief.

Into the trees, the energy of nature slowed his run, freeing a little of the compulsion.

Shattered sounds of wood on wood grew louder from beyond the ridge.

Rounding the top of the trail, he caught the full view of his men in formation, drilling staffs like spears, pivoting and adjusting in the tough mountain terrain.

Men attacked and defended strikes and stabs, learning the art of the spear.

Khan barked an order.

A horn blew.

The auxiliary broke into six groups, scattering onto the different slopes and into adjacent tree lines. Forming instinctual tactics, they attacked each other.

Fights sprawled over the ridges with groups splitting up. They yelled commands, the defeated trying to adjust to the ever-present stress of being broken apart.

Before any winner could be declared, the horn blew, and the chaos came to a halt.

Those who yielded regathered themselves and were commanded to drill attacks and defense, and with no break, they were forced to work harder still.

Those who won gained the prize of the day. Water.

The strong got stronger.

In most cases, the weak, weaker.

The odd warrior fought back from losing and turned a personal tide of the fight to regain their dominance.

In the pauses between action and assessment, Virtutis's forearms tensed with the impression of the general. He found himself shaking his head in torment.

Catching his thoughts, he took a long, deep breath, trying to move through the emotion. It was difficult. Solving it with violence was much easier than negotiating the inner turmoil a Spartan warrior faced when having to break instinct.

In a final attempt for intervention, he ventured farther into the line of sight, allowing his presence to be seen by Khan.

Lifting his hand in beckoning, he made the ox run uphill.

Huffing and puffing, he eventually arrived. "That's a good hill to run." Khan tried to control his breathing.

Virtutis looked down at his broken nose, resisting judgement. "You have done well, Khan. They are learning. Keep the drilling and fighting for tomorrow morning."

The compliment caused Khan's lips to curve into a big smile.

"Give the men an hour's rest. Then we move to the next phase. They can have water—food if they need it. It is time to hunt as a pack. Let's put our runners to work."

"This is where you kill an ox, isn't it?"

"No. This is where the ox is reinvented."

"Ha! I like that!" Khan paused his enthusiasm. "It's good to see you didn't get bit by the snake."

With a nod, Khan turned off down the slope, not giving Virtutis a chance to reply. The immediate action made Virtutis comfortable that Khan was taking a larger initiative toward action. He watched Khan halt training and give the order for water and rations. The men looked relieved.

Virtutis squatted, collecting dry dirt, then rubbed his hands together. Still trying to put the morning behind him.

He rolled his hands over a few times, then gently slapped off the dust.

Well rested for the moment, Virtutis signaled to the runners for their briefing.

Bounding easily up the hill, they arrived without heavy breathing. He laughed to himself at the contrast between the group and Khan but wiped off his expression before they could notice.

"Brothers. Are you well?" They nodded, keen to get to work, looking almost inspired. "Khan will lead a heavier, stronger group back down the hill toward the camp. It should take them three hours. They will take the shields, batons, and wooden swords. Their mission is to arrive at the camp intact with this as their banner." Virtutis removed his cloak, giving it to Stoades. "Give this to Khan. Tell him who arrives back with the banner wins the battle and to enjoy the fighting while he is fresh. He will like the challenge."

Virtutis drew three squares with the tip of his spear and a line showing the trail back to the camp. "The rest will be broken into three cohorts. The Ursus, Canis, and the Capra.

"They will ambush the Oxen along the way with staffs, using the element of surprise and the natural terrain. If they capture any weapons, they may use them. They must hit and run to dismantle the heavier-armed core. As runners, you are to relay information and coordinate the attacks at will. If the mobile forces do not work, you are directly responsible and must find a way to adapt. Understood?" He stared long and hard around the group to make his point, knowing very well the general's encounter would have lent extra tense energy to this address.

"Stoades, you are to take tactical lead. I will observe. Give Khan until the top of the trail, then hunt them down. Yields and captures are kills. Those who are dead will be sent directly to me in the upper trails. Any questions?"

Although a little reluctant, Stoades responded, "No, sir."

"Good."

Virtutis waited until the runners were occupied with the organization before lifting his head to gain Mercalis's attention, giving him a signal toward the tree line above, showing him where to meet when the chaos began.

They drew together, huddling close, kindling a battle's fire. "Mercalis, I have this message to be delivered to the general— urgently." Virtutis handed off a small leather folder containing a single piece of paper.

"Yes, sir." Mercalis gathered the message in two hands and began his run up the hill.

Virtutis looked to the runners. "Return with my cloak quickly. It's going to be a cold night. I will seek its warmth." He spoke this slowly and with force, reminding them it was something personal and significant.

The runners finished their plans and bolted to their positions.

Stoades glided down the hill to give Khan the orders, handing him Virtutis's cloak.

In a matter of moments, the ox was organized and on his way, heavily armed.

"Ahhhhhhh!" Khan roared through the valley, hoisting Virtutis's cloak on a spear shaft, accepting the challenge.

The Oxen reached the ridge for their descent back to camp.

The Ursus, Canis, and Capra disappeared into the mountain terrain, taking different paths in pursuit.

Virtutis gripped his spear and headed to the upper trails to observe, eager to see if his experiment would work.

Cutting out a steep climb, he scaled a small rock face so as not to backtrack, finding Mercalis waiting for him.

Virtutis scrambled up with spear in hand. He looked over Mercalis's face, reading for any possible changes in attitude or responsibility. The ease of his company unfurled his tension.

"Brother. Thank you for your composure. We have to get above the clearing before they start to attack."

"What exactly are we trying to do?" Mercalis asked, stopping Virtutis briefly.

Taking time, he explained the plan to his protégé. "The Oxen are the Romans, and the three cohorts are barbarians. If we can see any actions, patterns, or behaviors, we gain insight."

Mercalis nodded, taking in the plan.

"You are to gather those who yield and bring them back up to me. They will then start to eliminate our mobile cohorts as I order."

"So, all this is so we can learn how to prey on those who prey?"

"Yes. Some of these men could have been barbarians. They will not be far from the reality we will encounter." Virtutis shifted the subject quickly. "Is there anyone or anything I should be aware of?"

"For the most part, we are winning over those who doubted you." Mercalis huffed a laugh. "Either that or they are too tired to complain.

The men look happier, even though they are confused with your orders. They are learning to just do what they are told and figure it out."

"Good." Virtutis adjusted his spear to mid-grip, ready to move. "I need you to watch this battle closely. But keep hidden until you find the yielded. If we are to be successful, we must eliminate the threats before they know they are being attacked."

"Sir, my pleasure."

Mercalis winked a confident eye and rock-hopped down to a trail in pursuit of his mission.

Virtutis strode along the upper ridges, waiting.

The sound of men yelling and clashes of wood on wood filled the valley.

Khan was defending adequately, but probing attacks rendered him unable to move the Oxen forward.

Virtutis sat on his heels, watching. Something had to give.

The Ursus had them threatened from the front, giving time to the Capra and Canis to round the opposite flanks down the trail, waiting in ambush.

The runners were relaying messages back and forth well.

Stoades stopped the frontal attack, opening up a narrowed trail. Attempting to thin out the Oxen by giving them an opportunity to move without confrontation, looking to reduce the wide foundation behind their shields to isolate and attack.

With time pressing, Khan chose to move the Oxen, thinning their formation. They moved forward slowly, keeping their pace controlled, swords at the ready.

Virtutis ran ahead to see what they were planning.

The Capra had pushed loose rock and smaller trees onto the trails, forcing uneven ground, making it harder for the Oxen to maintain a shield wall.

If Khan were to pass, he would have to risk either narrowing his men even further or trying to clear the obstruction.

Either would open them up to suffering.

Virtutis smiled. It was all the elements he had hoped for.

Spinning his spear in his hand, ready for action, he descended from his vantage point, ready to start a plan of his own.

Closing in from behind the Canis, Virtutis watched their camouflaged bodies crawl into the upper tree line, ready.

Khan tried his best to consolidate his men over the debris, but there was no way around it.

Virtutis heard him yell.

"Oxen! Retreat!"

But it was met with a hail of rocks, and the trail was littered with small falling boulders. He was locked into a confrontation—one Virtutis knew the ox would love.

Attempts to breach the Oxen's shield wall at first did little to render success until Stoades and two other men approached the shield wall with a long tree trunk they had cut down. Almost twice as long as a Roman spear, they ran its end straight into the back end of the shield wall, collapsing two of the Oxen to their backs. The debris stopped the wall from closing fast enough, leaving it briefly vulnerable.

The hidden Canis launched a fierce attack. They managed to separate three of the Oxen as more Canis members piled over to yield the Oxen helpless.

Shortly after, two more long trunks were added to the assault. They hammered the shields again and again.

Virtutis watched Khan's head bob along the wall, looking for a solution.

"Arrow!" he yelled. He had found some plan to hold on to.

The Oxen formed a triangle formation, pointing up the hill. The three shields at the point were covered by a fourth so that it became well protected.

In a rush, they pushed their way onto the highest ground possible, sheltering under a rock ledge, protecting at least one side, and stopping the upper momentum of the battering trunks.

However, the successful move did not come lightly. Khan had lost more than half his men.

In the distance, Mercalis called the yielded men up the hill, pointing them toward the trail that met Virtutis.

Virtutis ordered the first few, "Wait here. Once we have more that have yielded, I will issue your next mission. Rest up, brothers. You will have some fun shortly," he said, giving purpose to the defeated.

Confused but ready to fight, they rallied, waiting for revenge, some bleeding and battered, nursing swollen knuckles from wood clashing with hands.

Virtutis returned to find the action in full swing.

The Ursus, losing their ambush advantage due to Khan no longer moving forward on the trail, decided to launch an attack from below and from the side. It was now a slog-fest that delivered more to Virtutis's cause.

He looked over the defeated men he had steadily collected.

"Come here, all of you. You are to take out the runners. Find them and make them yield. Next, start coming in from behind the Capra and Ursus. While their attention is on the Oxen, eliminate those who are susceptible; only attack those you can easily yield. Be patient. After they submit, send them to me. Remember, only fight when you know you can win; be swift."

It did not take long before Virtutis stood above the battle with growing numbers behind him. Every so often, he would send reinforcements to keep the momentum of the battle in his favor.

Khan stood his ground, his opponents dwindling more and more until there was little left to try and infiltrate the shields.

Khan popped his head up. "Cowards! Where did you all go? Are you scared?"

Stoades looked around, scratching his head, trying to figure out what had happened.

Rarely heard so loud, Virtutis boomed his voice from the top of the rock above the Oxen. "Halt! Regroup at the trail."

The men returned in a big, unorganized cluster.

They laughed a little, exchanging stories, some throwing themselves down on arrival, exhausted from the fighting, sad at their losses.

Virtutis gathered Khan and Stoades together.

"You all did well. Get the men back to camp well before dark. The faster they get there, the more time they have before tomorrow. But they cannot use the trails. They must move above or below them, through the trees and around the cliffs. If everyone arrives before sunset, double their goat meat and tell them to rest well. Tomorrow, we have more."

Khan looked confused. "So, who won?"

Virtutis smiled. "Not the goats, if you get back in time."

"No, they are going to be in tonight's stew!" Khan replied, almost overexcited.

Virtutis waited in silence, which eventually brought him back to reality. "Tomorrow morning, refine the shield wall with everyone. Focus on the defense from arrows and fire. Choose ten of your best men and break up the work for yourself. Let them lead a little. Just observe and refine."

Virtutis looked over Stoades's still-confused face. "You set us up, didn't you?" Stoades said.

"Yes. But you did well, brother. You are creative for a mere messenger. Make sure you mix more with the men tonight and enjoy their stories. Tell the runners to do the same."

"Sir?"

"People will listen to and trust more in those they know. If your voice is foreign, it will not bring comfort in battle. You are more than a runner, Stoades. Have confidence."

Seeing Stoades was still uncomfortable, Virtutis tried to ease his mind.

"We must form a way that is different. We must know we can trust each other. We are already under threat and pressure from the outside. The last thing we need is more tension from within. You are a good man—and you make good stew." Virtutis grinned, trying to lighten the responsibility. "We will do much more with inclusion than with isolation and fear. Not all warriors kill for pleasure—purpose is also a motivator."

"Sir." Stoades frowned and looked at the ground. No doubt he was still figuring out why and how it was his responsibility. "I think I understand. So, I share my stew?"

"Yes. Share your stew."

Stoades laughed. "Runner. Messenger. Battle commander. Now cook?"

"If you want a man to fight for you with everything he has, and it takes hot stew and a welcoming fire, so be it." Virtutis put his hand on Stoades' shoulder. Looking at Khan to ensure he was hearing, he said, "We must fight for each other. It just so happens I was ordered to prefectus to command, but I command my way. We must create a brotherhood, so we can face death as a service, not a command. I would rather die for my brothers than be tucked under a Roman commander's tunic sucking on a milk-less nipple, knowing he has no affection for me."

Khan launched his head back and laughed. "Ha! If I don't die in battle, I would most likely die here listening to you!"

Virtutis lifted his eyebrow. "Yes. You will most likely run out of air and suffocate yourself with that delicate nose." Khan placed his hand, checking his nose.

Stoades could not help but laugh. The energy of their leadership soon lightened the normal Roman tension.

"See you at the camp, brothers." Virtutis ended their humorous exchange. "Dark will be here before we know it. And you have stew to share."

Khan returned Virtutis's tunic. "For your nipples, sir." He shook his head, laughing.

Virtutis did not react, but the comment was too close for comfort. He gripped his spear, then released the tension, remembering that he had created the gateway for such comments, and Khan had meant nothing by it.

He waited while Khan gave orders for the return to camp—and for his head to clear of the day's events. He looked over the trees below, remembering his sons, Cynisca, and Urion.

Loneliness entered his heart briefly. In the spaces of emptiness, there lurked a sadness, but the occupation of recent events had left him distracted.

Readying himself by adjusting the spear to mid-grip, he took an off-trail run back to the camp. It did not take long before he was overtaking his men; some he offered words of encouragement, others just a casual glance.

Together, they ran like wolves through the rough terrain.

The general had given Virtutis a disbanded group. Now he ran with a quiet, developing pack of killers.

At the camp, Virtutis took to his usual shadowed comfort, surveying his men. They were mixing better with each other. There was a sense of belonging.

Moving in the shadows of the trees, in the dark ahead, he saw two shadows talking with caution. Lifting his hood to cover the whites of his eyes, he rounded the trees slowly.

It was Khan.

The second in command was meeting in secret with someone deep in the darkness.

Suspicion slowed his breathing, listening for any detail.

Using the cover of the trees, Virtutis approached with light footsteps.

Losing sight of them briefly, he risked getting closer, only to arrive to their disappearance.

Searching hard and fast, he glimpsed Khan returning to his campfire alone.

Unsure, Virtutis stood in the cover of night, choosing not to confront it. It was something for Mercalis to discover. Once he knew what the truth was, he would not hesitate to carry out a sentence.

Removing his hood, he watched from the trees for a short time to make sure no one else lingered. With stealth, he rounded the back of the camp to a random warrior's fire site, pulling his hood up over his head again. "May I?" He requested to the group.

Instantly, they opened their circle, watching him closely, not knowing what to say,.

Virtutis did not want to think anymore. Not willing to sit alone in the depths of his mind, he sought solace by a warrior's kindred fire.

"So, my brothers. How is the stew this evening?"

CHAPTER 16

Virtutis returned to his campfire. Khan and Stoades waited, the warmth comforting against the chilly night air. Straight to the point, Virtutis sat. "The last two weeks have passed quickly. Each man has become more proficient with the spear, short sword, shield, and bow. You both have done well. The days have been long and hard."

Virtutis offered wine from an amphora. Khan and Stoades looked at each other, nodding. He poured it carefully into their cups, giving the last droplets a final twist to not waste any.

Khan shifted in his seat, excited.

Virtutis studied any reaction that seemed out of the ordinary. Whatever Khan was up to in the middle of the night, his boyish behavior appeared to be authentic. But betrayal is often where it was least expected.

"I have received an order from the general. Tomorrow I will leave for ten days. Maybe more."

Khan snapped his head from his cup. "They are setting you up."

"No. I am going on a mission, nothing more." Virtutis calmly sipped from his cup.

"More snakes if you ask me." Khan's mouth twisted.

"Maybe, we will see." Virtutis felt the reality of Khan's warning in the back of his mind. "I appreciate the concern, but we must continue. We cannot stop." Virtutis leaned forward with his elbows on his knees.

"Keep the days the same. Each morning, drill the technical aspects of learning and practice weapons. Each afternoon, use tactical applications as cohorts in both defensive and offensive positions. But now, you vary the situation more and use different leaders. We must keep training, half like Romans and half like barbarians. Nothing must stop us from being more capable than any soldier in the Empire."

Stoades looked concerned.

"What is it?" Virtutis asked.

"Do you know where you are going?"

"It is a mission directly from the general. He did not give me any details other than to the sea."

Khan shifted again, this time with more concern. "Shish-snake. Watch out for those snakes."

"Yes, of course." Virtutis sat upright, biting his lip, tired of the warnings. "It will be what it will be. You both are in charge and need to keep working together. Khan, you will act as commander while I am away. Stoades you are second in command."

Both looked down at their cups.

"Do not fear what you cannot control," Virtutis advised. "Focus on daily assessments and look for improvements to build from. Never underestimate the intelligence of the men you lead. Let them lead you as well. I will be back. You have my word. If I do not return, there is no breath in my lungs, and I will see you in the afterlife." He swirled his cup. "I am sure the wine is better there."

Khan smiled. "The wine, the women—and my nose won't be broken. How sweet they will be in the afterlife. Not like my wife." He turned to Stoades. "Stoades, have I told you about my wife?"

Virtutis almost rolled his eyes, saving Stoades from a story three times told. "How is your training with Mercalis?"

Khan perked up. "Training? What training?"

Virtutis bit the inside of his lip.

Stoades smiled. "Merely how to run messages, Khan. We are learning. Who knew the man had such skill as a messenger." He covered their hidden practices of survival and assassination well.

Virtutis added diverting information. "Yes, he has a talent for observation and delivery."

Pushing Khan further from the subject, Virtutis looked straight at him. "Brother, there are two types of running. Offensive and defensive. Offensive is where you know what the situation is, so it does not matter the noise you make. Defensive is where we must listen in between breaths to hear what surrounds us. There is a rhythm to being a good runner."

"The ox knows one way. Always has, always will," Khan muttered.

Virtutis grinned. "Ox tastes good when the kill happens without him knowing it."

Khan shook his head. "I am no runner."

"I can help you, Khan," Stoades offered. "If I can teach you how to run, I can teach anyone!"

"Offer accepted," Khan said, looking bullied. "And I will teach you how to make stew!"

They laughed for a moment, then fell quiet.

Virtutis sat still without emotion, eyes on the flames, a world away.

"Brothers, I must get some sleep before tomorrow's orders. Be well while I am away. Trust your judgement."

Khan stood first, waiting to embrace forearms—Virtutis was caught by surprise. Khan launched a bear hug attack that almost lifted him up.

"Ah!" Khan roared. "We will see you sooner or later, in life or death. Sssssssssh."

Virtutis tried not to respond to such affection and distanced himself as soon as Khan let go. "Snakes! Watch out for those bloody snakes!"

"I will, Khan."

Stoades simply nodded. "Night, sir. We will wait for word of your return."

Virtutis listened to their banter while they returned to the inner campfires. He sat in his tent for a short while until the fire burned down before he lifted the tent flap and walked into the night.

As he passed through the nearby trees, he heard a whistle.

Mercalis.

He diverted toward the sound, seeing a shadowed figure deep in the dark.

"Chilly night, Sir?" Mercalis asked, hushed like the wind.

"Yes. But it's better than the heat. Not that I sleep anymore. Did you find out who Khan was talking with?"

"No, he has not had further contact," Mercalis replied.

"Watch him closely. It could be nothing, or it could be something that tears us apart."

"Yes. I will keep an eye on him."

"And the general? Any movements in the camp?"

"Nothing unusual. Just his normal midnight boys and his early morning maids. However, there was a very unique arrival early this morning before training."

"Unique?"

"She was beautiful, too good for him."

Virtutis did not respond. Any more conversation about the general could create a sleepless night filled with planning assassinations.

Virtutis scanned the night for anyone who could be listening. "While I am gone, keep your ears open, keep watching, but offer nothing; just play your role. If I am not back in thirty days, you are to inform my sons that I will see them in the afterlife."

"Sir?"

"It is that simple. If I am not back, I am dead."

"Yes, Virtutis. As you wish."

For some reason, in the cover of the night, Virtutis felt he could trust Mercalis without caution. It was as if the moon's presence held security.

"Mercalis, I started off wanting to know how close to death I could get. Wanting to practice the warrior's way, determined to find myself. Now, I am here in the dark, talking riddles. I woke up one morning with men under my command whom I don't know whether I can trust. And tomorrow, a demon himself could well determine my fate as a man." Virtutis filled his lungs, confessing. "Life has a way of leading us to places that we never imagined, in ways we could never have dreamed of. Nothing is more truthful than the day we must look death in the eye while the Black Wolf rounds from behind our back, wanting to feast. This whole quest is now layered with a responsibility I was never prepared for and a future beyond tomorrow I may never see. Every day, the world changes its shape on me. I could very well be in the wolf's jaws already, without knowing."

A wind blew in to stop the silence, then Mercalis scoffed in humor. "I was a skinny warrior; now I am a runner and a spy. I understand what you are saying."

"Yes, no doubt you do." Virtutis fought to stop his words. His mouth had begun to run like an open river. "Brother, get some sleep. There will be much to observe while I am away. Be well. We will see each other soon."

They gripped forearms.

"The bond is strong."

"The bond is strong," Mercalis confirmed.

Reassured, Virtutis walked back to camp.

He laid in his bed trying to sleep, but gusts of reality tormented his tent with tempest threats.

By midnight, Virtutis had already packed away supplies and sharpened his weapons.

He tried to sleep again, but Stoa's and Augustus's faces were embedded behind his eyelids.

"Virtutis," called the familiar voice of Mercalis from outside his tent.

He rolled to his feet, gathered his spear, and cautiously opened the tent flap. "What is it?"

"It's Remus," Mercalis whispered. "I was returning to my tent when I saw a torch light in the trees. So, I followed it to see what was happening. The Romans had captured him. They dropped him down the hole with his hands tied behind his back. I waited until they left. I could hear Remus wheezing; if he's not dead by now, he will be soon."

Virtutis checked his knife belt and crossed his hand to rub the opposite side of his neck out of discomfort. "Find me a rope and a torch, but make sure we only light it at the hole, not before. Wake Stoades, but do not disturb Khan. Meet me at the edge of the trees. It will be dawn soon, and there will be nothing we can do after it breaks."

Virtutis did not see Mercalis leave as he ducked back into his tent, realizing there was nothing else he needed outside his own courage.

In a steady, silent stride, he rounded the outskirts of the camp to the trees and waited, hoping they would arrive soon so that he had no more time to think.

With good fortune, Stoades and Mercalis arrived through the night.

"This way," directed Mercalis.

Fog drifted through the trees as they followed him to the drop.

"They pushed him down here." Pointed Mercalis.

Virtutis slid to his belly over the long dark hole and listened. There was still a slight wheezing sound; he was alive.

He stood, not letting himself create any more fear. Without wasting time, he took the rope from Mercalis.

"Tie me off; when I call, pull me up." He secured a knot around his waist and opened his hand to Mercalis. "Torch, flint." He put the flint rocks in his pocket and tucked the torch into his belt.

Stoades passed the opposite end of the rope around a tree trunk and tied it off.

With Mercalis and Stoades standing securing the rope, Virtutis stepped over the edge, leaning backwards, trusting his brothers not to let him perish into the unknown darkness below.

The rock was damp and slippery under foot as he inched his way down far enough to stop at the end of the moonlight and carefully lit the torch with the flint. However, the depth also stopped the breeze of fresh air; it was replaced with the foulest odor that made him want to vomit. The stench was so putrid that he had to only pull air through his mouth.

He looked down and around. It was long and dark, marred by sharp jaded walls.

Short wheezing breaths became louder with desperation as he descended.

Each time Mercalis and Stoades released the rope, his feet slipped more and more, almost making it impossible to control. Trying to keep his feet, time and distance became an afterthought until, eventually, the light revealed the bottom.

"Stop!" He called urgently.

Hanging from the rope two body lengths from the floor, Virtutis's eyes widened in a vision of terror.

Remus had fallen directly onto a shattered tree trunk that stopped him from hitting the bottom. A large splinter had impaled him, entering through his back and protruding out his stomach. He was suspended above a sea of decay; below him, twisted corpses of the dammed were scattered on top of each other. Rats and insects crawled away from the light and hid in the crevasses of rotting carcasses.

Remus groaned and scrunched his eyes at Virtutis. Although alive, he was unable to talk.

Virtutis did not look past his purpose; his only focus was on the last moments of his fallen brother.

With a cautious push, he swung away from the edge to catch a branch of the fallen tree.

"Ease me down." He called. The rope gave enough slack for him to balance on the trunk next to Remus. He placed the torch between the shattered splinters above them.

With Remus's hands tied behind his back, it left him arched and his head dangled back. Virtutis gently lifted the back of his skull for some last moments of relief.

"Don't try to talk." He said as calmly as his voice could muster. "Brother, this is the end. But you are not alone. You are far from Hades and as close to the heavens as any man has ever been."

Remus looked up at the torchlight and coughed.

"Yes, brother, I have brought you the sun." Virtutis talked slowly. "A gift from Rufus. He is waiting for you."

Virtutis caressed his head gently before pulling his dagger. "Soon, there will be no more pain. Only peace."

In a coordinated motion, Virtutis let Remus's head drop back a little as he slit his throat as clean as he could. Saving him more pain of death's passage, giving him a death with belonging and nurture.

He held Remus's head gently like he held Augustus's and Stoa's. Warm blood passed over Virtutis's hand and ran down his elbow, dripping into eternity, as the other sheathed his sacrificial blade.

There was no flinching, no sound, just a floating peace suspended over a pit of Hades that Remus was fortunate to have never seen.

Unable to remove Remus's body, Virtutis bent a branch back under his head to stop him facing what was below, then cut his hands free he crossed them over his chest.

With a delicate embrace of Remus's head, Virtutis cut the long tail of hair from the back of his head and threaded it through his belt.

He touched his forehead on the side of Remus's temple. "Forgive me, Remus. Your death is mine to own."

Virtutis looked up at the two shadowed figures looking down. From the back of his closed throat, in sadness, he spoke a single word towards the moonlit sky.

"Up."

He dared not look back, only upwards as time seemed to disappear into numbness.

He recalled walking silently through the trees towards the river.

Without removing his clothes, Virtutis walked into the water alone and fell to his knees. He removed the tail of hair from his belt. He rubbed it, letting the strands unravel and drift away from his grasp. "Your soul is free, brother. May the waters return you home."

He washed himself clean, letting the river carry away Remus's blood, then eventually stripped himself naked.

Holding his wet clothes in one hand and his knife belt in the other, he walked back to his campsite and stoked his fire high. He placed his clothes to dry and sat in the nude.

Stoades wrapped his shoulders with a blanket.

Mercalis had carried Virtutis's spear and placed it at the tent opening. He threw the rope in the flames, burning away his own emotion, then joined Stoades. Three men of a kindred bond sitting alongside the fire.

Virtutis could not stop the thought of the smell as he pulled the blanket further up his neck.

With a low voice driven by emotion, Mercalis began to sing.

"My ancestors see me through my warrior life,

They fill my heart and stand by my side,

I can feel them on my skin,

And a gentle breeze when I think of them,

Through the winter days and all of the summer rains

I can feel them all taking me back home again,

Taking me back home again.

And when I die, they'll take me home again

Home again."

His voice faded into the sound of crackling flames as they watched the firelight, each man with his own visions to resolve.

CHAPTER 17

Sleepless and fatigued, Virtutis slung his shoulder bag, latched his shield, and picked up his spear. He let the shaft roll down his palm, causing the tip to spin. It rotated, picking up light that glittered; he slowed it with a gripping of his fingers.

Amber dawn gave his day the folktale warning of an unforgivable heat followed by a storm.

"Red dawn warriors, be warned," Odigos would say.

He missed his faithful friend and took the memory as a warning, knowing he needed to be cautious not to let the events of last night influence his judgement with the general. Although ultimately, the general would have sentenced Remus to death, the consequences of desertion remained the same regardless of how anyone had arrived at the decision. If anyone was to blame for the death of the twins, it was himself.

He dug a hole deep down in his soul where he buried his feelings, knowing very well that one day they would rear their head from roots thick with anguish, watered in the blood of innocent men.

He sipped from his waterskin and swallowed with a nod of ownership.

He left Stoades and Mercalis asleep by the campfire and arrived well before he was due at the general's tent.

Guards mingled at the main gate, trying to pass the time. Praetorians stood at the general's mercy in grueling unwavering attention, having almost finished their watch.

Virtutis stood, wanting to shake off the visions from the hole of Hades. He waited until his wits were ready and approached steady-minded.

A praetorian broke his stance of attention and turned to face Virtutis front on. "Wait here, Spartan!"

Virtutis, knowing he needed to ground himself, decided to force a confrontation to focus his mind and sharpen his tongue. Turning his hurt to cunning, he capitalized on the soldier's inability to act out of order. "How was your night? That helmet a little cold in this weather? It must freeze your obedient brain."

"I'll have your head, Spartan," the praetorian said through gritted teeth.

They exchanged a moment of hatred, only to be broken from inside the tent.

"Let the Spartan in!" the general shouted.

The praetorian moved to the side and whispered, "Cunnus."

Virtutis snickered back during his slow walk. "Oh? How you talk so pretty. About as pretty as your sword that never sees the light of day being the general's pet? Does he hide his dagger away in your back pocket?"

"I will see your neck opened someday, bastard."

"Open as is your ass, Roman. Wide open." Virtutis grinned before he stopped outside the tent, putting down his shoulder bag, laying his shield and spear atop, gentle and slow, buying himself time to scan for anything out of the ordinary. He double-checked that the praetorian was still at attention.

Running his hand past his hidden dagger, he stepped into the tent.

"Virtutis! The Spartan! Come. Sit with us."

The general lay sprawled on his Persian carpet, propped up over pillows, drinking wine. He sat upright, trying to show proper posture.

Next to the general lounged an extraordinary-looking woman. Virtutis could not help but agree with Mercalis's statement; she was too good for the general's company.

"Ahhhh! Meet our Macedonian Princess, Liliana."

"I am no princess." She snapped her head toward the general. She looked back at Virtutis, summing him up and down. "So, this is my escort? A real Spartan?" she ended gently, curious.

The look made Virtutis uncomfortable, so he remained focused on the general. "I mean no disrespect, but I am no escort. I am sure one of the praetorians would be better to accompany her."

The general almost spilled his drink while attempting to stand. "Absolutely not! I have sworn to the emperor himself that I would protect Liliana, and she will not fall into the hands of a mere praetorian. And besides, I have beheaded all my other guards." He giggled, rather like a small girl.

Virtutis fought his curling lip.

The general turned to Liliana.

"I executed them for their complacency. Two of them pissed on the enemy and died from a dagger up the dick!" He erupted in drunken laughter, his excessive spit forcing her to wipe her face.

She lifted her chin without paying attention to the drunken display and focused on Virtutis. "I assure you I can ride better than any man. If not, better than you."

"That was not my concern. I mean no disrespect." He looked to the general, who was trying to fix his robe, all thumbs.

"Sir, my men are in training, and I feel it would be more effective if I stayed rather than wasting a week as an escort."

Staggering, the general stood back to his stage where his chair sat high, making sure he leaned over Virtutis's gaze. "Let me explain something to you about heads. The thing about heads is that when you throw them down a hill, they all roll the same."

Virtutis's eyes flickered to the vein on the general's neck, his hand shifting toward his dagger.

In his drunken state, the general withheld nothing. "Roman, Barbarian, Greek, Babylonian—and I am sure even Spartan." He threw his head back, laughing.

Then at once, the general stopped. "Praetorian! Come here!"

Two praetorians rushed in.

Virtutis rotated with his back to the woman, sweeping his tunic away from his dagger.

"Take off your helmets, lay down your swords, and drop to your knees!"

Without hesitation, they obeyed.

The general walked over and ran his hand over one man's head in jest. "You see these men, Virtutis? They will die at my hand. But you. Yoooou, Spartan, would never submit to such betrayal of self-dignity. You would rather die than be told to kneel like these... slaves."

Virtutis kept his muscles tense and ready. Nothing this man said could be trusted.

The general danced across the room and touched just under the princess's jaw.

She jerked her head away, retracting her posture.

"Ahhh, come now. I don't bite. Much," he coaxed with a laugh. "You see, Virtutis. Liliana is a very rare jewel in a world wanting to be beautiful. A world that is just a pigsty of deviatory. You will escort her. I will look after your men well enough. I won't even kill whoever is spying on my camp from the auxiliary."

Virtutis's brain fired into action. If the general caught Mercalis and had him tortured, his sons would be in jeopardy. "If there were any spying from my men, General, I would know about it. I assure you."

"Well then, what am I worried about?" The general opened his arms, almost losing balance. Then he frolicked around, collecting a scroll from his table. "This will grant you safe passage if anyone should stop you. You have my word. Make sure you get her to the sea within five days. There will be a ship waiting for her." He extended the scroll to Virtutis. "Your horses are prepped and ready. Here is your map and route. You will leave within the hour. That is all." He arched his back and scratched his groin, forcing Liliana to look away. "Now, both of you leave. I have to piss."

Virtutis scrunched the scroll in his hand; he had had enough.

Being told what to do, the disrespect, and the godlike attitude converged all at once. Virtutis looked around the tent; the praetorians, he would kill them first. The general's sword was at his chair. Being drunk, he would not be as fast, and his arrogance would delay him even more.

The seconds slowed, pulling a smooth breath into his lungs. He dropped his hand to his dagger and stepped forward.

"Virtutis." From behind, Liliana's hand covered his own on the dagger. It was a simple and gentle touch of class amongst the harsh darkness of minds climbing the ladder of a snake pit. "Let us take leave. Shall we?" She moved in front of Virtutis with confidence. "We appreciate your hospitality." She nodded toward the drunkard. "General."

"Gracious as always." General Lucio nodded back. "Princess."

Virtutis let her lead the way toward the tent's opening with a courageous posture, not looking back, her actions forcing him to follow.

Intrigue replaced his urge to kill.

CHAPTER 18

Virtutis eyed the princess. Though her frame was small, her assertiveness in pulling the saddle into position on the loaned Roman horse was impressive. She carried a strength but also a refinement that made her even more attractive than he'd first thought.

Withholding a smile, Virtutis could not resist commenting, "I see you know how to strap a horse well."

Without acknowledging him, she replied sternly, "My father taught me how to ride and how to draw blood. My older brother, meant for the throne, is weak and not fit for much more than a show—rather than taming the stallion, he tamed stable boys."

With ease, she pulled herself up into the saddle, revealing the soft whiteness of her thigh. Virtutis held his breath, jerking his eyes toward the heavens for assistance.

He caressed the smoothness of his saddle with an edged mind. It had been a long time since he had laid eyes on a woman's flesh—even more so a woman with such confident elegance.

It stirred a primal instinct he had not felt in years. He watched her adjust her long, braided hair behind her.

"Spartan." With a cynical tone, she snapped him back to reality. "While my brother was shoveling shit, I, on the other hand, learned to break men's souls and sever their manhoods from their worthless brains with the blunt dagger of my attention."

The statement caught Virtutis off guard as he visualized such an image.

"I am joking!" She rotated her horse, making its head bow. Impressed by the ease at which she controlled the beast, he stared, mesmerized. "Did Spartan humor also die three hundred times over in the Battle of Thermopylae?" She dug her heels in, leaving him standing, for once not knowing how to act.

He didn't know if he should be offended or if it would be a smart move to banter with such a formidable fast attack of wit.

Choosing the latter, he laughed under his breath. He strapped down the last bag and swung into his saddle, using one hand while balancing the spear in his other. "Easy, boy. This is going to be one interesting mission." He watched the princess circle her mount ahead of them with expert control.

Perhaps the same control she used with men?

He latched the spear alongside the saddle and gathered the reins in one hand, leaning forward and patting the horse's neck out of habit. "Good luck to us both. Easy, boy." His actions, his words, made him realize how much he missed Urion.

Shouts at the gate jolted him from thoughts of his past. Liliana almost trampled two guards, not breaking pace as she rode on.

"Slow down! Whore!" one of them shouted.

Virtutis followed fast, giving one of the guards a nudge from behind, making him fall on his face.

Under more flurries of curses, his horse snorted in pursuit as they closed in on the princess.

"You took your time!" she toyed.

"Well, if you keep up this pace, you will kill our horses, and we will be walking the rest of the way."

"Sounds like a challenge to me." In defiance, she kicked her horse into a gallop.

Virtutis would not be baited by her nonsense. He reduced his gallop to a trot and cut through a meadow while she valiantly sped the long way around.

He entered the road again, keeping a casual speed, and postured up.

Liliana raced from behind, the hoofbeats telling him her horse began to canter down.

He grinned when she came up alongside. "You took your time?"

"Shortcuts are not allowed!"

"Neither is killing our horses." He led, relaxed and assured. "It's time to calm down. Farther through these trees, we need to be more careful. Stay by my side. You never know who we will come across. Racing is a luxury in these parts, so let us not draw any more attention than we already have."

"What attention? The fact I am a woman that you need to cheat to beat in a horse race? You have precautions larger than your speared ego, Spartan," she baited.

Virtutis fixed his eyes in the direction they headed, pretending not to hear, pretending he had never encountered a woman with such a vibrant personality. He rode on, reining in his animal, shifting in his saddle, ready for a subject change. "We will stop beyond the ridge for another supply bag."

In the distance, the sound of his auxiliary drilled combat sequences. It became louder as they approached the crest in the road.

The runners huddled together with Stoades's planning.

Virtutis pulled up close enough to get Mercalis's attention.

Mercalis's gaze flickered over the princess, a slight widening of his eyes the only sign of his surprise. "Skinny, bring me that dagger," Virtutis said, motioning to the weapons that lay upon the ground.

Mercalis nodded. "Sir," he said, looking confused as to why Virtutis had chosen to return.

"See that all the weapons are cleaned and accounted for this evening. The general is paranoid these days. Even chamber boys have been known to be accused of spying."

Mercalis handed over the dagger, nodding his head in understanding. "Yes, sir. All weapons will be accounted for."

"Good. See you in ten days." Virtutis hoped he had given Mercalis the necessary warning and enough information about his return.

"Sir, ten days." Mercalis stepped back, ready to return to his instruction.

"Princess Liliana"—Virtutis said her name loud enough for Mercalis to hear—"this dagger is for you. Keep it well hidden. You never know what we will encounter on the way to the ocean."

With all manners and politeness, Liliana accepted the dagger. "How kind of you, of course. I will put it alongside my other dagger if that is adequate for you?"

She gave him a maiden's smile. Shock and curiosity rattled his brain—among other parts of his body that he gave no attention to.

"How many daggers do you have?" he queried.

"That is a woman's prerogative to know and for the brave to find out."

Virtutis flinched, his tension rising. She took advantage of every opportunity to tease and taunt, even when she spoke no words.

Reality jolted him back to his mission—the entire auxiliary had stopped to drink water, their eyes fixed on the sight of a saddled princess accompanied by their addled commander.

"We must go. We have wasted enough time here." Virtutis whipped his horse around.

"If you say so... Commander Virtutis." Liliana guided her mount to follow.

Before there was another chance to philander in more tension, he kicked his horse into a trot.

They rode side by side. Seeing a trail that led up through the mountains, Virtutis guided his horse against Liliana's, forcing her off the mapped route.

"This is not the main road the general advised." Liliana frowned.

"If the general advised you to sit on his lap, would you?"

She squirmed uncomfortably in her saddle. "Of course not!"

"Then why would I follow any route of his to seduction?"

He peeked at her from the corner of his eye; she was calculating her response.

"Very well. You have reason not to trust the general."

He looked back down at the trail entrance. No one had followed. He felt her eyes upon him but ignored her altogether for the sake of the mission.

"How you are growing on me, Spartan."

Letting her search his face, he did not dislike the game, and like everything that had led him here, there was a sense of destiny in this day.

Virtutis looked in her direction without eye contact, cutting her short.

"It is time to reduce the chatter, princess. These trails have ears and hold many perils. Concentrate."

"How serious," she provoked sarcastically. "Very well, commander."

Virtutis refused to engage.

They wound their way over many passes and down through the narrow mountain trails. The climb was steep, forcing them to navigate their horses over rocks and streams, slowing them for a few hours. Hours filled with the creak of leather, the gritty tang of forest air, and their horses blowing snorts in their efforts onward.

Virtutis broke the long silence. "Night will soon be upon us. We will stop at the next ridge to rest. There is a stream there if you wish to bathe."

"So, you can spy on me? How uncouth!"

Virtutis laughed. "It is so you can maintain your dignity, princess, and not smell like the general's stable hand."

"Barbarian!" she said, feigning offense.

"Princess." He looked over at her and smiled, obedient. "My apologies."

She returned a grin that warmed him in a way he did not expect after his calloused warrior life.

Coming upon the final ridge, the sun gave a spectacle that drew Virtutis to a halt.

She reined in. "What are you waiting for?"

Virtutis motioned toward the sun. "Do you not see the beauty the sun displays for us?"

"Well, it could be that the sun is announcing the arrival of the more spectacular moon?"

"It could be. How long do you think the sun and the moon have chased each other?"

"It is more about who is chasing whom, Spartan."

"Do you always attempt to riddle minds with your catapult of words?"

"Yes." Her grin widened, making her eyes glint with mischief. "It is a gift I was born with. Did you say it was getting dark soon?"

"I did."

"Then what are we waiting for—the general to tuck you in?" Liliana walked her horse on.

Virtutis followed. Not liking her taking the lead, he rode a little in front of her. "There will be no tucking in tonight." Virtutis held her inscrutable gaze.

Below the ridge, between two large rock formations, sat a small tree line. Beyond, Virtutis could hear the trickle of the small mountain spring. A mountain oasis he'd learned of from his runners who scouted the area for the auxiliary.

He moved them onward, reining in his horse by the steady cool stream. He scanned the area. There was only one way into the mountains. If someone was there, they would be easy to spot.

The way was clear.

Campfire rocks had been left by travelers, along with the added generosity of prepared kindling and firewood in its center, sheltered from the elements under a battered animal skin. The ground was swept clean.

"How cozy. I never took you for a romantic, Spartan."

Ignoring her barb, Virtutis dismounted and offered his hand to the princess. She slid off the horse's opposite side.

"I am quite capable, thank you." She thudded lightly onto the ground, holding her footing.

Offended, Virtutis defended his offer. "It was not an offer of capacity but rather of etiquette."

"Trying to swoon me will cause only your own heart to ache."

Almost having enough, Virtutis scoffed behind her horse, loosening its leathers. "It will be dark soon. If you want to bathe or relieve yourself, please do so quickly. Use only the area toward the stream to the right and not behind us. I will start the fire and prepare our food."

He ignored any more of Liliana's jests, gathering his spear and shield and placing them beside the fire stones.

In frustration, his attraction had changed, her attitude and common manners creating a second opinion of her. But, independent of how he felt, leaving a woman unattended was not right. He pulled the saddlebags off his horse and prepared a blanket for her.

Sparking his flint rocks, the fire soon crackled into comfort, its flames offering a familiar calming.

Liliana returned from the river half wet, the setting sun silhouetting her body in a dress that clung to her skin. He was unable to see her shadowed face.

"Have you never seen a woman before?" she toyed, breaking his daydream.

He steadied his eyes on her face, offering no apology. "I am often in deep thought. I was looking, but I was a long way from here."

"Thinking about your wife, I presume?"

His eyebrow lifted in a subtle defense of his dead wife's honor. But when he searched Liliana's playful look, for some reason, it relaxed him.

"No. My wife has passed."

"I am sorry to hear that. And children?"

Virtutis looked at the ground, not wanting to divulge any more information. "I am alone on this journey."

"Oh, you are mysterious, Spartan. I know there is more."

"There is no mystery."

"Are you afraid to open your life to me? Do I look Roman to you?" She scrunched up her nose, poking it in the air.

Virtutis allowed himself to seek out her face—struck by her humor. But he could not lower his guard.

"Rome has many faces. As people have currencies."

"Currencies?"

"Information, position, power, ego—they are all currencies."

"I do not understand. You will have to educate me in your wisdom."

Virtutis leaned back, studying her face. For once, he could not guess her tone, her intention—whether she was in jest or plotted. As royalty must. "Everyone wants something. Even you, princess. It is time to sleep."

He laid down and settled himself, his spear at the ready. The night air dropped its temperature.

"Virtutis?"

"Yes."

"I am cold."

Virtutis sat up slowly, then crawled over to the fire. Taking a knee, using his blanket to protect his hand, he loosened a rock from the campfire, opening up space, so heat could escape in her direction. Then, in fluid motion, he stood and flung his blanket out over her body. "This should keep you warm enough. Good night, princess."

"Thank you," she rebutted, seeming offended.

Unimpressed by her effort, he returned to his position upon cooling clay.

He pulled his cloak over his head. "Rest. We have a lot of ground to cover tomorrow."

But he lay awake, not wanting the Black Wolf to interrupt any relief of a peaceful night and a warm fire.

CHAPTER 19

Onto the plains below the mountains, the heat hammered, unforgiving and relentless, leaving the grass tall and dry. Horses' legs swished in rhythm, slogging through the crackling growth.

Virtutis, impressed with Liliana's stamina after a full day of riding the day before, relaxed his defenses, offering an encouraging smile.

Her posture remained tall in her saddle, majestic.

She did not talk like she had the first day. Her silence was becoming, not falling into an unnecessary conversation for distraction. She was tough, determined, and though direct in her opinion, she never complained.

By afternoon, she began to adjust herself in the saddle more frequently.

"Are you tired?"

"I am fine. These plains will no doubt have an end to them sooner or later. I am not sure what is more worn—this saddle or my thighs."

Virtutis smiled. At least her response was genuine.

"We are almost through to the woods. From there, it will be cooler until the coast. This is a more direct route. Forgive me for the harshness of the journey."

"How sympathetic you are—" She threw him a grin over one shoulder. "Much after the fact, I may add."

"There is little choice in our route. I do not trust anyone, and I never said I would take the general's route. I said I would deliver you safely."

"Do what you must, commander."

It needled him, her using that phrase again. Commander.

He drew in a breath, and it held tight.

As if any man could command her.

"For a moment, you seemed submissive, princess? You must be tired."

A test of her wit after a long day, in his peripheral, he watched for her reaction.

"I am not sure you would be interested in submissive." She placed her hand over her dress, lifting it to show him the dagger he had given her. "Ha!" she laughed. "Oh, the games we play."

"I do not play games," he said, knowing he should not have entered into conversation. "We will camp for the night shortly, princess."

They arrived at the end of the plains where the trees started their dominance and a freshwater stream divided nature. They moved slowly through the shallow water, taking refuge in the shade. Virtutis dismounted and held her horse by the reins. He waited while she hooked her leg over to the opposite side—again reminding him he was not in control.

He led the horses to the water, checking back and forth, scanning the surrounding area. It was calmer, not as hot here. He hoped the refreshing climate would cool off both of their attitudes.

With the horses tied to a nearby tree, he removed the bags and his spear. Taking his shield, he scraped out a hollow for the fire.

"You should sleep as soon as you can. Tomorrow, we must start earlier than today. It is the last stretch. We will arrive one day before the ship."

"Why are we in such a hurry? We could go slower and enjoy ourselves. Or are you wanting to get rid of me?"

"It has nothing to do with you. We cannot trust anyone. We must get there early, so I can do my due diligence."

"How safe you make me feel. With your big shoulders and spear."

His blood boiled with the bite of her sarcasm. "Enough. Finish your food and get some sleep."

"Yes, commander." The tone, again seductive. Hinting at things his mind should be barricaded from.

"That is enough."

"Enough of what?"

"You know what you are doing."

"Yes, I do. But the question is, do you? Are you always going to ignore the obvious?"

"The obvious?"

"For someone so self-assured, you are filled with doubt."

Virtutis's gaze snapped to hers so quick he heard his neck crack.

Her lips turned up at the corners in a slow, knowing smirk.

He averted his eyes, slid his dagger from its sheath, and flipped it between his fingers, giving himself something to do. She was right.

He favored his duty, but that duty was intertwined with a burning want to have his way with her.

She brought him back to reality. "That scar across your eye, what was that from?"

"I was sixteen. Another tribe raided our village. They came in the night to kill us. When I ran out the door to fight, I ran straight into a barbarian. He swung at my head, and I pulled back as the sword almost severed my skull."

"Did you kill him?"

"No, someone else did."

"And the scars down your cheek?"

"From a wolf. When I was younger. We were hunting, and he attacked me. I killed him with my spear."

"And your neck? Did someone try to cut your throat? That looks very personal?"

Personal like your questions. But he entertained her game with little to hide from his warrior life.

"We were tracking thieves who stole our goats in the forest. One jumped me from behind. I threw him off. He got up and ran. I chased him but do not remember anything. I passed out—I didn't even feel the blade. I woke up days later to my wife nursing me. If my friend Odigos was not with me, I would have bled out."

"What happened to the man who cut you?"

"Months after, I walked into his village late at night. I woke him from his bed and cut his throat."

"You are a killer, aren't you?"

"I am a warrior." He looked at her and saw no fear at his truths. "And you, princess? Are you a killer?"

"I am not."

"Then why the dagger? You are prepared to kill. If you are not a killer already, you soon will be."

"Perhaps, in defense. But not in revenge."

"What is wrong with revenge? Is it not justice?"

"That depends. We can set out on justice or revenge, but who is to say those we choose to serve consequence actually feel remorse? Maybe they are willing to die for their cause and welcome it as if they have found their ultimate purpose. Revenge has many delicate layers attached to it. Just because we feel a certain way that drives us into action. We must also consider that there are many truths in the act of revenge and justice. We are all in some way blind to the truth we do not see."

Virtutis stopped, unsure how to respond. How many mistruths had he acted upon?

Liliana giggled, breaking the silence. "I think that's enough talk for tonight. Don't you?"

She stood up from her blanket. With one smooth movement, she removed her dress, showing him her perfect curves. Curves calling for his grasp.

An eruption of chemicals filled his veins after so many years of celibacy. He sat up, lifting his chin, filling his lungs, opening his chest.

"I think it is time we removed whatever it is between us, don't you think?"

Before he could breathe, Liliana stood over his hips.

He placed his hands behind her legs, running them up as she sat down open, vulnerable.

Her hands felt endearing, an unexpected gentleness in her fingers wrapping around the back of his head. He nestled his mouth into her neck.

He gently bit the softness of her skin, forcing her to lean back. She pulled his head into her breasts; then, she searched to remove his shirt.

There was no return.

Her weight sat perfectly upon his waist, and he took control, spinning her over and onto her back.

She groaned softly, only half surprised—like she knew what he would do—it gave him the confidence he needed.

After he placed his hands on either side of her head, her legs wrapped around him.

She removed his belt, briefly releasing her clamped legs, only to strip him naked.

Drawing breath, all nervousness and doubt left his mind, his body relaxing for an unpredictable moment. Unpredictable comfort with her.

Her hands caressed his triceps, rounded over his back, and pulled him down unresisted.

Her brown eyes softened further, preparing for their first kiss.

"Virtutis!" she interjected. The urgency in her voice killed all passion.

He rolled her with him to the side—hard and fast.

A blade cut deep into the space they had left.

Releasing Liliana, he maintained a grip on her arm and launched to his feet, pulling her up and scampering into a run.

"Kill them! Don't let them escape!" The declaration broke through the trees and their scurrying sound of desperation.

He pulled the princess along, trying to keep her balanced.

Naked, they darted in and out of the trees. His eyes still adjusting to the darkness, he steered them back down toward the river.

His voice was hushed with focus, "Into the water."

He looked around, making sure she could hide without discovery.

He leaned close and touched her cheek. "Stay low, get under the weeds as much as you can. I will come back for you."

Liliana slid effortlessly into the cold water without a sound.

Virtutis stopped his breathing. Crouching, he listened for an opportunity to retaliate.

More than one set of footsteps approached. Silent, he retreated into the water, his hands searching to find stones heavy enough to stun or kill.

From the trees and into the moonlight appeared four large figures.

Barbarians.

Changing his plan, Virtutis silently released the inadequate stones and slipped further back into the water, into the deep where the current could take him quiet and quick downstream. Back to the campfire.

He needed his spear to confront such large, armed men.

Seeing firelight flicker through the brushes, he swam to the riverbed and waited, observing.

His spear sat on his saddle bag, his dagger in his belt on the opposite side.

Silent, low with caution, he emerged from the water's edge.

His feet finding dry land, he exploded toward his spear.

The balls of his feet scarcely touched the ground at such pace, and like a flame flash, he gathered his spear and disappeared again into the darkness.

He rounded back where he had left Liliana. A cluster of men searched the river.

The barbarians probed the water's edge, tracking where his footsteps had entered the water.

They were almost on top of her.

"It's a nice night for a swim, don't you think?" Virtutis snorted. "I can smell you from here."

The barbarians turned.

Seeing a naked Spartan with only his spear in his hand, outnumbered four to one, they laughed.

The biggest, boldest shadowed figure returned the challenge. "We will make bait out of you, Spartan."

Virtutis took a stance, holding the spear in two hands, pulling it toward his back shoulder more like a staff.

His enemy spread out, giving them an initial advantage of attack.

Coercing them, Virtutis inched his way forward, inviting them to act first. To attack.

All four were within his vision.

He steadied his breath, relaxed his front hand on the spear, and tightened the back, ready to adjust to any needed strike.

The first attack came from the largest barbarian. With his sword high, he shifted it to a lateral slice.

A common attack of a swordsman.

Virtutis felt the change in motion.

Using the downward pressure of his front hand, he spun the spear in reverse, ducking at the same time. The shaft of his spear caught the sword from behind, guiding it over his body as he ducked around the large window of attack.

With an easy advantage, Virtutis regripped, reversing the strike. He extended his arm and ran the man through from one side of his neck to the other. Releasing the spear with his right hand, he added a quick spin back-to-back and restored the hold with his left—pulling it all the way through.

He left the dead man to fall on his face.

He slid his hand over the shaft, squeezing the blood away, and finished with a flick of the wrist that scattered warm drops onto the moonlit sand.

All three attacked at the same time.

It was a familiar dance.

With ease, Virtutis's spear stabbed and sliced its way to conquest, dropping each man in a rhythm of their own footsteps on the passage to death.

The sand littered with bodies. Virtutis lowered his head and searched the night for more attackers.

None could be seen or heard.

He paused, filtering through the sounds of the night—nothing.

He postured up, his muscles taunt, his skin lathered in blood.

The water's edge splashed with movement, and Liliana appeared. The moonlight silhouetted her slender walk.

His eyes searched her nude figure, like a goddess rising from the oceans of Zeus.

On the far bank, there was stumbled movement—a bowman shifting to gain balance—aiming long.

Spinning his spear to regrip, Virtutis lunged forward, launching his spear like a javelin. It glided over Liliana's shoulder, slicing strands of hair beside her ear before sinking its weight into the chest of the bowman.

He arched upwards, his arrow thrusting into the trees above. The sound of his body falling was drowned by the steady rhythm of the river.

Liliana, having glanced over her shoulder at her falling hair, moved with confidence. Not breaking stride, she thrust herself into his arms as though she had a thousand times.

Comfort and reward filled his heart. His hands circled around to the small of her back.

He gentled his tone, whispering against her ear. "We must move quickly. There could be more."

Breaking their embrace, he searched for her hand that fell into place like it had always been there.

She laced her soft fingers with his own—calloused and hard.

Through the trees, they rounded back to the edges of their campfire and crouched in the bushes.

He squeezed her hand. "Stay here. If you hear or see anything, get back into the river."

Virtutis darted into the light of the dying fire and gathered his dagger, shield, and their clothes. He rushed to get dressed before returning to her and offering her clothes and, once again, his dagger.

"I need to get the horses saddled and the bags tied. Stay low until I tell you."

He tied the saddles first. He stopped, listening hard.

Nothing.

He then fetched the bags and returned to the horses.

Once strapped, he dipped his head, listening into the night.

Staying low, he walked the horses toward the princess.

"Let's go. Quick. We have to cross the river for my spear first. Then we ride."

They mounted in slow motion, avoiding more noise than he needed, then entered the water, staying low in their saddles.

Leaning off his saddle, yanking his spear away, Virtutis led them on.

Through the midnight forest, they kept a silent, slow, steady pace. He could hear her horse close behind. The sun began to peak its way through the trees.

After long hours of riding, attentive to potential threats, they came upon a small clearing by a stream and stopped to rest the horses.

He dismounted first, catching her reins. She threw her leg over the front of the horse and slid down the saddle into his arms, wrapping her arms around his neck and burying her head in his chest.

They were engulfed in their own world.

With dried blood covering his face and hands, he kissed her for the first time. He finished with a gentle bite of her lower lip.

She pulled back, smiling. "You're soaked in blood. Into the water with you, commander."

"As you wish, princess."

Virtutis released her waist, giving space to lead the horses to drink. Having tied them off, he stripped off his blood-soaked clothes and walked naked into the river.

He felt her presence, watching his every move.

Making short work of it, he passed water over his head and body. He returned, snatching up his tunic and throwing it over his shoulder.

He paused for a moment.

"A warrior's life is short," he consoled himself, giving him confidence in his actions.

Then, dominant, he rushed her, picking her up from under the legs, carrying her into the tall grass for cover.

CHAPTER 20

They rode side by side into the small coastal town; it was thriving with fishermen, spice traders, and merchants. The salty ocean breeze was a far cry from the dryness of the interior wars raged by Rome.

"It seems we are an unfamiliar sight," Virtutis murmured as they rode past the docks.

"These people have every right to be unsure. Who knows when they will be overrun by a bottomless Roman pocket?"

Ignoring the twisting of heads in their direction, he had other questions. "Why would you leave from here?"

Looking straight ahead, she replied just as cautiously. "It is Father's plan to keep me safe. So far, it has worked. Don't you think?"

"You have not made it to the ship yet, princess."

"It will arrive tomorrow at dawn," she iterated. "It is to stop only briefly to collect me." She spoke like it was a warning.

Virtutis felt a small, desperate pinch in his stomach.

"Will you miss me, commander?" she said with a sly smile.

"It depends. Will you torment me to no end until you leave?" he toyed back.

"Why would I do anything else?"

"Then, yes." Their banter raised a polite smile on his face, disguising his happiness. His expression fell. "I will miss you." He watched her lips give a requited curl.

Abrupt and cautious that his mind was wandering from his mission, he stopped their horseback passage. "I have seen enough. We had better not draw any more attention to our presence here. It is best that we find somewhere out of town to sleep for the night. We will go up into the cliffs."

"Yes, commander," she replied, serious for once.

It did not take them long to climb into the mountain foothills; setting up camp in the late afternoon was slow from lack of sleep.

Liliana laid on her blanket, curling one arm beneath her head. "How is it that you never look tired?"

"I am tired, but I am too concerned to sleep." He wanted to tell her of the Black Wolf and his nightmares. But if what he felt could be true, perhaps love was a way to dampen the demons and silence the wolves. Maybe a new conquest would lead him to be old and gray.

Liliana sparked back. "Concerned to sleep? How can the great Virtutis be concerned?"

"Liliana, you have entered my life like no woman has before." He thought of his wife and how they were so very opposite. "You are different."

"Does that make you afraid?" she asked as she searched his face. He stared back without fault.

"It makes me concerned that I will never see you again. But who knows if I will survive?"

"Don't you have to pursue your quest as a warrior?" She lay back and swayed her bent knees from side to side. "And your dutiful death to discover?"

"I do."

"Then why the fuss?"

Virtutis cracked his neck. "Are you coaxing me to close my thoughts to you—is that all you want? A game?"

"Are you offended, commander?"

"No. Confused. I do not play games. I am not entertainment for royalty."

"So, you have feelings for me?" She stopped moving her legs, looking serious.

"Of course. I am an honest man. And I do not enter into anything lightly."

"Honest?" she scoffed, pointing toward his waterskin. "I want you to give me a drink of that water."

He handed it to her; she gulped it back, wiping her mouth with her arm, slobbering over herself on purpose. "Can't get more royal than that, can we?" She giggled at his seriousness. "Virtutis, would you honor me with a walk?"

"Of course," he replied, cleaning her arm with his tunic while maintaining a straight face.

The sun started its familiar run, leaving orange scorch across the ocean waters below their walk along the cliffs.

She broke into an assertive, serious tone. "Tomorrow, when I leave, we will not have time to talk. I am to board as soon as the boat touches the dock. It will not tie ashore—it will not even fully stop."

The information sparked Virtutis's interest. "Why the rush? What is this mission you have?"

"It is diplomatic. I am to find an agreement to secure peace between Rome and Macedonia. Last night was not the first attempt on my life since I landed in Roman territory. I would ask you to come with me, but it is not the time. When you are done with your quest, you may come find me." Her eyes genuine, her words without any veil of protection, he started to fall into her ocean. "You can lay your shield and spear down. You will always belong with me if that is what you choose." She pulled her hair behind her head out of the occasional wind gust, tying it off with a length of leather.

The invitation left him speechless.

"Are you... here?" She forced him to stop, her face a map of concern.

"Yes. Yes, I am."

"Are you troubled?"

184

Maintaining his honesty, risking more than his life, he risked his heart. "I feel for you beyond duty. Beyond anything I have felt before."

The words of his wife entered his mind. Love is as fleeting as time itself.

He knew she wanted him to find happiness again and that if he found love again, it would only bring her joy to see him live full once again.

"Are you sure you want me to find you?" He confirmed.

"Yes." She smiled with joy of reassurance, tapping his chest with her hand, making sure he knew. "Virtutis, I do not know you, but I love you all the more for that."

"I am a warrior. I have nothing more to offer."

"You have everything I need. You can want other things than being a warrior, Virtutis. You can expect to live a long life—you are allowed to love. That, too, is okay. Or would you rather die on a battlefield somewhere alone?"

Virtutis looked into the distant waters, he knew what he felt, and at least both women - regardless of being alive or dead - agreed.

"Death is death. It is neither here nor there. We could fall off this cliff if the gods willed it."

"What a tragic end!"

"Tragedy is a man never finding purpose."

"Well, tragedy or not. I am sure. Are you?"

"Upon my life."

"Then what proof do you want?" She held his forearm, her eyes burning with the passion behind her words.

Beyond the barrage of banter between them and the layers of protection she needed to survive in the turmoil of Roman negotiations, he knew she was worth more than he could ever imagine.

What he felt was different. He had learned to love through habit, out of commitment. After his many wars, his heart and perhaps his mind had been calloused over, hardened from loving, scarred from his wife's torment.

The only real honesty he had known for the last ten years had been between the rapid choices of life and death. Death was not the worst thing that could happen to him—seeing the death of others and losing them had been the worst torment.

He thought he had lived the greatest of loves, breathed its hope, but he had also crawled through its anguish, raw and exposed.

This was something entirely different. What he had with Liliana… was surrender.

Without the confinement, without reason, he fell into a future possibility that severed his heart one way and his duty the other.

She shook his arm. "Virtutis?"

"Yes. Yes, sorry. I was just thinking."

"So much so that it is almost tomorrow." She gave him a gentle caress on his cheek with her hand. "Let's eat; I am starving. And we have many interesting matters to discuss before dawn."

After they ate the last of their rations, Virtutis lay back on the blanket. He pulled his dagger from its sheath, placing it away from his reach.

"Why would you be so far from your blade?" she asked, curious.

"Sometimes instruments of death should not be so close to something so alive."

In truth, he was concerned, not wanting to fall asleep in comfort, only to wake in a nightmare of hurting her.

She laughed. "We are so alive because we have been so close to death."

Virtutis stood looking over the glistening water's edge from a full moon. Her hands wrapped around his waist from behind, giving him an uncomfortable comfort, a place of belonging.

"I thought you were asleep?"

"There is much to think about."

Gathering his thoughts, he released her, looking down at the waves crashing against the rocky shore for a different kind of courage. The courage of duty.

She extended her arms and opened the space between them. Her voice was assertive. "I have packed already. We must make this fast, for both of our sakes."

"I am at your service, princess."

He turned, cutting talk short to save the rocks from hammering at his heart before they must. He wanted to kiss her but knew it would cloud his mind even more.

"If we are to be there at dawn, we must leave now," she said.

"Yes, the sun waits for no man, beast, or demon, and if we are to face any of them, let it be earlier rather than later."

"And that of goodbyes," she added with a wink.

Her humor about their reality made him want her even more as he bit the inside of his lip.

In silence, they checked their horses.

With a final glance, he mounted into the uncertainty. His heart ached at the thought of never seeing her again.

Cracking his neck, he clicked his tongue at the horse and led them down the cliff. Slow and with caution, they entered along the back of the town to the docks. But everything seemed faster than it was.

The sun began to break over the ocean, the brightness forcing their eyes toward the arriving ship.

"Virtutis." Her eyes held his with desperation swirling in their depths. "I will be waiting."

Emotion left him unable to speak.

The ship bumped the dock, and the grinding of wood-on-wood ricocheted arrival down the wharf.

He scanned around, looking for anyone approaching. Out of the corner of his eye, he watched as she dismounted and pulled the saddlebag off her horse.

They exchanged a brief look. She did not wane, holding her confidence, her trust.

Her chin lifted, and her eyes widened.

With a slinging of her possessions over her shoulder, she turned and ran to the boat. Placing her hand on the rail, she disappeared over the side of the ship, severing the connection cold.

Virtutis remained mounted, watching the ship slowly drift away before catching sail. Somewhere behind its wooden embrace, below the cover of duty, what could be the love of his life dipped its way out of sight.

Turning the horses away from the town, he recognized his heart emptier than he had remembered. For the second time in his life, his heart felt ripped away. A space that hummed a silence only he could hear. That he could only explain to himself as falling into a void, where if he let himself, he would continue to be floating through time.

He pulled the horse around, entering a trot. Replaying the days they had spent together and the intensity between them confused his outlook on the day.

He remembered how she maintained her calm with the general.

The vision of her walking out of the water—the spear flying past her head without her so much as flinching.

Her composure when following his lead in the confrontation with the barbarians.

Then, he replayed the words the barbarian spoke.

We will make bait out of you, Spartan.

How did he know he was Spartan?

A rage filled his veins, his heart accelerated, pumping a cold chill through his body.

The only man who knew of their plans was… "Lucio! The bastard general!"

He kicked the horse into a canter.

With a snort, they hit a rhythm.

Fueled by revenge, Virtutis rode on with rage.

CHAPTER 21

The Roman horses weakened after two days of hard riding and barely any rest. Virtutis knew he was pushing their limits. He slowed down and came through the trees, eyeing the auxiliary camp. It was barren; no smoking fires, no movement.

With two reins in one hand, his spear in the other, riding cautiously, he entered.

Virtutis surveyed everything with suspicion before climbing down and awakening his land legs.

He rotated his shoulder and cracked his neck. He faced the horse, rubbing the nose of his brown companion with gratitude. "We are here; you can rest."

Hitching the horses to a post over a water trough, he adjusted his spear in hand. Trusting nothing.

The wind gusted, blowing dust across his path. Then, it fell still. In the distance, the legion's tents had been dismantled, and their encampment was completely empty. His gut dropped.

He had been deceived.

His men had been overtaken.

His skin crawled. The auxiliary's tents still stood, indicating they would not be coming back. Somewhere in the general's plans, they would be used as a dispensable force.

The general had betrayed him. Had betrayed his men.

Who knew the extent of what was to come?

Virtutis's veins ignited, tightening his hard grip on the spear, not his usual spinning contemplation.

The auxiliary was at the mercy of a power-hungry narcissist, an egomaniac disguised by the banner of Rome.

Virtutis walked through the camp in search of clues.

Stopping at Khan's campsite, he nudged over a bowl containing half-eaten stew.

Hanging on Khan's tent was a rag. Pulling back the tent flap with the tip of his spear, Virtutis looked inside. By chance, the rag fell onto the ground, revealing something written in charcoal.

Oxen move slowly into the morning sun.

They were moving inland, and Khan was trying to slow their movement.

Virtutis left his fatigued horse and mounted Liliana's stallion in the hope it would bring him favor in his pursuit. Searching the outskirts of the camp, it was not hard to find Roman tracks.

He kicked the horse into gear. "Ha!" He gritted his teeth, following the beaten-down trail over the meadows and into the mountains in pursuit of vengeance on the ungratified dismissal of his command and the attempted murder of Liliana.

Before the end of the meadowed plains, he found the first reminder of the general's leadership.

A young runner lay stabbed in the belly, the trail of blood suggesting he was gouged and left alive. He must have crawled, attempting to hang onto life. A life that was no longer his the moment he signed his name to the empire.

Virtutis wanted to spit out the taste in his mouth, but out of respect for the boy, he held it in and swallowed it once again.

"Rest well. When I am finished with your general, not even maggots would eat his putrid mind."

The horse let out a cough and twisted his head, no doubt feeling Virtutis's mounting tension.

Virtutis thought of his men lining up to be slaughtered.

He rose in the saddle, leaning forward and kicking vengeance into action. "Ha!"

Galloping the wider upper trails, he soon found campfires that had turned cold.

By nightfall, he first came across the wafting stench of an allocated latrine site, then farther along—camp's fires holding their last breath of smoldering warmth.

With the horse weakening by the hour, he dismounted for a short recovery.

Despite Virtutis's fury, they were covering vast amounts of ground. Perhaps too quick. Remembering Urion, he touched his forehead to that of this poor steed, offering his respect, knowing this would most likely be this horse's end. He would not endure the final push.

"It's two days ride ahead on a normal day, but these are desperate times." Virtutis patted the heaving beast's sweaty neck.

Retrieving his waterskin from the saddle bag, Virtutis poured it into his palm under the horse's nose.

"Drink what you can in peace. By morning, without a break, we will have made up the ground. I am sorry, my brother. This will hurt, but we have little option; many will die. May the gods bless your deeds in life and in death."

Virtutis mounted thirsty for what could only be quenched by blood.

"Tit tit, let's go. Easy now." Virtutis leaned forward, whispering in the horse's ear, giving him an extra pat. "Together, we will gather in this night."

His pace was steady without pressure over the mountain passes.

As the plains began to lengthen, so did their moonlit strides, knowing that the day ahead would bring an unforgiving heat. If they were to make up ground, now was the time in the cool morning air.

The sun rose at their back, followed by louder snorts of stress steaming from the horse's nostrils.

Before long, heat beat down upon the tracks of the general's army. They had become fresher and narrowed for some time, meaning they had not stopped for many hours in the heat of the day. For some reason, the army was in a hurry.

Perhaps the general's anger catered to his own ego and pushed away all logic.

They were not far.

The horse nodded his head, frequently coughing—an almost choking sound while trying to keep his legs moving over a dry grassy plain.

"Easy, boy. We are not on our last breath yet."

Virtutis tried slowing the horse a little, but he was already in another world, pushing himself through the limits of life.

The horse's grunting eventually became like a chant creating a synchronism, Virtutis finding perfection in pained movement.

The steed had made up his own mind about how his story would end.

Long square shapes came into view, the occasional shine bouncing off clean armor.

In the distance, the backs of the legion's rank faced upward toward a barbarian force in perfect formation.

Between them stood Virtutis's outnumbered auxiliary.

The barbarians exploded—screaming down from the natural fortress of the tree line, drowning the sound of Virtutis's own breath. They charged with anger that stirred the Black Wolf's thirst, salivating at man's own desperation for self-destruction. Anger against the insults of the Roman empire.

Rage shook the earth of men running to defend their way of life, their family and tribe.

Virtutis dug in his heels. "Ha!" He forced what energy was left in his steed and kicked him into a fuller stride.

Virtutis gripped the reins, his forearms rushing with blood. Gritting his teeth, a vengeance swelled his mouth too thick to swallow.

The horse began to grunt and groan.

The sounds of metal on metal screeched, the grunts of his men bracing their shields changing the pitch of destinies, death in the air.

Virtutis closed in on the rear of the Roman legion. At the rare flank, safe from harm, the general sat upon his horse, watching.

Virtutis's blood scorched his veins.

He reached for his spear.

Surrounded by little protection, Virtutis could easily divert his course and make little work of the general. But the moment became clear.

Virtutis held an oath to his men, and they were more important than the poisoned snake himself.

Either way, the general had signed his own death sentence.

Taking one last look at the general's veiny neck, Virtutis declared to the gods.

"You can wait. No god will recognize you when I am done." He refocused his eyes forward. "I will have no mercy on you."

His horse snorted harder, gasping from the depths of his dry throat.

Not diverted, Virtutis looked for the fastest way to the auxiliary.

From behind, they sped through the small passageways between the legion's perfect alignment.

Unconcerned with the occasional collision that knocked the odd Roman over where he stood, leaving mayhem in his wake, he concentrated on his objective.

Khan had the auxiliary in arrowhead formation in an attempt to fortify against the first collision of the barbarian force.

But he had left the back open. If he did not close it, they would be exposed and slaughtered. If he closed it, he would be outflanked and overrun.

Almost at the battle, the horse began to falter.

Barbarians ran wide, attempting to enter the back of the arrow formation.

Virtutis let loose his spear, blowing an unsuspecting victim off his feet. It did not slow the assault; with the obvious opening, more were threatening.

Khan struggled to maintain the front and lateral impacts. They were being driven back. Soon they would be off balance even though they repatched the holes.

Virtutis felt the change in his horse's balance and knew the limit was reached. He reduced their speed with a half-halt and gathered his shield with his free hand.

He pulled the reins gently, sensitive—their journey at an end.

He pulled again. "Easy, boy."

Almost at a full halt and using the momentum, he threw his shield upwards and launched his feet from the stirrups—propelling his body to catapult over the side of the saddle and into an off-balanced run.

His body weight continued to fall forward, and he converted the energy into a roll—collecting his shield mid-movement.

With full force, he rammed the first body.

The impact cleared enough space to gain orientation. Removing his dagger, he hit and sliced until he was able to remove his spear stuck upright from the dead weight of his first victim of the day.

Staying low, using the falling barbarians like an extra shield, he began his dance. If killing was no option, it was sufficient to slow the thrashing tide by maiming.

Spinning—stabbing—shielding, he fought in a three-hundred-and-sixty-degree sphere. Every move he made, he knew, would get him closer to the auxiliary.

No time existed, just slice-stab-spin.

He drew a steady breath while drawing men's blood. The clunking rhythm of defense and attack beat a perfect drum.

Dodging a sword, he ducked below, stabbing into a barbarian's waist. Within a spear-length distance, he saw the common sandals of his men side by side.

He had made it to the rear of the auxiliary formation.

Adjusting his focus, he placed his back to the security of his men and continued his attack, sealing the weakness.

"Close the rear!" Khan ordered.

"Close the rear!" Stoades repeated.

Virtutis looked over to Stoades; he, too, had been ordered to take up shield and sword.

Yelling and groaning of opposing forces collided, pressuring the formation. The strain of life and death efforts echoed inside their shields. There was little space to breathe, less to move. With the added blind spots, it made it difficult to predict where the force of the attack would strike next.

Khan turned around to Virtutis and let out a roar. "Now, you bastards will know what an ox feels like when he steps on your throats! Tighten shields! Hold like the stubborn mules you are!"

Together, amid the fierce thunder of battle, Khan, Stoades, and Virtutis managed to gather back-to-back inside the eye of a tornado that whirled with the hacking of axes, swords, and hammers against their defensive wall.

They all knew without words. The formation was becoming fragile.

"Khan! We have to move! There is no way back!" Virtutis slid his spear over the shoulder of one of his men, jabbing a barbarian in the throat. "Forward up the hill. Take the high ground. Now!"

Khan bellowed the cadence. "Arrow! Tight!" Daylight pierced the wall. He jabbed a wild defense through with a random sword from the ground.

The men tightened, listening beyond the commotion.

He ordered directions. "Forward! Tight!"

"Forward! Tight! One, two, three. One, two, three." The men shouted, reinforcing their comrades, gathering momentum.

"Stay on your feet!" Virtutis stabbed his spear through any gaps in the shields. Slowly they crept upwards, but it was still slow progress.

Virtutis pushed his way low to the front of the arrow formation, stepping over dead barbarians.

"Khan—with me!"

He glanced back at Stoades. "Keep the flanks and rear strong!"

Virtutis drew a double shot of oxygen through his nose, ready. He spat defiantly onto the blood-spilled ground, spinning his spear ready.

"Ready the tip to open on my command! Open front!"

Khan pushed his shoulder into Virtutis's. They stepped into Hades with their tempers hot.

The point men pushed out, then folded back a step, allowing Virtutis and Khan to attack in controlled space.

The shields held a lateral defense at their side. Together they raged into a clash of wills against an enemy, equally funneling the fury of survival.

Side by side, the two fought to open a narrow corridor out to lead the arrow.

They opened space with extended jabs and sharp attacks, extending the confrontation directly up the hill.

"Flat tip!" Virtutis screamed, using all parts of his spear to maim, kill, and defend, trusting Khan would hold his own.

The flat arrowhead wedged behind them, covering their backs.

They fought out in the open, chipping away in a sea of slaughter.

The two fought under barbarian shadows, cutting toward a light. A light they hoped existed and risked everything to find.

Stoades yelled commands from the back, keeping the wall moving. "Forward! Tight! Cover that gap!"

Virtutis spun his spear, regripping for his strikes with a single hand, holding off blows to his shield. Slowly, the terrain changed under his feet. They had climbed higher off the plains and into the tree line.

Soon, the attackers were spreading thinner, forced by uneven terrain and thick trees at the rear.

Sensing the opportunity, Virtutis changed the wall shape.

"Rec-tan-gulum!" he boomed in a deep command.

The arrowhead maintained its flat head; on either side, the shields filled space alongside until the wall formed an oblong shape, just deep enough to preserve space in the middle. The outsides folded in, making the rear of the rectangle two deep in defense with a higher wall if needed.

The bold move slowed the barbarians, forcing them to regroup to the rear and begin to fight uphill.

Virtutis's victims fell less frequently, giving him time to notice Khan's area was secure.

Khan was using a barbarian's axe at full extension, spinning and whirling, keeping the attackers at a distance. Attackers that solely focused only on the two easy targets.

"Khan! Retreat to cover!" Virtutis yelled.

"Bastards!" Khan yelled, throwing his axe at the closest barbarian, dropping him backwards with the axe buried deep into his forehead.

Seeing Khan had disappeared, Virtutis stood his ground for a moment before he retracted into shielded protection.

Men groaned, shoving, pushing back against the attacking bombardment of attempts to fracture the wall from the outside. Sandals slipped, gripping for traction, gripping for life.

Crouched safely behind the wall, Virtutis laughed as Khan kneeled, gasping for air. His mouth wide open, he wiped blood from his face.

Virtutis could not help himself. "What? Did you drop your sword? First you lose your spear, now your sword?"

Khan let out his energy. "Yeah! It's stuck in the face of one of those thieving barbarian bastards!"

They both laughed, releasing their minds from the intensity of the fight.

Khan stopped laughing abruptly, a worried, washed-out look overcoming his face like he was going to faint. He heaved in more air.

Virtutis snapped back into focus.

Stoades was leading the fortification well. Mercalis was in the middle of the newly reinforced front wall using a spear, probing and defending.

"Khan! Replace Stoades. Keep defending! Wait for my word."

Khan crab-crawled to Stoades and tapped him on the shoulder—pointing back toward Virtutis.

He returned, eyes wide, flustered.

"Brother!" Virtutis slapped a hand on Stoades's shoulder to the tune of the clashing of metal on metal that now came in waves. "Well done. You saved us thousand times over!"

"I think I pissed myself!" Stoades yelled back.

Virtutis laughed. "Better out than in, brother! It's a great day. So far, you are alive to talk about it." Virtutis tried to bring Stoades back to the present.

He placed his hand on Stoades's shoulder. "Are you with me?"

Stoades nodded with a smile of relief, helping his complexion return to almost normal.

"Ahhhh!" Screamed a barbarian war cry beyond the wall.

The yell caused Virtutis to instinctively scoff at the belated challenger.

It was not only time to fight back—it was time to terminate the threat altogether.

CHAPTER 22

Men grunted, holding on for their life as all types of weapons continuously collided against the shield wall. Kneeling in the middle of men's desperate willingness for life, Virtutis took a moment to clean away dirt and blood that had lathered his spear.

He looked at Stoades, then over his shoulder. Above, a warrior stepped backward under the pressure of the barbarian attack and almost fell over the top of them. Virtutis exploded above Stoades, using his shield and spear to brace his weight, giving the man time to gather his balance and return the integrity of the wall.

"Stoades, take Mercalis and two runners. Get high into the tree line, away from the fighting. Look for any advantages we can take to get us moving as a pack. I will call a sprawl. It is time we stopped defending and started attacking. It won't be long until they find a way to hammer us down from the back."

"Sir." Stoades sighed, relieved, welcoming the opportunity.

He crept down and took Mercalis and two more runners from the reinforcements. Keeping their heads low, they crawled back to Virtutis.

Mercalis winked, catching Virtutis's eye, breaking into a knowing, vengeful smile. The chance to attack had arrived.

Virtutis nodded in encouragement. Their dirt-ridden faces now gleamed with the focus of revenge.

"I will clear a path. As soon as it is open, get to high ground. Stoades knows what to do; follow his lead. Do not stop. Understand?"

They nodded, dropping their swords, drawing their daggers, so no weight would slow them down. Virtutis lifted his eyebrows at Mercalis, who embraced his sword, then drew his dagger, being the warrior he needed to be at this moment.

Virtutis stood briefly, looking for the best exit. Ducking low, he moved with confidence. "Come, this way."

Leading them to the right flank, he crouched behind the wall and tapped one of his men on the shoulder with his spear. "Open when I say," he yelled, making sure he was heard over the din of battle. "Close after they leave. Watch for me; I will be back."

Virtutis checked back over his shoulder to Mercalis and Stoades. "Ready?"

"Promptus," replied Stoades.

Spinning his spear, the grit of dirt twisting within his grasp, Virtutis forced an involuntary smile of a warrior's belonging.

He cracked his neck. "Now!"

Breaking into the thin exposed barbarian flank, Virtutis sliced his foe to immobilize, not taking the time to kill.

Mercalis came up behind and launched his own lateral attack, cutting through what was left to strengthen the plan.

The commotion cleared for a second.

"Go." Virtutis scanned the distance. "Go now!"

The runners launched into the woods and scattered. They dealt with every oncoming attack using the techniques Mercalis had taught them. Leveraging their speed, they ran from approaching threats beyond any logical consideration that made them invisible to boiling barbarian blood.

Virtutis looked beyond his opponents to make sure the runners were safe while thrusting his spear, and he finished off his retreat with culling everything in his way. But he took time to look over the battlefield.

The Romans still had not moved.

The barbarians were unorganized and started to break apart. Some rushed toward the legion's waiting formations. Rushing to their death.

Virtutis had seen enough and returned behind the shield wall.

The numbers were almost even. They could attack, but there was a cleaner way.

"Khan!" Virtutis shouted over the sounds of war.

Khan looked up from his command.

"To the trees. Sprawl!"

"You want to make this old ox run? Ha! I knew it!" he shouted back and grinned.

"Tighten!" Khan commanded.

"Tighten! Tighten!" the auxiliary echoed.

"Push! Then, sprawl!" Khan ordered.

Tight, together, with grunts and shouts, the auxiliary expanded in a powerful push in all directions—as if it were lungs taking a breath in, holding, then exploding like a powerful hurricane.

It pushed the barbarian attack to the back foot, off balance.

Gaining a small space in time, the auxiliary then broke apart, scattering.

Virtutis sprinted up into the tree line amid the sounds of men running in armor.

With no threat close, he paused, scanning back.

His pack sprawled over rocks and fallen trees; leaving the battle with a sudden silent exit, he disappeared into the woods like mist.

The barbarians stood confused by his escape. With no auxiliary to attack, their silence turned into a downhill rage to reinforce their tribesmen against the Roman legion.

Virtutis heard Stoades whistle from above. He made his way over a small trail to encounter his men, armed and ready for war. Even the wounded stood at attention out of respect for their commander.

Stoades came bounding in from behind, almost out of breath.

Virtutis dipped his head, attentive and listening, offering his respect. "Stoades, what did you see?"

"The legion is strong to the left flank; there is little attacking there like they are being spared from the battle. They are not engaging at all. The right flank is where the main barbarian force is attacking."

Disgusted with the general's handling of his auxiliary, the turning of Virtutis's gut told him he had to respond.

"He's waiting for them to be depleted to finish them when they are weaker. Let's not give him the glory."

Virtutis lifted his head and eyed his warriors.

He looked straight into Khan's eyes. The energy between them turned cold, cutting away human compassion, ready to condemn the souls of men. "We will round the trees to the left. Start your attack where they are thinner on the flank. Do not stop on open ground."

Virtutis looked over his men. "Be aware. If they run, do not follow them into the trees."

He looked at a young warrior half his age. "Cut them clean. Show no mercy!"

Virtutis' voice boomed loud with an unforgiving-calloused black heart.

Turning his back on his men, he then ran into the cover of the shadowed trees. His men close behind, their light footsteps rustled through the foliage like a sudden wind. Not even a clunk of misplaced metal could be heard. They overcame the terrain like a swarm, and they hunted like a pack.

Virtutis broke from the tree line into the sunlight.

The battle raged against the Romans. The sound of clashing wills hit like a wall after the cover of the trees. He led his men straight into the enemy's weak and exposed, leaving the Romans to defend dead bodies.

Slow and precise, Virtutis's auxiliary cut their way across the battlefield, consuming all the living on their path to victory.

In the open, the auxiliary found their strength against the barbarian masses.

Virtutis pulled back his own attack, letting his men flood past him like a broken dam. A dam that carried a million of the sharpest of blades, drowning out all hope for the barbarians.

The fight turned into an inhalation. Virtutis nostrils filled with a sharp metallic tang of chipped steel and the odor of blood.

Overwhelmed, the remaining barbarians scattered into the forest. His men gave chase across the plains. Then they slowed, stopping before the trees.

Virtutis stood alone on a littered battlefield between the dead and the dying, his sandals sinking deeper into a fresh swamp of warm blood.

He wiped his eyes clean, uncovering the scar across his brow and down his cheek.

Resting his shield against his thigh, Virtutis squeezed the debris of war down the shaft of his spear; it dropped off his hand and back into the earth.

He turned his head over his shoulder, looking from the corner of his eye at the entire Roman legion standing mostly unscathed, remaining in their formation.

The auxiliary formed a square, not leaving their backs open to any barbarian retaliation, acknowledging the new threat: the Romans.

Virtutis snorted the battle-filled air and faced down the hill toward General Lucio, who sat high on his horse, chin elevated behind the safety of his personal guard.

Virtutis stood in defiance without any gesture of his intention.

Tension grew on both sides. A silence that caused the dying to pause their death in anticipation of a bigger wager for the gods.

Down the hill, armor glistened in the midday sun. The only obstacle between Virtutis and General Lucio's ego was dead bodies.

Groveling from the ground, a barbarian caught Virtutis's attention.

"Help me," he pleaded with an outstretched hand drenched in blood. His other hand holding in his badly wounded stomach.

Virtutis rotated his spear to an under-grip, holding the spearhead higher. With a smooth blow, he struck the man's head, rendering him unconscious.

Virtutis spoke under his breath. "Be calm, brother; you won't remember a thing."

Rotating the shaft back into position, he then plunged the spear through the man's heart, ending his life.

The barbarian twitched, followed by a gasping release of air. The deed was done.

Drawing back his weapon, Virtutis watched a centurion on a white horse run back and forth behind the legion's battle formation, giving orders.

He dropped his head, listening hard, but it was beyond his hearing.

To the side of the battlefield, his brown horse-companion rolled from his side to his hunches and staggered to his feet.

Like a sign that they would all live another day.

Urion, Liliana, and his sons entered his thoughts. Thoughts like these in battle were unsettling, causing a brief hesitation.

This is not a good situation; the timing is wrong.

With his men already fatigued and the only sweat the Romans had broken from the heat of their armor.

From afar, the general boiled Virtutis's blood. But now was not the time. There was too much at stake—he must wait.

Turning to his auxiliary, Virtutis dug his spear deep into the blooded earth; it sucked at the blade. "Auxiliary! Form at attention!"

Silence fell upon the battlefield. The wind rose again, causing a slight whistle around Virtutis's spear.

The whistling stopped, overridden by Khan's voice. "Auxiliary! Form at attention!"

Shields retracted and filled the air with the sudden stop of sliding metal, the shield wall of protection dismantled. With precision, the auxiliary shifted into lines. Together, without doubt, they stood down. Loyal under the command of their leader.

The battlefield maintained its tension.

The centurion on his white horse galloped between the Roman columns. With a steady stride, he came toward Virtutis, trampling limbs of the dead without regard. His clean shining armor almost blinding.

Virtutis stiffened his gaze to counter the squint and avoid revealing any discomfort.

The centurion pulled a little too close for comfort, his leg almost colliding with Virtutis's chest.

Virtutis did not shift.

Warlike and blunt, the centurion stated his business. "Spartan. You are to finish off any survivors and report to the general tomorrow morning at first light."

Virtutis lifted his head with a slight tilt, not able to refrain more animosity towards the Roman. "It would be my pleasure. Should I wait for you to crawl from his tent first? Or will you still be there, unashamed of your sword cleaning his duty?"

The offended centurion's nostrils flared; he tightened the reins to sweep the horse's head in a subtle attack. Anticipating the move, Virtutis reached to secure the bridle in his hand, preventing the horse from turning.

The centurion fought with the horse as Virtutis eyed him down to size.

"I will have you at the end of my sword, Spartan scum!" the centurion yelled.

Stepping back, Virtutis smiled, then released the reins. "Enjoy the comfort of your saddle while it lasts."

The centurion spat toward Virtutis, then cantered away.

Unsure of what tomorrow would bring, Virtutis knew he had bowed his head for something greater.

Pulling his spear away from the earth's suction, he looked over the waiting auxiliary.

Khan broke rank toward Virtutis, weaponless, covered in blood.

Virtutis shook his head. "Again? You still haven't got your sword back?"

Khan just shrugged, knowing his habit was the truth. "I like to throw weapons."

"Keep the men here until the Romans leave. When they are clear of the battlefield, the men can rest." Virtutis lifted his eyebrows. "Then find your sword. But stay out of the trees and in the clear. We will make camp over the ridge by the river—away from the main camp for now."

Khan looked uneasy. "Sir, the Romans wanted to end us."

"Yes. But they didn't."

Shouting caught Virtutis's attention—as the legions made their exit; three men were attempting to force Virtutis's horse along by pulling his reins and beating his hind legs.

Virtutis ran down the slope, leaving Khan breathing hard, playing catch up behind him. The horse who saved his men would live out his days in peace.

Cursing and frustrated, done with beating the beast, a soldier drew his sword to cull the bewildered stallion.

The man's attention, so focused on controlling his strike, did not see Virtutis coming. With the blunt end of the spear, Virtutis struck the man in the side of the leg. He fell to the ground, spilling his sword, clutching his thigh.

The horse bolted a short distance away, staggered, then stopped.

Virtutis followed, slow and gentle.

Khan rushed past him, ready to attend to the other men shouting abuse.

"That horse is the property of the empire!" one shouted. Virtutis looked over his shoulder.

"So is this dagger!" Khan snapped back, flipping the blade around, ready to throw. "Would you like me to return it to your skull for safe keeping?"

The horse steadied under Virtutis's familiar voice. "Easy, boy. You have run your race. No one will come near you. Easy."

Standing to one side of his neck, Virtutis softly took the reins back with no pressure. Rubbing under the long chin, he could sense the confusion and vulnerability. "Let's go. Let's get you some water and food; you can rest easy." Again, he peered back to see the Romans leaving, intimidated by Khan's presence.

Virtutis walked the horse up to the auxiliary who were preparing to leave. The sound of men talking startled the stallion, and he jerked against Virtutis's hold. "Easy, boy, you're at home now."

Virtutis looked toward his men's blood-soaked faces. Thick mud clung to their feet and legs from all types of battle remanence. There was no telling who they were as individuals; each man had carried himself through the fight and wore the rewards of victory. As dirty as they may be, they were still alive.

He flooded with pride. They had proven to each other resolve, courage, and most of all, they had survived a significant test under the demands of war, whereas in the past, they would have crumbled.

Virtutis stood with his recovering horse as he lifted his spear above his head.

There was no war cry, just a silent salute to a humble victory.

Proud and respectful, his men lifted their swords, returning the gesture. A gesture so powerful Virtutis could feel they galvanized with a greater bond. The bond he hoped would be enough to survive the cunning of a twisted Roman general.

"Khan. Finish off the dying. Make it quick. See that none suffered unnecessarily. We will camp farther up the river; make sure we are on high ground tonight and we rotate men with the runners on guard, so they all can rest and have less time on duty."

"Sir." Khan nodded.

The night closed over the bodies being stabbed and tested for life, then left to be absorbed by nature.

Virtutis led his horse up past the men to make camp, far enough to have his space, close enough if he was needed.

Exhausted, he wrapped himself in his tunic to sleep. It did not take long before he woke, unable to swallow, his throat choked with sand and the sound of slave chains rattling.

He rolled over to his side, looking into the trees.

The horse startled, shifting its feet. Staring back at him through the night, hazel eyes gleamed; the Black Wolf stood watching over his prized Spartan prey.

Staying on his side, Virtutis took his dagger from its sheath and pricked his finger. He squeezed it, making blood drip over into his palm to make sure he was awake and what he saw was real.

"Come, my little black pup. Is this not what you have been waiting for? Can you smell it? Do it now, or leave me be. I have no time for your games."

Snarling, the Black Wolf edged backward into the trees, his eyes fading away into the darkness.

Virtutis closed his eyes, trying to recover. Distant guilt for loving another other than his wife entered his thoughts briefly. But the thought of Liliana—her smell, her humor—outweighed any prolonged hesitation about a new possibility, a new pathway.

There was a sense of something other than the pull of his quest to live closer to a warrior's death. He now longed for belonging, even if it was peaceful.

He fell into a deep sleep; his body twitched and jolted, always moving.

Fire crackling in the middle of the night woke him abruptly.

He tested his finger; there was no sign of the dagger's truth.

CHAPTER 23

"You surprised me yet again, Spartan," Lucio said. Uneasy, ready to launch at the general, Virtutis studied the tent. Six centurions stood just inside the entry. General Lucio sat behind his table that held a freshly opened map. His dagger held the weight on one end and his wine cup on the other. Small eagles had been strategically placed toward the ocean, clearing a path for the empire's expansion.

A familiar shadow lurked in the background behind a curtain. A figure of a man who still did not want to be identified.

Rolling his shoulder with a small twitch, Virtutis cracked his neck. His tunic covered his left side, hiding his hand that at any time could reach for his razor-sharp blade. Smaller weapon in a cluttered room had the advantage of attack.

Virtutis breathed deep and steady, his mind calm and clear—no longer finding the situation intimidating. His heart maintained a slow pulse, his awareness of his surroundings sharp.

Not shifting his eyes from the general, Virtutis replied, "Surprised I've risen from the dead?"

The general rocked forward in his seat, squinting his eyes like they were out of focus, wanting to see more. Pushing forward with his own agenda, he continued, "Your entrance to the battle. It was tremendous. I have never seen anything quite like it. To confront such a force with no fear, to break them through the middle, to take their ground. Tell me, what was it like?"

"I do not remember. I'm not sure what you want to know," Virtutis replied, buying time—assessing the room, planning the assassination.

The general sat back in his seat and opened his hands. "Come now. I am merely trying to understand the way a tactical intellect thinks, from one tactician to another."

"Like I said, I do not remember. I simply acted." Virtutis grew suspicious, now defending himself. He rubbed his thumb inside his index finger, trying to figure out the general's motives. "I arrived, and my men were outnumbered, sent to be slaughtered. We fought to survive. Then, we fought to eliminate the threat."

"Slaughtered?" The general leaned forward in his seat again. "I was in complete control. I knew the barbarians would split in two. I had planned to send a legion around to flank them and dismantle their attack while the auxiliary held center." He jolted back against his seat. "That was until you rode through the middle of my ranks and spoiled the plan! It was you who almost slaughtered your own men by leading them too far away for me to order any lateral attack."

Virtutis replayed the battle. Could he have made a mistake?

Lucio was lying. He had to be lying.

The general stood and threw his robe over his right shoulder, bearing his battle armor. Evidence there was no trust between them any longer. He was no longer taking any chances—he was under threat, and he knew it.

Virtutis held a smile in check. General Lucio's protection was out of fear, which made him even more guilty.

The general looked at the map without seeing it.

He snapped his head up. "Your own agenda to chase death overcame all logic. Heroic you are—a great fighter, an able tactician." Standing, he rounded the table toward Virtutis, making himself an even easier target. "Memory loss does not serve you well, Spartan. Let me remind you of something."

They came face to face. Last night's stale wine tinged the general's breath.

Virtutis touched the handle of his dagger, searching for the cut that did not exist on his finger, reminding him of the Black Wolf's trickery.

"You see, Spartan," the general spat. "Sparta is a failed institution of war consumed by its own thirst for an unsustainable legacy. Like a demon consuming its own tail. Death is all they knew. So, tell me, Spartan, is death all you know?"

"I know I am not afraid of death. Nor do I fear its unknown." Virtutis did not waver. "I have felt its calling many times."

The general turned back toward his table, revealing his veiny neck. "Obsessed! You are obsessed with death!"

Virtutis remained calm. "How a man prepares his life to face death is the only true test. At the end of each day, he must balance the accounts of his life so that he is able to live well enough to die with no doubt of who he is. Have you balanced the accounts of your life, General?"

"Who are you to say death is the only true test? Who are you to question my account or accountability? What makes you so righteous?"

"The answer of accountability is a personal opinion. I am a warrior. I merely want to meet a humble death that is not driven by an ego that will never quench its thirst."

The general straightened, his spine stiffening. "What are you implying?"

"I am not implying anything. If there is something that fevers your blood, maybe it carries some kind of truth for you. I am merely saying there is a difference between men. I know who and what I am. I do not chase death—I observe it closely and with a curious eye."

Behind the curtain, the shadow shifted.

Virtutis felt his patience replace itself with thoughts of his dagger. "Is there anything else you would like to discuss?"

"If there is something to discuss, I am the one who decides when and where." The general looked him up and down. "Not you. If you were not an interest of Rome, I would have your head."

"You are welcome to it. But you would have to take it first."

The general slowly clapped his hands together several times, then opened them wide. "There he is! My favorite Spartan! Unbelievable!"

Virtutis slid his fingertips around the ivory handle of his dagger.

The general shoved himself into Virtutis's space, his breath as foul as before. "You are by far the best auxiliary commander we have had. Though raw." He tipped his head to one side. "And you know nothing of the true order of the military. Yet beyond expectation, you have united your men." He lifted his finger and pressed it under Virtutis's nose.

"And!" He paused, his stale breath almost causing Virtutis to gag. "You defeated the barbarians against the odds."

Virtutis tapped his fingers from the dagger, curious. "If I am that good, why did you take my auxiliary without any notification?"

"Opportunity of war does not wait. It is nothing personal. The barbarians had to be intercepted."

"General—you left their tents back at the main camp. Such an order only shows there was no coming back for my men. They are not sacrificial lambs."

"No coming back? They were lucky they were with us at all!" The general frowned, his beady eyes forward. "We had to find your men first—they were up in the mountains, playing with their wooden toys! There was no time to bring the comforts of home, commander. War waits for no man, let alone his tent."

The general rounded his table and took his seat. "Your questions, though very direct, are bordering on insulting."

He leaned back and interlocked his fingers. "The princess? Did she arrive safely to the ship?"

The mere mention of Liliana turned Virtutis cold. "She arrived safely, despite challenges." He punctuated his words, stepping closer. "We were attacked by barbarians in the mountain pass."

"Mountain pass? You did not take the route I ordered?"

"We decided it was better to arrive early and not draw attention to ourselves."

"You took the princess over unprotected terrain?" The general sat back and hooked his thumbs under the opening of his chest armor. "Have you ever followed an order?"

"I follow my instinct."

Virtutis studied every spec of Lucio's face, looking for any clues to confirm his suspicion.

"We both remember our agreement, don't we? Your failure is your life? You did not fail, so you maintain your life. What is done with the princess is done. As long as she arrived."

Virtutis watched the vein in the general's neck throb.

Was General Lucio a man of his word? Was his word all that was keeping him alive?

But he was still guilty. He had to be covering his lies.

With bloodshot eyes, the general looked down at the eagles on the map. "Here!" He ran a crooked index finger over the map's terrain. "Between the plains of the lowlands, up into the hinterlands, and through the mountain passages that connect the trade route to the sea. You will keep your part of the auxiliary patrolling these areas until further notice. Anyone and anything that is not Roman is to be destroyed."

The general looked up; his eyes narrowed in unpredictable, pent-up rage. "You are to remain prefectus of your makeshift auxiliary until further notice." He lifted his finger from the map and pointed at Virtutis. "And remember. You are in the service of the empire, and I expect your best death!"

Confused, Virtutis showed no emotion.

The general dropped his tone. "You leave tomorrow; collect the supplies you need. That is all. You are dismissed."

Virtutis turned toward the open tent flaps.

"Oh, and one last thing," the general added.

Virtutis looked over his shoulder, unable to hide his disrespect.

"You may keep the horse. But steal the property of Rome again, and I will personally mount the steed and trample you to death."

A surge of regret burned through Virtutis's veins. At the first opportunity, he should have used his dagger. Again, the general had no inhibition against throwing insults or pouring more oil into an open volcano.

Replaying the battle and his decisions, Virtutis walked through the legion campsite. His thoughts were broken by General Lucio's soldiers drilling sword strikes, barely battle-worn—unlike his own auxiliary.

There is nothing like men who are battle-hardened, and he would take his men over the centurions any day.

They stopped their drilling. Virtutis felt the Roman soldiers' eyes fixated on his every move. He shrugged it off. There were obviously no orders for his head because he would have been dead already, so he did not fear such looks.

Just outside the camp, a whistle came from within the cover of the foliage.

Mercalis signaled from a crouched position, hiding from anyone on the path.

Virtutis checked behind him, then followed Mercalis far enough into the thick trees, so they could not be seen.

Virtutis looked around, confirming they were alone. "Did you see anything different from this morning?"

"The same as earlier. The general pissing, a boy leaving, seven centurions in and seven centurions out."

Virtutis snapped his attention, reading Mercalis's face, whose eyes had started to become darker, somehow more emotionless. "How many centurions?"

"Seven."

"Are you sure?"

"Yes, I am sure. Why?"

"There were six guarding me, not seven. Whoever this ghost is, he is hiding amongst the centurions. At least now we know."

"But why hide? It makes no sense."

"When it comes to the general and the Romans, nothing makes sense." Virtutis heard the distinct clunking of foot soldiers walking through the trail. He paused, hushing his voice. "Keep watch for another day. Maintain your distance, gather what information you can, and then return to us at the main spring in the mountains. Take my horse. He is yours. I will leave him on the other side of the river."

"As you wish."

Virtutis extended his arm to his trusted brother. "The bond is strong."

Mercalis returned the gesture, held firm, forearm to forearm in confirmation. "The bond is strong."

Virtutis made his way back onto the trail and to his camp.

Khan and Stoades waited around a midday fire, roasting a rabbit and talking of their adventures. Virtutis sat sniffing the sizzling meat. "Brothers, we have our orders."

Not trusting Lucio, Virtutis again laid his own way within the general's plans. "Send a small unit back to the main camp. They are to bring us supplies, then meet us up in the mountain springs in three days."

"And the rest of us?" Khan said.

Virtutis ignored his inquiry in favor of an assessment. "Are there any badly injured? How many dead?"

"No injuries that would stop us from moving. Eight dead," Khan said.

"Good. Then we will take a more direct route to the springs." Virtutis allowed a grin. "Tell them to travel lite up the ridges to the thinner trails. They can hunt what they need for food. Anyone who captures a barbarian is to bring them to me. If they refuse, kill them. None of our men are to enter villages, and they are to stay off the main roads. We must only be seen if absolutely necessary, not even heard if possible."

Stoades scratched his balding head. "Our orders are to be invisible?"

"No. But to live through this, we have to be. For now. To survive the eagle, sometimes you need to become a wolf."

Khan broke into his usual mischievous look. "Auuawww, from an ox to a wolf. Who'd ever thought."

Virtutis was not amused. He stared at Khan until his smile disappeared into submission. "Move quickly. Orders are to be followed immediately."

He pushed past the desire for freshly cooked meat and walked through the camp before crossing the river. He sat in the tall grass, unseen, watching his men.

Within the hour, they had formed small groups and made their way toward the mountains. Stoades and the runners were the last to leave.

Virtutis gathered his bag, slung his weapons over his shoulder, and crossed back to the barren campsite. The runners looked at each other, perhaps expecting Virtutis to stay his usual distance.

"If I may, I will climb the trails with you?"

Stoades nodded. "Of course, commander."

"Thank you. Stoades, you lead. I will follow your pace; you know your men and when they should stop."

"Sir." Stoades smiled with a humble nod.

Virtutis joined the group, knowing it was worth protecting. Stoades had proven himself an able tactician, but without Mercalis, they were vulnerable and too valuable to leave unattended.

Stoades led them through rough, narrow trails. They climbed where it was steeper; then, where they could run, they floated effortlessly across the easier terrain.

The trails were eventually lit by a strong full moon. They took advantage of the light and the cool of night air to advance up into the denser forest.

Stoades slowed, pointing upwards. "We will stop there for the night, up behind those boulders. No one will see the fires from above or below. We can rest there until dawn."

The men scrambled up the rock face and over the boulders to a flat submerged and protected from the wind.

They lit their fires and prepared food together. Around a larger middle fire, they sat as a family, filling their bellies and sharing tales.

Virtutis sat with the hood of his cloak over his head, enjoying the presence of humble men void of any agendas, only serving the best version of themselves for each other.

Stoades sat next to Virtutis. They remained silent for hours, just listening.

In a quiet voice that even made the flames seem loud, Virtutis spoke for Stoades only.

"Brother, I meant what I said in the battle. You have grown to be a good leader. You were out of your familiarity, yet you made many correct decisions." Virtutis rubbed his hands toward the warmth of the flames. "Any man can find his weapons when there is light. But only a leader can find a way to adapt and survive in the darkness. You made some very good decisions under pressure when many would have failed. These men owe you their lives." Virtutis looked directly at Stoades. "So do I."

"You, too, have saved us." Stoades pushed a stick into the flames. "In so many ways. We all know there is a war going on that is greater than the battle we just faced."

Virtutis ran a hand over a week's growth on his chin. "I have no idea where this is leading us. Or if I am leading correctly."

"Perhaps. We will see. You sway battles with your spear, a far cry from other commanders we have had."

"A man who knows only how to use his spear will meet a narrow death. And slaying men of lesser skill is an easy solution to a narrow mind."

"You sound concerned?"

"Of course. There is too much uncertainty, and the Romans cannot be trusted."

"So, what is the plan?"

"We make these lands our home. But first, we need to secure the hinterlands. But we don't have enough resources or men to do it. The only way is to unite the mountain tribes by an alliance, or we will be defeated. But we cannot do it for Rome. We must do it for ourselves, for a new purpose. We cannot kill innocent people."

Stoades raised his eyebrow. "That is treason against the empire."

Virtutis drew a line in the dirt with a stick. "Treason here." He pointed to one side of the line. "Treason there." He pointed to the other side. He then circled the line entirely. "Treason everywhere."

Stoades nodded. "Truth."

"I am here because of treason. Some of our men killed the commander. There can be no illusion. We continue to cheat ourselves every day somehow. The only thing we can do is live beyond the threats of the empire and toward something that is our own. We must find our own way."

Stoades pulled his cloak higher over his shoulders to cover his neck. "Some of these men have been in the auxiliary for more than ten years; it leads to citizenship and a better life. They are nearing halfway. Not all will be happy."

"They can leave. They will never make the twenty-five years, not under Lucio. We all saw his lack of action yesterday. You were all put forward for slaughter. No matter what the general may say."

"What did he say?"

"That he had a plan, and I interfered. We cannot trust him. No one can."

"I have never met him, so I cannot say. But I trust you." Stoades nodded, placing his hands on his knees and rolling his shoulders. "What do we do now?"

"We protect ourselves. The Romans cannot control this region; they will be very reluctant to enter here in peace, so they will burn everything in their way. We are better off taking a stand and governing it ourselves. But we must make peace with the tribes and help them understand that we only want to serve and protect." Virtutis rubbed his hand over his head in contemplation. "Tomorrow, I will need you to deliver a message to Benductos; he is over the western mountain ranges with his men."

"His men? Didn't you kill the hostages?" Stoades said, wide-eyed and shocked. "You set them free, didn't you?"

"Yes, I set them free. They were no threat. And the boy would never survive without protection. It was my word to his father to see that he lived. I hope they have been recovering their numbers. We must make an alliance with them. Maybe we can convince Rome we have the region under control; meanwhile, we build a Kingdom under their noses."

"You planned all of this?"

"No. It is a thought. Tomorrow, I will know if there will be any truth to it. At the moment, I do not see any other way. I am not going to kill innocent women and children in the name of Rome. I joined the auxiliary to better my understanding of the warrior way. Not to rape the helpless and destroy people's lives. I am haunted enough already."

"Haunted?"

"I wake at night choking on sand, seeing my men dying in front of me." Virtutis looked over the flames. "I am haunted by the Black Wolf."

Stoades sighed. A sigh that gave Virtutis comfort. Someone understood.

"There is nothing anyone can say about the dreams that haunt a man. Who knows if it is the reality of the future calling or a distant memory that one day makes space for new memories? I would be a fool to try to counsel any man on something I do not know about."

"You already have, brother. The dreams are mine to own. For the most part, whatever it is, it only happens when I sleep. So, I guess I have already lived my life twice over while others are sleeping." Virtutis smiled at his torment.

Stoades smiled back, rubbing his runner's knees to warm them. There was a reminiscing in his voice. "You know, as a young man I dreamed only of wanting beauty in life. So, I chased it—only to conclude the greater I uphold duty and service, the more I see how beautiful life can be. Chasing only beauty in life makes the beauty fade quicker, and it eventually becomes unattractive. Today, I saw a sunset in a way I had never seen before. I tasted water from a stream that was so sweet it lifted me to the heavens. It would never have been obtainable without the battle of the day before, when I pissed myself with fear. So, whatever you require of me, no matter the hardship, I know it will only bring me a greater appreciation for new wonders and beauty of life."

"Truth. I, too, have found beauty in service." Reaffirming his quest to find his way back to himself, Virtutis sighed, somehow knowing he was in the right place. "Brother, I am grateful for your loyalty."

"Virtutis, it is our bond. Mercalis and I shared an oath—he said an oath with him is an oath to you, and if he was to die, then I would take his place in whatever is required. There is nothing that can come between what must be done to keep that bond pure."

Virtutis offered his forearm. "The bond."

Stoades gripped—surprisingly strong for a runner. "The bond is pure."

Virtutis softened his posture in comfort he had not felt in many years. A comfort reserved for friendships that would last for an eternity, so he sat for longer than usual.

He sensed Stoades's curiosity. He heard a deep breath, no doubt about to risk a question.

"Virtutis, you have children?"

For the first time, Virtutis did not feel threatened to answer. "Yes, two boys."

"You must miss them."

"I do. But I had to follow my purpose and give them space to grow toward their identities as men. They deserve more than what I was giving them, and I did not want them to live under the shadow of a Spartan father. They know of the virtues. Now with space, they have a chance to be men before manhood finds them unprepared. They have been loved, cared for, and shown right from wrong. They are half Spartan, so they have the right to choose their pathway."

"That must be difficult."

"Yes. But I was not who they needed. At the time, leaving them was the right thing to do. A normal Spartan would have held on, like the very Spartan culture that inhaled themselves. We must evolve beyond who we are. I know only war and death; it had always been my choice, my illusion."

"Your illusion?"

"The illusion of truth."

Stoades scratched his head. "Is truth an illusion?"

"Sometimes, I think it is. Nothing is what it seems. There is always something bigger that imposes itself on us. Our truth is subjectable because we cannot see more than our own life. So, how can we hold anything as the truth? What is truth today is the mistruth that leads us to destruction tomorrow. We are specks of dust, waiting for a storm that we never considered."

"If we are specks, what is the use in any of it?"

"That's what I am trying to understand. Our body is feeble; with one cut, we are bleeding to death somewhere. The same will happen to our children and our children's children. That's if they survive. Sparta was built on the legacy of death, and it is dead. Who knows if it will ever be remembered? Perhaps none of us will."

"So, why not do what we can see as right in the moment?"

"Exactly. That is all we can do. But I do wonder, when I die, will it be for truth, or will it be for an illusion?"

"Well, I guess we will see when we get there?"

"We will see."

"You love your sons, don't you?"

"I do. But they must breathe into their own appreciation for life."

"Yes. My village says: How a man leads is an extension of how he leads his family." Stoades laughed. "You let men breathe and grow. Unless you don't want them to breathe at all." He placed his hands together in a form of sincerity. "I wish your sons fortune."

Virtutis sighed, missing Stoa and imagining Augustus chasing his big brother's shadow. "Thank you, Stoades. I am going to rest. By morning, I will have made up my mind, and we will plan accordingly."

"Sir—we will be here waiting."

Virtutis collected what he needed and walked away from the fires. He settled below a bush, nestling his back to its base, its branches falling over his cloak to keep him warm. He rested his head on his folded right arm, feeling the tenderness of his spear shoulder.

He slept while he could. It was not long before a new dream woke him in wonder. The roar of a thousand voices screaming his name. It was deafening but, at the same time, exhilarating.

He rubbed a closed eye with his palm and bit his lip to be sure it was a dream.

Rolling from beneath his cover. He moved to his feet slowly at first, stiff from running the day before. He climbed high until he looked over the campsite.

One runner kept guard, walking the perimeter while his brothers slept.

With relief, he released a breath and sat crossed-legged.

He thought of his sons again. He missed them more at night, in the silence, and even more after opening his life to Stoades.

He pulled his cloak up and over his head and fixed his eyes where the sun would break, hoping to find the solution to his biggest quest yet—how he would save the innocent and protect the fatherless? Knowing some were now orphaned like himself from his own hand that fought for a Roman wage. How would he resolve such conflict that still alluded him? Moreover, he knew he must not let his guilt intimidate the right decision.

He cleared his mind, reasoning with his traitorous plans.

Was he killing all the virtue he aspired to possess?

Liliana wandered into his mind again, and the thought of her stimulated his groin. He would do what he could here; if he lived, he would follow her calling.

There was no telling if the general was trying to assassinate her, but he could not take that chance.

The sun crept into a new day, and slowly, he formulated his plan.

The runners stirred below.

Virtutis climbed down and issued Stoades his orders. "We are to stay the course and meet at the mountain springs. There, we will assess and see who arrives. From that, we will know who we have left. We will openly discuss a plan, so the men can decide their fate."

Stoades replied with a nod. "We will leave as soon as we can. We have to run while it is still cool. It is half a day to the springs."

"You lead, brother. I will follow."

Stoades gathered his things and turned into a slow jog, warming up to the climb. After a steep incline, they started to run the narrow trails over ridges that dropped, unforgiving to the valleys below.

After hours of cautious walking, running, and climbing, they rested.

Virtutis stood with Stoades, in awe of the scenery, for once admiring the beauty of the natural contrast of the plains below and the steep cliffs they stood upon.

Virtutis adjusted the shield on his back. "This height will test the men's nerves. Your command to stop last night before climbing this terrain in the dark saved a lot of potential misfortunes. Men plummeting to death over a cliff is far less appealing than being killed in battle."

"All men plummet," Stoades replied. "However, not all of us scream on the way to the bottom."

With a heavy heart, Virtutis thought of Rufus falling out of sight and Remus's demise in the hole of death, undeserved.

He rubbed his hand over his head, wondering when it would be his own time to plummet.

CHAPTER 24

The grueling last climb to the springs took its toll on Virtutis's legs and lungs. He placed his shield and spear down over his shoulder bag while Stoades called the runners to drink first, then come to council.

Ten men gathered at the center of the campsite.

Tempting treason, Virtutis unshackled the words from his mouth. "Brothers, I must declare myself to you. I am no longer loyal to Rome. I am going to serve and protect this region from General Lucio."

There was no movement. No emotion.

Distant sounds of flowing water filled the silence. Virtutis adjusted his stance, studying the faces of the runners.

"I offer you the freedom of choice; you may stay or leave."

Again, no one moved.

Stoades elevated his chin a little more than normal. "Virtutis, it is unanimous. We are with you."

"You all understand?" He made eye contact with each man. "You understand you will be hunted until the day you die?"

"We understand," Stoades affirmed.

It was almost too easy. The weight of reality, of his decisions, crushed down Virtutis's spine. His influence inspired these men to uproot Rome's road to dominance. If he failed, their bones would be scattered, buried under Roman stones along with hundreds of thousands of nameless men. Nothing would mark their graves; none would gather to mourn their lives; their winning or losing would dissipate without regard.

He searched their faces; it seemed these lean men already knew the ramifications of their choices. They stood determined and loyal to his cause that had now become their own. The men who previously looked young were now hardened and flint-like.

The youngest of the runners looked at Virtutis.

"The bond is strong." His eyes gleamed with pride and surety.

"The bond is strong." Virtutis held out his arm—removing all Roman-led barriers.

One by one, the men showed their allegiance, extending their forearms. Virtutis moved between them, one to another, each grip as firm and heartfelt as the other.

"I am honored." Virtutis lowered his head, taking a deep breath.

His voice broke the water's fluid sound, standing in its own intention. "We must search the surrounding areas for any threat to the men while they rest. Once we secure the area, you will watch in pairs over the trails leading here. Stoades, you will remain with me and prepare to inform the rest of the men of their choice." Though happy with the decision, Virtutis could not smile. Responsibility held him in a grip far greater than the eagle's talons. "Over the next day, the men will climb the last inclines to the springs. We must be ready."

With a nod, the runners scattered to do their scouting.

It was not long before the springs hustled with life. By the following nightfall, campfires extended well around the water's edge and up into the rocky cliffs.

The atmosphere was one of unity and brotherhood.

Virtutis rubbed his chin in contemplation.

He looked at Stoades, who was cooking rabbit, wondering where he had got it from.

"Some of the men have captured barbarians," Stoades said, looking up. "There are ten tied up near the central campfire. There is no way for them to escape. They would have to run through half the men still arriving."

A familiar gruff and panting paused their conversation; Khan's broad frame came into view between the fires.

He slowed his run, opening his arms wide. "Brothers!" He gasped. "The young mountain wolf that used to be an ox has arrived!" He lumped himself down on the ground by the fire, struggling with the thin air at such an altitude.

"That was some climb." He looked at the fire. "What's for dinner?"

Stoades and Virtutis could not help but smile at the relentless strength of the personality Khan processed.

"You may have even earned your mountain rabbit legs for that entrance!" Stoades provoked more humor. "Rabbit, kind sir? It's fresh and hot."

"Why, yes, sir! I love a good rabbit!" Khan accepted with a huge smile, grabbing at the flesh from the fire stake with his knife.

Virtutis let him finish his dinner in peace, waiting until he was happily licking his fingers.

There was no easy way to say what he had already instigated.

"Brother, I am no longer loyal to the Romans. I no longer serve the empire."

Khan looked long and hard into Virtutis's eyes. He let out a deep "Hmmmm." Thinking.

Not blinking.

Not breaking his stare.

Khan held a sterner face than most men. It was even harder to read in the firelight.

Khan wiped his hands and knife on his cloak, still not breaking eye contact.

"Twelve years I have been in the auxiliary." He pushed one hand into the earth to straighten himself up crossed-legged, not dropping the knife. "Twelve years! I have fought every type of man and beast in the name of the empire. Those bastards have killed my friends, my brothers, cousins, nephews, sons, and even their distant relatives. I have served under Roman tyrants and murderers. Even with a broken nose, there is no end to their stench!"

Rolling his shoulders, arching back, he cracked his spine, making his face scrunch up.

"The emperor pounds people to peace with a hammer of war and expects loyalty? The thought of another eight years alone breaks my back."

He slid his knife into its sheath.

"But, these last few months, I have never had so much fun!"

His smile grew bigger than his appetite.

"I am with you! Do I get to kill some of those pompous pricks?"

"There is a great possibility of that, yes," Virtutis assured.

"Where do I sign, commander?"

Virtutis stood, putting out his forearm. "There is no signature that bonds brothers."

Khan scrambled to his feet like a bear.

Before Virtutis could adjust, Khan grabbed his shoulders with each hand in a solidness worthy of a brother's assurance.

"I am at your service in life and death." He pulled Virtutis into a hug, crushing his ribs and squeezing the air from his lungs, making him uncomfortable. "We are bound by battle and wager of a free man's gluttony due to this tasty rabbit!"

Bouncing on his toes, he released the bear hug and squeezed Virtutis's shoulders before letting go. He looked at Stoades.

"Now, who's got the wine?"

Virtutis did not know how to respond to such joy, but the strange assurance put him at ease.

Eventually, Khan quieted, and Virtutis explained his plan.

"Tomorrow, we inform the rest of the men. We will split them up between us. Those who want to stay will continue their oath. Those who wish to leave or return to the Romans may do so. I do not want a meeting. I want us to visit each camp and deal with this personally. There are no orders from me unless the men are willing."

Khan was sitting, still smiling. "Of course. Now, what's the rest of the plan?"

Virtutis, Khan, and Stoades spoke into the depths of the night, clarifying anything that needed to be said. By morning, they started their rounds, informing the auxiliary well into the night.

Some of the discussions were long. Others were short and to the point with little questioning.

Returning to their campfire after a day longer than that of battle, somehow Khan had acquired another rabbit and was skinning it for a second dinner.

Virtutis sat watching Khan cut with precision. With one pull, he shed the skin; their meal was ready to be impaled.

Stoades looked on with interest.

"How were the men you talked to?" Virtutis asked.

Khan did not look up.

"Oxen are always stronger together. They will stay."

Stoades rubbed his bald head.

"Everyone is staying. It is like we are the makings of an army without trying."

"Well, that bastard Lucio used us for barbarian bait," Khan said, twisting the rabbit and positioning the stake. "He gets what he deserves. The men are more than willing to do what it takes." He shoved the stake all the way through.

Virtutis tilted his head at Khan, taking pride in his preparation of the rabbit before he placed it over the fire like it was his most prized possession.

Stoades shifted uncomfortably.

"Sir, do I need to assemble the runners quickly? They can walk the camp or use the shadows to know what the men are saying."

"No," Virtutis responded without hesitation. "What is worse than being deceived by your friend is doubting his loyalty. The men have stayed this long; they have kept their oath. I have no reason to doubt them now."

"A risk." Stoades scratched his head. "But I trust your judgement."

Khan wiped his knife clean, then spun it through his fingers. "The word of a man is only as good as the blood he is willing to spill for it." He flipped the blade toward him and threw it into the dirt, sticking it clean. "It's up to them if they want to spill theirs, and it will not be quick."

"So, what is next?" Stoades asked.

"We need to talk with the barbarian tribes; they are our only hope of keeping the Romans out of here long enough to reinforce any kind of stronghold. Khan, take some men and free the prisoners, give them food and water. Treat them well. Make sure you get enough of our men to sit with them through the night, so they do not run but do not tie them up again."

"And if they want to fight?" Khan lifted his eyebrows, no doubt hoping for a violent reward.

"You can take care of it if need be. No killing."

"I would like nothing more than to show a barbarian my ox tricks!"

Virtutis smiled. "Remember, we need to build, not break. These men need to understand our intentions and deliver our message."

"Of course," Khan said, reminding himself. "No breaking barbarians."

Virtutis stood gathering his spear. "I will be back in the morning."

"As always," Khan said, "I don't think you have spent more than a few nights within the camp since I have known you. I understand." He shrugged. "If it's not planning, it's fighting demons. I, for one, am tired of living with demons because they are always inviting more."

"Demons?" Virtutis asked.

"Our minds can be worse than any man's intention. We must put the demons to rest, or they will pile up at our doorstep. When men like us are alone, we are either fighting demons or making plans. Just be careful not to make plans with the demons; that's nothing but trouble.

Every leader needs solitude; that's why I am not a great leader. I like wine, food, and company way too much!"

Virtutis and Stoades exchanged looks across the fire.

"I swear, Khan"—Virtutis shook his head—"I have yet to know a man like you. I still am figuring out what is in that head of yours."

"Oh, trust me! I have been asking myself the same question." Khan laughed, turning the spit, cooking the rabbit evenly with great intent.

"I will see you at dawn, brothers," Virtutis assured. "Rest well."

"I can't promise the rabbit will be here. But I will be." Khan said, almost eating his bottom lip.

Virtutis slipped into the night, climbing the rocks above the camp. Standing at the zenith of the world, he searched the stars, pulling his cloak hood over his head.

He lowered his vision to the flickering flames.

The runners still made their rounds on the outskirts of the camp against any unannounced arrivals.

There was a scrape and scuffled footsteps behind him.

Virtutis snapped his head around, crouching, grasping his spear, prepared for whatever was coming in from the cold of night.

"Mercalis." He relaxed. "Brother, I am glad to see you."

"Yes. It's been a long few days." His voice was strained, dry.

"You must be tired? Water?"

"No, not yet. We must talk." Mercalis's eyes looked more withdrawn, with purple bags beneath them from lack of sleep. "There is little time for rest now."

"What has the general conspired now?" Virtutis's heart pumped adrenaline, making his veins ignite.

"The general is only the beginning. There is someone else."

"The seventh centurion?"

"Yes, but he's not a centurion. I don't know who he is. But he has control of most of the legion, and they are heading here to cut you down."

"General Lucio is Medusa. He's twisted versions of truth from his lips so convincingly that he could sell a blind man darkness and deaf man silence." Virtutis shook his head. "Which way are they coming?"

"From the east, so they don't narrow themselves too much."

"Clever. And General Lucio?"

"He is back at the main camp." Mercalis looked concerned, frowning more seriously than he had been before. "Virtutis, whoever is after your head has over two hundred men, and they are armed well. But they have no archers."

"That makes no sense at all. If they wanted to defeat us, that would be their best attack."

"I know. I overheard Lucio's guards wanting to skin you alive when they bring you back with your spear up your ass. They are out to finish you."

While offended, Virtutis also found the statement humorous. "Only those bastards could think of buggery and revenge at the same time." He snickered. "Romans."

Virtutis gazed around the lookout, making sure they were alone.

"Sit."

Virtutis sat cross-legged, resting his spear across his shoulder. From his bag, he handed Mercalis his leather water flask.

"Drink, we are not fighting any battles yet. You have time to rest. Who knows what tomorrow will bring?"

"Truth." Mercalis opened the flask, taking a swig. "Thank you, brother. I followed you for most of the night, and this was the only time we would not be discovered talking. I was not sure who to trust."

"You did well. You are right to be careful. The stakes grow with each day."

Virtutis looked up at the constellations.

"So, the general sends his men to do the dirty work?"

Mercalis gulped down more, wiping his mouth with his forearm. "They never had the intention to let any of us live."

"No. But why let me live this long? He had his opportunities to kill me more than once."

Mercalis shrugged. "The man is twisted; we know that. And the shadow who joins him must enjoy twisted company. Snakes slither around anything that looks like food if given the chance."

"Yes. But why?" Virtutis watched Mercalis sip water from the corner of his eye. "How did they know we were here?"

"I am not sure yet. But I will find out."

Virtutis cracked his neck to the side, releasing tension.

"I should have known better. We were left on our own too much. I see that now."

"Alone, how so?"

"They never gave us any other orders or guidance. Silence amongst warriors is comfort and belonging, but silence amongst Romans is conspiracy or war. We were intended for something, but not survival. Our own arrogance may have very well saved us."

"So, what do we do?"

"We have to prepare and attack, or we will be defeated by pure mass. They have us at least four to one. We know nothing of who is leading; the men are tired and need another few days rest."

"Run and recover?"

"I am not sure yet. There is much to consider. The men will fight regardless." Virtutis looked back down over the camp. "Go get some rest, and I will issue the orders in the morning. Khan and Stoades have food; sleep there in comfort; you can trust them. But be gone before dawn to join the runners."

"Thank you. I need to sleep."

"Yes. Mercalis, you have done well. Not bad for someone so skinny," Virtutis laughed.

"It helps me hide behind blades of grass while someone kills men pissing."

Virtutis pulled his head back with curiosity, smiling.

"You saw that?"

Mercalis shook his head, grinning, "Someone has to watch your back."

"Truth. And thank you. The bond is strong." Virtutis held out his arm.

"The bond is strong," Mercalis returned his oath.

It did not take Mercalis long to rock-hop down to the base of the springs, timing his movements between the runners keeping watch. Virtutis studied the shadow assassin's every move, impressed with his ease and ability not to be seen; he was becoming a formidable spy.

Adrift in the engulfing tide of events, adding the general's undercurrent of deceit, Virtutis looked to the constellation Carina, asking for guidance. He thought of the navigator Canpolus, who braved the greatest seas for his Spartan King Menelaus.

"Please, show me the way through the things that I cannot see. If I am to drown in this storm, I swear General Lucio is coming with me."

His attention became drawn to men shuffling about in the center of the camp.

A scuffle started, followed by yells filling the air.

No doubt, the barbarians were in revolt of their hospitality.

Seeing it as a sign, Virtutis smoothly gathered his shoulder bag and spear.

He paused, appreciating the star-lit mountain.

The barbarians were something he could attend to now and not concern himself with tomorrow. The Romans were closing in on his every breath. There was no time for delicate negotiation.

Without worrying about being seen, he set off on his run down the boulders, sliding on his rear, leaping from the steep declines, and breaking speed using the end of his spear. Hitting level ground, he sprinted directly through the campfires to the center of the camp.

With the intensity of his pace, he sensed his men swarming in behind him, mob-like.

He arrived to Khan, trying to fight five barbarians by himself. Khan flipped a barbarian over his shoulder. Half the auxiliary stood ready behind him.

Seeing the mob appear, the commotion abruptly ended.

"Brother," Khan panted. "I had it all under control."

Virtutis had no patience for games or humor.

"Who is the most senior here?" he asked the barbarians, who no doubt feared for their lives.

"I am!" a barbarian yelled, lifting himself from the ground. "If you are to kill anyone, kill me first!"

"I am not interested in killing any of you." Virtutis stood his spear on end. "If I wanted you dead, you would be already."

"What! Am I supposed to be grateful? You bastards have already killed half the tribes here."

"Yes, I know. There is nothing we can do to resolve that, not now. But you need to understand something." Virtutis stepped forward, almost nose to nose with the man. "The Romans are coming from the east. All the villages in their path are at risk. They will annihilate everyone in their path. They are not here to be diplomatic. They are here to kill everything that moves, so nothing can oppose the empire."

"Why should I trust a Roman auxiliary?"

"We are no longer with the Romans. We are exiled. We are here to help secure the region from the general's plans of genocide."

"Exiled? You mean you have brought the Romans to our lands looking for you?"

"In a way, yes. But there is something greater happening that we do not know. One thing is for certain, if you do not warn your people, they will perish."

"Why should I trust you?"

"You don't have to. But the threat is real, and your people will die. We will meet the Romans head-on and buy you time to organize, but you must decide if you want to fight or retreat. They would have come regardless of us being here or not."

Virtutis tightened the grip on his spear, quickly growing tired of explaining.

"You have two days at the most before they arrive. You can save the tribes a day away toward the east; anyone any farther than that, they are already dead. If you go west to the edge of the river valley, you will find Benductos and his men. If you want to fight, that would be your best chance. If we survive, we will come and join you to galvanize the region. The Romans will never stop. Never, ever trust the Romans, even in peace."

"Benductos is only a boy," the barbarian spouted. "He knows nothing about war."

Virtutis's voice grew harsh.

"Do not underestimate him. When this is over, you will find us at his side. It is your choice; you can run or face the Romans alone. It is not my concern." Virtutis leaned farther forward, eye to eye with the barbarian. His energy was intense, adjusting his spear, balanced stern at his side. "Your time is limited. I would leave now. Take your weapons and supplies. You are free to go."

Taking the opportunity, the barbarians quickly scampered away.

Khan stood guard over their every move. Satisfied with their exit, Khan scoffed at their departure as he dusted off his tunic.

Virtutis knew there was a confrontation coming beyond anything he had seen or fought against. Somehow, he had to ignite his men into a greater expectation of themselves. He rotated his spear slightly in his hand. Their eyes pinned him on the spot. Even though the trails had been harsh, and they were tired, there was no going back; there was no rest other than tonight to be had. But instead of easing their minds, Virtutis decided it was time he pushed them into a trance of purpose that even the sleepless would never want to dream again.

"In the coming days," he bellowed, "we will encounter something fiercer than you have ever faced. You should know that death is almost certain. The Romans have begun their hunt. They hunt us all. If we stay here after tonight and they make it to the top of the trails, we will be starved out and destroyed. We have to meet them down in the valley."

He gripped his spear, flexing his arm, forcing it to rise, a motion embodying his words.

"Remember this well. It is better to accept you are dead already; not even fear can influence your actions. You will not doubt; you will be stabbing a man while he is trying to gouge your eyeballs out with his fingertips. This is war!" Virtutis studied the faces of his men. "War against a beast that has tormented and conquered for over one hundred years. It is a beast that has never had mercy on itself or anyone else." He walked farther into the group of men, not waning his voice or intensity. "When you cut off a Roman head, five more will grow from its neck, each one more cunning and evil than the other. We must show! No! Mercy!" Veins in his arms pulsed. His words forced his body to prepare for war. His Spartan blood slowly shifted his brain toward a merciless human-animal ready to kill.

A howl echoed through the dark mountains.

"My black pup," Virtutis whispered under his breath, searching the trees suspiciously. This howl was real.

His thoughts flooded with how the Black Wolf had intimidated him and threatened the life of his sons. It filled him with even more defiance.

Virtutis opened his arms, lifting his head, and he yelled at a volume that caused everything on the mountain to pause.

"Ahhhhh!" he screamed. "I welcome the Black Wolf! I am the Black Wolf!"

He hunched over, rounding his shoulders, gaining all his Spartan strength.

From the deepest depths of his soul, he launched his head back with a scouring howl.

It echoed alone through the mountains.

Before he had stopped his howl, his men followed the power of his lead, releasing their voices, howling their own defiance. They howled so powerfully, it jolted the forest.

He lifted his spear strong and silent high into the air.

Without a sound, his men reciprocated, lifting their weapons high. Each man gripping with an intention so tight that Virtutis could feel the energy. The energy of where human resilience meets the steeled and defiant minds of men with nothing to lose.

Scanning each face, he had found belonging once more. And with it a purpose that flowed a sense of confidence through his body.

Together, they lowered their salute.

They knew the time they had was precious, and rest was needed to prepare for the days ahead.

"Brothers, sleep; after this night, we may never rest the same again. Tomorrow, we will drive helmets down the Romans' open throats. Do not waste time fighting the battle before it is due time. Return to your fires, eat well, cherish your moments."

There was a pause. Then, confidently, the men dispersed to their campfires.

Stoades, Mercalis, and Khan remained.

"Stoades, we need to confront the Romans to our advantage. At first light, I need you to send the runners to scout the territory, confirming their pace and location. While we don't know who is leading them or how they will fight, we must know where they are and what they have."

Stoades stepped forward. "Sir, if we go now, we will reach them by dawn. By tomorrow night, you could have the information you need."

Virtutis nodded, liking the cunning. "Running the ridges at night is dangerous. Take your precautions how you wish. I need our runners alive."

"Sir." Stoades turned in haste, not wasting a second thought.

"Skinny, you still need to rest. You will stay here tonight. If I have information, tomorrow you can run it to Stoades."

Mercalis nodded, happy with the arrangement.

Over Khan's shoulder, Stoades and the runners quietly absorbed into the night beyond the trees.

Virtutis and Khan returned to their fire. There were no words around the camp, just the sound of weapons being passed over sharpening stones.

Mercalis ate some leftover meat and lay uncovered in the night.

He shivered while he slept.

Virtutis took off his cloak, laying it over his loyal friend. The mountain air was cold, but there was enough heat in Virtutis's boiling veins that would warm him well this night.

Virtutis cupped cooling ash from the fire, mixing it in a bowl with drips of water, turning it black.

In the name of his sons, the wisdom of his dead wife, and the fortitude of Liliana. He spread ash over his chest and heart.

Spreading ash over his face and arms, he thought of how Lucio had planned to kill them both. He replayed how he was a pawn in the sick general's game all along.

Intrigued, Khan followed the darkening.

Their bodies were soon covered in black.

The white of Virtutis's eyes glowed in the dark.

He drew his dagger, cutting three lines along his forearm, then lathered more ash over his open wound, mixing with his blood with a permanent pact of revenge.

Khan could not withstand questioning the ritual. "For the Black Wolf?"

"No." Virtutis did not look up. "Three lines. For the three times I should have stuck my dagger into Lucio's spineless neck." Mixing ash further into his stinging-bloody flesh, his eyes watered with tears of revenge. "Now, there will be no hesitation." The ash stung the cuts. He imagined its blackness flowing through his veins. "My heart is turning black, and there will be no remorse."

He spat upon his sharpening stone again. Sitting cross-legged, he began rocking back and forth; he groaned as he swayed. He fell into the depths of death's trance.

Trees rustled, branches snapped. Dark energy caused Virtutis's skin to crawl.

Blinking his eyes, the Black Wolf walked between the campfires. His growl aggressive, he snarled, baring his teeth.

The hair along the ridge of Virtutis's back stood on end; the beast had returned to fight.

Virtutis looked without wavering directly at death's messenger. He lowered his head slightly, wanting to release a fury of his own. "What?" Virtutis growled.

The Black Wolf rounded his front.

Virtutis bit the inside of his mouth, forcing blood to rush over his tongue. He swirled it around thick. Lifting his chin, he spat it at the wolf.

The wolf dug into the dirt with his claws, then shook his head from side to side.

Furious, growling, the wolf paced his way back and forth until he settled directly in front of Virtutis's face.

They locked glares in a stand-off, and time stood still.

Knowing it would go no further, Virtutis sat upright in his tranced defiance. "One thing I am learning quickly is that you let man's weaknesses do your killing. Because you are unable to kill anyone yourself. You are a scavenger of the weak."

The wolf snorted with harsh stale breath. Virtutis stared into his hazel eyes.

"Again, you lack the kill." He searched the depth of the wolf's soul. "I will pierce your throat with my dagger." Virtutis placed his blade under the wolf's chin.

The wolf backed away, shaking and dipping its head, thrashing from side to side. He sprayed drool and shivered like it had just been leashed. In frustration, the Black Wolf faded into the distance.

Jolted by a crackle of the fire, Virtutis opened his eyes.

He tested the sharpness of his blade.

Covered in black, he lay back with the whites of his eyes gleaming toward the stars. He held his dagger across the middle of his chest under a caring, gentle pressure of both hands.

He closed his eyes, now without any fear of the Black Wolf.

Virtutis imagined that this was how his body would be positioned when he was done and dead. With it, he smiled.

CHAPTER 25

S moke smoldered from campfires drifting, its way toward the midmorning sun, mixing with the already smoky ash covering Virtutis's body, the inside of his nose sensitive, raw. His men stood ready. Their once maroon uniforms had been rubbed deep with ash, turning them all black. They smelled like fire. Fire with an appetite wanting to settle the score of betrayal.

"Are we waiting for Stoades?" Khan asked.

"No. There is no time." Virtutis replied, cold. "We run the ridge and get as far down the mountain as we can."

"But we are at a higher advantage. The Romans will be forced to thin out," Khan consoled.

"We have to meet them where they least expect it." Virtutis looked deep into Khan's soul. "There is timing and there is time. Romans misuse timing because they are too busy trying to control time, and they often force themselves into mistakes. To defeat them, we take their timing away. They are built on routine and order; without them, they will scour to the shadows. If we let them climb higher, they will no doubt come with a plan. They want us to stay. As long as we control our strike, adjust the tempo of attack, and take our opportunities, we have a chance. If we can cut away at their structure where they would perceive themselves as secure, we will destroy them."

Khan deliberated, scratching at the dry ash over his head. "Less questions, more ox." He broke into his normal self. "The sooner we can kill these bastards, the better." He itched the back of his neck. "And the sooner I can wash this ash off."

Virtutis ignored Khan's dilemma.

"The men must move light. No supplies, only one shoulder bag with two days' rations and water." Virtutis looked into the trees on the other side of the springs. "When the wolves are hungry, they will hunt." He looked back at Khan. "If we want to eat, we need to consume the Romans and take what is theirs."

Virtutis took one last glance over his men before the day would speed into an unpredictable labyrinth of decisions. Decisions their lives depended on.

After this moment, there was no thought of the past or future; the way to victory was with Virtutis's instinct. An instinct to win. The smaller increments of a plan were a set of consequences beyond his control; therefore, overthinking would only dilute his ability to adapt to the chaos.

Pulling on his shoulder bag, hitching the shield, and regripping his spear, he started a slow stride out from the springs onto the upper trails before starting the descent. The pace was easy to conserve energy. Footsteps were the only sound carried by the wind, occasionally echoing from above.

The trails were even, with good width, until the high ridges became narrow.

Virtutis slowed with caution.

He could hear the ox's panting steady behind.

Talking over his shoulder, not taking his eyes off the terrain, he warned, "Easy now, Khan. Keep your distance when you follow. Relay it to the men. One false step, and they are dead."

Virtutis could hear the initial message being relayed, but his concentration soon drowned out anything other than sure steps over the sudden drop.

The occasional rock slid and tipped over the edge, bouncing its way out of sight. Its rhythm and percussion not at all comforting.

Virtutis was conscious of the midday sun beating harsh heat upon the warriors, but there was little to do other than carry on.

Finally, from the ridge, he broke first into the woods with a nearby stream. He quenched his thirst from the water's edge and filled his waterskin.

Khan arrived, smiling. "Legs like mountain goats and a head like an ox! Thirsty like one too!"

Virtutis did not look up. He walked across the river downstream to keep the water pure for his men. He started a slow jog up to a small hill covered with trees. Unless he had something to say, there was no conversation.

Virtutis studied the area, waiting for Khan to arrive.

"Keep the men here until nightfall. They must stay away from the river and stay hidden while they rest. I will be back."

Virtutis sensed Khan's discomfort, not being his humorous self. Swallowing his vengeful personal spite toward the Romans, he connected, knowing his second in command was a jester but always battle-ready.

"Brother, soon you will be able to flatten Romans with your bare hands."

Khan looked up, shocked. His tension released with a showing of his uneven teeth and a nod.

Virtutis looked up over the tree line. Dropping his shoulder bag, he took easy strides up the hill and into the dense trees.

He fought to cut a pathway up through untraveled terrain, and he used his spear shaft to sweep foliage and launch himself over debris. His black figure was easily lost in the density of the forest cover.

The hatred for General Lucio raged, and it flowed like fuel through his veins. Each gained step required determination—his breathing heavy with effort.

At the peak of the hill, he gathered his bearings, checking behind him at the carved path up into the steep hill that overlooked a valley. Below him, through the cover of the trees, held a plain extending to the river, making it a perfect Roman campsite.

With care, using his spear for support, he descended to the bottom of the hill. A fast route that provided good cover. Hitting the bottom, he braced his legs, stopping in a crouch. He cleared his mind, devising more of his plan before he carefully exited the cover of nature.

Once secure, he exploded, striding out toward the river, imagining the strike of battle. Downhill was quick and easy to navigate.

Experiencing enough, he adjusted his run, entering into the shallow stream leading back to his men.

Ahead in the distance, familiar men ran scattered across the flats toward the upper stream under the trees.

As they promised, his runners had arrived and, he hoped, with information that would conclude his plans.

Hidden with stealth, Virtutis followed the runners, playing a game of his own, stalking friendly prey.

A sudden movement caught his eye from the trees.

Two shadows stopped and started. Someone was tracking his runners.

He sharpened his vision, the suspicion correct.

Roman messenger spies.

Virtutis scoffed at their nerve.

The games had well and truly begun.

Submerged using the riverbank, Virtutis watched before making any decisions.

Looking back, he saw no movement, making sure there were no signs of more trackers.

Leaving the riverbank, heading straight for the opposite tree line, he picked up the trail of the spies.

The sound of the wind provided cover, and he risked short open bursts, making up ground.

Two men huddled behind a large fallen tree.

Virtutis settled under low brush on his belly.

A spy would peek up intermittently, looking for direction, listening for information.

Virtutis stalked.

His runners had been intercepted by his men. They stopped at the river and began to climb to join the rest of the men.

The spies whispered, then took a route to higher ground for surveillance.

Virtutis crawled backward from his cover, then took an even higher vantage. He moved slowly, sure not to disturb any loose rocks or fallen branches. From this higher vantage point, he could see them using the slightest cover to crawl downhill to the stream, closer, attempting to listen to every word they could.

His men sat relaxed, unaware.

Without a sound, Virtutis closed down from behind the unsuspecting spies. He thought he caught the general's scent drifting across his path, provoking anger, turning him cold.

He rotated his spear for throwing, then drew his dagger. Holding his breath, starting his run, he closed the distance at pace. By the time they heard him, it was too late.

Virtutis let loose his spear, its momentum forcing his dagger hand backward. Once the shaft left his hand following through, he exploded his opposite arm forward; the dagger flew end-over-end in a rhythmical motion.

The spear buried deep into one of his target's chest.

The dagger following entered deep under the clavicle of the other, choosing a strike to keep the spy alive.

Before the Roman could even lift his opposite hand to check the damage, Virtutis was towering over him. He jammed the side of his foot into his victim's soft throat, pinning him, rendering him helpless. The pressure caused the Roman to squirm in pain and gasp for oxygen.

With pleasure, Virtutis asserted a harder stomp before letting up his sandaled impression. He bent, grabbing the man by his throat, leaving the dagger for extra discomfort.

Virtutis dragged the spy along toward his men; they stood, now alert, with weapons drawn.

"It's a little late, don't you think?" Virtutis threw the man on his back up the hill.

The spy screeched in pain, his eyes darting around as he tried to understand what was going to happen to him.

Virtutis checked back over his shoulder. Khan and the runners came forward, looking embarrassed.

"If you let someone crawl this close to you, you might as well cut your own throat."

Virtutis focused on the spy.

"You are the messenger for General Lucio, aren't you?"

The man cowered away, not making eye contact.

Virtutis towered above him.

"You summoned me to the general, and they attempted to assassinate me." He thought of Liliana, how close she came to death.

The compassion he once held for the man had gone. A cold current of revenge now surged through his veins. The spy still refused to make eye contact.

"Very well. If you wish to search for a rock to crawl under in your final moments, so be it."

Virtutis sprawled over him with his knees on either side of his torso, forcing the man to look up in shock.

"What? Now you want to look?"

Virtutis placed his hand on his dagger's handle; the other hand pinched the man's cheeks together, making his face flinch in pain.

"You have one chance."

Virtutis pressed down on the blade handle, the man squirmed and coughed.

"Who is leading the legion?"

He pressed the dagger harder.

Blood ran from the corner of the man's mouth.

He gargled and spat, trying to clear his throat. The spray warmed Virtutis's forearm.

"I-I don't know." The spy coughed, cringing in pain. "The general ordered me directly."

Virtutis searched deep over the messenger's face. He gripped the dagger, slowly removing it from deep within sensitive flesh.

"Then, you are no use to me."

The wound began gushing Roman red.

Virtutis placed the blade across the Roman's throat and let his body weight fall forward, slicing everything in its path.

Virtutis enjoyed every ounce of pain, fear, and torment that crossed over the spy's face.

With a flick of the wrist, he ended any doubt of obstruction to his death.

Virtutis hovered over the body, watching him bleed out and the life fall from his eyes. He wiped the blade through the grass beside the spy's head and placed it in its sheath. The revenge seemed shallow. It offered no information, leaving nothing but emptiness.

CHAPTER 26

Virtutis stood looking down at the dead spy as Khan bellowed orders that shook his attention toward their vulnerability. Now that they were out of the hinterlands, surprise was the only element of war that would favor them when they encountered a superior force.

"Sweep the area again but higher and wider," Khan yelled. "If anything moves, catch it and bring it back."

Virtutis shook his head, knowing Khan was trying to regain his authority after their potential discovery.

"Khan." Virtutis remained focused on information. "What did the runners report?"

"The Romans are headed straight here. They will be here by tomorrow at noon."

"Then we must entice them to camp here and not continue."

Khan's embarrassment turned to curiosity.

"Send twenty men to make fires with river stones," Virtutis instructed. "Light them as soon as you can, let them burn well, then smother them out, remove the wood that did not burn through, as if they have been left for some time." Virtutis etched a design with his dagger in the dirt. "Place the fires this way. Cut the brush leading down to the riverbank on the plains so it is open and easy to access. Remove all the cuttings, leaving it clean, but bring the cuttings back bundled."

"Sir," Khan replied with a smile. "You and your fire bundles."

Virtutis continued, uninterested, "All the rest of the men are to follow me. We have some trails to make before tomorrow. Send the runners back toward the Romans to keep watch; they must stay in front of their scouts." Virtutis looked at his men.

"Skinny!"

Mercalis appeared quickly, emotionless.

"Get Stoades back here as quick as possible. I need him. Stay hidden until tomorrow and observe all Roman movements throughout the night."

"Yes, sir."

"Khan, an opportunity will only be here for a short time. We have until dawn to prepare, so the men must work through the night. We need ten long trunks cut and left up in the tree line." Virtutis pointed to where he had stalked the spies across the river.

Turning around, he pointed in the opposite direction.

"I have cut a trail up the hill that backs down to the beginning of the plains. Clear eight or ten paths down the hill under cover and create areas behind the trees before the plains, and make sure they are well out of sight for the men to hide tomorrow. They will need to keep their weapons hidden in the clearings until we return tomorrow night, and there must be no chance of noise as we get into position. But they can keep their daggers until then."

"Sir." Khan turned and started barking orders.

Virtutis started walking back down to the river to collect his spear. Placing his foot upon the lifeless chest, he took time to study the valley, his eyes seeing it differently. The natural hillside became his fortress and the valley a death pit. Even if the Romans did not make camp, this is where everyone would meet their fate.

With no regard toward his speared victim, he yanked it free.

Night fell, and Virtutis and his men cut their moonlit way through the trees. They cleared away their areas, readying for the strike, and laid their weapons under foliage. With stealth, they returned up to the top of the hill by the river in single file.

It was an airy and fireless night. Men used bushes and ferns for their beds, trying what they could to keep warm.

Virtutis sat above them by a large boulder, and a single figure walked from man to man, handing out ash from the fires of the morning. The men began darkening themselves once more until they were all black.

Laying his shoulder against a rock, he took whatever rest he could.

The Black Wolf tried to haunt his dreams, sniffing around the beds of Stoa and Augustus. Liliana kissed his head gently and slid a dagger behind his back. She pointed at a sea filled with snapping wild dogs as a warning. It was jumbled. Restless. Finally, the sound of shackles stirred him awake. Again, he choked on dry sand that did not exist.

Sitting up, reaching for his leather waterskin, there was little movement anywhere, his men resting while they could.

After taking a small sip, his runners rounded the river. They stopped to keep watch, then fell away into the night.

The sun peaked her fiery eye over the distant mountains.

Virtutis made his way down and woke two men in silence. They, in turn, woke the others. Soon, they were all on their feet, waiting. Before the sunlight shone on the hill above the river, they began their walk back into the trees along the ridge of the hill.

They hid on the upper trail well out of sight. Not a word was spoken into midmorning.

Virtutis stalked the lower tree lines, spotting a lone runner coming through the valley, cutting away from the plains and returning up into the trees.

Virtutis smiled. Stoades had returned, which meant the Romans were not far behind.

Signals from hidden men intercepted Stoades as he soon entered the tree line.

Virtutis huddled in a narrow line along the ridge amongst his men as Stoades arrived.

"Brother," he greeted, "I am pleased you made it."

"I see you have made yourself at home." Stoades grinned. "Glad you decided to come down from the springs and not wait. They were going to burn you out up there."

"I knew they would find a way to unsettle us if we waited."

"They will be here in a few hours." Stoades removed his dagger from its sheath, cleaning half-dried blood off with a large leaf. "The hills are alive with spies. You are well hidden here; it's not a direct route, and the cliffs will hide you well from the Romans above," he confirmed.

"We need them to camp here."

"Yes, I saw your welcoming gift. I just hope it is not too obvious."

Virtutis briefly doubted his decision. But there was nothing he could do now.

"Well, if not, we will have to deal with the situation as it arises."

"If they stay, we will attack well after midnight. You need to settle in and rest. We do not know what will happen after this starts."

Virtutis handed Stoades his shoulder bag with food and water.

"Did you find out who is leading the Romans?"

Stoades stopped rummaging through Virtutis's bag and looked up.

"No. Whoever it is, he is amongst the legion somewhere. It is strange for a Roman not to show his authority."

"Yes, it is. It does not matter now either way. There is no going back. We are here, and we fight regardless."

"They are well prepared. They have good supplies, and their pilums have been extended. They will want to fight to their strength."

"We will not give them the opportunity to find stability," Virtutis vowed.

The day passed slowly without a breeze.

Khan scrambled his way along the line toward Virtutis.

"Sir, the men are almost out of water." Khan's brow was pouring sweat from the humidity. "The trees are giving us shade, but the heat is draining. Can I take a small group back to the river to get more water?"

Virtutis studied Khan's face. "No. We must hold the men firm. The sun won't be threatening much longer. The men must keep their resolve."

Stoades intervened by poking his head around Virtutis.

"There are runners everywhere. If we move from cover, we'll lose our element of surprise."

"Stoades." Khan looked shocked. "I did not see you. Did you bring any of that goat?"

Virtutis sighed, not happy he was caught in the middle while they continued their banter.

Like the gods intervening, movement stirred down the bottom of the hill in the tree line, saving Virtutis from any more discomfort of chatter.

A runner came panting up to Virtutis.

Out of breath, dripping with sweat, he gasped out information.

"The Romans are here." He wiped his forehead. "They have stopped on the plain by the river. They are making camp as we speak."

Virtutis raised an eyebrow.

"Are they using the fires we set out?"

"Yes, sir. They have started to set the fires alight."

Virtutis rubbed his hand over his head, relieved.

Khan became excited. "What have you got planned?"

"Where there is fire, there is smoke, and where there is smoke, there is cover. We will attack from out of the trees directly into the middle of the camp but stay within the parameters of the middle fires. There are twenty in total. Five wide and four high. Attack upward through the center, then outwards from there. Know you can always come back toward the middle."

Virtutis picked up cut brush from the trail cleaning. "Each man is to carry some of these or the cuttings from down on the plains. Khan, we will carve our way with the majority of the men. Just hit and move. If any man gets a chance, stoke the fires, and make as much smoke as possible. Remember, go straight through the middle of their camp; it will keep our men fortified. If there are too many problems, head for the trees and up the hills. Stoades, you will select ten men and wait for me. I will lead the main attack, then double back. We will attack all easy targets on the outside and watch." Virtutis looked side to side at both Khan and Stoades. "Both of you. The men are to be silent. No yelling. No talking. No battle cries. The sound of killing is all we want to make. We hit everything that moves and get into the trees. We do not stay and fight long if they start to have the upper hand, understand? However, if we can, we finish them."

"Quiet as an ox," Khan said, not meaning to say it out loud.

Stoades became concerned. "So, we attack sleeping men?"

"Those men would gut us like pigs and watch us die. They have no mercy for us and never have." Virtutis shook his head. "There is a time for elegant warfare, and tonight is not one of them. I, for one, will not die at the hands of the entitled. I am not concerned with honoring an army that outweighs human decency, to begin with. Those men walked themselves here with the intention to burn us out. They are a long way from their mothers' coddle."

Stoades took out his dagger again, checking its sharpness with his finger.

"Truth."

The sun drifted beyond the trees and over the high cliff faces above, bringing with it a welcomed relief.

The night closed with deeper darkness than normal.

Virtutis gruffed. It was time.

He nudged Khan and signaled to Stoades to start initiating the descent to the clearings using the cover of the trees.

Virtutis checked his men slipping into the shadows, their black ash matted in sweat and growing hunger in their bellies, making them unformidable. Making them an unforgiving deadly force.

They sat in the trees, watching the Romans by their campfires' light. Virtutis could hear them laugh, making his stomach turn. The smell of left-over stew wafted. While the Romans filled their bellies with food, Virtutis filled his with revenge, and no doubt, it filled his men with more hatred.

The moon sat at a quarter, clouds drifted in, covering the stars, blocking more of the low light, and the night had just become deadly.

Virtutis tapped Stoades on the shoulder.

Staying low, he crept from the trees.

A long black shadow appeared beside him, extending the tree line forward. A deadly shadow ready to engulf all that stood in its way.

He scoffed, whispering toward the Roman camp.

"How you take for granted your guardian eagle."

He listened to the silence of a secure sleep. A sleep that was about to become a slaughter.

He sounded the cry of the night hawk, then started a steady run toward revenge.

They crossed the plains without disturbance, slowing to a walk into the rustling river, its sound covering their slow steady footsteps.

Climbing the shallow riverbank, Virtutis increased his speed toward the middle fire.

Two Roman guards stood looking directly at the river. They did not see the shapes appear until it was too late.

Virtutis let loose his spear, ripping into the chest of one. Someone near him had launched their dagger with precision, penetrating the head of the other.

Gathering his spear on the run, he did not slow. The river provided the necessary disguise for their approach.

There was no movement, and they were still undetected.

254

The Roman tents held the occasional snore, and the fires dimmed dull light. Virtutis rotated the shaft of his spear to regrip.

Entering deep into the camp, he stopped in a crouch.

Nothing stirred.

He slowed, turning to his men.

They crouched poised.

Khan held position right behind him.

Virtutis swept his spear across his midriff, signaling the attack. Men disappeared into tents. Others spread out laterally toward the outer fires, ready for the waking dead.

Virtutis and Khan held center.

"We are under attack!" a Roman roared.

Screams alarmed energy through the night.

Shouts and calamity of steel on steel soon followed. His men worked their way out and back, slicing and stabbing on the run.

They pushed toward the northern trees, not extending beyond the outer lateral fires.

Virtutis's heart raced with adrenaline, and he wanted to fight, but he waited for the ultimate prize. Wanting to discover the seventh centurion. He needed to find the man behind the general.

Virtutis motioned to Khan.

"Keep them going toward the trees."

Roman screams and scurried fighting intensified.

The outside of the camp was awake and responding to the middle attacks. His men used the center as their stronghold.

Virtutis twisted and turned, looking, listening for any hint of discovering his rival. The Romans, in chaos, quickly became easy prey for his men.

Perhaps whoever was leading was already dead?

Virtutis whipped his head around. Frustration was building, and he was about to explode.

There was no organization, and there were no shouts to order.

Gritting through his teeth, he gave the final order.

"Khan, finish them. Finish them all."

"Sir." Khan launched his own command style, attacking with his usual fury, the men following suit.

Remaining on his mission, Virtutis returned against the flow of battle down to the river, spearing the occasional Roman, hoping it would release some of his pent-up anguish.

At the river, Stoades waited with his men, looking ready to deal whatever blow they were required.

"I need you to scour the fringes and stay out of combat. We need to know who is leading."

Stoades shook his head in understanding.

"We are not to fight?"

A fire burned through Virtutis's veins.

"No, we must find the leader."

They were destroying the Romans tonight, but there would always be the question. A question that burned more than the desire to kill.

"This plan is to break the beak of the eagle. Then, I will cut out its tongue and send it back to Rome, where it came from." Virtutis spun his spear in his calloused hand.

"Let's go."

Virtutis and Stoades combed the outskirts together, watching through the chaos for any sign of authority, but through the smoke, he only witnessed mayhem and murder.

The battle would be over too quickly.

Between the fires, only dead bodies and scattered groups fighting remained.

In prone positions above the plains, they studied the Romans.

A group of Romans secured an area to defend. They shouted to each other, containing their resources, forming barricades from the river and northern trees.

Still, nothing became obvious to Virtutis.

"Where is he?" Virtutis asked.

"We should finish them while they are weak," Stoades insisted.

Virtutis knew the move was correct. There is no sense in leaving any Roman intact to potentially regroup again at greater strength.

"Very well, as you wish."

Stoades scurried back. Virtutis heard his footsteps fade away into the darkness.

Not wanting to give in, he continued to search through the remaining chaos.

Khan eventually flanked the camp, the men pouring deadly shadows into the weaker lateral barriers.

Disappointment and depression overcame Virtutis, and he rolled over to his back, looking up at the stars in disbelief.

The wind blew its whistle, and with it, loneliness entered his heart. The victory was without difficulty, without challenge. It all left him empty.

Rolling back to his stomach, pressing himself up for a better view, his men had begun to raid the camp's food stores while screams of Roman soldiers being finished off filled the valley.

Scanning the terrain, a lone figure came running through the plains at speed.

Recognizing the posture and velocity that the figure approached, Virtutis knew it was Mercalis. There was something more.

Gripping his spear and shield, he ran toward the camp. Virtutis darted, leaping dead bodies to meet Mercalis in the middle of the smoldering Romans.

Mercalis, almost out of breath, delivered the news.

"This is not the full force. There are reinforcements coming, and they are no more than a day away." Mercalis arched his back, putting his hand over his shoulder, bringing it back covered with blood.

"You are bleeding." Virtutis stared with concern at Mercalis's hand, drenched, dripping. "Is it bad?"

Mercalis looked at his hand. "I don't think so. When you attacked here, messengers scattered back to the main force. I stopped some of them, but there were too many. The message will have gotten through by morning."

Khan and Stoades arrived, sensing the importance of the informal meeting.

"How big is the force?"

"Three hundred, maybe four." He placed his hand over his shoulder and grimaced.

Virtutis, concerned with the amount of blood coming from the wound, rounded his back.

"The seventh centurion is leading the other force. But the general, he is not there," Mercalis added.

Virtutis listened while he took a look at Mercalis's back. A deep cut started at his trapezius and finished below his shoulder blade. It needed immediate attention.

Virtutis motioned to Stoades. "We need to bandage this now."

Stoades sped toward the Roman tents, scavenging for linen.

Mercalis, unfazed, continued, "Virtutis, I have never seen spears like they had."

"Are they longer than normal?" Virtutis asked.

"Yes. And they have archers."

A loud scream followed by cursing from Roman survivors being slain interrupted their conversation.

Virtutis brushed his head with his palm. "We are outnumbered three to one, plus archers and new weapons." He gripped his forearm, putting pressure over the three self-inflicted cuts, hoping the sensation would bring some clarity. "We must stop them before they get here. But we have to let the men rest a little."

"Yes. We don't have many injured, less dead on our part," Khan said, turning to leave. "I will check again."

"Khan." Virtutis briefly halted him. "The men can eat what they can find and replenish their bags. Pull back into the trees and recover. We will have to leave before first light. We will need to find somewhere to confront them to our advantage. Whatever chance we had here is gone. If we stay here, we are done for."

CHAPTER 27

Virtutis walked through his men scattered amongst the trees, resting. Khan lay on his back with his feet up and a rag over his face. "Are the men rested enough?" Virtutis asked.

"I don't think there was much rest for anyone," Khan replied, peeking out from under the rag, obviously no longer startled by Virtutis's presence. "They are tired, but they know we are at a point of no return. These last days have taken their toll. Most of them just want to face what they need to and get through it now. We lost ten and have fifteen injured."

Virtutis stood looking over Khan, asking himself if he could trust him fully now that he seemed comfortable. "Can the injured move?"

"Yes." Khan ambled to his feet, stretching his back with a groan. "Most are still able to run if they need to."

"Bury our dead now, then we move," Virtutis ordered. "By the time the Romans march, we want to be well over halfway to meet them. I know where we need to confront them. But the men will suffer; we must cut over the pass to the valley."

"Cut over the pass? That's almost vertical." Khan scratched his head. "Well, if I fall from anything, let it be a lofty mountain with an axe in my hand." He puffed his chest in acceptance. "The sooner, the better."

"That's if you don't lose your weapon first." Virtutis used humor to soften the order, hoping Khan was reiterating the men's general attitude and that a lighter side could drive motivation through the men. However, the attempt left Virtutis feeling at odds with himself; there was no choice but to trust him.

Under the breaking night sky, Khan wandered through the men as orders went out quickly to try to beat the sun's unforgiving heat, using the shade while it lasted.

By the time the sun gifted her light, with tired legs and heavy eyes, Virtutis started his run. His men scattered throughout the foothills, finding their best way through the trails toward the harsh climb.

The terrain steepened, and Virtutis could feel his sandals slip and slide over the loose shingle rock. The hard sandy incline forced him to latch his shield and spear, using his hands to maintain balance so he did not topple backwards.

The incline made his legs scream for relief; the consistent grind to the top exposed the depths of his lungs rarely felt in his lifetime. All logic to yield was overpowered by the thought of revenge. The type of revenge that blocked recognition of pain. There was no second thought, he could muster the energy needed to wage war for all eternity to settle his stakes with the general.

He pushed on with calloused hands, often gripping loose rock, wasting more energy, making him grunt up the grueling slope, but Virtutis held nothing back, scaling the slope quickly, which he hoped meant a greater possibility of winning the battle.

As he neared the summit, the sun rose with an unforgiving beam of heat directly in his face; the crest of the valley glanced down at his men, breaking through dusty rays of sun.

The closest men looked upwards; their eyes bloodshot from exhausting efforts forcing them beyond their limits. Virtutis refused to sigh, withholding any expression, knowing they had not even faced the worst to come. The pained passage for each warrior would take its toll today.

Mercalis, though injured, was amongst the men, the slower pace not normal for him, but he was moving.

Virtutis, satisfied with his men's effort, pushed on to the summit. With each step, he gasped a full breath under the screaming strain for oxygen. His hope and anticipation were to create a plan before the Romans arrived.

With his heart pounding and legs screaming, he conquered the top of the pass.

Cusping the crest of the basin below stood a small clump of trees; the rest was littered with boulders and bushes, giving enough cover to gain an unseen advantage, giving him a small sense of relief.

He unlatched his shield and spear and rested them against a boulder.

"Symbolic location, don't you think?" Stoades joined at his side. "In winter, it holds little sunlight, and in summer, it swelts like a windless pit."

Stoades motioned his head toward the road that carved its way through the middle of the valley, upward to a steep incline before winding down to the plains they had come from.

"Seems like a good place to bury Romans."

"In more ways than one," Virtutis replied. "This is the only way they could get to the mountains, correct?"

"Yes. They have to come this way or leave their supplies behind," Stoades confirmed.

"My concern is if any scouts saw us climbing over the pass."

"Well, if they did, they would have to pass through the valley in front of us. We took the fastest route. The runners will take care of anything that comes this way."

"Very well, Stoades. I trust your judgement." Virtutis surveyed the valley. "We need to cut down more trunks, make sure they are twice as long as the new Roman pilum, if not more. The Romans will be here in a matter of hours, if not sooner. Use the thick trees at the back of the valley over there." He pointed down to the clump in the valley. "Remember, cut the ones at the back, and do not disturb any cover at the front. Quickly, brother. Our lives depend on it."

"Sir."

Stoades gathered ten men and instantly headed down the valley.

Khan approached from behind with his telltale breathing. Virtutis stood calmly, letting the ox gather his composure.

"Khan, what do you think?" Virtutis studied the gradient.

"I think I am getting fitter."

Virtutis delivered a look that soon brought Khan's comments into line.

"We could not have kept going for much longer and fight. This is good. The men are tired, but at least they are not hungry; they ate well this morning and have more food, for now, thanks to the general's generosity," he said, chuckling, then wiggled his armor to seem more serious. "We have the right advantage here if we can block the Romans in. Especially if we can stab at them and not go direct until we can divide them. The men want to end this."

Virtutis analyzed Khan's face, nodding.

"Waging war was one thing. But humans are unpredictable when pressured. We need to test them, keep them under strain by making them stay stagnant for a good amount of time," Virtutis added.

"Agreed, brother." Khan looked up at Virtutis. "Mercalis told me they are outnumbering us four to one?"

"Yes. That's better for us," Virtutis assured. "They will try to stick together longer for security. They won't attack outward initially. When the time is right, you will have your way. We will open them up."

They stood in silence, observing more of the pit, soon broken by the chopping of wood.

"But I do have a concern, sir," Khan said.

Virtutis caught the ox biting his bottom lip. He pulled a high-pitched sucking sound into his mouth in contemplation.

"The archers. We don't have any way to defend against them."

263

"Yes, I was thinking the same thing. We need to finish them before they gain cover from within the shield wall of the legion. Our first strike has to be focused on separating the two. We will see how they are grouped when they enter the valley. The archers should be at the back before the supply wagons."

"Can we send a runner to confirm?"

"No. We cannot risk giving away our position. We must get out of sight soon. We have to adapt to what we see. Let's finish off the archers first if we can, but we need their bows and arrows if we are to reverse the advantage."

"How do we split our men?"

"You will have to block the advancement of the Romans, so they can't take advantage of elevation at the front. Take twenty men, mainly the injured and fatigued. Have them each carry two shields if they can, so you look larger than you are. I will take the rest and swamp the archers, but you cannot be seen until the archers are well within the valley, or they will retreat at the back, gaining higher ground. Their arrows will pick us off." Virtutis rubbed his hand over his head. "The gods will have to help us with timing."

"Gods?" Khan chuckled. "People go looking for the gods and find coincidence instead. I will hold as long as we can. Even with my human mortality." Khan chuckled. His face fell deadly serious as he pointed to his eye. "I will wait until the tip of their spears are at my eyeball if I have to."

In awe, Virtutis looked over Khan's face. He had proven himself loyal to the bone. He still wondered who Khan had met with in the dark of night. But through the trials and tribulations of their own experiences in war, he decided that he was seeing the true Khan.

He decided to put any doubt about his second in command to rest.

"Send Mercalis to see me; then he will rejoin you, but he must not be in this battle."

"Anything else?"

"It's a good day for a sauna," Virtutis grumbled.

"A what?" Khan's head tilted, confused.

"You will see. Let's get rid of the archers first." Virtutis extended his arm, dipping his head in respect. "I am grateful for your loyalty."

"The bond is strong." Khan returned the grip. He squeezed firmly, without his usual humor. His eyes flooded with sincerity. "Virtutis, we will prevail. The Roman snake was always going to slither down the pole eventually. The day had to come when we would all meet in the snake pit and battle it out. I will do everything I can to control Medusa's head for you. Then, you cut it off. Bite it off if you have to!"

Virtutis nodded, motivated to do either.

Chipping and chopping sounds in the trees caught Virtutis's attention; they had begun to trim fallen logs.

Virtutis looked at the tree line.

Stoades bounded his way up, ready for instructions.

"We are almost done. What do you want me to do with them?"

"Lay them flat and cover them midway down the slope. When I give the word, you will need to use them to strike at the shield wall like you did in training."

Virtutis looked back at the road.

"But first, we must stop the Romans. After you position the logs, take the runners around to where the last of the wagons will enter the valley. When you see the opportunity, get control of the carriages, get them burning, and ram the archer's formation from the back so they scatter. We will try to stop them from forming to organize their strikes. Take two men with you to hold shields for protection while you ride. Once you get close to the legion, get out of there and back to higher ground. Observe, plan, and reinforce if you need to." Virtutis considered his plan in more detail. "Where do you think the Romans last camped?"

"I'd say they last camped two days ago. And the last watering hole would have been a day from here, so they would be almost out of water in their waterskins. Only the water in the reserves would be left."

"And knowing the Roman command," Virtutis added with a scoff, "they would try to get them through the valley without stopping because the terrain wouldn't favor them."

"I agree. Here they would be at their weakest; it's no-man's-land, there is nothing but snakes and scorpions," Stoades affirmed.

Virtutis nodded, then placed his hand on Stoades' shoulder.

"You will lead the timing of the attack. When you strike, so do we." Virtutis held no quiver in his voice. "If we are being slaughtered, run."

"Sir, my place is here with you," Stoades said, calm, self-assured. "It is my oath."

"You no longer have an oath with me," Virtutis said. "Not all of us must die early to favor death's destiny. If you live after this one request, go live your life while you can. We are already on the way to death, no matter if we fight in this battle or not."

"I appreciate your offer." Stoades lifted his eyebrows. "But I am already resolved in the world. Besides, what would I do? Be a runner for the Romans?"

Virtutis's cheeks wrinkled in a smile.

Stoades took a breath. "And who knows how many innocent people these men are destined to kill if we don't stop them first."

The comment swayed Virtutis's own personal vendetta to hold even more purpose. "Truth. There is not much time. Take the men you need and do what you must."

"Sir." Stoades nodded. Turning quickly, he hand-picked men on the run, soon disappearing.

With the sound of fast-moving feet, Mercalis approached.

His posture was broken, still suffering greatly from his laceration.

"Are you going to live?"

"Yes. I am fine. It is just uncomfortable. Every time I straighten, it seems to rip it open again." His face grimaced with pain, trying to pull his shoulders back. "I will be better if we see tomorrow."

Virtutis had invested greatly in the skinny assassin, with good reason. He was resilient and composed.

"If I am to fall here," Virtutis confided, "do not hesitate to carry out the plan. Save my sons."

Mercalis flinched, his cheek in pain, as he extended his arm.

"The bond is strong."

Virtutis reduced his normal grip in a gentle reply.

"The bond is strong. I just wanted you to know that I am grateful for you."

"And I for you."

Over Mercalis's shoulder, Virtutis noticed his men gathering on the ridge.

"Go with Khan," he requested. "We will see the outcome of this soon enough."

Virtutis looked over his men. The battle-worn soldiers stood, eager for orders.

A pressure came and went through Virtutis's chest.

A deep breath released some tension.

He studied the few clouds blowing by quickly, looking for a sign.

Embracing the sun's heat, he relaxed.

Augustus came to mind, his enthusiasm and naiveness of war.

"I am afraid, Father," he said. "I am afraid we will have to kill them all!"

Rolling his shoulders back and popping his chest forward, he cracked between his shoulder blades.

He rubbed his hands over, then separated them with a flick, scattering dirt like an invisible blessing, releasing the past and future he bought upon the present.

Clearing his passage to death.

This pit is where he was destined to encounter something he knew was a pinnacle.

Firmly, he gathered his shield and spear and walked toward his men on the hill.

The wind gusted at his back, a messenger from the gods sent to carry his orders.

"Today, you must fight with a deep, dark hunger. But!" He waited for the wind to blow his message stronger. The rasp in his voice added strain to their cause. "We also need to be patient enough to make decisions that will determine our fate by using our intelligence. First, we must create mayhem, forcing the legion to close their walls hard and fast. Once they are closed, do not continue to fight. Harass them! Use rocks if you must. Once they have formed their defense, do not let them open and gain high ground!"

He gripped his shield, his voice becoming husky, deep.

"There will be archers. We must eliminate them as soon as we can. Leave none alive. Stoades will find a way to scatter them from their cover."

Virtutis pointed to the center of the men, sweeping his spear to the right.

"From you outward, you will be responsible for the archers. Divide yourselves evenly, half on this side and the other on the opposite side of the valley entrance. Remain hidden until the time is right. Kill the archers, take their bows and arrows, then retreat to high ground. If the legion's wall wants to peak, fire arrows into the opening."

Virtutis looked over to the other half.

"The rest of you hide from midway by the road. You must keep the legion occupied until we gain control. After that, hold your ground and wait for more orders. We will have our way with these Roman bastards once and for all!"

Virtutis could feel the wind increase its pressure on his neck. His stomach churned with the thought of the general, the betrayal. His mouth was dry and gritty from the climb, becoming raw the more he increased his volume, his throat sounding harsher.

"Up here, we are greeted with a gentle breeze and comfort of homeward winds."

He tried to swallow, but a thickness formed in his mouth, motivating more mercilessness in his voice. He gripped his spear with all his strength, pointing to the bottom of the valley.

"Down there, there is no wind. It will be hotter than Hades. You will boil while you wait for the chance to fight. But know this! For every second you suffer, we will make them suffer tenfold. On this day, we will bleed them dry, one way or another. We will walk from this snake pit, dangling a dead eagle by its feet."

The men stood tall.

They refrained from yelling, the stakes too high. They all knew their actions had become louder than any battle cry.

"You are all good loyal men. I have no doubt you will do what is right. Get into position early. Hide well. Stay off your feet while you can. When the time is right, there must be no hesitation!"

The wind stopped.

A shift of tension hit his chest.

Something was coming.

He had to finish what he needed to say.

"Remember! When you strike your sword, make it count! We are outnumbered four to one. If you are going to die, take as many with you as you can!"

Their energy became restless.

"While some wolves seek the safety of the night and howl at the moon, let us be the wolves who engulf the sun!"

Virtutis lowered his head, listening. What he heard was beyond human recognition.

He snapped his head to the side, cracking his neck.

"Go." He glared over his men. "Now!"

The men scattered into the valley, slipping behind boulders, bushes, and trees. They hid in gullies and tall grass along the roadside. From above, Virtutis could see their shapes, paused, ready.

He took one last look over the surrounding mountains before descending into a pit that would hold an armlock of wills, his only real advantage. Surprise.

Down the hill, closer to the road, Virtutis saw a large rock half covered by a small bush.

His approach was silent so as not to stir any creature, big or small.

One of his men lay close to his position. He looked back with a nod.

A hard realization hit Virtutis. The man's face, he did not recognize nor know his name.

Was he so far removed from his men with the occupation of the general and the seventh centurion?

What else had he missed?

In the sweltering heat, prior to the biggest battle of his life, Virtutis realized how self-consumed he'd become.

Virtutis placed his spear down. He whistled quietly, getting the man's attention; lifting his waterskin, he threw it soft and precise, landing on the man's chest as he turned upwards.

The man guzzled what he could, wanting to throw it back, but Virtutis held up his hand, refusing its return. Not risking any more disturbances.

Keeping his diligence, Virtutis listened hard, looking at the sun lifting higher and more powerful in the sky.

Slowly maintaining his hidden vantage, he checked around the boulder and down the valley for movement.

Heatwaves began to sway, and he knew his men would suffer in a way few could tolerate.

He scanned the ridges for Roman runners.

Nothing.

Stoa came to the forefront of his mind. He reminisced of a day by the river under the heat of summer; they had paused their training to drink and talk.

"Stoa, there is no other sensation like the dance of death. Dealing with death is man's greatest quest. Eventually, you will face the Black Wolf alone. No one will be there to protect you. He's been waiting since the day you were born. He will use whatever fear you have living inside you. The revenge you seek, and uncontrolled anger, will bring you to his cause. He wants you to come closer; he also wants to invoke fear of death."

Not forgetting his priority, Virtutis pushed himself forward into a crouch, looking around the boulder, scanning the valley again.

A heatwave from the sun hit them more intensely.

"They will be here soon," Virtutis muttered to himself, returning to his spot.

He contemplated more of the conversation with Stoa and how it reiterated his own attitude toward his situation.

"The way of the warrior is to accept death, to understand that each moment we are stepping closer to it. I've seen many brave men dance in the fires of the wolf's footprints." Virtutis remembered looking deep into Stoa's eyes, having his full attention. "One thing is for sure, the Black Wolf will hit you; he will knock you down. Because that's what happens to us all. He will climb upon your chest, forcing you to smell the stench of his breath. You will feel his weight crushing your ability to breathe. Threatening to feast on your flesh, he will want to intimidate you; that's his role in life's final acts before death. When the Black Wolf looks down at you, into your eyes, you will taste his drool dripping into your mouth. Swallow it like it was your own. Become a part of him. Keep your wits about you. Remember, while we accept that death is coming, do not accept the manner in which it arrives so easily. While he opens his jaws to bite, he will tilt his head and close his eyes for a second. He will shift his weight." Virtutis had stabbed his words with fierce eyes at his son. "You will be able to take a breath. Take the air. Find a way out. Twist. Weave. Cut and stab. Move. Get to your feet and fight. Do not stop. Search for a way out. Live. Understand?"

"Yes. Yes, I do, Father," Stoa had replied.

"Son, few men use their brains under pressure. Fewer people have the capacity to navigate their emotion close to death." Virtutis had rubbed his hand over his head. "It is a journey I am still trying to understand myself. Now get up, and let's drill. Defend. Attack. Defend. Attack."

Virtutis was jolted from his memory by the general's face.

Would killing him earlier have changed the outcome? Either way, if he lived through today, General Lucio would be a dead man.

The sound of a hawk echoed through the valley. Virtutis's pulse became intense. He peeked toward the entrance.

Three Roman runners came sprinting into the open. One stayed on the road while the other two split up over the terrain.

If any of his men were discovered, the plan would fail.

With the distance between Virtutis and the road, he was of no use to get to the runner.

He crawled on his belly, closer, hoping his men would eliminate the threat.

The runners on either side of the hill disappeared without a sound.

Alone, the scout on the road stood, looking for his companions.

He shielded his eyes from the sun, looking up into the ridges.

He turned and twisted around.

Like a relaxed rag, he dropped to his knees and to his side. The distance making it look gentle, almost peaceful.

Virtutis's heart pounded.

One of his men had thrown a dagger deep into the scout's upper back, taking the air from his lungs.

"Get to him, finish him," Virtutis muttered in frustration.

A knife in the back is not enough to kill a man. If he screams, the plan is ruined.

From the cover of a side ditch, a black figure crawled onto the road, sprawling over top of the victim. They smothered the scout's mouth with one hand, the other holding the knife in place so as not to spill blood.

Unseen pressure filled the valley from a hidden audience. An audience whose lives depended on the smooth removal of the dead. In silence, the black shadow quickly dragged the man off the road and up behind a boulder.

Relieved, Virtutis checked the entrance.

A sparkle hit the top of the road.

The gold eagle, high on its standard, announced the entrance of Roman presence.

Virtutis shook his head, swallowing a thick thirst, his heart pounding, refusing to be intimidated by an eagle that has delivered decades of destruction.

Careful to maintain his advantage, he crawled back into cover, kneeling, preparing his spear.

His forearm pulsed beneath the three deep cuts.

Cuts that reminded him that unresolved revenge is a labyrinth that can quickly descend below dignity. And without finishing off the very threats to the lives of the ones he loved, the dignity and virtues, he knew he had no chance of survival. His quest shifted from the fascination of death, to the protection of life.

Spartan ancestry set his blood on fire.

A defiant, deep growl from the back of his throat broke its whisper to the gods.

"Today, no eagles will survive this pit."

CHAPTER 28

Virtutis clutched his shield, bending his wrist as much as the tight straps allowed. It cracked a familiar crack, releasing tension in the joint. Affirming a war-torn comfort, he strapped it over his back. He took one last look over his battered spear, and with care, he ran his fingertips over the nicks and rivets of past battles before he started his assault.

Slow and precise, he crawled, working a way around the boulder, making sure he did not unsettle any dust. Lifting his head, he surveyed the land between his position and the road, trying to judge the time it would take to deliver a strike.

Roman standards shone high, carried by a centurion on a white horse, closely followed by cohorts of the legion. Unaware, they were not battle-ready. In a long progression, they marched four abreast. They stomped in time, grinding over the ground like an impenetrable manmade machine. A grind that caused an involuntary scoff from the back of Virtutis's throat.

When the legion reached halfway through the valley, the archers appeared.

Virtutis laid prone counting—over sixty archers walked four abreast. He dipped his head to relieve the tension in his neck. Closing his eyes briefly, he hoped for the wagons, wishing for an easy target somewhere amongst the enemy. He opened his eyes to a scorpion walking on the ground in front of his nose. He waited until it passed under his armpit before lifting his head to oxen pulling wagons over the ridge and into the valley.

The corners of his mouth broke into a smile that narrowed his eyes as he scanned the entire progression back and forth. Paused in anticipation, he held his breath, counting on Stoades to strike when the first three carriages made their way to the top of the hill. It would give them a downhill advantage of speed that would scatter everything in their way.

The rhythm of men marching kept its echo through the valley. The Romans were almost three quarters of the way through the valley. Frustration and anticipation started to seep their way into Virtutis's veins.

"Come on, brother," he whispered, looking down at the hard clay sand, resting his neck briefly again.

With a blink, he cleared his eyes, seeing the last wagon come to a subtle halt, then start moving again. The next in front stopped and started. From the distance, there were only small pauses from the carriages, but enough for Virtutis to know the plan had started.

The progression of the Roman machine was almost about to start its climb out of the valley when the wagons burst into flames, turning it into an eye of a volcano.

Virtutis exploded to his feet to the thundering of his men's voices, sending a shock down the valley. Men with intentions beyond that of a common soldier roared, their voices no longer silent.

Virtutis's feet raced over the hard rocky terrain as the hillsides swarmed with the black shadows of his men moving directly at their targets. Trusting his feet, he glanced toward the ridge in the road; Khan had created a barricade of shields that looked unformidable.

Adrenaline peaked while Virtutis pumped air in and out through his mouth. The wagons picked up speed. The closer he came, the more arrows started to sail in all directions, forcing his senses to be fully alert.

The sound of stones on shields rang true as the legion's ranks closed hard, protecting themselves from a hailstorm of rocks. The move, as predicted, left the archers unprotected, forcing them to scatter.

Within seconds, Virtutis was sprinting by the roadside past the Roman wall, uninterested in attacking the defensive legion. He needed to sever the archers from gaining protection, or organized arrows of Hades would hail on their heads.

Shield braced in front; adjusting his spear to the ready, he gained speed.

His men pounded to taunt the closed Romans from the front and sides.

Zzzzzzzttt! An arrow whistled past his head.

Zzzzttt! Another scraped his unprotected calve.

Tat! Tat! More bounced off his shield.

The closer he got, the harder each arrowhead became against his shield, jolting his arm against his chest. Defensive, he ducked his head for cover. Bracing his shoulder, he launched himself into a screaming mass of confused archers.

Hitting something solid, the impact opened his body; arrows and short swords came from all directions. He defended, pulling back slightly, adjusting the grip on his spear, gaining balance. Attacking, he stabbed at red-covered armored bodies, spinning in a fluid motion, striking with no mercy.

The ground shook under his feet like the gods had cracked the earth.

Whack!

His shield was hammered by a force that blew him off his feet so fast he was unable to control his body. Landing on his back, his head crashed against the hard ground, twisting his neck awkwardly.

The back of his skull burned before darkness folded over him, rendering him unable to console any manner of self-protection.

Blinking with stinging eyes, he tried to swallow, but dirt gritted against his tongue, its taste making his throat dry. He coughed, the jolt making his ears ring. He focused on his awareness that grew to hear men scream. He had somehow ended up face down in the dirt.

Unknown feet scuffled around him. Unknown feet meant he was vulnerable; he had to move. With a heavy head, he widened his eyes, forcing them to life. He flexed his hands, then his feet. The back of his head pounded.

The familiar warm sensation of his blood had crept over his shoulder. He shook his head lightly, it made him feel heavy, and darkness threatened its cloak; he resisted.

Get up! Get up now! Move!

He forced himself, staggering, to his hands and knees. The position made blood rush over his head into his eyes. He balanced, wiping his face with his forearm, and snapped his vision around.

My body will have to manage.

He crawled, fumbling for the security of his shield. Gripping it in a crawl, he searched for his spear. It was nowhere to be seen.

Unable to attack, he drew his dagger as another force hit, tossing him up in the air with a thunderous grunt. He landed on his back. Only one beast could have that power and rage.

Oxen!

Unsure, with blurry vision, he located what looked like a ditch. He rotated to his stomach and exploded forward, diving shield first, then he rolled, pulling it over him facing upward.

Peering out from below his defensive position, another powerful beast burst past him, pulling a wagon in flames. The chaos he had intended for the Romans had turned against him. The gods favor no beast nor man in battle; only the skilled live above their will, he reminded himself. There is no passage to death that is certain.

Virtutis gathered breath. It tasted like dust and smoke amongst the screams and clashes of metal that rattled a familiar rhythm.

Enough waiting!

Pivoting a hand behind, keeping his shield in front, he buried his dagger knuckle first into the earth. He propped his opposite leg in base, shifting his free leg underneath his hips; he lifted to a crouched stance, darting his eyes for an advantage. He scanned once more for his spear that remained somewhere in the chaos.

Zzzz-tat Zzzz-tat!

Arrows ricocheted off his shield. Two bowmen fired and entered into the Roman wall.

For the plan to work, he had to cut the archers off. Virtutis exploded toward the rear of the wall, filled with recovering archers. Colliding with a thud, the impact knocked over an archer. He stepped over his body, covering them both with his shield, stabbing under the archer's chin with his dagger.

Zzzzzzt! An arrow zipped past his ear. Staying here meant certain death. Darting forward, he hammered his shield at an archer about to let loose, throwing him off balance. He fell face down. Seeing an exposed leg, Virtutis stabbed deep behind his thigh. The archer turned and bellowed a screech as Virtutis pounded his head with his shield, caving in the archer's face.

Pulling the shield back, he looked down to check his strike as more blood began to pour past Virtutis's eyes, blurring his vision. He wiped his face again, then ducked backward to defend any potential attacks. He had to get out of the chaos to gain visibility of the battle; he had to command.

He moved through the battle as bodies thudded, and men grunted, lashing steel upon steel.

Archers dropped around him. Some crawled, some screamed for mercy, others were dead on their feet before they hit the ground.

He had to push through the middle to higher ground. With his shield, he hammered, spun, and launched himself forward. He cut and stabbed his dagger, making the most of opportunities on the way to the opposite side of the road.

Like breaking free from a river's current, he broke free from the confusion and scrambled to higher ground, turning his back on the mayhem.

Zzzzzztat!

An arrow just missed his head, and another hit the inside of his shield; someone was targeting him from behind. He re-gripped the shield, placing it over his shoulder for protection.

Zzzzzztat! Zzzzztat!

Arrows meant for his back deflected and fell away.

Making sure the hill above was clear, he spun the shield back, turning at the same time, kneeling for cover.

Zzzzzztat! Zzzzztat! Zzzzzztat! Zzzzztat! More arrows meant to end him hit and ricocheted away.

Under cover, he wiped more blood from his face with his forearm. There was silence behind his shield; the arrows had suddenly stopped.

He poked his head out to see his men zig-zagging their way over the road and up the hillsides. Some Roman archers had given up their backs in an attempt to kill him, breaking the fortitude of their defense. His men cut them down.

Now able to survey the valley, he summed up the battle; to the left, smoke smoldered from burning debris from the wagons as two oxen bellowed, caught halfway up the hill with a flaming cart behind them. To the right, the Romans controlled their position, remaining closed and defensive. In the middle, dead archers littered the valley road.

As planned, his men began to form on all four sides of the wall. From a distance, they threw rocks, while others swiftly scavenged bows and arrows off the dead. The plan, until now, had worked in some capacity. But almost a quarter of his men lay wounded or dead.

Virtutis knew he held control of the battle for the meantime, but that could shift at any moment. He pulled up his shield, covering his front, and stood in order to see more.

A blurred lone figure ran across the road, heading straight for him. He pulled his dagger back, ready to throw. His vision cleared; it was Stoades.

"It worked! It worked!" Stoades shouted.

Virtutis could not respond. His eyes became blurry again as he lost focus; the earth shifted beneath him. He collapsed backward, hitting the dirt. His head pounded, and he blinked in pain as the blue sky turned black from the corners of his vision.

Liliana pulled at his hand, her soft eyes turning, determined. "Virtutis," she demanded. "Virtutis. Get up."

Blinking his eyes open, Virtutis realized Stoades had him seated, supporting his back.

"You were on the other side, brother," Stoades said in a quiet, reassuring voice. "Your head is cracked. We have to bandage it to stop the bleeding."

Virtutis nodded as he closed his eyes briefly, opening them to the sound of ripping fabric that the pain exploded in his head even more. He wanted payback, but Stoades held the back of his neck. "Stay with me, brother. You have to stay upright," he insisted.

Virtutis could feel the earth shifting again. The gentle pressure of the bandage started on his forehead and slowly wrapped around the back. Then came a hard tightening, and with it, a sharp pain that shot through his skull, forcing tears from his eyes.

"Virtutis, breathe. Breathe," Stoades coaxed.

Virtutis pulled air through his nose, forcing his brain to work, forcing clarity in his plan, wanting desperately to finish this.

He cleared his eyes. "Help me up."

Stoades gripped him by the forearm, standing close by his side.

The Romans were trapped in the middle of the road, unable to move without breaking formation.

Intolerable pain shocked his skull. The valley turned gray, losing its color.

On his feet, he floated as voices came and went.

"Is he dead?" Khan asked, concerned.

"No," replied Stoades. "He's here, and then he's not."

"What do we do?" Khan asked.

Strong light fluttered through blinking eyes, and pain forced his hand over his face.

He found his voice through an array of dirt and debris, making his words strained and husky.

"H-hold the Romans. Get the trunks ready." Darkness threatened his consciousness again. Determined, he fought it away. "B-batter the wall and send arrows when they breach. Make them stay tight." Pain radiated to the base of his skull, forcing him to close his eyes. "Khan, this is the sauna. Make them suffer."

"Ha! Sauna!" Khan yelled, elated, but his voice grated Virtutis's very soul. Then there was the scrapping of Khan's footsteps. "I get it!" he yelled as his voice faded away into the distance.

A familiar hand held him upright by his elbow.

"Rest if you must. We are in control," Stoades assured.

Reality seemed to disappear.

Pain pounded his strength away.

"Virtutis?" Stoades called him from the darkness. "Water, drink some water." He placed a leather pouch to his lips. He had fallen again.

The rejuvenation of fresh water filled his mouth.

"Easy, sip it," Stoades instructed.

Energy started to crackle through his body. He focused through watering eyes.

Looking down, his spear lay at his feet.

"Someone found my spear?"

"It was on the road. You were hit by a loose carriage, then almost trampled by the oxen. You are lucky you're alive. With a little more luck, the carriages would have smashed into the wall as well."

Spartan instinct surged. The fight flooded its way back into Virtutis's veins. He stood with Stoades assistance.

With strained eyes, he studied the Romans. Blinking constantly, regaining long-range focus.

"Stoades, they won't hold for long. We have to start attacking them now, or they will break for higher ground."

Loud lumber battered the wall. Khan had started attacking the opposite side with trunks and threw anything that burned at the Roman shields, increasing the heat surrounding them.

Arrows stripped from dead Romans flew, attempting to breach the tightly shielded wall.

In the middle of the man-made fortress, a single shield slid slightly open and closed quickly.

Virtutis grunted. "They are planning a move." He opened his hand, keeping his eyes fixated on the wall. "Give me my spear."

Stoades placed the spear in his outstretched hand.

Pain shocked his head.

Reaching for his shield, he used its stability to stand.

Stoades's firm grip steadied him from under the elbow.

"We must cut out their eyes," Virtutis grunted.

He stumbled, careful not to shake his head as he focused his eyes on the gap in the wall, opening and closing.

Pulling a double pump of oxygen through his nose, he adjusted his spear like a javelin and commanded his uncertain legs. He hyper-focused on a small gap between the shields.

Blocking out the pain, he broke into a slow downward run.

He cocked back the spear, adjusting his stride, guiding the spear backward, and balancing mid-weight of the wooden shaft.

The shields opened again. Using fluid power, Virtutis launched. The spear glided off his fingertips as he finished the touch with a caress, letting it fly through. Virtutis stumbled, then regained his balance, watching as it cut and rotated, sailing effortlessly through the air.

The spear spun with precise timing over the distance, the tip severing between the small space of the two shields. The sharpness of the blade plunged into his prey's eye. The weight of the shaft smashed the man's skull, jolting him backward.

Screamed orders and panicked movements closed the gap.

Virtutis turned his head to listen, searching for the result. An eerie hush blanketed the valley.

The wall reshuffled again.

In a slow downward walk, Virtutis studied the Roman wall.

Dirt crunched behind him under fast footsteps as Stoades arrived at his side. "They are panicking."

Virtutis's vision was fading again, making him stagger.

Stoades caught him by the arm, helping him reaffirm his stride.

"Your shield. Here, take my sword," Stoades demanded, placing the handle in his hand. "We must finish them."

The grip of the sword handle and the familiar comfort of his shield ignited Virtutis's core.

Stoades was right; it was time to end this.

Walking onto the road, Virtutis and Stoades were soon joined by a small band of his men. From over Virtutis's shoulder, the Zzztat-Zzztat of recovered arrows hit shields, forcing the Romans tighter.

"Bring the trunks onto the road. It is time to open these bastards up."

Runners broke away laterally with the orders.

Grunt and snort came from behind.

Oxen.

Initially startled from his last encounter, Virtutis readied his sword, twisting into a crouch to see Khan walking behind two huge beasts bound by a yoke. He struggled to hold the reins but maintained a smile of conquest while the oxen trotted and groaned.

"The ox and his oxen have arrived!" Khan yelled.

Virtutis welcomed the sight, raising his sword high with a growl of attack and turning back toward the Romans.

Energy filled his mob of vengeful men.

Virtutis sparked final battle orders. "Hammer them! Do not stop! Put power behind the trunks! Let loose every arrow we have. When they break, we scatter them up the hill, so they have to fight upwards to the rest of our men. Each man must wage his own war."

Men flooded past him.

Trunks rammed each barrage more intensely and more concisely. Arrows and rocks hammered any shifting space.

"Stoades, get fire from the wagons. Find a way to burn Hades at their backs; we want them off the road and onto unstable ground. Throw it, roll it; it does not matter. Burn this pit."

"Sir!" Stoades disappeared up the hillside.

Virtutis stood on the road, waiting for the right time, waiting for his men to soften the wall. A thick stench of smoke wafted its way over the wall.

Khan had somehow covered the oxen's heads. Blind, their agitation increased. Virtutis knew he could not control the beasts much longer.

Virtutis had regained his vision. He placed his hand over his neck—the blood had begun to dry, so he moved the bandage higher on his head.

Twisting his head from side to side and with a subtle jolt, he managed to crack his neck for relief. It shot pain across his forehead, but the pain was tolerable.

Flames crept high on the opposite side of the Roman wall. The sight made Virtutis open his mouth wide, stretching his jaw like he was possessed by the Black Wolf himself. The veins on his arms throbbed. He lifted Stoades' sword and let it slowly fall forward. Giving the signal for an all-out final attack.

"Hee-ya!" Khan yelled. The cracking of whipping reins drove them on.

The sound of Khan's yell and the bellowing oxen seemed to energize the attack even more.

Khan raced past, running behind, holding the reins, almost losing his footing. Virtutis and his men instinctively spread to give space, giving chase behind the battering ram as it passed.

The oxen drove through the Roman's defensive spears, colliding with shields, sending them screaming.

The impact opened space big enough to capitalize on. Now Virtutis would take his chance.

Virtutis focused on the gap in the defense as he broke into a run, covering the ground fast. In a fury, he launched himself deep into the Roman wall. He steadied his feet, standing over fallen bodies cluttering for order. There was a sense of relief, a transcendence into a rage, releasing the suppression of leadership. Now the merciless fight could begin.

He stabbed-sliced everything he could. Spartan ancestry pounded its way out through his sword. Rarely using his shield, he attacked cold-blooded, leaving men dead before they hit the ground.

Khan burst into action at his side, screaming bloody murder, slashing at anything that moved.

The pit had become Hades itself.

With clashes of steel on steel, Virtutis and his men ravaged the Romans from the inside until they finally broke outward. He strode through the battle, severing men's lives and limbs without mercy. Together with Khan, they slaughtered anyone remaining on the road. From the corner of his eye, Romans fled to find easier combat; however, that was not the case.

With little option, some of the surrounding Romans scurried away, only to be met by more of his men waiting on high terrain.

Although Virtutis's men were outnumbered, the crimson tide crumbled, succumbing from the chaos and psychological disadvantage. The battle was quickly coming to a halt, the orchestra of two sides sliding into the silence of a single victor.

Covered in blood, the thirst for vengeance lingered in his mouth; Virtutis stopped without opposition. He roared in frustration, wanting more. Nothing satisfied his unwavering desire for revenge. No matter how many times he turned to attack in all directions, satisfaction did not arrive and relieve his anguish. The familiar shaft of his spear stood, buried in a man's head amongst littered bodies.

He walked slowly, lowering his shield, tempting fate. He wished the dead would wake, so he could finish them off again. He grunted in disappointment as he stood over the dead body that held his spear.

He kneeled over his victim. The tip buried straight into his eye. Placing his sword on the ground, the spear remained standing straight toward the sun, propped up by the weight of the skull.

"He's a pretty dresser, isn't he?" Khan noted, out of breath. "Noble?"

Virtutis studied the Roman's clothes and armor in disgust, controlling his anger.

"I have no idea." Virtutis spat out blood and dirt. "He's more than a soldier; that's for sure."

"The seventh centurion?"

"Could be, but who really knows?" Virtutis could feel his frustration building again. Answers, he wanted answers. Or had he just killed them with his spear?

Khan motioned his sword to two yielding Romans on their knees. "One of them might know."

It was an opportunity Virtutis could not let pass. He stood while letting his voice carry pent-up anger.

"Stop! I want them alive. Bring them here. Now!"

Tussling in resistance, the Romans were dragged under their shoulders on their knees, then thrown in front of the impaled face of their commander. Virtutis kneeled on the opposite side of the dead body, making sure they could see his face. He searched their expressions.

With a closed mouth, Virtutis sucked in his cheeks, rolling around granules of dirt and blood before he swallowed, making his voice rougher still.

"Rome's great centurions," he huffed in a husky tone. "Carrying the oath of death and loyalty. I know you will not break easily. But break you will. You both know there is no escaping death today. I have no problem with you, but I do have questions. Questions you will pay the price for if needed."

Virtutis adjusted the tunic on the dead corpse, then patted over his dead heart, an insinuation of false respect.

"Who is this man?" He paused. "What is his name?"

The two Roman prisoners remained silent. Virtutis tilted his head sideways, wondering what was passing through their heads.

"Khan, put a dagger to their throats. Hold them still."

Khan stepped forward, unsheathing two daggers from his belt, each hand placing pressure with his blade under their chins, ready to slice throats. Virtutis's men quickly secured the Romans' arms, so they could not retreat.

Still, the captives did not flinch.

"How well Roman soldiers face death? Your sweet commander would be very aroused at the effort, especially with you two being on your knees. Don't you think?"

Virtutis's face dropped, and he signaled to his closest men.

"You four, take your swords. Place them on the heels of our guests."

The captives shuddered with shortened breaths while swords almost pierced through the soles of their sandals.

Virtutis smiled at their discomfort, focusing on the game of cut and tell. He peered behind their backs, hinting at the swords poised to stab their feet, teasing. The pressure of torture dripped sweat down their foreheads.

"If you live your life on your knees, who needs feet in the afterlife, right?"

Virtutis toyed with the shaft of his spear still dug into the eye of the unknown Roman. It wobbled, not coming unstuck.

"You can choose your fate. Fall forward and cut your own throat, or we can butcher you slowly. It is up to you."

The corners of his mouth lifted in an intentional devious smirk.

He nodded to his men on the heels of the Roman on the right. When the pressure of the swords cut through his feet, he jerked forward toward the dagger, trying to take his own life. An easy death was not what Virtutis had intended for these two.

Like a game, Khan withdrew the dagger from the man's throat, letting him fall face down, as blades of the swords cut through his sandals and deep into earth, pinning him. He screamed in agony while his face was buried into the dead corpse, making the spear shift back and forth.

Virtutis, calm, reached out to stop his spear from wobbling.

"Did you really think I would let you die at your own hand? You have to earn that right. When you are ready, the questions remain."

He knew this small victory was his. In turning the men, the choice of death over torture would be something he could bargain with.

He turned to the other kneeling centurion, so far unscathed.

Virtutis, not wanting to raise his voice over the moaning of his comrade, pushed the feet-impaled Roman's head further into the corpse to muffle the disruption.

"I have higher expectations of you. Who is he? What is his name?"

The Roman broke.

"The pompous prick came out of the general's tent two days ago and assumed command. We do not know who he is." He gulped under the pressure of Khan's blade. "But, know this, Spartan scum. All of Rome is coming for you. Everything you touch in this region is already dead. These lands belong to the empire."

"Dead, is it? Not while I am alive."

"You are the one killing it, Spartan! Rome will flood this land to find you."

"Really?" Virtutis did not believe a word tumbling from his mouth. "A Spartan is of no concern to the empire."

The Roman scoffed, "You raped a princess under the protection of Rome. They want your head."

Virtutis's mind slowed down to catch up with the insinuation. He looked up at the faces of his men. The allegation switched the calm interrogation to releasing the depths of his suppressed anger.

"And who would accuse me of such a crime! The honest, law-abiding general!?"

"It does not matter. Such a crime against Rome is punishable by death. They will hunt all of you down. They will kill you like the Spartan bastard you are!"

"You lie!" Virtutis shouted, but the dirt in his throat turned it even more husky as high blood pressure burst the clot at the back of his head, forcing a hot river of blood to run down his neck, streaming over his shoulder and down his arm.

"Your tongue has a snake wrapped around it! Twisting tight with lies!"

He stood, placing his foot on the dead noble's chest. Gripping his spear, he yanked it free in one motion.

"Let's see where such lies take you in the afterlife?"

Khan stepped aside, no doubt unsure of what was about to happen.

Virtutis took an underhand grip of the spear, grabbed the Roman by the hair, and held the razor-sharp tip at his mouth.

"Open!"

He did not.

"Very well."

The Roman's eyes widened in fear.

All Virtutis could see was the general looking up at him. Bloodied rage trickled down Virtutis's arm, over his hand, and down the spear shaft.

Without bringing the spear back, he punched it forward, breaking through the centurion's teeth. He increased the pressure, continuing to pierce the tip of the spear through his head until the Roman buckled backward over his heels, his body unable to hold resistance. It twitched and fell limp as the spearhead entered the earth below.

Unapologetic, he placed his foot on the man's throat, pulling his spear free, then he spun his spear and whacked the other Roman prisoner on the back with the shaft.

"Khan, turn him over," Virtutis ordered.

His men ripped the swords from his feet as Khan buckled him backward, slamming him on the ground. He gasped for air while Virtutis stood over him, his shadow casting long in the late afternoon sun.

"Who is this man? What is his name!"

The Roman shook his head, regaining his breath.

"I do not know!" His eyes grew wide. "Nobody knows!"

"Then what use are you to me?" Virtutis shrugged at Khan. "Take him. Do what you will."

The Roman screamed insults in his final seconds, but it came to an abrupt halt.

Virtutis's mind instantly became fixated on finding the general, wanting to settle the truth. He tried to calm himself to think straight.

He looked up at the valley from the road. Flames still raged, casting a smokey haze. The air changed its direction, uncovering packs of his men who scoured the valley, finishing off any Roman survivors.

Virtutis placed his hand over his shoulder, feeling the mix of wet and crusty dry blood.

"Virtutis. Virtutis?" Stoades called his attention from behind. "Are you good?"

He turned his head, adjusting his eyes to focus on Stoades.

"I am fine." But the pounding in his head had returned. "We have to get out of here soon. We cannot wait."

"Where are we going?" Stoades asked, offering water, but Virtutis declined.

Sharp daggers shot through his forehead, forcing him to close his eyes; the Black Wolf shocked his image in the darkness. He snapped his eyes open, trying to stay composed, forcing himself to continue.

"Back to the river. We must get water and supplies so the men can recover."

"Agreed," Stoades said. "At least it's downhill."

"The sun will set soon. Call Khan."

Stoades placed his hand on his shoulder. "Virtutis, he's already here."

Virtutis blinked his eyes, regaining reality. Where did time go?

"Khan, give the order to move. We cannot stay here."

"And the injured?" Khan asked.

"Find a way to get them out of here." Virtutis cleared his eyes. Smoke wafted in and out of the valley, revealing scenes of sprawled dead bodies while wounded oxen groaned in agony. "The valley is littered with drowning souls," Virtutis said. "No man alive or dead can rest here." An ox groaned again in desperation. "And make sure you take care of the oxen; they do not deserve to suffer."

"Virtutis," Khan said. He held up the golden eagle from the empire's broken staff upside down, swaying it back and forth. "Dead and dangling, sir."

"It is yours, Khan." The eagle was not what he was after. "Do with it as you wish."

Khan snickered. "Oh, I have just the place to put this."

CHAPTER 29

Battle worn and fatigued, Virtutis's legs became less dependable, forcing him to lean upon his spear from time to time as they climbed out of the valley and wound down trails.

"Water?"

"Thank you, Stoades." Virtutis stopped, unable to walk and drink. The water refreshed his mouth, but when it hit his stomach, the urge to vomit made him double over with his arms wrapped around his center.

"Are you well, Virtutis?"

"I am fine," he replied, shaking his head a little. His hearing became sensitive, and he was unimpressed with himself for showing any more signs of weakness. There was a commotion from the valley; he thought he could hear the Black Wolf howl, followed by the snapping of jaws and muffled grows mauling, most likely over flesh. Shrugging it off, he scoffed, knowing it was all in his head.

"They are dead men anyway," he reassured himself.

"Excuse me?" Stoades looked at him, confusion knitting his brows.

"Nothing. We must move on." Virtutis squinted, making sure it was Stoades, no longer able to discern reality from figments of his imagination.

"The runners and I will run ahead and assess the trails and valley."

"Thank you, Stoades. We will follow soon enough."

After hours of slow moving, his calf began to swell and bleed from the arrow wound. It was a welcome pain away from his head.

At the entrance to the plains, the smell of last night's fires still burned.

Out of the darkness came Stoades, slowing his run. Not trusting his eyes at first, Virtutis adjusted his spear. He shifted his stance, edgy and uncomfortable, knowing he was losing his usual instincts. Before he could refocus properly, Stoades was in front of him, looking concerned while delivering his report.

"There are still Roman bodies scattered through the plains. Should we cut over to the trees and take the trails?"

Virtutis bit his lip to sharpen his mind before responding. "The fastest way to the upper river is through the plains. Our men need rest. The dead are departed by now. We go through the valley."

"Sir," Stoades responded, uncomfortable. "I will lead us through."

In a tight line, they walked through the battlefield, submerged in the dead of night. The air shifting thinner with the early stages of rotting flesh. In the distance, animals chattered in excitement, eager to satisfy their hunger, erupting in the occasional fighting frenzy.

Virtutis and his men remained silent, passing through the maze of soulless bodies. The last hill held a type of security for Virtutis. Far from the pit and away from the plains behind him, the familiar ground held essence, healing. The tension in his head relieved itself enough for him to stop and appreciate the starry skyline without the earth spinning while men walked past, slow, exhausted.

Uncontrolled and erratic, his stomach sank in overwhelming loneliness of missing his sons. Such thoughts were that of a man dying, and he knew it. The quest of death's passage, the Black Wolf, and revenge against the general were suddenly dwarfed by the thought of losing his children. He had never before felt such emotion.

"Brother, we are almost there," Khan said, coming to a stop. "What's the plan?"

Virtutis brushed his new vulnerability to the back of his mind.

"It's not over. We need to meet as soon as the men organize camp. Call Stoades and anyone who wishes to attend."

Fighting to stay in reality and juggling new conspiracies, Virtutis pointed to a clearing under the trees, selecting a meeting spot. "We will meet there. Bring me water and some of your stew."

Khan smiled and walked away.

Virtutis rubbed the front of his head; there was a large ball from being battered.

Khan's stew? I must be dead or dying.

Virtutis sat with his men around the comfort of a warm fire for the first time in days. He peeled dried blood from his neck, then cleared his throat, still tasting dirt even though he had washed his mouth out countless times. He ran his tongue over his newly chipped tooth.

"The allegations about me raping the princess are not true. If anyone here wishes to question, they may."

Silence was the answer he had hoped for, but he searched through the flames for eyes of uncertainty.

"If any of you wish to leave, you may sever your oath in peace. None of you are bound by anything. If you wish to fight more, you will have to join the barbarians. I would say Benductos is the future of the hinterlands and mountains. If you wish to return to your homelands, go over the springs and go by sea. If you go inland, you will be slaughtered. The Roman valuables we have captured are yours to divide and share. It should be more than enough to maintain your lives for years. I want nothing of it."

Tension from his injury and the quick contemplation of his plans forced him to crack his neck.

"There is no telling if the Roman centurion spoke the truth about the empire intending plans to hunt for me, but we cannot take the risk. There are only so many surprises and tactics we can use against greater numbers. I chose to confront the Romans in the pit because they would have destroyed everything standing in their way. If we did not meet them early, they would have destroyed everything toward the springs, including us. But now, a surprise is not an advantage, and the last thing we need is to give them information about our position. If we can, we must distract them away from here to give the tribes of the hinterlands more time."

"Sir," Khan interjected.

Virtutis nodded, glad for the time to rest his throat.

"I agree. Misinformation is the best way. Send messengers, spread rumors, and even attack away from this region."

"Yes. But we cannot stay here." Virtutis became sterner. "We must disband."

Men shuffled, confused, and muttered amongst themselves.

Stoades lifted his arm to speak.

Virtutis raised his hand, calling for calm. "Brother?"

"Is it better to know for sure if the Romans are coming? We can get more information, then we can make better decisions?"

"I understand. But whatever the truth is, by the time we know it, we will be dead. If any runners are caught returning to us, we will lose the information, and we remain in the same position, waiting. This is not just a battle we are entering; we are entering into a greater world of deceit and lies that would take months, if not years, to understand. Even then, our chances are slim to none."

Flames flickered and embers launched from the fire.

"He is right," Khan stated. "We have no idea what we are facing. But, is it not better that we stay together?"

"Yes. In an ideal world," Virtutis agreed. "The only way we can survive is if we grow our force fast enough to counter the Romans. But we also become more vulnerable. It will take time to make deals with the barbarians. Apart from Benductos' men, we will have to risk with people we do not know. We are not large enough to not suffer from internal sabotage."

Khan shook his head, scoffing in agreement. "Truth. The Romans will turn the best of men into traitors with the promise of a kiss, only to have them bent over a log without a head."

His comment caused an uneasy silence.

Virtutis sensed the tension, and men shuffled uncomfortably with the notion of a traitor amongst them.

"If I stay, it will only bring more death and destruction to innocent people who have no idea what they are in the middle of." He coughed, clearing his throat, the force jolting pain over his forehead. He squinted across the fire. A mirage of the general seated, looking back at him, appeared. Virtutis's veins ignited. He blinked hard, then returned to reality; the general's image disappeared.

"We all know the general has set us up from the beginning. He had no intention of letting us live for long. We have been in a game since the beginning, I am going to find out who I killed in the pit."

Virtutis found that by letting himself speak freely, a plan also started to emerge.

"If any of you wish to stay with me, I am taking ten men. I am going to kill General Lucio. The rest of you can either stay with Stoades and join Benductos, or you may be relieved of your duty in peace." Virtutis scanned his men's faces. "This is my request. Not my order. I must do what I must do. You are all free to do as you choose."

The stillness of his men concerned him, but they, too, were exhausted and needed to rest.

The fire crackled.

"The truth is. I do not know where my decisions may lead me. All I know is that betrayal comes in many forms, and I do not want to betray any of you with my ignorance of the world. You must find your own causes and your own way."

Over the flames, in the dark of night, the Black Wolf's eyes pierced through the darkness. Uneasy, riddled with his personal discomfort and the mounting pressure of survival, Virtutis continued to close the meeting.

"If there is anything anyone wants to say, now is the time."

The men remained still, each contemplating their own futures.

"Very well." Virtutis stood, his legs shaky from concussion and fatigue. "Brothers, I am grateful for our passage together. Gods willing, we will not reunite again, and you will live a life of peace."

Exhausted, he could not think anymore. He walked into the night to find a place of solitude. He headed up into the trails, where he found a clearing and sparked a small fire.

"How is your head?" came a voice from the darkness.

Even though Virtutis recognized Mercalis's voice, it startled him enough to reach for his spear.

"It's pounding," he replied. "How is your back?"

"Better, it has stopped bleeding, but still tight." Mercalis entered the fire's light, his head covered by his cloak. He removed the hood, his face withdrawn, pale.

"We do not have much time," Virtutis warned. "Follow us tomorrow and wait for the outcome with the general. If I die, you will return to my sons and tell them the truth of what you have seen. Tell them the quest for death and freedom and the ambition to be an accomplished man can be found behind a plow just as much as on the battlefield. But they must still carry the ways of the warrior." He coughed. "If I live, we will stay the course." A heaviness fell over his eyes. "Now leave me. I must rest."

Totally exhausted, he did not see Mercalis leave. He pulled his cloak over his battle-worn body; the dark night closed in, and the flames died away. His eyes fluttered, knowing he should have sought a safer form of solitude.

Unprotected, he fell into a deep sleep.

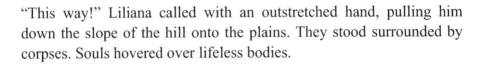

"This way!" Liliana called with an outstretched hand, pulling him down the slope of the hill onto the plains. They stood surrounded by corpses. Souls hovered over lifeless bodies.

Screams echoed through the valley. The Black Wolf snapped his powerful jaws, crunching men's souls, shaking them from side to side in a fury, rendering them helpless, devouring them whole.

"Virtutis," she echoed. "Here is the key."

She opened her hand over a Roman body.

"Here, you will cut open the door to Rome."

Virtutis jerked awake. Sitting up, confused, he gasped for air. The sudden movement made his head pound and his heart race. He quickly searched to get his bearings; only the familiar flames of a dying fire provided a notion of where he was.

The dream was a sign that made sense. Awkwardly, he forced his weary body to its feet. Struggling to walk at first, his feet carried him back to the main camp.

He listened intently into the night. Khan's snores made him easy to find. He stomped over, hoping the sound of his steps would wake him. It didn't work, and he had to crouch and shake the ox's shoulder.

"Wake up," he said with a gentle shake. There was no response. "Khan, wake up." He shook harder.

Khan gasped for air, and his eyes burst open. He rolled away in panic. "What the hell?"

"It's me," Virtutis assured. "We have work to do. Let's go."

Khan, still in shock, ambled to his feet.

"Where are we going?"

"To scavenge souls," Virtutis replied, stern-faced. Then he smiled, perhaps a little insanely.

Khan rubbed his face with his sleeve, clearing his eyes.

"A moonless night, and we are scavenging souls." He dusted off his arms and legs. "Lucky I am not a superstitious man. And since when did you ever say anything with a smile?"

"Since you knocked over your stew and sat in it."

"Ah? And now a sense of humor?" Khan scratched his head. "This is just plain confusing."

"Let's go before it gets light." Virtutis returned to seriousness.

Vision adjusting to the dark away from the firelight, Virtutis's eyes were straining to focus, but his time-sensitive plan could not wait. Through the cover of night, they scavenged Roman uniforms, weapons, and shields from the dead.

Virtutis looked around; taking advantage of Khan being occupied with stripping down a corpse, he took a knee next to a man with a badly beaten and cut face.

He bent over, whispering quietly, "Forgive me, brother. I know you have already given your life. I mean no disrespect."

Picking up a scattered sword, in a smooth motion, he severed the head. It rolled away as if not wanting to leave its body. Virtutis gathered it calmly, drew his dagger, then proceeded to slice and stab it before placing the head in a shoulder bag. He wondered if the man's soul was offended, and when it was his own time, would his present act of dishonoring a corpse be reprimanded in his final moments.

Virtutis checked to see if Khan had noticed, but he was busy humming his low tunes to keep himself company through their scavenging.

Virtutis blinked his burning eyes as light broke, threatening to shed light on his not-so-honorable plan. He slung the bag over his shoulder and finished collecting what he needed.

He returned, stepping over dead bodies, and dropped a bundle of swords at Khan's feet.

"Not one of the prettiest moments in my life," Khan said

"Nor mine." Virtutis felt equally conflicted. "But it's done now."

"What's next?" Khan yawned.

"We need to select some men who have small injuries that would not stop them from running or fighting. Then, we see how good the general is with a sword in his hand."

"Sounds painful. Everything that involves running ends up painful." Khan nodded his head repeatedly like a happy ox. "I'm ready."

Virtutis walked a small hill to Stoades, who waited for a farewell before leading the rest of the men up through the mountains toward Benductos. He reflected on how well the old reluctant runner embodied leadership with loyalty and how he had shown courage over his fears on numerous occasions. He became a respected warrior and commander in his own right.

He extended his arm to the faithful runner, perhaps for the last time.

"I hope to see you soon, brother. If not, that all may end well with you in this life."

"The bond is, and always will be, strong, prefectus," Stoades replied. "I hope to see you with your sons in the heavens, if not, over some goat stew."

"Thank you, Stoades. I am grateful for our friendship." Virtutis smiled warmly. "And for the stew."

They exchanged a look of respect and brotherhood. Virtutis was proud of their endeavors, proud he had trusted his instincts many months ago.

They held a gentle, authentic stare before Stoades turned his back and parted ways.

"I'll miss you too, you old goat of a man," Khan yelled. "One day, I will teach you how to cook proper stew!"

Stoades did not look back; however, he did puff his arms out to the side and bellowed like an ox.

"You two will never stop, will you?" Virtutis snickered.

"Stop?" Khan said. "He started it with his goat legs and his bald head."

"Are the men ready?"

Khan nodded in the direction behind him as the men assembled, ready for orders.

"Very well," Virtutis said. "Let us pay our General Lucio a visit."

With the morning sun breaking strong through the trees, Virtutis and his men began their descent back to the plains, where weapons and uniforms were quickly distributed.

"You can leave the shields," Virtutis instructed, latching his own shield to his back. "Bring your personal daggers, but carry only Roman helmets and swords. We won't be stopping, so whatever you take, make sure you can carry or strap on. Do not clean the blood off yourselves or the uniforms." With a brief look over his men, knowing he was leading them on a suicide mission, he sucked air through his nose and let it out with a huff. "Khan, you will lead. Let's go."

Khan smiled with pride, but it soon dropped. "Oh, I understand, the slow runner at the front, so no one has to wait."

Virtutis nodded politely.

They started a slow run. As they warmed up, Khan settled into a surprising pace toward the camp.

Virtutis noticed Khan's broad figure looking back from time to time. Focusing became harder as his head throbbed and trickles of blood dripped over his shoulder. Mixing with sweat, making his clothing sticky, it began to rub his skin raw from the poorly fitted Roman uniform. Weight from his weapons and the Roman head in his bag took their toll on his energy. So fatigued, not even vengeance energized him, he let himself slip into another world beyond the physical.

They ran for hours, and hallucinations filled Virtutis's head. He swore he ran side by side with his nemesis, the Black Wolf. But it also created a place where time and pain disappeared, so he did not question more. Rather, he let the wolf reside.

Virtutis did not recognize where he was until he heard Khan's call to stop. They had reached the thick cover of trees just outside the Roman's camp; they had run through the heat of the day.

Khan offered him his waterskin. Virtutis took a sip and poured a little water over his head.

He searched the taut faces of his men. "You." He motioned to the biggest man amongst them. "Take my spear and shield." The man looked confused, unsure why Virtutis would give away his security. Virtutis then drew his dagger and looked at the blue sky above the trees. With a flick of the blade and a slight flinch, he cut a slit above his eye. Blood instantly covered his face and chest. "I will keep my dagger." Without looking, he placed it back in its sheath.

He spat blood, then lifted his shoulder bag up in front of him, offering it to Khan. "In this bag is my head. Be proud; carry it well."

Khan studied it frowning, "I do not want to know."

As Khan lifted the bag from his grasp, Virtutis instantly felt a strange lightness coming over his body, and he could breathe again. Then, he tore his Roman tunic, giving the strip to Khan. "Bandage my face. Then we walk straight to the front gate. Remember, you are Roman. Only remove your helmets if you need to."

With little light entering the bandages, Virtutis walked with his hand on Khan's shoulder.

Underfoot, Virtutis could sense the forest floor change to a dirt road as heavy horse hooves came galloping toward them.

"Halt!" a centurion shouted. "Declare yourselves!"

"We have been defeated by the rebel auxiliary. We are all that's left," Khan replied. "We have walked from the plains in the mountains. Everyone else is dead. We have not had food or water in days."

"What's in the bag?" the guard demanded.

Virtutis could feel the tension rising.

"It is the head of Virtutis," Khan replied.

"Virtutis? Who killed him? Declare yourself!"

"I did," Virtutis announced blindly. "I cut him down like the dog he was, but not before he almost took my eyes."

"Centurion." Khan insisted they kept the game moving. "We need rest. These men are wounded, and this one could go blind if we do not clean his wounds with fresh water."

"Very well." The centurion sounded suspicious. "Most of our men are still re-posting. You will have to attend to yourselves, and there is no one to care for the wounded. Around the back, there are open tents. There is food and water. I will inform the general of your return."

"Centurion," Virtutis called, feeling a wave of emotion, knowing Lucio was here. "Please tell the general I would like to deliver Virtutis's head personally. I am sure I will be justly rewarded."

"Reward? For your duty to Rome? Good luck addressing that with the general!"

The horse scuffed its hoofs with a snort.

"Open the gates!" the guard called.

Khan led Virtutis in a slow, steady walk. Blinded by the bandages, the confinement seemed to calm him. He listened intently to the surrounding sounds.

Khan tried to whisper, but his booming voice strained to be quiet. "We are almost at the tents."

"Make sure you all eat and drink," Virtutis replied. "Bring me water, but keep my face covered."

The coolness of the shade lifted the heat away from Virtutis's head; they must be in a tent.

"Here is a stool." Khan guided him to sit.

He heard the chink of his shield and spear being leaned against the tent pole. He cracked his neck, the darkness under the veil serving him well to rest his eyes and pounding head.

His self-inflicted swollen eye stung, giving him a distraction from the abrasion at the back of his skull. He closed his eyes lightly, focusing, trying to clear his mind as his body begged to rest on the ground.

CHAPTER 30

"In here!" a centurion yelled, followed by a tent flap opening with a slap, breaking Virtutis's moment of peace.

"You! The general will see you now. Bring the head."

Isolated, alone, every sensor burst into life, a surge of adrenaline hit his veins, but Virtutis managed to gather his composure. "Are you talking to me?"

Where did Khan go?

Alone and without his sight, he needed to buy time. "Centurion, I am almost blind and need your help. I cannot walk alone." Virtutis tried to sound weak.

"Where are the others?" the centurion grunted. "I serve Rome, not a blind man with tall tales."

"If I could see, I would tell you where they went." Virtutis still played coy but brushed his hand over his dagger to make sure it was ready if needed. "I am sure they will return soon."

Virtutis regulated his breath, listening for any sign that would reveal how many centurions there were.

Seconds crept passed slow. He wanted to attack but could not risk any uncertain move that would alert the general of his presence.

"Aren't you popular!" Khan entered, breaking the tension. "Six centurions sent to find a blind man. Can I at least give him water first? We can't have him losing his voice as well as his sight."

Virtutis leathered skin grinned underneath the cloth—only six centurions.

"Very well, make it quick." The centurion folded to Khan's request. "Then you both will come with us."

Virtutis felt a small relief, but his hand still laid upon the only thing he could control, his dagger.

"Easy, now," Khan reassured. "I have water for you. Drink slowly."

A cup touched his lips, water flowing instantly, refreshing his brain.

Knowing he still needed to bide his time, calming the Spartan urge to attack, he waited. Once in the presence of the general, there could be no hesitation. Lucio would not escape his dagger. He had to die.

"We cannot keep the general waiting. Move!" the centurion barked.

Virtutis stood, letting Khan lead him out into the open with his hand on his shoulder.

"Do not forget the spear," Virtutis interjected. "I am sure the general will love the story of how I pried it from Virtutis's dead hand."

"No weapons!" the centurion shouted.

Virtutis instantly pushed his hand under his cloak, knowing there would be no chance without his spear in the general's tent.

The centurion's energy pushed past his shoulder. "I will take it to the general," he boasted.

Virtutis smirked at the suicidal offer.

"And I will take the shield," Khan offered, attempting to be disgruntled. "I have carried it this far. It's not going to be for nothing!"

"Hurry up then!" the centurion yelled, hitting Virtutis in the shoulder with the shaft of his own spear.

Virtutis reacted with a smile, knowing he would impale the arrogant Roman in due time.

Soon the clink of armor and sandals crunching on dirt pathways drowned out any indicators to help orientate him. Virtutis had to trust Khan's lead.

Just as Virtutis was going to try to signal for information, Khan began to hum.

"Hmm, hmm, I look at the trees, and what do I see, six black birds looking at me." He sang low and off-key.

"Quiet!" the centurion ordered. "The general has been drinking all night. He will have your head with that racket!"

Virtutis pumped two short breaths from his nose to clear his head, adding up the odds against them: six praetorian guards, plus six centurions and General Lucio.

The centurions were not difficult, but the praetorian guard, if given the chance, would be a threat.

Khan cleared his throat.

A change was coming.

"In here!" a Roman voice called.

What light came through bandages in the daylight now turned pitch black. There was an odor of stale wine and sweat from sex lingering in an unnatural putrid warmth, then a familiar voice cut through the darkness.

"This is the man who killed the Spartan?" The general's tone made every hair on Virtutis's body stand on end.

"Yes, sir. He claims this is his head and spear," the centurion replied.

The sound of the spear clunked on a table directly in front of him, meaning the table was setup the same as before.

The general must be in his usual refuge behind the table.

A thud of the head being released from the sack silenced the room.

Virtutis brushed his inner wrist over his dagger under his Roman cloak.

He waited for Khan.

"I saw the kill," Khan said. "He stabbed Virtutis twice in the stomach. Once with his sword and another with his dagger. When the Spartan fell to his knees, six men impaled his back with spears to make sure he was never to return alive."

The stomach. Khan again gave him another code. Virtutis added two guards facing him, and another six behind them, with twelve outside.

Virtutis took his hand off Khan's shoulder with a gentle motion, pulling him behind, hoping he would understand to take the men at the back, but Khan's hand trapped Virtutis's forearm to halt any sudden moves.

Virtutis waited.

"This is Virtutis's shield. May I?" Khan asked.

"You may," the general said.

Khan separated their connection.

"Now!" Khan screamed, shoving Virtutis to one side.

Virtutis ripped off the eye covering and gathered his balance. Light shocked his eyes.

The general scurried up his chair, jumping over the side toward his sword.

With a clatter of shield on steel behind him, Virtutis dodged the blade of the closest guard. He lunged toward the spear, drawing his dagger, holding the blade in reverse to cover his forearm. Clank! He defended another sword strike, the impact blowing his arm backward. Using the momentum, he spun to the opposite side of the table with enough space to secure his spear. He ducked and saw a shin; he immediately stabbed his spear under the table. The tip cut through bone and muscle, dropping the guard where he stood.

Around the side of the table came another attack. A high sword threatened from above. He blocked it with the spear shaft, kicking hard at a Roman kneecap. It buckled backward, leaving the Roman moaning on one knee and trying to stand using his sword as a prop. Without defense, Virtutis sighted his exposed abdomen, pushed off the ground, and stabbed his spear long, hitting his target. He retracted quickly, then backed around the table low and slow.

From his peripheral, Khan swatted anything that moved with his shield, causing chaos amongst the praetorians, but he would not hold them back for long without a weapon and support.

A figure came from the side, shoving Virtutis with a shoulder. Falling, he tucked and rolled spear first. Rotating his body with a twist, he bounced back with a stab to the Roman's chest, followed by a slash across the throat with the tip of his spear. The body fell silent.

Khan was on his back, covered by his shield with praetorians hammering him. Virtutis tried to move in his direction, but a side sword strike came hard and fast. He scooped away the blow with his spear. Using his dagger, he closed space and stabbed under delicate ribs. He spun away from the confrontation and started to attack the multiple threats over Khan, using his spear to assault and counter. It gave Khan time to scramble to his feet.

Virtutis did not stop, stabbing two more, dead.

Khan gathered a sword and started pounding his way in revenge.

The tent fell deadly silent.

"General!" Virtutis snapped. "Where are you? You coward!"

He had escaped behind the chair and into his private chamber.

Guards shouted from outside the tent flap, their footsteps pounding.

Khan stopped in his tracks. "I will take care of the crows." He smiled with a sinister grin, "Go!"

Putting away his dagger and picking up his shield, Virtutis slowly entered the back of the tent. A brawl erupted behind him, but it was soon drowned out by the dimly lit danger of the cunning general. Virtutis licked his upper lip; blood poured from the open wound over his eye, over his mouth, and off his chin. The laceration on the back of his skull had opened and was bleeding again, like warm vengeance running down his back.

Focusing, he scanned the room. Smoke wielded from blown-out candles, and a statue of the emperor's head sat on a pillar in the corner. Sheep-skin rugs were laid across the floor up to a large bed decorated with whips and chains. A putrid odor that made his eyes water filled his nose. Slowing his breathing, searching for sound, he waited, low, just inside the entrance. His shield lifted to his chin, spear ready in an under-grip.

A figure jolted frantically from the right corner. Virtutis stepped backward, not reacting to mere impulse. It was a naked boy. His eyes wide with fear, his body bruised and cut.

"Leave," Virtutis growled, leaning aside, giving him space to escape.

Virtutis entered deeper into the room, sweeping his body from side to side without opening his defenses. A flapping of light drew attention. The tent had been sliced open at the base in the right corner.

Virtutis remained alert. With his guard up, he retracted with a backward step, not putting anything past the general.

A voice erupted outside. "Burn the tent!" the general screamed, frantic. "Now!"

Virtutis lifted his stance to hear a snort as he twisted a spear ready to attack, only to see Khan covered in blood, trying to exhale someone's blood from up his nose by holding his finger over one nostril. Behind him he had left the praetorians littered, lifeless.

"Which way?" Khan asked.

"This way, before we get burned alive." Virtutis spun back around, leading the way. "It backs to the fence. At least there's cover on one side." He sliced open a new exit at the side of the tent with the razor-sharp tip of his spear and exploded through, ready to fight. But there was no one there.

The general's voice continued to yell. "Burn the tent, or I will have you all hanging dead by morning!"

Cautious, Virtutis and Khan crept around the corner to see the general ordering Virtutis's disguised men.

The camp was well and truly deserted.

Virtutis and Khan exchanged a look of surprise.

"Well, that was easy." Khan laughed.

General Lucio, still dressed in his nightgown, lifted his sword in shock.

"Kill him! That's an order from the emperor himself!"

No one moved.

He turned toward Virtutis's men. "I will cut your balls off myself!" The general sprayed words, losing his mind. "Kill him!"

Virtutis walked directly to the General without losing stride. "Let me introduce you to your exiled auxiliary." He gruffed.

The general exploded, "You Spartan bastard! I should have killed you while I had the chance."

"I was thinking the same thing," Virtutis responded, spinning his spear in hand.

The general steadied his stance, lifting his sword, threatening to attack. "Spartannnn..." He launched his blade, delivering three accurate strikes toward Virtutis's head and torso. But they were standard Roman strikes and overly predictable.

Virtutis deflected them with ease, feeling even more disrespect for the man. He toyed with the general, throwing away his shield and letting him try his best for a moment. He then rotated his spear around the general's sword, jamming his wrist hard, forcing the sword to fly from his hand.

"I will still have your head!" the general yelled.

"No, it is I that will impale yours," Virtutis replied calmly. "But first, I have some questions for you."

Unarmed, the general tried to attack Virtutis's legs. But Virtutis side stepped away without much as a touch laid upon him. The general landed on his stomach in a pile of dust and screamed, scrambling to his feet. "Barbarian Spartan scum! I would die before I'd entertain any more dialogue with you!"

"Oh, you will die. But not before I get what I need from you." Virtutis closed the gap between them, drawing his dagger while using the end of the spear to sweep the general's legs out from under him.

The general once again crashed hard into the dirt with a thud, winded. As he searched for air, he crawled away backwards.

Virtutis jammed his spear between the general's legs, cutting through his robe, pinning any more of the coward's movement. Blood quickly stained the privileged white linen, making him clutch his inner thigh.

"Looks like I just missed your snake. Lucky, I have my dagger."

Virtutis forced his spear deeper into the dirt through the robe, making sure his prey did not escape.

The general screamed in pain. "Bastard!"

"It's funny. You feel pain? However, I feel nothing for you."

Leaving his spear dug in, Virtutis stepped around it and straddled Lucio. Like a pathetic drunk, the general tried to punch and slap his way free before Virtutis delivered two Spartan slaps to the head, so hard it made his own palm sting.

Struggling to find more energy to fight, the general spoke with pointless threats. "You will be hunted and slaughtered. Do what you will. You will get nothing from me."

"We will see," Virtutis said, flicking his dagger through his fingers and grabbing the general's ear. He sliced the tender flesh off.

The general's scream echoed through the camp and beyond like the screams of the many men he had tortured and killed for false allegations.

Clashes of steel rang as a fight broke out behind him. Virtutis glanced over his shoulder. The gate guards had come to defend what was left of the general. Khan and the others disposed of them easily.

The general squirmed, becoming the focus again. With a bloodied hand over his ear and tears watering his cheeks, the general knew the worst was yet to come. Virtutis yanked him by his nose, threatening the dagger across his cheek.

"Who took command of your men? Who said I raped the princess?"

The general laughed. "I will never talk. I want it to burn inside you until the day you die. Like your sons will burn. Like everything you touch and everyone you know will suffer because of who you are."

Anger flooded Virtutis's brain, his wound behind his skull reopening with more pressure, and blood trickled over his shoulder onto the general's face. "You will talk!"

Virtutis stood, snatching his spear and stabbing it into the ground beside the general's head.

He grabbed Lucio by the throat, making him scramble to his feet. Virtutis forced him to scuff and stumble backward under the strain, ramming his back against a pole used for executions.

"How about we settle some business in the name of the empire, shall we?"

The general erupted like a wild cat, striking and kicking. With an open hand, he connected a strike over Virtutis's ear that made his head ring. Virtutis replied with a vengeful snarl, opening his mouth wide like the Black Wolf stretching his jaw before he eats.

Anticipating a repeat palm attack, Virtutis wove his head around the general's arm, trapping his wrist between his head and shoulder, holding the pressure with his chin. With his dagger, Virtutis stabbed under his armpit, slicing down to the elbow.

More screams filled the barren camp.

Almost touching nose to nose, Virtutis whispered, "Things just keep getting better for you, don't they?"

Placing the dagger into the collar of the general's linen robe, Virtutis sliced it open.

He reversed the grip on the handle, digging it into the general's chest, diverting over his ribcage so as not to pierce vital organs. He proceeded without mercy, adding another incision in his lower belly, cross-cutting from one side to the other, causing pain that death would not save him from.

The general gasped for air; unable to scream, he shuddered.

"You see, General, there are many ways to die. Unfortunately for you, a fast death is not something you will have the privilege of experiencing."

The general's body shivered. He let out a muffled groan under the pressure of Virtutis's grip around his throat.

"Virtutis," Khan said. "Mercalis is coming. He's in a hurry."

Virtutis hesitated as he processed Khan's words, then let the general slump to the ground. "Keep him here," he replied, not diverting his focus on reading the general's beady eyes. "See that he does not go anywhere."

Mercalis approached in full flight through the camp. Something was wrong.

"It's the Romans," he called. "There are too many to count. They are almost here."

Hearing the news, the general erupted, "Ha! They will kill you. They will kill you all. You are dead, Spartan." He spat blood, changing his tone. "Or... we can make a deal if you let me live."

Remaining calm, looking over Virtutis's shoulder, Mercalis pressed quieter. "We must leave, now."

Virtutis glanced back at the general like a wolf in a fury. He strode over to him, grabbing his collar.

"Get up! You are coming with us," he snarled.

Khan stepped in his path. "Virtutis, he will only slow us down," he cautioned. "We can't take him."

Frustrated, Virtutis wanted to throw Khan out of the way, but he knew he was right.

The general smiled. "If you kill me now, you will never get answers to your questions. Who betrayed you? Who spun lies?" he paused, looking as if he felt he was gaining control. "When will we kill your sons?"

The general's voice irritated Virtutis almost beyond reason. He wanted to ram his soul into Hades and back. He looked at Khan, searching his face for more options, but there was only one.

Virtutis sighed, "Put him against the pole. No need to tie his hands." He retrieved his spear from deep within the empire's falsely claimed earth, then faced the man who had layered lies beyond his imagination, who now had found some kind of courage, wanting to stand his ground while his back was against a pillar of death. Dominant in his cause, Virtutis reduced Lucio to his pending doom once again by cutting across his other cheek with his spear tip, then cuffed his mouth with his palm, keeping his scream quiet. The warmth of fresh blood seeped through his fingertips and ran down his forearm.

Virtutis pressed the general's cheeks together, making him pucker and opening the cuts further. "I joined the auxiliary to serve the Roman ideal. But that all changed the night you raped my friend and sentenced him to death."

The general shook his head. Virtutis released Lucio's cheeks, letting him speak. "That was you? I should have known!" The general's voice was muffled under Virtutis's palm. "He should have been executed as a spy." Virtutis tilted his head like an animal analyzing its prey, letting him talk. "The boy offered himself up by trying to look at my map and the questions about the auxiliary..."

Virtutis processed Lucio's words. A fast and very different reality pushed Virtutis's thriving revenge aside. Could he have been the reason Arquitos was raped and beaten? This whole journey. Was it, in fact, a consequence of his own misjudgment?

Khan moved to Virtutis's side, reigniting more tension to the situation. "Virtutis, we must go."

Lucio snickered through his pain with pleasure. "The boy, he was asking for you, wasn't he?" Even under torture, the general searched for some sick form of satisfaction. "Ha! It was your doing! The information, it was for you! He must be dead by now. You killed him! Haaaa!" The general coughed, but the smile quickly returned to his face.

Virtutis looked at the general in disgust. His upper hand made Virtutis want to stab him in the eyeball. Now it was too late for his own resolution, making a wave of anger shake through Virtutis's veins and the wound at the back of his head burst even more. Blood gushed down his back and ran over his legs as he exploded into a rage.

"Roman bastard!" he spat. "You murdered innocent women and children. You insulted my culture and ancestors."

Virtutis's voice became deeper, anguished. "You tried to assassinate Princess Liliana," he snarled and headbutted the general across the nose. "You tried to kill my men." He continued to grind his forehead against the general's face before pulling back to stare into Lucio's eyes. "Your part in this game, General, has come to an end."

Virtutis pulled his head back, opening his mouth, the Black Wolf within him wanting to feast on the general's soul. He placed the tip of the spear under his chin, then placed his other hand at the back of the general's head.

The general squirmed his legs, but he was trapped between a Spartan's wrath and a weak existence. Virtutis gripped the spear's shaft extra hard, squeezing all the pent-up emotion, then pushed it upward while forcing the general's head down. The general resisted, pushing back into Virtutis's hand at first, but the measure of Virtutis's revenge was too strong, and he eventually gave in. The spearhead penetrated the general's throat through his mouth. Virtutis watched as the general's bloodshot eyes widened. Emotions curled deep in Virtutis's belly, turning to anger that surged to a deep Hades-like bellow. "I will piss on your corpse! You putrid bastard!" His voice dropped to a whisper, "You lose..."

He rammed revenge, driving up into the general's head with an untamed hatred until the tip of the spear pierced the back of General Lucio's skull.

Stepping away, Virtutis snapped the spear back, letting the general fall ungraciously and lifeless to the ground. Virtutis stood in a pool of blood. He searched his thoughts as the anger within him somehow subsided. The revenge, the finality of the moment he had been waiting for, was not what he thought it would be. The greater picture of deceit crept into his mind at the questions unanswered, leaving him unresolved. Liliana was right; revenge and justice are not all received as we intended.

"Virtutis," Mercalis urged, "we must leave now!"

Virtutis saw Khan's eyes wide and concerned for the first time; the men were agitated.

"My sons. Mercalis, you must get to my sons," Virtutis replied, recalling the general's threat.

"Yes. But first, we must all get out of here, or we will be trapped," Mercalis urged.

Virtutis started to plan their exit; he looked toward the gate at the far end of the camp. It was too far away and not worth the risk. "There is another way out, but first, we need the general's papers. Mercalis, come with me. The rest of you, we will meet you at the back end of the camp."

"Let's go." Khan led the men away in a trot.

Virtutis and Mercalis sped toward the tent and frantically turned it inside out, snatching at what papers they could. Virtutis yanked a leather satchel full of documents from beside the general's chair.

"We have to go!" Mercalis warned.

Overpowered by desperation, Virtutis snapped back, "Meet me at the back of the camp. I need to check the general's chamber."

"There is no time," Mercalis pleaded.

Driven by his one-sightedness to uncover answers, Virtutis ignored all logic as Mercalis cautiously checked outside the tent.

The search turned violent. Virtutis flipped chests and tables, looking for more papers and maps, but found little to nothing.

"They will be at the gate by now," Mercalis whispered. "We must get out of here."

Wanting to scream, knowing he had to listen, Virtutis kicked over a statue of the emperor before they exited through the hole in the back of the tent.

In a low run, they made their way behind the encampment. They passed the naked boy, who sat watching, his face blank, confused. The boy exchanged a blank look with Virtutis like his soul had been detached from his eyes. As a witness, he should be taken care of, but Virtutis shook off the feeling; he did not kill innocent children.

They rounded a tent to find Khan and the others waiting for them crouched by the fence.

"This way," Virtutis whispered as the sound of Roman scout horses galloping closed in.

"They must have seen the gates unguarded. They know something is wrong," Khan said.

"Stay low," Virtutis ordered. "This way."

They scrambled between a gap in the fence and into the low-lying bushes just outside the camp and sprinted up into the hills, taking cover in a small clump of trees.

Virtutis watched as the camp became flooded with Roman troops. Orders screamed through the commotion that echoed up through the trees.

With blood drying over his torso, Virtutis watched the soulless boy from the general's tent being dragged toward a Roman commander, then being interrogated with the back of a hand.

"He will fold," Khan said, just as the boy pointed in their direction. "I knew it." Khan spat on the ground.

Frustrated, Virtutis shook his head for leaving him there; he could have at least taken him out of the camp; now, they were under more pressure. "Spread out," he said. "We have to climb."

They scrambled up the hilly forest terrain that led toward the mountain passes and scattered, trying to maintain cover. But it did not take long before the sounds of Roman horses snorted and closed in on their position.

Almost at the mountain trails they knew so well, Virtutis looked back to see Khan duck for cover under a log. Roman horses groaned above while Khan lay trapped, looking at Virtutis. He waved his hand for him to carry on.

Unwilling to leave his friend behind, Virtutis took cover and waited.

317

A praetorian guard almost rode over the top of the ox, causing him to cover his head with his hands.

Like a dark wave, more figures on horseback followed, spreading out through the trees. They swayed through the terrain as Virtutis let out a scoff through his nose, realizing the situation was now becoming even more unpredictable. The emperor must be close; these were not your typical Roman guards.

A hawk called over the valley from afar—Mercalis had sounded the intention to attack.

Virtutis sent a closed fist signal for Khan to stay hidden. For the life of his brother, there was no hesitation in what needed to be done. Not knowing how many threats there were, he took the risk.

Virtutis dropped his loaded shoulder bag and cracked his neck. Gripping his spear with a bloodied, calloused palm, he gently tapped his shield three times.

For Stoa. For Augustus. For Liliana.

He took two quick breaths through his nose before he stood staunch into the open. His body was beaten, and the stress of the journey had taken its toll. This was a fight that would be his greatest challenge. While the general's sword was weak, now the scales had tipped far from frail. From the depths of his stomach, he called out to Rome's famed sons of war.

"Praetorians!"

CHAPTER 31

Standing at a slight height advantage with his back to a low bank, six praetorians enclosed Virtutis with a half-moon formation. Deciding that the closer they came, the better for his spear attack, Virtutis waited. Unsure when Mercalis and his men would be close enough, it was inevitable he would have to act.

In the distance behind the half-moon, he saw more praetorians gracefully guiding their horses through the trees. Virtutis resigned to the fact that these moments could be his last, he steadied his heart rate. If he were to face the Black Wolf, he would do so with the utmost clarity of mind.

"Declare yourself!" a guard shouted.

Virtutis looked into their shadowed eyes behind their helmets; with nothing to read, he used his peripheral and focused on a guard to his far right. He slowly rotated his spear tip facing down. "I am Virtutis."

"Virtutis!" the guard shouted. "You are wanted for crimes against the empire. Surrender, and you will have a better chance for a fast death."

He could not think of anything worse than a fast death. He smiled as more black horsemen arrived, and the situation became direr. There were now twelve. He knew he had to attack before they could settle into a formation.

Virtutis lifted his spear, already in a javelin grip. He sighted the throat of the praetorian on the right flank and launched it. The impact threw the praetorian off his horse. Following the flight line of his spear, he exploded, using his shield for cover in a race to regain his weapon.

"Kill him!"

Virtutis's feet barely touched the ground as he focused on his objective. Almost within reach, he dove, snatching the spear under the cover of his shield, and rotated to his feet.

His whole body was thrown backward, rammed by the powerful chest of a horse. It sent him thudding to the ground in a heap. He quickly regained his sense of direction, flipping backward over his head, crouching, looking to attack, searching for an advantage.

The horseman swept his horse around to strike him again. Stepping back and spotting a turning thigh, Virtutis stabbed his spear hard and sure.

There was a scream of agony.

"Ha!" a second horseman yelled and came directly at him.

Virtutis inched back in preparation. He stepped laterally, using the shield against the side of the horse's head, diverting and spinning around the mass. He reversed his spear, still spinning with the horse's momentum, and used a backhanded stab. The tip penetrated the side of the praetorian as he rode by; the horse carried him a few more steps before he fell dead.

Distracted by the clashes from the horses, Virtutis had given the other praetorians a tactical advantage. "Surround him!" yelled the horseman in front of him.

They distanced themselves, enclosing him, more alert, making surprise attacks impossible.

Virtutis pulled strong breaths through his nose, forcing his brain to think—he could not let them gain total control. To attack another flank was too predictable.

"Don't let him out!" a praetorian yelled.

Virtutis did not need more of an invitation. He launched his spear with full power at the Roman's chest; the force unsteadied both the rider and horse, and the spear ricocheted off but gave Virtutis enough time to chase. In a low run, he drew his half-covered dagger. A praetorian spear hit his shield. Another blew past his head.

The horseman in front almost regained his balance. Virtutis jumped high to the side of the horse's neck, burying his shoulder into the waist of the praetorian. Together they plummeted to the ground. Rolling, making sure he finished on top, Virtutis trapped his victim between the shield and dagger. Knowing the soft targets of the guard's armor, Virtutis stabbed hard and fast. Then, he rolled away with his shield for cover and sprawled into a sprint.

Horses grunted, and hooves pounded around him. Spearless, he had to find better ground. Two horses galloped directly at him. He dove to the side as the horses clipped at his ankles, spinning him mid-air, tossing him recklessly. Rolling in a tumble, he tried getting up, but one of his feet did not respond, making him hop to regain balance. With little choice, he flipped his dagger, gripping the blade between his fingertips, ready to throw. Shouts for diversion echoed from the trees.

At last, Mercalis had arrived; spears and daggers flew. The welcomed sound of swords clashing meant the fight was truly for the winning.

Virtutis glanced over at Khan, who led a barrage of attacks at the remaining praetorians.

A horseman with his sword drawn came directly at Virtutis. Accepting the challenge, he steadied. The snorts of the horse slowed down. The strides became predictable. Virtutis lowered. He let the rider anticipate a false point of contact, then exploded forward, diving to the side, rounding the horse. The rider's head followed, opening a facial target. With a flick of the wrist, he let his dagger go. Being so close and with only time for it to rotate end-over-end once, the blade entered directly into his cheek.

Virtutis landed in a heap, then scrambled away to gain perspective on the battle.

From the corner of his eye, he saw the praetorian with a dagger in his face cantered down and slumped, eventually stopping.

"Virtutis!" Khan yelled, throwing his spear. "You lost something!"

The spear stabbed into the ground at his feet. Virtutis glanced down with a smirk.

"You're welcome!" Khan called, laughing.

Wrenching the spear from the earth, Virtutis took advantage of the praetorians who were now under attack and began choosing his confrontations. He did not consider any target unacceptable or without honor, all opportunities were taken. Together, Virtutis and his men culled the praetorians from all directions. With no rules of engagement, it became suited to his men in an all-out brawl that ended abruptly.

Virtutis stood alive amongst the best of the Roman elite. While they lay dead and dying, he savored the moment but quickly came back to reality. They survived this confrontation; the next may not be so favorable. Before anyone could stop to think, Virtutis ordered action, "Get the horses! Quickly!"

The men gathered the scattered horses as Virtutis hobbled to find his shoulder bag.

A horse snorted in resistance. Mercalis rode a Roman horse with another one's reins in hand, cutting through the trees and stopping to the side of Virtutis. Without looking up, he gave orders.

"Skinny, they will not stop coming. Tell the men to ride two to a horse if they need to," Virtutis continued, slinging his bag. "We have to get as far up the trails as we can."

With a limp, he stepped up to gather the reins from Mercalis and straddled the horse.

"Let's go."

With some men doubling up, they rode the horses hard over the trails, gaining distance from the camp.

Virtutis placed one hand on the saddle for support. He struggled to balance, and his head began to ring. After two hours of harsh narrow trails and following steams up the river, he followed Mercalis's lead as they cut through dense trees, finding refuge in a clearing far from any trail. He dismounted to his legs almost giving way, forcing him to sit to check his ankle, but his vision was too blurry, and his eyes burned for relief.

A horse snorted in the near distance, bringing his attention to two men who dismounted, bleeding. Mercalis and Khan raced to attend to the injured.

Behind them, another one arrived, slumped in his saddle, dead. Virtutis forced himself to his feet and gently guided a dead brother down from the saddle, placing him on the ground on his back. He looked over him for a moment, then with the palms of his hands, Virtutis paid his respects by closing his eyes for him. "I hope the gods favor your journey," he said.

The wind blew a gentle breeze through the trees, followed by a distant howl. Virtutis, without energy, laid back briefly, finding a strange comfort being beside the dead, thinking it was better to lie in the company of a dead brother, than live in the midst of betrayal.

Virtutis woke to Khan and the others working in silence, placing wood and rocks in preparation for burying a warrior's body. With shaky legs and his mind still regaining focus, Virtutis stood and started to help.

Sunlight struck through the clouds onto their clearing as the remaining ten men gathered around the grave. "There is not much time," Virtutis began, breaking the silence. "The horses are easy to track if we all ride together, so those in better condition to run will ride and lead any trackers away. Take what bags you can; when you dismount, fill them with rocks to keep the weight the same on the horses, so the trackers continue to follow." His eyes became blurry, but he wiped them clean with his forearm, leaving a crusty feeling over his face. "The rest of us will have to break up and go through the hinterlands."

"We should stay together," one man said.

"No, brother," Virtutis objected sincerely. "We need to spread out and find our own pace. To keep another man's speed if we are unable puts the other at risk." Virtutis noticed the clouds forming overhead. "The rain will help mask our tracks if we act now. We will meet in the town that sits below Mount Versus to the east. There is a farmhouse that was built next to a large rock formation just outside of town. Find the large barn used for slave traders; enter only at night and use the sound of the night hawk before you open the door. I will meet you there in ten days. The Romans are after me, not you, so the choice remains with you; you have no obligation to continue."

"I will meet you at the town," Khan said.

"And I," the men said individually.

Virtutis looked across their faces, then nodded in acceptance. "Very well. The bond."

"The bond," they replied.

"Leave as soon as you can," Virtutis said. "We will talk again in ten days. If the Romans catch you, take your own life, as it will not be worth living; spare yourself."

The men nodded before starting their preparations.

Exhaustion became heavier within Virtutis's body as he walked away. He desperately needed to gather his energy, but he was overcome with curiosity to try to solve his dilemmas that could well plague his mind forever. He walked toward a fallen log and sat awkwardly with his war-torn body.

Khan appeared out of nowhere with a waterskin from a Roman horse.

Virtutis, knowing he was losing reality, managed a smile that it was not a Roman who caught him unaware. "Thank you." He refreshed his mouth and returned the waterskin.

Khan took it back and placed Virtutis's hands together, then began to pour water over his palms.

Virtutis tilted his head, looking at Khan, trying to understand why he'd wash another man's hands.

"Rub them together well," Khan said with a smile. "It is good to wash your hands, no matter how long they have been dirty. Who knows when we will ever wash our hands in peace again? And I am nowhere near as beaten up as you." He laughed.

"Truth," Virtutis confirmed. "How do you always seem so happy, Khan? Amongst all of this?"

Khan frowned. "I like to fight. Why I fight, how I fight is a complexity I leave to you to figure out. I trust your judgement," he said matter-of-factly. "We have not lost yet, so I have made some good choices. But if I die, I die full. If I live, I live full."

"Full?" Virtutis asked curiously.

"I have a son and a daughter, so if I die, I don't die. I know I will die, but I won't be dying empty." Khan scratched his head. "Even if I were in the darkest of gallows, they would never take my soul, never take my fullness because my fullness is bigger than me." Khan placed his hand on Virtutis's shoulder. "Prefectus Virtutis," he said with a soldier's tone. "You are riddled with the bigger questions of life. I don't really have the mind to understand the philosophers. I don't seek virtue or fame. I seek adventure; I think you are true to who you say you are, the rest is none of my concern, and it's better that way. A good fight. A loyal friend. A good stew." Khan frowned. "That reminds me,"—he grunted to his feet, walking away, talking over his shoulder— "you will need some food. Let me see what the sweet praetorians have in their bags."

Virtutis flicked water off his hands and rubbed them on his tunic. Then began another piercing headache as he tried to contemplate Khan's simplistic view of life. In a certain way, Khan represented a pure quest, but through all the changes, Khan managed to keep it simple; whether he fought for the Romans or against them, Virtutis realized Khan would have followed, regardless.

A roll of thunder in the distance interrupted his thoughts and brought him back to his plan. Through blurred vision, Virtutis looked for Mercalis, who was patiently waiting for instructions.

"Skinny," he called, rubbing his eyes to try to stop the burn. By the time he finished, Mercalis had already sat silently beside him.

"After you have rested enough, take two horses," Virtutis said. "You know what you must do."

"I will leave now," Mercalis replied, standing ready to go. "The bond."

"The bond," Virtutis said, knowing it was in his best interest not to delay Mercalis' mission.

Mercalis bent to secure forearms, a gentle, sincere grip. In a jaded reality, he crossed the clearing to gather two Roman horses. Virtutis watched as he guided the horses halfway through the trees, then ran, towing the horses, so it looked as if they had been spooked, leaving false tracks. Virtutis watched until he disappeared, knowing his life and the lives of his sons depended on one man to deliver two messages in the grace of time.

Knowing he had to get himself ready to leave, Virtutis stood and tried to walk, but his leg almost gave way, his ankle was swollen, his severed calf ached, and the stinging at the back of his head turned his stomach. He sighed, peeling more crusted blood off his face from his cut eye. With all the discomforts adding up, he latched his shield over his back and braced against his spear in a hobble, knowing the days to come were going to be rough, especially without the adrenaline of war and the fleeting purpose of revenge being dismantled. Forgetting about Khan coming back, he limped away toward the edge of the tree line, leaving his men to attend to their own fate. He took off his shoulder bag and laid his weapons. He sat in the long grass, rummaging through it, searching for anything important. Some of it he did not understand. There were maps and sealed scrolls, no doubt for the emperor. He looked for his name or Liliana's, but there was nothing. The lack of information created frustration in his already deteriorating mood. He opened a map that showed Rome's expansion to the sea. His decision to fight against the Romans was justified—they had already set plans in motion to conquer the tribes of the hinterlands by any means. At least that's part of the puzzle, he reminded himself.

At the bottom of the bag, there were two more scrolls. He grabbed them, their seals already broken.

His stomach turned as he read the first.

Wanted Dead or Alive

Virtutis – Spartan

Commander of the Auxiliary

Charges:

Kidnapping and Rape of Princess Liliana

Conspiracy and Murder of a Roman Commander

Treason

Confused, he let the papers blow away in the breeze as a strain crept over his eyes, a strain of trying to understand why he was not just executed. A mix of emotions made his swelling ankle bulge bigger and the pain somehow worse. He ripped part of his tunic and wrapped it around his ankle for support. He lay back to look at the deep gray clouds rolling below the blue sky, threatening their downpour at any moment. He had to move; he rolled to the side. In a struggle, he sat up.

"Worse for wear, brother?" Khan asked softly, stopping briefly before he sat beside him.

"We have been in the snake pit since the beginning," Virtutis replied, flinching as he pulled the bandage tight, forcing the pain to reflect his frustration. "The general was playing me like a pawn."

"You or us? And why?" Khan asked.

"We were already guilty of treason and the murder of the commander." Virtutis touched the back of his head to check for bleeding. "The rape and kidnapping of the princess were a setup afterwards."

"So why did he let us live?" Khan rubbed his head. "The noble we killed in the valley?"

"Maybe, but we still don't know who he is. Maybe we never will," Virtutis scoffed. "I don't even know if the princess is alive or dead."

Khan snickered a cheeky laugh. "You really like that princess, huh?"

Virtutis held his tongue, not wanting to explain more of himself.

"Fair enough," Khan grumbled, looking down at his feet, knowing it was not a subject to be talked about. "I have organized the diversion to buy us time. Two men are going to take the horses and leave a trail for a few days. The rest of us will split up and meet you in the town. I will stay with you as long as my feet can keep up."

Virtutis faced Khan directly so he would understand his intention fully. "I appreciate the offer. But I am best to travel alone." Virtutis looked at the clouds again, squinting from the glare of the hidden sun.

"As you wish." Khan shrugged. "Sometimes, the more we know, the more we are conflicted."

Virtutis rubbed his palm over his face in thought. A sharp pain reminded him once again of the cut above his eye. "I killed the general too soon. It would have been better to stay there and die, knowing the truth. It feels like I have lost myself more than when I started. Have I resorted to what I swore not to be?"

"What is that?"

Virtutis looked Khan dead in the eye. "A mere savage."

"I'd rather be a savage with you than a crimson sheep in a Roman slaughterhouse." Khan laughed. "You are more than just a savage. But yes, you are a savage."

"Again, Khan?" Virtutis hinted at Khan's humor.

"That's why I am confused why you want to be alone on your journey," he replied. "I am great company."

Unable to muster a smile, Virtutis rubbed his left temple with his thumb, trying to reduce the headache. It was no use; everything he had been fighting for had taken its toll, even the company of his trusted comrade.

Khan sighed. "With each battle, we lose a little of ourselves; not all that glitters is gold."

"We are not talking about gold," Virtutis said.

"Land, power, glory, and gold. For us, it is something else."

"What is that?"

"Perhaps the occupation of ourselves in war eases the pressure to live a normal life? I couldn't cope with my wife, that's for sure." Khan scratched his head with a laugh, then dropped his face serious again. "There is something about being a warrior that separates him from the common man."

"I wish I was so clear. I thought this journey would bring me clarity." Virtutis extended his leg to rest his battered hip. "I thought it was complicated before all this. But now…"

"Ahh, simple is as good Stoades-stew." Khan giggled. Then, raised his finger with a forced gleam of wisdom for humors sake. "Better to be the one who eats, and not he who is the meat."

Virtutis grabbed the shoulder bag and turned it upside down one last time. A gold coin dropped into the grass between his legs. He picked it up, spinning it between his fingers, then gave it to Khan.

"Money, land, and power have never motivated me. What modern men seek to value is the furthest from my mind, and in that, I may have made the greatest mistake. Men are divided into two categories; that is clear to me now."

"How so?" Khan asked.

"I have killed hundreds of men. But Lucio, though he was weak with a sword, he killed thousands, if not more, than I ever could. So, is being a warrior effective at all? Does a man remain in the safety of the shadows under leaders who could consume the world and all its virtue so easy?"

"I, for one, cannot stand in the shadows," Khan said. "Neither can you, and that is why I am with you. As for the general, you killed a man who needed to be killed, or thousands more would have perished."

Virtutis sighed. "Truth. The bastard had to die."

Khan nodded. "What are the two categories?"

"The virtuous and something else that I am not."

"What is that?" Khan lifted his eyebrow.

"I have yet to define. Maybe I am just like the general?" Virtutis said, frustrated. Knowing he could not be satisfied with any words or conversation, he stood and gathered his shield and spear. "You are a good man, Khan. Who knows if I am right or wrong and what justice I will face for all of this? Take care of your feet."

"Justice is like an echo; sometimes, it is delayed. While we seek or wait for justice for one thing or another, somewhere, someone has already set in motion things we will never comprehend or see coming; like a third tiger, it will catch you unaware, justified or not. For a warrior to worry about such things will only dull his blade and dampen his judgment. While you worry about what has happened, be careful of what other tigers lurk your way. And avoid the fog."

Fog? Virtutis thought, unsure of the warning.

He heard Khan's words but found them hard to listen to. With more and more adrenaline leaving his body, the pain over his forehead became increasingly sharp.

"I need to be alone," Virtutis said, losing focus. "I will see you on Mount Venus."

Khan offered him water for his journey. "There was no food, sorry."

"Thank you, brother. Water will be enough for now."

Khan nodded.

Virtutis used the blunt end of his spear to help him start walking. He limped to the breath of tall trees, longing for silence, longing for resolve.

From the distance, he heard Khan shout, "The Bond!"

Virtutis carefully lifted his spear over his head in salute, not looking back. The gesture almost forced him to lose balance as he entered the sanctuary of the hinterlands. The coolness feeling safer, he disappeared into the upper trails toward the mountain passes that led to Mount Venus.

A silence soon started to buzz in his head in contrast to the intensity of navigating the noise of the last few months and the bombardment of his own personal vengeance. Vengeance that seemed instinctual and outweighed logic and the sureness he once had.

Stoa and Augustus flashed in and out of his head. He left them to grow uninhibited, but he knew now how far he had already influenced their fate; it all seemed like a boyhood narrative. A narrative he was concerned he had placed upon his sons; that was perhaps an obsolete expectation he did not know he was setting at the time, or was it? The world waged wars beyond his imagination in ways he never fathomed. This new reality seemed to haunt him more than the Black Wolf. It twisted its weight within his body, making it heavy, and placed a fog in his already aching head.

He was done with this game. If Liliana was still alive, he would pursue the offer of a new life, a new warmth for him and his sons.

His body ached with every step, but the thought of her helped him move. Her smile provided a true north to navigate a world of deceit, and from time to time, it relieved some of the burn of his torment.

Night covered the mountains with a different shadowed cloak, that of a man without a home. Heavy mist crept its way over the terrain, making it difficult to navigate. Initially, a freshness eased the strain on his eyes, but the cold snap pressured his head even more, causing him to squint and blink. He shivered as his muscles became taut and stiff. He staggered over the uneven ground until he could no longer feel his feet. He knew he was driving himself toward a dark and deep place.

He tripped, unable to physically respond. Time slowed as he fell face down in the dirt. He pulled a long breath into his lungs before closing his eyes.

A quiver racked his entire body as he shuddered an inward breath.

A familiar growl broke the ringing in his ears.

On instinct, he stood, no longer exhausted, gripping his spear and shield, scanning around in a slow turn; his heavy legs now flooded with energy.

Hazel eyes pierced their way forward without blinking. The Black Wolf approached at the zenith of death. Not resolved that this would be the way he would die, Virtutis dug his back foot deep into the earth.

The Black Wolf slowly walked into view, shaking his head from side to side. Something was wedged between his jaws. Whipping his head violently, he let loose an object, and it rolled straight to Virtutis's feet. It was the head of a Roman centurion he had cut off in the valley.

Virtutis looked closer. Attached to the back of its head was Remus's long strand of hair.

The Black Wolf snarled, his ridged back fired, ready to attack, as they stood face to face. The Black Wolf's tongue rolled in hunger, letting out a stale odor of the dead. "You owe me souls, Spartan," he growled.

Virtutis lowered his battle stance, cracked his neck, and rolled his spear shoulder, ready to fight. He widened his jaw in a wolf-like stretch, a challenge back to the Black Wolf.

A wolf pack encircled him, snarling, intensifying the confrontation.

Virtutis dragged in the midnight mist long and hard through his nose, then snorted it out two times as he squeezed his spear, poised for the fight of his life.

"Come, let me show you the dance of death, and I will sever your soul."

Made in the USA
Las Vegas, NV
02 November 2022

58637149R00187